Praise for Kris Clink's
Goodbye, Lark Lovejoy

"An uplifting tale about family, second chances, and the complexity of making fine Texas wine."

—KIRKUS REVIEWS

"Kris Clink takes us on a delightful trip to Texas wine country in her heartwarming debut.

—LAINEY CAMERON, author of *The Exit Strategy*

"With a confident voice, smart humor, and masterful handling of difficult subjects, this story is full of heart and has so much to love."
—Leah DeCesare, author of *Forks, Knives, and Spoons*

"Just the rosy dose of optimism and hope we need right now."
—PHOEBE FOX, author of *A Little Bit of Grace*

"Lark Lovejoy is fierce, funny, and unforgettable. Clink's debut is a heartwarming and uplifting story that reminds us it's never too late to go after your dreams, that age is just a number, and you can find love in unexpected places. I can't wait to see what Kris Clink writes next!"
—ALISON HAMMER, author of *You and Me and Us*

"You'll want to say hello to these charming, complicated, and refreshingly flawed characters."
—AMY E. REICHERT, author of *The Optimist's Guide to Letting Go*

Featured

ead This April"

SISSIE KLEIN
IS COMPLETELY
NORMAL

SISSIE KLEIN IS COMPLETELY NORMAL

A NOVEL

KRIS CLINK

The Enchanted Rock Series, Book 2

Published by SparkPress, a BookSparks imprint,
A division of SparkPoint Studio, LLC
Phoenix, Arizona, USA, 85007
www.gosparkpress.com

Published 2021
Printed in the United States of America
Print ISBN: 978-1-68463-099-8
E-ISBN: 978-1-68463-100-1
Library of Congress Control Number: 2021908644

Interior design by Tabitha Lahr

To my sisters—Julie, Amy, and Jamie—and to George Clink, the man who taught us to care about animals and all things in nature, to love without condition, and showed us how to be each other's best friends.

Contents

PROLOGUE 13

Part One

ONE. 17

TWO 24

THREE 32

FOUR. 38

FIVE. 46

SIX 54

SEVEN 63

EIGHT 72

NINE 77

TEN. 86

Part Two

ELEVEN 97

TWELVE 106

Part Three

THIRTEEN. 115

FOURTEEN. 121

FIFTEEN 129

SIXTEEN 136

Part Four

SEVENTEEN 149

EIGHTEEN 156

NINETEEN 165

TWENTY 172

TWENTY-ONE 179

TWENTY-TWO 185

TWENTY-THREE 191

Part Five

TWENTY-FOUR 197

TWENTY-FIVE 205

TWENTY-SIX 213

TWENTY-SEVEN 221

TWENTY-EIGHT 226

TWENTY-NINE 234

THIRTY 239

Part Six

THIRTY-ONE 249

THIRTY-TWO 257

THIRTY-THREE 264

Thirty-Four 271

Thirty-Five 278

Thirty-Six 287

Thirty-Seven 296

Thirty-Eight 302

Thirty-Nine 309

Forty 317

Forty-One 325

Forty-Two 335

Forty-Three 343

Forty-Four 349

Part Seven

Forty-Five 354

Forty-Six 360

Forty-Seven 369

Forty-Eight 375

Acknowledgments 387

About the Author 389

Prologue

Trouble had a way of sneaking up on me when I was looking the other way. Della Castro was like that too. She laid claim on me in kindergarten, and before I could say boo about it, she and I were like peanut butter and jelly. Pretending to be sisters came naturally with our dark hair and brown eyes.

But by the time we hit middle school, those resemblances faded. I grew a whopping seven inches over Della's "cute" five foot three. So long, peanut butter and jelly. We'd become Jack and the Beanstalk.

Our height differences had no effect on our friendship. I adored her, and when the chips were down, Della would've barrel-rolled over broken glass to be at my side.

During my junior year of high school, my guidance counselor urged me to consider my future and my purpose in life. I found neither in the college brochures he pushed my way.

I had hoped to find my answer when Della invited me to come along for an unofficial campus visit at Texas State. My parents weren't hip to the idea, but I talked it up as an educational opportunity. Dad was a hard sell, so I implored Mom to advocate for me.

She came through like a champ. "Thomas, they're just normal girls, exploring a college town," she told him. "Della's cousin will show them around the campus, maybe even take them to that cute bookstore. Don't be so overprotective. Worst that could happen? Sissie returns home with a sunburn from riding in Della's convertible."

You could've knocked me over with a feather when my dad agreed with his bland, "Hmph, I suppose."

Looking back, they were setting me free to make lasting memories with my best friend.

Memories were made that weekend, that much is true. I didn't visit that bookstore or come home with a sunburn, though. And what did happen triggered an unravelling of an otherwise normal life—a cautionary tale mothers would use to scare their daughters straight for years to come.

Part One

One

March 2003

....

Can't say which pulled me out of sleep—the knocking or the yelling outside. Memories of the previous night were clattering around in my head like broken china. I managed to peel my eyes open long enough to take in the source that had numbed my right leg—a naked, lifeless body.

Okay, Sissie, pull it together. I attempted to center myself. The room was sticky with humidity. A hit of Drakkar cologne sent a bilious pulse down my throat. My stomach roiled. I feared the movement required to vomit might tear me in two. I tried to relax and reconcile what I had done. Caleb was cute enough to date, but—

Don't think about it, Sissie. You're just a normal girl, hooking up with a cute guy. College girls hook up all the time.

Except. I'm not a college girl.

Della had begged me to leave the bar with her. Weird, since she was the one who'd bought our fake IDs. Who'd wanted to pretend we went to Texas State. Who'd wanted to go clubbing and meet college guys. All fine—until she'd decided our fun was over. And when Della made a decision, there was no looking back.

Not this time, baby. With rum and Cokes bolstering my courage, I held my ground. "Leave if you're tired," I'd told her.

Her face turned to stone, like I'd betrayed her. She jerked her purse over her shoulder and jutted out her chin, but I wasn't going anywhere. Finally, she let out a giant sigh and shoved her cell phone in my face. "Take it," she'd said, acting like she was my mother.

I had no purse. Where was I supposed put a brick-size phone? "No, thanks."

Realizing that might have been a mistake as my gaze made the slow, blurry climb along the wall to the water-stained ceiling as I reordered my memories—head-banger music in Caleb's car, plans to meet his friends—friends who didn't show—kissing on the stained brown couch, an Austin Powers movie, and the beers that dragged me to Blackout City.

"I know you're in there!" a man shouted and pounded the door, rattling the foil-covered window over the couch.

I tried to move, but needle-like shocks pricked my right hand, which was stuck beneath Caleb's body.

"Caleb." My whisper wasn't compelling enough wake him, so I tapped his shoulder with my left hand. "Someone's here."

"Mmm." Caleb moaned and shifted slightly.

I lifted my head, and a fresh rush of sweat crawled over my skin. The sight of his bare butt confirmed what was pressed against my leg. A chilly shiver juddered my backbone, shaking me to wriggle free.

The room was musty like my grandmother's basement. I rolled to the floor, and my knees landed on crunchy shag carpet. A dizzying swirl of confusion and raw ache held me in place, as a fresh riot of knocking began at the door.

Where are my clothes? My hands flew to cover my body while I scanned the room.

"Wake up," I demanded, kicking at Caleb's arm.

"Huh?" he mumbled in a raspy voice. "Oh. Hey-y-y." A smile crossed his heavy-eyed—and, suddenly, annoying—face.

Not so cute anymore.

"Somebody's here." I retrieved my jeans, puddled on the floor.

"Caleb, I'm taking my key back!" the man barked from the porch. "I'm hung over, I'm tired, and I need to get ready for work." More pounding.

"Caleb," I pleaded in a whisper. "I need to go home."

Home—didn't sound quite right. *Anywhere but here?*

He blinked a few times, and his heavy-lidded gaze trailed my body.

"Stop staring at me like that. Get dressed. Someone's outside." I bent to claim my bra and gestured at the door.

Wearing nothing but freckles and a smile, he groaned to standing, stretching his arms like a starfish. "Chill, will ya?" He pushed his strawberry-blond bangs off his forehead and squinted at me like he'd just discovered I was in the room. "You're hot."

A stale beer burp rose in my throat, and I covered my mouth.

His lack of clothing didn't stop him from moving toward the door.

"Wait. Not until I find my shirt."

"Don't stress. He's seen naked chicks before."

Ugh. How many girls has he brought here?

"I need to call Della. Where's your phone?"

"Hell if I know," he mumbled, still walking toward the door.

The door squeaked open as I slid into the kitchen to pull on my jeans in privacy—and then had to button my mouth at the sight of soggy food on dishes in the sink. *Disgusting.*

An almond Trimline phone hung on the wall. I lifted the handset. *Dead. What did I expect?* From the living room, there was a back-and-forth between Caleb and whoever had come in.

I fastened my bra as swiftly as I could manage. My eyes landed on an empty Jagermeister bottle sitting beside a flip phone. *Hallelujah.* I peeled it open and raised the antenna. *One bar of battery power. That'll work.*

Della answered immediately. "Where are you?"

"With Caleb. Can you come get me?"

"Yeah, but give me a sec. I wasn't up yet."

"Please, hurry," I whispered.

She exhaled loudly. "Fine. Where are you?"

"With Caleb."

"Duh. I got that much. What's Mr. Wonderful's address?"

"Hang on." With an arm covering my chest, I peered into the living room.

"Hey." A Black guy in sweatpants and a Houston Rockets T-shirt nodded from the couch, his elbows resting on his knees. Beside him, Caleb, now wearing jeans, leaned back with his eyes closed.

"What's your address?" I asked.

Caleb roused. "This is Sissie."

"The address?" I repeated, but Caleb didn't answer.

The guy slapped Caleb's arm and turned to me. "It's 149-B Mosely."

"149-B Mosely," I repeated into the phone. "Outside of San Marcos."

"Not San Marcos. Martinsville," he corrected, running a hand over his flat fade.

"Martinsville," I repeated.

"Where?" Della asked.

It was no use asking Caleb, so I turned to his friend. "Can you give directions?"

"Here." He held out his hand, took the phone, and introduced himself to Della as Jamal. While I searched for the rest of my belongings, he instructed Della when to get on the highway and where to turn left.

"Alright," he said to me and held the phone out. "Here."

"Thanks." I took it from him.

"Welcome." His warm brown eyes said he understood my uneasiness.

"Who was that?" Della asked.

"Tell you when you get here." I tried to keep my voice level.

"What's going on?" she pressed.

"Nothing." I spoke through my teeth. "Just get here." I slapped the phone closed and dropped it on the coffee table.

"You alright?" Jamal tipped his head and met my eyes.

I forced my lips into a smile and continued looking for my clothes. Recognizing my heels below Caleb's legs, I coughed to draw his attention, but he didn't seem to notice. "My shoes are under your legs."

He slid to one side, allowing me to snatch up the shoes while I skimmed the perimeter of the sofa for my shirt.

"Whatcha looking for?" Jamal asked, rising from the couch.

"My shirt," I mumbled.

"I'll help," Jamal said. When we both had no luck, Jamal smacked Caleb's leg. "Where is it?"

Caleb pushed a hand behind his back and retracted a ball of navy and white fabric that no longer resembled my shirt.

"Not cool." Jamal grabbed it, shook it out, and handed it to me, shooting a judgmental side-eye at Caleb.

I dropped the ridiculous shoes on the floor. *Who did I think I was last night? Jessica Simpson?* I'd go home barefoot before putting those things back on. I pulled the wrinkled shirt over my shoulders and attempted to fasten a button. *Where are all the buttons?* I got my answer when a memory of our clumsy make-out scene surfaced.

Recognition dawned, and irritation contorted Jamal's face.

I returned a weary smile, and moved toward the front door. Clutching my shirt together with one hand and opening the door with the other, I muttered, "Bye."

"Take care," Jamal said.

"*Adios*," Caleb said. Before the door slapped shut, I heard him say, "Pretty sweet, huh?"

The other side of the door was no less comforting. With wobbly knees, I passed Caleb's Grand Prix and a yellow two-door import with a name I couldn't pronounce. I moved to the curb, covered in shame and a torn shirt.

I wasn't a prude, but I wasn't a slut, either. I'd done it with my steady boyfriend last year before he left for college, but we'd waited until we'd gone out for a whole year. It had been different—so different from this.

I hung in the balance like a spider dangling from the thinnest thread until Della's white Mustang convertible turned onto the street.

"So, what's the deal?" She pulled to the curb, her hair in a swirling mess and still wearing her standby pajamas—a tie-dyed Fredericksburg High T-shirt and a pair of boxer shorts.

I fell into the passenger seat and closed my eyes. "I feel like crap."

"Must've been some night," Della said while making a U-turn, leaving Caleb in the dust.

May I never see him again.

She pushed in a cassette tape. One of our choir songs blasted through the speakers. "Sing with me."

I sank deeper into myself.

"Come on. You like this one."

"Seriously, I'm not in the mood."

Della lowered the volume. "Don't be mad at me. I was worried about you. For all I knew, you could've been raped—or worse."

Choking up, I covered my face with my hands. "I'm sorry." *Understatement of the year.*

"Wish you would've left with me. It was weird, leaving you there with a stranger."

"He's from Fredericksburg."

"I know. I heard him." Her voice was heavy with sarcasm.

"What's that supposed to mean?"

"Bragging about his football days? I was, like, 'Dude, you're out of college, get a life already.'" She laughed, but I didn't respond.

A minute later, she pulled into a McDonald's parking lot, switched off the car, and twisted in her seat to face me. "C'mon. You drank too much and hooked up with some dude you met in a bar. You'll live to tell the tale."

"Thanks for being so supportive." I rolled my eyes as a whiff of McDonald's French Fry grease hit my nose.

"Hey, whatever you did with Mr. Peaked In High School can't be that bad."

"Don't tell anybody."

"Who would I tell?"

"I don't know. Can we just agree last night never happened?"

"What, exactly, 'never happened'?" Della asked.

I glared at her.

"Fine. I promise. But a walk of shame isn't the end of the world." She bent her head and our eyes met. "Right?"

"Right." Saying it meant nothing. I felt dirty and wrong in a hundred ways.

"What happened to your shirt?" she asked.

"I don't know."

"What *do* you know?"

I crossed my arms. *Take a hint. I don't want to talk about it.*

"Sissie." Della's jaw tightened and one brow quirked. "Was he rough with you?"

"I'm fine."

She huffed and squeezed her eyes tight on me. "Why don't I believe you? Did he push himself—"

"It wasn't like that." My answer flew from my mouth. A few seconds passed, and I sat a little straighter. "I got drunk. We made out. End of story."

"That shirt tells a different story." She paused. "We could go to the hospital. We're in a whole other town, your parents'll never know."

"I'm fine," I ground out, wiping smudged liner from my eyes in the visor mirror. I slapped it shut and leaned back. "Please, just get me out of here and forget it ever happened."

Two

Junior prom, term papers, and summer plans distracted us from discussing our time in San Marcos. In a few short weeks, Della and I would fall into our summer routine, sneaking in afternoons floating down the river beneath towering live oaks and cottonwoods along our little slice of heaven in the Texas Hill Country.

Della worked at her parent's realty office every summer, and I locked in a job this year, too, teaching tennis lessons to bored kids at the country club three mornings a week. Not exactly riveting, but it satisfied my parents' wishes for me to earn my own money.

The week before finals, Della and I caught the same spring cold. Della bounced back quickly, but it did a number on me. Breathing was torture. My head pounded and I couldn't keep food down. Our family doctor put me in the hospital for dehydration. They slid me into a CAT scan machine and must've stuck me a dozen times.

A day of IV fluids brought me back to life, but the hospital drove my parents a little crazy. The nurse said they'd discharge me after the doctor made rounds. Until then, my dad paced my room like a Great Dane in a kennel.

Don't judge me, but I'd always seen my parents as dogs. Dad was a Dane, with his deep voice, imposing height, and haunting eyes. Flitting around him was a well-groomed Bichon Frise known as "Mom."

My brother, Brent, had won the genetic lottery and absorbed their good looks, smarts, and charisma—like a stately Weimaraner with gray eyes that drilled clean through you. When my turn came, Mother Nature overcorrected for her generosity and produced a mutt. *Woof!*

If Dr. Marlowe didn't arrive soon, someone was going to get bit.

HOURS LATER, I WAS SITTING crisscross applesauce, staring a hole through my English notebook when Dr. Marlowe finally moseyed into my room.

"Thomas," he said, meeting my dad's gaze. "I've got some news." A darkness had taken over his usually cheerful face.

I thought I was better. *Oh, God. It's serious. Am I dying?*

Dad raised one of his caterpillar eyebrows. Neither man looked at me.

Mom shined her trademark welcome-to-my-cocktail-party grin at the doctor before directing her optimistic spotlight on me. "I'm sure everything is normal."

My eyes returned to my trusted doctor. His had been a familiar face throughout my life. Whether I saw him for immunizations or spells of tonsillitis, he maintained a jovial tone and a smile. Today, his kind eyes looked older and his gray hair more disheveled than I remembered.

He confused me with his "we need to talk" tone and deflated expression. He inched to the edge of my bed and ran a nervous hand over the back of his neck. His eyes flitted around the room before meeting mine. "Sissie, you're pregnant."

The words echoed off the hard tile floor.

Give me a disease. Cancer—a curable kind. Anything but this.

His mouth made a flat line. "You understand?"

My eyes fell to a blue line I'd drawn down the middle of the page of my spiral, where I had noted differences between F. Scott

Fitzgerald's East Egg and West Egg. In that moment, I willed that line to crack open and tug me out of that sterile hospital room.

My father quietly excused himself, not even looking at me. When the door swept closed behind him, everything went fuzzy.

While my mother quizzed Dr. Marlowe about the reliability of the blood tests, convinced there was no way her daughter was . . . "with *child*," I thought of Della. A part of me didn't want to tell her. Another part wanted to run to her, hoping she'd know what to do.

Suddenly, my stomach flip-flopped and the nausea returned. Sayonara to the broth and crackers I'd eaten earlier.

A nurse helped clean me up and escorted us to Dad's Suburban— picking up, no doubt, on Mom's shock and Dad's anger. She patted my arm as I slid into the backseat and tossed me a reassuring wink as she closed the door.

Tension filled every square inch of our car. I waited for it to full-on smother me dead. My father cleared his throat, his call for us to "listen up."

"I'm talking to the both of you. You hear me?" he asked.

Mom responded with a faint nod.

"This is not to leave our family." He aimed an alarming glare at her. "Not to share with your bridge ladies, at the club, or with the neighbors. Hear me?"

"Yes, sir," Mom answered, childlike.

He turned to me. "Same for you. Not Della, not even your brother. We'll decide how we'll handle this situation."

You mean my *situation?*

"Priscilla?" He only used my real name when he was mad.

"Yes, sir," I managed.

He was done talking, leaving me to sit with my shame.

At home, Mom flitted in and out of my bedroom like the doctor had diagnosed me with the kissing disease, not pregnancy. She delivered trays of food I didn't eat and juices that turned warm on my nightstand without a mention of the obvious.

Dad's mandate put a steep wall around me, and I was as alone as I'd ever been. I played the part of a normal sixteen-year-old girl preparing for final exams as well as I could, but no matter how long I stared at my notes, I couldn't force the material to sprout in my one-track mind. *I'm pregnant.*

At times, I caught my hand settling on my belly, palpating and prodding for proof of life. A bizarre warmth filled my chest as I sensed the tiny being taking root in my body, and I harnessed a thread of comfort knowing I wasn't completely alone.

Sunday evening, Dad marched into my bedroom. I looked up from my trig problems. He might as well have been carrying his briefcase for all the courtroom swagger radiating from him.

"Thomas?" Mom called, chasing behind him. "She's resting—"

He raised a hand to pause her, and she froze in the doorway.

I wasn't resting, and I wasn't studying. Those trig problems could've been drawn in Sanskrit, and I would have understood them the same.

"Sissie?" his voice lacked the harshness I had expected.

"Your dad's talking to you," my mother said.

I'm pregnant, not deaf.

He took a seat on my bed and crossed his right foot over his left knee.

"Hey," was the most I could say.

He tipped his head to the side. For a beat, a thread of sympathy shone on his face. "How'd we get here, young lady?"

"I'm sorry."

"'I'm sorry' doesn't make sense of these circumstances. How'd we *get* here?"

Anxiety roped around my insides. I feared it might squash the life from my tiny being.

"Well?" he asked.

"San Marcos," I mumbled.

Disappointment settled on his face. "When you were with Della." It wasn't a question. He twisted to wag a finger at Mom. "I *told* you that Della was low-class. Should've pushed her into another friend group. Maybe she'd be . . . I don't know . . . dating a nice young man instead of . . ."

The reality of my situation seemed to be hanging in his throat.

"This happens to normal girls all the time, and they figure it out." Mom said in a tone that grated on my nerves. "Let's put on our thinking caps and decide—"

"You two are done making decisions," Dad snapped. "I'll tell you how we'll handle this."

I crossed my arms, bracing for turbulence.

"Kathleen, we'll take her to one of those clinics to take care of it."

"I'll call—"

"You'll call no one," he barked. "I'll find a place. One in San Antonio or Austin, where no one will know us."

"Brent's in Austin," Mom reminded him.

"God damn it. I know where my son lives. Austin's a big city, and I doubt Brent's been in the market for an abortion."

Of course my perfect brother wouldn't screw up his personal life or his career as an architect. He was the golden child, and I, especially in light of recent events, was the pariah.

As far as Dad was concerned, the poor choices I'd made negated my eligibility to participate in this conversation, even if my body was at the heart of the discussion. His unilateral decision scored my soul and inflated my resentment.

"Mom and I will let you know what we'll do next." Dad crossed his arms and didn't even look at me when he spoke. "Until then, keep it to yourself and study for those tests."

Love you, too, Dad.

On Monday, Mom dropped me off at school in time for my oddly scheduled final exam block. Before I climbed out of her car, she touched my sleeve. "Honey, just go about your business like normal."

Normal. Check. Like it's that easy.

"Dad and I will take care of everything." She leaned over the console and pulled me into her arms.

"Hey." Della appeared outside the car. Her frown questioned why I hadn't driven myself.

Mom smiled at her through the window. "Lunch this afternoon?" She asked, offering to repeat our end-of-the-school year tradition.

"Sure," Della said.

"Is that alright?" I muttered to Mom. "With Dad?"

"Of course." Mom painted on a bright smile. "Della, can you drive her home?"

"Yes, ma'am," Della answered as I exited the car. She asked me, "Why's your mom driving you?"

"Guess she's worried about me. No biggie."

That afternoon, Della drove us to my house, where Mom had set two TV trays in the den so we could watch *Days of Our Lives*. At some point, when Della stepped out of the room, Mom cleared her throat dramatically and tapped her lips—a reminder of my dad's mandate.

In our post-lunch sluggishness, Della and I lounged on the leather sofas, perking up when Mom popped into the den. "Will you ladies be alright if I take off for a few hours?"

"Don't worry about us," Della said, dismissing my mother without a second thought.

The garage door hummed to a close and Della shifted to my couch. "You and your mom are acting super weird. Spill it."

"Nothing." I fixed my gaze on the TV.

"My mom's been working her rosary beads to a pulp. Why didn't you call when you got out of the hospital?"

"I'm fine."

"Not gonna lie. You hurt my feelings. I went up there, and they said you went home. I left like five messages with your parents. Didn't they tell you?"

"I was tired. That's all."

"Bull." She stared through me, attempting to decode my secret. I had to look away.

When I glanced at her face again, it looked more pissed off than curious. *How can I lie to her?* A wave of emotions shook me till I could no longer control my expression or the tears cascading over my cheeks.

"Oh, shit." She looked me up and down. "You're so skinny. Is it HIV?"

"Nothing like that." I hesitated. "I'm . . ." *My God, this is too real.* "I'm pregnant."

"You're screwing with me."

"San Marcos." That was all I had to say and proof enough I wasn't screwing with her.

Her olive skin went white. Then, something came over her—something inexplicably maternal and kind, something I was in desperate need of—and she wrapped me in her arms. "We'll figure it out. Don't worry." She patted my back.

"Dad's making me get an abortion."

She pulled away from me and squared her hands on my shoulders. With a serious face, she said, "Sissie, you can't. You just can't. Besides the fact that it's murder, there are couples all over who can't have kids who would give your baby a happy life."

"I don't know if I can go through with it."

"With what?"

"Either one." My hand snapped to my belly. "Maybe I should keep it and raise it myself?"

Della smiled. "I could help, like a supportive auntie?"

"What about school?" I asked.

"I told you—we'll figure it out."

Who was I kidding? There was no way Mom and Dad would let me keep this baby. But Della's idea might be one way I could make something good come out of this mess.

Three

"Della, I don't know anything about adoption." The words clunked out of my mouth as I unpacked my feelings about incubating another human and then (this was the part I feared most) ejecting it from my body.

"Are you kidding?" Della's face lit up. "Catholics have adoption covered. One of my mom's friends at church works with an agency in San Antonio. They connect pregnant girls with people who want kids all the time." Della's expression said she was ready to run with the idea. Once she took off, there was no reining her in.

"I don't know about having it grow up around here, so close to me."

"I'll bet they give you a choice where the baby goes." She made it sound simple, like ordering a pizza. "I'll get her number."

"Wait." I clutched her arm. "My parents can't know. They can't even know I told you. Dad won't even let us tell my brother."

"He doesn't need to know. Relax." She bit her lip. "Sissie, did you tell the guy?"

"Why would I tell him? I hope I never see him again."

"Don't you remember that *20/20* we saw? About that baby who was ripped out of his home because the biological dad, who didn't know he got the chick pregnant, came forward? It made my heart hurt when they took the little boy out of his adopted mom's arms. You've got to tell him."

"What if he wants it?" I reconsidered my question. *There's no way Caleb could take care of a goldfish, much less a human.*

"You just have to tell him and get him to say he doesn't care what you do with it." She paused. "In case he comes back later and says he didn't know, I'll be your witness. Let's call him."

"I don't even have his number."

"You called me from his phone."

"Like two months ago."

"I saved it, in case I got lost picking you up." She removed that giant phone of hers from her backpack and began punching its keypad.

"Wait," I said, but she put her hand up, shushing me, and pressed the phone to her ear.

"Hi. Caleb?" She lobbed a big-eyed look at me. "Can you hold on?"

My stomach dropped to the floor when she shoved her phone at me. I stared like the phone was radioactive and heard him ask, "You still there?"

I dragged it to my ear. "Hello?"

"Who's this?" he asked.

"Sissie Klein? It's been awhile, but we hung out in San Marcos. In March?" *Please remember me.*

"Hold up. I remember you. Yeah. Pretty Sissie."

How many Sissies does he know? "Could we get together?" My heart pounded loudly while I waited for his response.

"What'd you have in mind?" he asked.

"Um. Are you coming to Fredericksburg anytime soon?"

"I'm here, hanging out at my parents' house."

Covering the phone's mouthpiece, I whispered, "He's in town."

"Tell him to come over."

"Now?"

"Get it over with," she whispered.

"What if my mom comes back?"

"You know how your mom shops. She's always gone longer than she says. We'll get him out of here by the time she shows up," she said with certainty.

Right after I tell him I'm pregnant, he'll run for the hills.

I moved my hand from the mouthpiece. "Can you swing by my house?"

"I need to shower up first, but yeah. Give me a half hour."

Picturing a perfect storm of his arrival coinciding with my mother's, I gave him the address and ended the call.

"He's coming." I bobbed my head, reassuring myself I could go through with it.

"Just tell him, and when he comes to, tell him you don't want anything from him and you're giving the kid to a good home. Once he agrees, you're golden."

I wanted to trust her, but it all sounded too simple. "He'll be shocked. Maybe mad, even."

"Why? You were tipsy. If he knew how to use a condom, you wouldn't be here."

"They're not foolproof."

She rolled her eyes and reminded me what to say to him when he arrived, but I was too nervous to make sense of her words—and she had so many words.

♋︎⤛

WHEN THE DOORBELL RANG, MY heart did a twist and my mouth went dry.

"I'll go," Della said, crossing herself like she did when she walked into mass on Sundays. "Get yourself together."

No "getting myself together" can prepare me to tell a guy I've only met once that he's the father of my baby. Our baby. I lingered in the hallway, hoping he'd just turn around and walk out that door. Instead, he asked about me, and he sounded genuinely interested in seeing me—not like the jerk I remembered the morning I left his place.

"Sis?" Della called, and I poked my head into our formal living room. She waved for me to join them.

Caleb panned the room and bounced on his toes. His hair was lighter than I remembered. He wore jeans, and his linty black Polo shirt looked like he'd washed it with a load of fluffy white towels.

"Hi." I gave a slight wave.

"Hey." He raised his hands in a surprised gesture and leaned toward me for a hug. "You're looking hot," he said as I pulled away.

Looks can be deceiving. I tried to smile but a whiff of his cologne revived my nausea and I had to close my mouth.

The three of us stood there, the room shaking in the silence.

Finally, Della pulled at my arm. "Go on. Tell him."

"Tell me what?" he asked, turning to me with a stupid grin on his face.

You won't be smiling for long, buddy.

"Why don't we all sit down?" Della said.

Caleb hesitated.

"As in, *sit down*," Della said, firmly this time. "This is important."

"Hope it's good," he said, falling into my dad's favorite wing chair.

"Oh, it's . . . something." Della's forehead pitched up, and I frowned at her. "So, anyway . . . Sissie, what were you gonna say?" Della tilted her head toward Caleb.

Caleb shook his keychain and tapped a foot against the edge of the coffee table.

"Well . . ." I shifted my gaze to Della.

She pumped her head demandingly and mouthed, "Just say it."

"Caleb . . . after that night, I got real sick. Sick enough to go to the hospital." My heart thudded and I wasn't sure I could force the words out.

"Oh, man. That sucks."

"And while I was there, I found out . . . I'm pregnant." I dropped my chin, keeping my eyes on him.

"Whatever." He pushed his hair back and laughed.

This is SO not funny. Please don't make me say it again.

"Hey, sorry you got sick, but that's not a good joke to throw at a guy."

"She's not kidding," Della snapped.

After a long stare down with Della, his face fell. "Are you serious? Like serious, serious?"

"Dead serious," Della said.

"Holy shit," he mumbled and flipped his gaze on me. "You sure?"

"They did a blood test, so it's legit. But I don't expect you to do anything," I said.

"She's giving it up for adoption," Della announced, a bit too confidently.

"Ah, that's cool." His voice conveyed relief, but his cheeks stayed flushed. "Are you sure?" Suddenly, he looked as sick as I felt.

"Yes," Della answered for me. "You don't want a kid, do you?"

"Shit, no." His eyes went wide.

"Sorry," I said, automatically, and Della's face contorted with displeasure.

"Why are you sorry?" Della asked. "He participated in the deed."

"I just mean, sorry to have to tell you. Pretty shocking, huh?" I waited for him to answer.

"He's fine," Della quipped.

"Whoa. Let's just back up," Caleb said. "You sure it's mine?"

I hadn't expected this. Anger bubbled up in my chest and I licked my lips. "The doctor said I'm between eight and nine weeks along. That's when I was in San Marcos, and there . . . hasn't been . . . anybody . . . else." Tears sprouted between each word.

"Alright. Calm down. So what'd your parents say?" He glanced around the house.

"My dad wants me to get an"—I was barely audible now—"abortion."

"Well, if you wanna go that way, I'll go in half," he said. "Heard it's not bad. Doctor takes care of it and zing-zang-zoom, done."

Guess I know his choice.

Della stood and looked at him like she might treat him to an enthusiastic throat punch. "You talk like it's a quick trip to the ATM, not killing a baby," she snapped.

He turned to me, his voice breaking, "Do you actually want it?"

"*It* is a baby, not a part on your car." Della's anger seemed to overflow then, and she released a villainous laugh. Her voice dropped a few octaves. "Gee, Caleb, the little lady you knocked up's gonna set you back a couple Benjamins."

"You're a bitch," he snarled. "You don't even know me. Screw you. This is between me and Sissie." He stepped toward me. "So, you're set on giving it up?"

"I guess." I hunched my shoulders. "I don't know what I'm supposed to do."

"No offense, Sissie—you're pretty as hell, but I'd make a terrible dad, and you don't want a kid jacking up your life."

A security chime indicated someone had entered the house, and I let out a groan.

"Uh-oh," Della murmured, her eyes flashing to me.

"Sissie, whose car's blocking my side of the driveway?" Dad hollered, his footsteps clambering toward us.

"Hi, Mr. Klein," Della called toward the hall between the living room and the kitchen.

Caleb frowned a question to me, and I whispered, "My dad."

"Shit." Caleb stirred in the chair.

"He's gotta hear it sometime," Della said.

"Hear what?" Dad's brows rose at Caleb's presence in the room.

"This is Caleb." Della pointed. "The father."

Four

Caleb's introduction left a crater in the middle of our living room that would be seen for decades.

At first, Dad pumped his head up and down while he digested the information. In those tense seconds, my heart nearly beat out of my chest.

Finally, he cleared his throat and waved a finger at Caleb. "The father? This guy?"

"He sure is," Della said. She crossed her arms and jutted out her chin at Caleb, stepping beside Dad like she might claim a reward.

But Dad didn't seem to notice. His glare fell on me like a white hot spotlight.

"Priscilla," Dad said in a low voice, rattling me to my core.

"I'm sorry," I muttered and dropped to one of the two stiff cream sofas framing the room.

Dad's head twisted to Caleb, who was slouching in his chair.

Slouching like that's gonna make Dad want to kill you even more, I telegraphed silently. *If you don't want to die today, stand up. Show him some respect.*

But Caleb wouldn't look my way. He just sat there, running a hand over his stupid face.

"On your feet, son." Dad said.

Here comes the boom.

"Step to it, I haven't got all day," Dad ordered.

Caleb rose, breathing like the motion had knocked the wind from his lungs, eyes fixed on the ground.

"That floor isn't talking to you," Dad growled. "Eyes up here."

Caleb pushed his hair back again and lifted his gaze to my dad who was at least a head taller.

Dad's eyes narrowed slowly. "I know you. What's your name?"

"C-C-Caleb. Caleb Dietrich."

Dad cleared his throat, mustering up a mess of something in his chest. His mouth bent to one side, and he released a derisive sigh. "Pike Dietrich's boy?"

"You know my dad?" Caleb's expression relaxed somewhat.

"Know *of* him," Dad said.

Crap! I didn't just mess around with the wrong guy but the wrong family, too?

"How old're you, son?" Dad's chest rose while he waited for Caleb to choke out a response.

"Tw . . . twenty . . . th . . . three."

"Know how old she is?" Dad held his fisted hands at his sides. He didn't wait for a response. "Sixteen. My daughter is sixteen is sixteen."

Caleb tucked his head like a puppy fresh off a spanking.

"What do you have to say for yourself, son?"

"She was at a bar, so I—" Caleb said.

Shut up, Caleb. Will you just freaking shut up?

"You in college?" Dad asked.

"Graduated in December."

"Hmm." Dad turned his back on him, reloading for the next attack.

"You knew how old we were." Della had to get a piece of the action. "You told us how you went to the same high school. Remember? When you were bragging about your football days? I think it was right after you bought her a drink." Eyeing Dad eagerly, she added, "He was probably getting her drunk so he could—"

"Della," Dad barked. "I've got this." He pinched the top of his nose and addressed Caleb again. "Know what they call a twenty-three-year-old man fooling around with a sixteen-year-old girl?"

"Not good," Caleb said.

"Not good." Dad grunted. "The law calls him a rapist."

"Sir?" Caleb asked. "She was into me."

"Doesn't matter what she was into. My pregnant daughter's a victim of statutory rape."

Caleb's face broke out in a sweat. "I didn't mean to—"

"Didn't mean to," Dad grumbled. "How long has this"—he pointed to Caleb, then me, then back at Caleb—"gone on?"

"Um, we just, um, got together the one time."

Ugh. He makes it sound so trashy.

Dad's shock of silence made space for the *tick-tick-tick* of our grandfather clock. For a moment, I fell into its hypnotic escape. Any hope of a peaceful conclusion vanished, however, when Dad pushed one of his wingtips forward in an intimidation-packed step. "Not too bright, are you?"

Caleb flushed. "I thought—"

"You thought, alright," Dad's voice rose abruptly, then fell to a mutter. "Certainly, not with your noggin." He shook his head. "Priscilla, of all the boys you could've gotten mixed up with."

Caleb's head popped up whack-a-mole style, "Who's Priscilla?"

In slow motion, Della pointed to me.

"Sissie is Priscilla." Dad explained. "Didn't bother to get her full name before you . . . Jesus Christ."

"Thought your name was Sissie." Caleb looked to me, but I didn't answer. He turned back to Dad. "Sorry."

Dad's eyes narrowed. "You're sorry?" Fury dripped from his face.

Caleb's gaze bounced around the room, searching for clues. "I know—"

"You know what? You know you shouldn't have helped yourself to my *daughter*?" A drop of spit flew from Dad's mouth.

"I, uh . . ." Caleb stuttered.

"Not making a lick of sense, son. You don't know up from down, do you?"

"Guess not, sir."

"Willing to bet that's the first truth you've spoken all day."

"Sorry, man," Caleb said.

"Sorry ain't raising my grandchild."

His grandchild?

"It's okay. She's giving it away." Caleb tossed a glance my way. "Right?" At Dad's groan, he added, "Er, or she'll get rid of it?" He pointed to me. "Sissie, tell him what you want."

"You think I'm gonna let this decision fall on a sixteen-year-old girl?"

"Yes, sir."

"What?"

"No? I mean, no, sir."

"Man of many words, are you?"

Caleb stared at his sneakers like he'd just noticed they were tied to the wrong feet.

Dad twisted around. We locked eyes, and he jerked his head at Della. "Sissie?"

The message in my name was clear; I gave him a tiny nod, pressing my feet to the floor, then grabbed Della. "Come on." I pulled her arm. Her feet moved toward the hall, but her attention remained fastened on the scene behind us. "Probably better if you went home." I pushed her over to the front door. "Come on."

At the door, Della stood firm. She wasn't going anywhere. I needed to give her something to do.

"Hey," I said, "while they talk, can you go home and call that lady from your church? Find out how it works?"

"Sure." Energy returned to her face. "Call me the second he leaves." She touched my belly. "Take care of that little peanut."

"Little peanut" created an identity to the being growing inside me. My hand grazed my waist, and a pleasant flash of warmth filled my body.

"I'm afraid to leave you." Her face rumpled and her dark eyes pleaded to stay.

"I'll be fine. I promise."

Once Della was safely out the door, I slipped into the living room and took a seat on the sofa.

Dad flicked his eyes toward me, and his expression eased. "Doing okay?"

I nodded and pushed my hair off my shoulders, appreciating how Della's departure had quelled some of the agitation she injected into the air.

Caleb leaned forward and offered a smile.

"Sissie, give us a minute," Dad said.

I frowned at him, but he ignored me.

"Caleb, follow me." Dad stomped to his office and Caleb followed, feet dragging. The door clicked shut—and dread flattened me.

My life's purpose was what? To send a guy to jail? How long before my parents send me away to preserve their reputations?

The storm of emotions grew too strong, so I retreated to my bed. I curled up beneath my comforter, praying for sleep, praying all that I'd witnessed had been a nightmare. Sleep didn't come, and after some time, Dad's office door clicked open from the hall.

Time to learn my fate—or Caleb's? I ventured down the hall and peered into the living room.

"You alright?" Dad asked, his face brighter and gentler than it had been earlier.

Caleb stood nearby, less fidgety than before, and I caught a look pass between them as if they were soldiers fighting for the same army.

"Your face is green." Dad nudged me toward the sofa.

I threw a hand over my face as Dad left the room.

Caleb walked over. "Can I do anything?"

I kept my mouth shut and shook my head.

He twisted his hands and looked down at me. Then he pointed to the space beside me. "Can I?"

At my nod, he joined me with unfamiliar gentility, watching me like a pot that might boil over. "I gotta apologize about being a jerk when you left that morning. Shit, Sissie . . . do I call you Sissie or Priscilla?"

I mouthed, "Sissie."

"Cool. I like that better. Anyway, I gotta say I'm sorry for screwing up everything."

"It's okay." Was it though, really?

Dad reappeared with a sleeve of saltines. He passed it to Caleb, and again I sensed a sort of softening between them. Caleb pulled the plastic seam of the saltine pack apart, clumsily dropping crumbs on the sofa.

I took a cracker from his hand and held it on my tongue. I was surprised by how the saltiness offset the acid. *How did Dad know?*

"Hellooo," my mother announced her arrival from the other side of the house, accompanied by a commotion of plastic shopping bags. "Do we have company?"

The cracker lodged in my throat. I coughed it loose as my Dad left the room.

Ladies and gentlemen, prepare for round two.

"Did the doctors tell you anything else? Besides . . ." Caleb glanced at my belly.

"Not really. I'm worried he . . . or she . . . might have problems. Before I found out, I took a bunch of medicine." Guilt brought a crescendo of tears to my eyes. "What if I, like, ruined—?"

"You couldn't have known." His hand moved to my face and a shaky finger wiped tears from my cheek. "Don't cry. We'll figure it out."

"How?" I asked.

"I don't know exactly, but don't worry." He patted my shoulder like we were down in the last quarter of a football game. He leaned back, his eyes drifting upward. "Guess I'd better start looking for a job around here."

I wasn't sure if he was talking to me or to himself. "Caleb, aren't you moving to Austin?"

"Still don't have a job there." He huffed. "Doesn't matter. Can't leave you to do this alone."

"If Dad has his way, it'll be over soon."

"Ah, he's not gonna make you do that. He scared the hell out of me at first, but once we talked, he's not so bad. He wants us to talk about taking care of it—the baby—together."

Sweat raced down my back. "Earlier, you said you wouldn't be a good dad."

"I was talking out of my ass—you'd just told me, and I was hoping you'd tell me to screw off." He touched my hand. "Listen, your family's not like mine. My dad's cool, but he's not home a lot, and . . . my mom's got problems. I'm an idiot about babies. Don't know anything about them, but I'll do my best."

"I'm still in high school—"

"Yeah, that sucks but what if the big guy's sending a message?" He gestured overhead. "Like this kid's here for a reason? What if our kid's like, our destiny?"

My immediate destiny was supposed to be teaching tennis to whiny kids, not incubating one. "What, exactly, did my dad say to you?"

"Um, he's worried about you . . . finishing school and all that . . ."

Mom sashayed into the room, missile-locked on Caleb. "Hello. I'm Sissie's mother. Call me 'Kathleen.'"

I was so grateful when Caleb stood and held out a hand. "Nice to meet you."

"Nice to meet you, too," she said.

Dad frowned at her. "Well, 'nice' isn't why we're here. Let's have a seat."

And . . . he's back.

Mom propped herself on the arm of the sofa beside me and stroked the back of my hair.

"Mr. Klein, um . . ." Caleb pushed back his hair and gestured to me. "I told her I'd help take care of her . . . the baby, too."

Anyone care to ask my opinion?

"How would that look?" Dad asked.

"Um, like you and I were talking . . . back there?" he pointed down the hall.

"What?" I asked, but it was like no one heard me.

"Having kids isn't an amusement park ride, son. They cry and get sick. They need things. Things require money. As I recall, you don't have a job."

"No, but I'll—"

Dad waved a hand at him. "Kids need a house. They need stability."

"Well, you and her mom'll be here, and—"

"Her mother and I weren't in the market to raise a teenager and a grandchild at the same time."

"You wouldn't. I'd raise it with her," Caleb said, glancing at me with confidence.

His dedication was a gift I wasn't sure I wanted. My stomach churned, and I covered my mouth with the same hand marked by Caleb's touch and his cologne. The scent increased my urge to purge.

"Big talk." Dad scrubbed his chin. "Wasn't but a little while ago you were squirming. Now, you're ready to raise a child with this girl you hardly know?"

"I am." He gave a hard nod. "Sir, I'm responsible. I can be. I will be. I will take care of her and our baby."

Five

I didn't stick around to hear Caleb's defense. In fact, I barely reached my bathroom's white tile before those saltines came back for an encore.

"Oh, dear." Mom appeared behind me and patted my sweaty face with a damp cloth.

"Thanks, Mom," I said with a moan. She stood over me. Something was different about her. "Did you cut your hair?"

"Three weeks ago," she said.

I hadn't noticed, but I hadn't noticed many things while I was sicker than a dog. The Jennifer Aniston hairdo framed her face nicely and made her eyes look bigger. But that wasn't all. She seemed thinner than usual and fragile, like a bird with a fractured wing. *Did I do this to her?*

"Make room." She dropped to the floor beside me. "Tell me what happened."

I closed my eyes, aligning the clunky pieces of my short history with Caleb. No matter how I turned them, they wouldn't form a satisfying memory—none I could bear to tell her.

Anything she'd learn would only magnify her disappointment. Mom always wanted me to attend her alma mater and get into her sorority. If my disinterest in her high-society standards hadn't killed my chances already, the baby growing inside me would certainly do the trick.

"What's he like?" She ran a rosy painted fingernail along my right arm.

I paused, considering what to share. One thing for sure, I'd spare her the grisly details of sneaking into a club, getting drunk, and waking up at that duplex the following morning.

"Kind of a goofball, and—"

She must've read my expression because she changed the subject. "This baby might have the luck of the Irish." At my lost expression, she added, "Red hair is lucky."

Some luck.

"Maybe we should give it away? Della knows a lady who does adoptions, giving babies to people who can't have kids," I said.

"Is that what you want?" she asked.

"I don't know. I don't want to . . . get rid of it. But having a baby come out of my body seems freakish. Even if I could go through with it, I'm not sure I could give it to a stranger."

"Babies are work." Her face split into a peaceful smile. "But they're pretty wonderful."

"Were you scared when you had Brent and me?"

"Definitely."

"Having a kid moving around in you—like an alien." I grimaced. "Don't even want to think about how they get it out."

"Well," she breathed out a long breath. "Much the same way it got there."

That's what I'm afraid of.

"But once they're here, you forget that part. You're overtaken by love for their tiny hands, their wiggly feet, and . . . oh, the smell." Mom sighed. "Like nothing you've ever sniffed before. They're so clean and sweet. Ahh. Babies smell like heaven."

I shrugged, not seeing anything heavenly about my situation. "I'm so confused."

"Girls like you—young women, I mean—find themselves in situations like this all the time. Pregnancy is completely normal. It's how humans continue to exist."

"No offense, Mom, but nothing about this is normal."

She placed a hand over mine. "I'll tell you a little secret, but you have to keep it between us. Promise?"

"Yeah, sure. Promise."

"When I married your dad, I was in the same shape." She knocked her chin upward. "I was eighteen."

"But Brent's—"

"Not Brent." She winced and her eyes fell to her hands. "A girl, Audrey. She came almost three months early. So tiny." Mom held her hands together like she was imagining holding my sister.

"Does Brent know?"

She shrugged. "You dad might have told him. I'm not sure."

"Huh." I nodded, picturing *that* conversation. "Is she why you got married?"

Her mouth twisted to the side. "Maybe."

"But you were, like, twenty-five when you had Brent?"

"We were in love. We waited until after law school to have you and Brent."

"What did Grandma say when you told her . . . about the first one?"

"She threw a hissy fit. Then, after a while, she said, 'What are we gonna do about it?' She started planning a wedding before your father bought me a ring."

"Can't imagine getting married . . . at my age."

"Have you and Caleb talked about it?"

"I barely got the chance to tell him when Dad walked in and pulled him into the study. Caleb came out saying he wants us to raise the baby together." An image of us passing a baby back and forth made my stomach churn. "Surely, he's not talking about getting married?"

"Well . . . " She paused. "Let's put you in your baby's place. Would you want to grow up with parents who didn't live together?"

I didn't answer.

"I've always felt sorry for those kids—never really feeling grounded?" She met my gaze. "What about later? When you and Caleb get married to other people? Your baby will have to contend with stepparents and stepsiblings?"

"Man, I wish I could just go back and not do it."

"You're learning that grown-up choices can lead to grown-up problems."

Her soft-spoken admonition compounded my shame. I leaned into her lap.

"Oh, little lady," she repeated, rubbing my back in circles like she had when I was little.

As we sat on that cold tile, my mother's admission made me question every detail of my life. I'd always worried I'd disappoint her. She was a social butterfly. I was an introvert. She was crafty and fiercely competitive on the tennis court. I was neither.

The woman I'd seen in our family albums looked like she'd been born with loads of confidence. I wanted to return to those photos. Beneath Mom's tacky perm and clumpy mascara, would I pick up on her secret?

I didn't ask how it happened. I mean, I knew how it happened, obviously—but I didn't ask for details surrounding the incident. Did she laugh too loudly at Dad's jokes, trying too hard to be cool? Did she drink too much? Did they love each other before it happened? Or, had they decided to fall in love when they learned they had a child on the way? My assumptions about my straight-and-narrow parents began to sway and bend. Who were these people who raised me?

❦

THE FOLLOWING MORNING, I LINGERED in my bed, slightly less nauseated even if the worry was just as strong. My flannel pajamas warmed me as my mother blasted the air conditioning unnecessarily. *What's her sudden fascination with turning the house into a meat locker?*

With a knock on the door, Mom's face peeked into my room. "Okay to come in?"

The door opened wider. Della's smiling face appeared, delivering a flicker of palpable relief.

"I'll leave y'all to catch up." Mom tossed me a wink.

Della promptly stomped on that flicker as soon as she closed the door behind her. She pulled on a serious face. "What the heck, Sissie? You said you'd call."

"Sorry. I got sick and went to bed."

"What'd your parents say about the baby?"

"We're talking about it, still. I'm not going to have a . . . you know."

"Thank God," Della said, waving her hands over her head. "They okay with adoption?"

"Not exactly." I paused, wanting to be careful with my words. "I'm probably going to keep my baby." Saying it made it terrifyingly real.

"So your parents are helping you?"

"They are . . . but Caleb will be involved, too." I closed my eyes to avoid her response.

"Yuck." Her top lip rose like she'd just sniffed rancid eggs.

"Don't be like that. He's growing on my parents."

"Like mold," she snarled.

"Del, you've got to stop that. You're talking about my baby's father."

"Two days ago, you hated the guy. Now you're defending him?"

"Keep an open mind."

"What about school?"

"Haven't gotten that far, but Mom's looking into how to get a GED. Then maybe some online college courses before the baby gets here."

Della frowned. "You sure put some thought into this since yesterday. Why can't you stay in regular high school?"

"What am I supposed to do with a baby while I'm at school? Put him in my backpack?"

"My mom can babysit. She's just answering phones all day at the agency."

Leave my baby at the real estate agency where your mother smokes all day? No, thanks. "Della, it's complicated."

"Complicated, huh?" She gnawed on her bottom lip. "What

about *him*?" She didn't have to say Caleb's name—I knew who she meant. "You know? The guy who got you drunk and pregnant?" She crossed her arms. "Now he thinks he can be someone's dad?"

"He *is* someone's dad. Look, he and Dad talked. It's okay."

"You sure he didn't slip your dad a roofie?" She huffed. "Jesus. How can you even consider doing this with him?"

"Do what? Have the kid we made? You're the one who said I should keep it."

"For adoption, not to raise with him."

"Della, it was also your idea to call him, remember?"

"To get him to sign off, not to move in with you and your parents." She stared through me. "Why are you looking at me like that? You're not thinking of moving in together, are you?" Her voice hardened. "Say you're joking. Right now. Say it."

Words wouldn't rise to my lips.

Della's voice wavered, and her eyes glistened with fresh tears. "I can't lose you."

"You're not losing me. I'll be right here."

"Not if you're with *him*."

"Nothing'll change between us."

Her lips moved, but no sound came out. Then she found her voice again. "What? Are you going to become one of those women who stay home all the time? Like—"

"Like, my mom?"

"Well, yeah, I guess." Disgust had made itself at home on her face.

"What's wrong with being like my mom?" I asked while my pulse ticked faster.

"Really? You're the one who said she has a boring life. Come on. The way she follows your dad around like a sad puppy? You don't want that."

I *had* said it, but hearing those words fly out of her mouth sliced deep. And she wasn't done yet.

"From what I hear, Caleb's just like his run-around dad."

"Who said that?"

"My mom," Della spat out.

"How does your mom know about Caleb's family?"

"Yesterday, after your dad found out, I told my mom so she could help us with the adoption thing."

"You told her?" I pinched my lips together. "Who else did you tell?"

She rolled her eyes. "Nobody else. We're Catholic and all that, but expecting my mom to believe you're a virgin and that kid's a divine miracle would be stretching it."

"What'd she say?"

"Crossed herself a hundred times and cried. Oh, and she asked how you were doing. Then she started grilling me—like I'm going to be the next one to get preggers. After that, she pulled out her rosary and prayed some more."

Della kept pelting me with questions, but I wasn't in the mood. I summoned up my courage and said, "Hey, can we talk more about this tomorrow? I'm so tired."

I wasn't fooling anyone, but she got the hint. She offered me a cool hug and left.

A LITTLE WHILE LATER, I CAME out of my room and overheard my parents in the den. Dad was terrible at whispering.

"Come here. It's going to be alright, Kathleen."

"I never wanted this for her," Mom cried.

"I know. Like a punch in the gut when Marlowe said that word. Broke my heart, then and there."

Broke my dad's heart? Talk about a punch in the gut.

"But . . ." Dad exhaled a heavy breath. "We can't pretend it away. A baby's coming. The timing's hell, but I'd like to believe there's a reason, like you and me?"

So that's where Caleb got his divine rationale.

"It wasn't easy on us. She's so young," Mom said.

"Young like we were." He cleared his throat. "Caleb's not so young. He'll take care of her."

"And the baby?"

"And the baby. When we meet him—"

"Or her?" Mom said.

"Or her." He relented. "His, or *her* . . . untimely arrival will make more sense to all of us. And mark my words. She'll be a great mother. She'll have to be. She learned from the best."

Mom gave a tittering laugh, then paused. "And Caleb?"

"From what I hear, the kid hasn't had a strong foundation at home. When I pulled him aside, he admitted as much. We can shore him up, Kathleen."

Deserving of an opinion in their conversation, I stepped into the living room.

Mom froze, and Dad turned to face me, asking, "Feeling better?"

"Yeah." I glanced back and forth at them. "I heard what y'all said about Caleb and me."

"Honey, we were just talking," Mom said.

Dad locked his gaze on me. Not sure I'd ever looked so closely at Dad's face. Behind his eyes was the sadness I had put there. I'd broken his heart wide open.

"Dad?" my voice quavered. My chest ached with heaviness.

"Come here." With glassy eyes, he pulled me closer. "Sissie, we love you more than you could ever imagine. You'll know that kind of love one day, when you're looking at your little guy . . ." He tossed a wink at Mom. "Or girl. And Mom and I will do everything we can to help you and the child."

"'The child.' Sounds overwhelming," I said.

Dad ran a soothing hand over my shoulder, then thumbed a tear from my cheek. "We're here. Don't worry, honey. You'll do great."

Reassuring words coming from a man whose motto is "walk it off." "You really think so?"

"Know so." His eyes rose to the ceiling and he sniffed. "Alright. Let's pull it together or Mom'll think we're a couple of softies."

Six

Around five on Saturday, Mom entered the den with a dust rag and pushed my feet off the coffee table.

"It's spotless, Mom," I said, thumbing through *What to Expect When You're Expecting.* Mom had bought two copies so we could read it together. "Wanna look at this with me?" I pointed to a drawing of a kidney-bean sized baby in utero.

"Later." She didn't lift her head while she dusted the table. "Your dad asked Caleb to join us for dinner tonight."

"*Dad* asked Caleb?"

"That's what he said." She shrugged. "Why don't you change your clothes and fix that hair. It'll make you feel better."

"I'm okay."

"You'll *look* better, then."

Climbing off that couch was the last thing I wanted to do, but Dad had made plans. Considering how I was involved, I pulled myself off the sofa to straighten myself up before dinner.

An hour later, the scents of Mom's cooking welcomed me as I left my bedroom. I followed the sounds of men's voices discussing the chances of the Texas Rangers winning a pennant. *Who else did they invite?*

I rounded the corner and entered the dining room. To Dad's left was a man in a starched white shirt and a brown western-cut sport coat. His cheekbones were high and sharp, and gray strands flecked his dark hair. He held a crystal lowball glass filled halfway with amber liquor, identical to the one in Dad's hand.

"Sissie," Dad covered me in an unsolicited, scotch-scented hug.

"Well, she must be our girl." The man's toothy grin and enthusiastic laugh made me take a small step back.

"Our girl?" Who the heck is this weirdo?

"This is Caleb's father," Dad said.

"Hello, pretty lady." He offered a hand. "Call me Pike." Skin wrinkled around his warm chocolate eyes as he bent to look at me. "Darlin', we're here for you. Anything you need. The wife couldn't make it tonight, but we'll put you ladies together real soon."

I heard Caleb's voice coming from the kitchen, where I could only imagine he was bonding with my mother. Just as I was debating whether to go in and say hi to him, he appeared before me, sipping what looked like beer from a pilsner glass.

"Hey, Sissie." He stepped toward me, and I'm pretty sure I squinted at him. *Caleb's drinking a beer in my house. His dad's yukking it up with mine. My planets are colliding in the weirdest possible ways. Should I be comforted or freaked out?*

"Hey." I took a measured step toward him, and he gave me a side hug.

"Meet my dad?" he asked.

"Yep." *Won't soon forget him, either.*

"Almost ready," Mom called from the kitchen.

Dad pointed to the hunter green parson's chairs surrounding the dining room table, and Pike slid into my usual spot. "Sissie and Caleb, why don't you have a seat here." Dad gestured to the chairs across from him.

Caleb pulled out my chair, and I lowered myself into it. Facing Pike's hundred kilowatt grin creeped me out a little. I changed my mind and stood. "Mom might need help," I said, and edged my way out of the room.

Mom looked up when I entered the kitchen and smiled. "You look pretty, honey."

"When did y'all invite Caleb's dad?"

"Dad thought it would be a first step, bringing both families together to talk. We didn't want to stress you out with the details." She turned toward the oven.

"I thought Dad didn't like Caleb's family."

She whipped around like I'd broken a prized artifact. Shushing me and glancing around like she might be overheard, she led me to a corner of the kitchen. She whispered, "The Dietrichs have their problems. I'm not saying we haven't had our share of snags here and there, but the Dietrich's are a whole other animal."

One with shiny, white teeth? "What? They don't have money?"

"They have money. New money. He spins around in that flashy sports car wearing that tacky pinky ring." Mom buttoned up her eyes as if she was blinded by the gaudiness of it all.

Fitzgerald's East Egg-West Egg meets Fredericksburg, Texas. Mom's family puts us in the East. Caleb's lands him in the West. Huh. That dumb book makes sense now.

Another picture became clearer now, too—the way my parents' expressions changed when Della came around. When we'd run into Della's parents, Mom and Dad greeted them with the same insincere politeness they wore to run off a door-to-door salesmen.

Della's parents had always treated me well. They had to work harder than most people to enjoy the same lifestyle my parents took for granted. Della's dad immigrated to the United States, taught himself English, and took night classes to sell real estate. He changed his name from Pablo to Paul to fit in. Judging by their large house and luxury cars, he did alright. Just not quite good enough for my parents.

"Smells g-o-o-o-od!" Caleb poked his head in the kitchen.

"There's the guy I was looking for." Scuttling to face him, Mom pointed a red fingernail at a basket of rolls. "Caleb, honey, would you mind taking these to the table?" The woman could think on her feet, I had to give her that much.

Caleb carried the basket away, and Mom fanned herself. "That was close. Don't worry about your dad. He gets along with just about everyone."

If by "getting along" you mean "sorts them by class and snubs them in his own East Egg way," then sure.

Mom filled plates with salad, Chicken Cordon bleu casserole, and lemony green beans, wiping the edges of the plates like she was sending them out to diners at a fancy restaurant. "The bigger portions go to Caleb and his father," she instructed me.

I rolled my eyes at the heaping plates. *What is she trying to do? Commit murder by Chicken Cordon bleu?*

THE DINNER CONVERSATION THAT evening was a surreal back-and-forth, mostly between the men, and mostly about Caleb. Dad encouraged Caleb to update his resume while Pike bragged about his son's "vision for business." Caleb nodded, speaking only about Mom's cooking.

"Sissie, please try to eat." Mom stage whispered to Pike and Caleb, "She's had an icky tummy." Translation: Please ignore our daughter. She's been puking her guts up.

I pushed the food around my plate, forked a green bean, and took a bite.

"Son, did you tell Sissie about what her daddy's doing for you?" Pike asked.

Caleb looked lost. Then, as he swallowed a hefty bite, realization clicked. "Your dad's hooking me up at Voyce Brothers."

"Hell of a company." Pike gestured with his fork. "Hands in everything from oil drilling to artificial hearts. Surprised they haven't renamed this town Voyceburg—their name's everywhere."

"That's great," I said, trying to be encouraging. Honestly, it was hard to focus on what Pike said. The man was big—big grin, big eyes, big personality, big talker. Listening to his big stories was like watching TV during an electric storm—lots of flickering and hard to follow. He'd flash his own version of an applause light, tossing out, "Don't need to tell ya—'twas a hoot," if we didn't laugh.

In between hoots, Dad stepped into the other room to open a bottle of wine. Pike got up to follow him. "Lemme help with the choosing," Pike said.

Dad waved him along, although I suspected he preferred to go it alone.

Caleb leaned in toward me. "Your dad's cool."

My dad . . . the man who was going to throw you in jail . . . is cool?

"Yours, too," I said, trying to be polite.

The men returned and, after Dad opened the bottle, Pike offered to "do the pouring." And pour he did.

"You just rim it, don't you," Dad said, twirling a finger over the top of his glass.

"Saves ya time that way." Pike raised his glass to toast to his own cleverness.

"Indeed." Dad clinked his glass as Mom delivered dessert—individual bowls of mint sherbet topped with almond-brickle.

As soon as she was seated again, she jumped back into the conversation. "We should start our search for wedding venues."

"What's that?" Caleb asked.

"Venues are places to get married," Mom explained in a voice she'd use for a small child.

Our parents swapped glances, and Caleb raked a hand through his hair. "Um, Sissie, our parents think we should prob'ly get married before . . . um . . . before?" He swallowed and made a production of glancing at my belly.

My eyes returned to my plate, and the room began to tilt. Sweat dampened my skin, and my last forkful of Cordon bleu made a run for the door. I bolted from the chair, ran into the kitchen, and bent over the sink.

"Here." Caleb appeared behind me and passed me a towel.

In between retching spasms, I noticed he had passed me one of Mom's hand-embroidered tea towels. It read, "Children make your life important. Erma Bombeck." *Thanks, Erma, whoever you are.*

"You okay?" he asked.

I nodded and righted myself. "You really want to get married?"

He shrugged.

"What about love and all that?"

"Yeah, I hear ya. We can have love. Ya know, even pregnant, you're pretty hot." His brows shot up.

I frowned at him.

"I think we can make it work."

How romantic.

"Caleb." I shot him a "be serious" look, and we stood there for a minute. "What if we didn't get married? Just raised the baby as friends?"

"Nah." He shook his head. "Kids shouldn't bounce around."

Where have I heard this before?

He brushed my arm and rearranged his face. "Serious as a heart attack, and I mean this—after talking to your dad, I think I'm ready to do this. Landing a job, getting married, having a kid. Sounds awesome."

For you.

"Hey, don't look so disappointed. Not how I thought it would go down, but shit happens. We're having a baby together. That's pretty cool."

"Cooler if I wasn't sixteen."

"You're sixteen now, but when he gets here . . . wait. When's your birthday?"

"November 18."

He counted using his fingers. "You'll be seventeen."

"How do you know it's a boy?" I felt the edges of my mouth turn upward.

"You're right. It could be a girl."

Glad we got that settled.

"If so, she better turn out like you." He covered his face with a hand. "Or she'll be one ugly son of a bitch."

"You're cute," I said, and he blushed a little. "Either one will get the best of both of us." I wasn't sure what I was saying; I supposed I was trying on a shade of optimism. "How would we make it work? You and me?"

"Before the kid gets here, we'll spend time together," he said. "It'll click."

"Huh," I let out with a sigh.

"Don't worry. I'll be here for you and our kid." Hope glistened in his eyes, and I decided to believe him, but the prospect a relationship with Caleb was overwhelming. Another wave of emotions made landfall, and tears slid over my cheeks.

"Aw, don't cry." He leaned in and put his arms around me, clumsily trying to comfort me. "It's crazy, what happened here, but our kid's gonna be freaking amazing. You'll see."

❧

CALEB WASN'T MESSING AROUND. Within a few days, he'd cut his hair, shined up his shoes, bought two new ties, and followed up with Dad's friends at Voyce Brothers. He seemed genuinely stoked about the bright future unrolling before him.

I was happy for him, but tying my future to his meant anchoring myself to my hometown and a guy I barely knew. Our child, meanwhile, would frame and limit my choices. And if that reality wasn't enough of a buzzkill, my body began betraying me on a daily basis—my stomach refused to settle, my boobs hurt, and I was tired all the time.

Della called every so often to check on me, but our conversations were shallow versions of the ones we had once shared. Laughs were rare. Mostly, she kept asking the same questions—how I felt, if Caleb was behaving, and if I had reconsidered adoption. Growing tired of her second-guessing my choices, I started avoiding her calls altogether. Not long after that, she stopped calling.

It would've been lonesome without Caleb to keep me company. We watched movies and took frequent hikes around Enchanted Rock, Cross Mountain, and the cabins at LBJ park down the road in Johnson City. It was nice getting to know him and seeing places around town I'd overlooked. *Getting stuck here might not be so bad*, I caught myself thinking one day.

He wanted to know more about my family. He asked to see my baby pictures, and we took photo album trips down memory lane.

"You were such a cute baby," he said. "So cool how your mom kept all these pictures." A thread of sadness diminished his curiosity. "You're lucky to have a normal family."

My normal family was a godsend for many reasons, but they were my lifeline when Caleb landed that job at Voyce. His absence during the day amplified the radio silence from my high school friends, who weren't jazzed to hang out with a girl carrying a baby in her belly. I caught myself wondering what might happen if I lost this baby. Would they welcome me again?

Caleb picked up on my sadness and surprised me one Saturday. Hauling a picnic lunch packed by my mother, he took me to Enchanted Rock, one of my favorite spots in the Hill Country. By far, it was one of our best days together.

On our way back, I spotted a group of my old friends climbing out of a car. My heart rose, and I turned to Caleb. "I'll introduce you."

When we approached them, though, they offered simpering smiles and waved, then turned toward the trail like they hardly knew me.

I tipped my head down to hide my tears, but Caleb caught on quickly and put an arm around me. My situation placed me in a suffocating chamber—one most of my old friends wouldn't enter.

"I've known some of them since kindergarten," I said, sniffling. I tipped my head to hide my tears.

"You've got me," he said.

※

MOM AND DAD EMBRACED CALEB, and I hoped my brother would, too. They had been in high school at the same time—at least they'd have that in common. But when I asked Brent why he was so quiet when I mentioned Caleb, I got more than I wanted.

"He was a sophomore when I was a senior," Brent said, his tone indifferent. "He was a partier, a class clown. Kind of an ass. Hope he's grown up."

Yeah, Me, too.

Brent envisioned another option for me—one that would limit Caleb's involvement. "What if you came here?" he suggested. "Stay with me? You could take classes at Austin College after the baby's born."

"You never invite me to visit. Now you're asking me to live with you?"

"Work gets in the way. Sorry. Just think it might be healthier for you to get out of there, put the baby in daycare, and get your education."

"What about Caleb?"

"Austin's not far. He can visit."

"It's his baby, too."

"You don't need to lock it down with him just because you're having a kid together."

"That's not what Mom and Dad think."

"They see things through old eyes—the way they were raised. You get knocked up, you get married. You don't have to go down the same road they did."

"Nice to know they told *you*. I didn't know until recently."

"It was Dad's way of warning me about having sex in high school."

"I didn't get that talk." *Not that I would've listened.* "I'm probably gonna stick around here. Brent, give him a chance. He landed a great job and really wants to be a part of our baby's life," I said, trying not to sound overly defensive.

"That's what I heard," Brent said, unconvinced. "Look, if all that doesn't pan out, just know I'm here. Let it all sink in before you jump into a lifelong commitment with him. You have options."

Seven

Brent thought he knew what was best for me, but he hadn't been around to see how our parents rolled out the red carpet for Caleb.

Mom loved having Caleb join our nightly dinners, and Caleb wouldn't have missed one. She picked up on his favorites and bought groceries with him in mind.

One Friday night in June, my parents had invited Caleb's parents to a cookout. Caleb's mom couldn't make it, but Pike accepted.

While Dad grilled our steaks, Pike discussed the merits of charcoal versus piped-in gas. If the man got on Dad's nerves, he didn't show it. Then again, Dad had always wielded a steady poker face.

At some point, I pulled Caleb aside to ask, "When can I meet your mom?"

Caleb screwed up his face like he had a toothache. After a long moment, he lobbed his head back toward the house. "Um, can we go inside?"

Once inside, we moved into the den where we could be alone. His voice was low, and he kept an eye out for anyone who might be listening. "When I was little, my mom was a normal mom. She'd play with me and all that. When I was in third grade, though, she had these surgeries on her back." He paused. "They gave her some medicine for the pain, always giving her more. She was never the same. Anyway, I've always had to keep an eye on her."

"That must've been so hard on you."

His mouth flattened into a reluctant line. "Didn't have a choice, right?" Another nervous laugh. "I think I turned out alright."

"Sure you did," I said, hoping I sounded reassuring. In that moment, so much about him made sense. The part of him that should've been easiest to reveal—his family—dredged up humiliation.

I patted his hand. "Every family has its problems."

THE DIETRICHS MIGHT'VE HAD THEIR problems, but Caleb wanted to do right by our baby. He attended my doctor's appointments. When the doctor let us hear the heartbeat, Caleb teared up, and he did again when we learned we could expect our little peanut to land in December.

"Merry Christmas to us," Caleb said, pride all over his face.

The following Friday afternoon, Brent drove in from Austin, saying he had big news for our parents. Mom made spaghetti, and I introduced Caleb to Brent.

Brent was polite but reserved. Nothing new there.

At dinner, Caleb seemed nervous and barely touched his food. Suddenly, he stood. "Dropped my napkin," he said loudly, and knelt on the floor.

I took another bite of spaghetti.

"Sissie," Mom said.

I looked at her. She nodded to my right where Caleb was looking up at me, holding a box in his palm.

"I know we already talked about this but, a girl should have a ring. So, officially, will you . . . um . . . marry me?"

I almost choked on my pasta. *Are we really doing this?*

Caleb bit his lip, and Mom whispered to my father.

After a long pause, I answered, "Yes."

Caleb pushed the ring on my hand awkwardly and kissed me in that "our parents are watching" way.

Dad smiled, and Mom teared up.

Brent, looking like someone had dumped his spaghetti in his lap, said, "Congratulations."

SOMETIME AFTER MOM delivered plates of Brent's favorite dessert—Key lime pie—to the table, she asked Brent about his job.

"Well, I've been waiting to tell you since we sat down, but . . ." He tossed a glance at Caleb. "Hard to top Caleb over here. Probably not that big of a deal, but you know how we talked about Irvine and Lowell, Dad? In Chicago?"

Dad nodded.

"They offered me a position."

"You're taking it, I hope," Dad said.

"Yes."

"You didn't tell us you applied," Mom said.

"They came after me. Moving to Chicago in a month."

"That's wonderful, but . . ." Mom pulled her napkin to her face. "It's so far away."

"Kathleen, he can't turn down an offer like Irvine and Lowell because it's far away from his mother," Dad said. "This is huge. I trust you're getting a big pay raise?"

Brent scanned the table. "I'd rather not talk about that here."

"Don't worry, I'm not gonna tell anybody," Caleb said. "How much do they pay you to draw up houses?"

Speaking slowly, like Caleb might not understand, Brent explained, "Commercial architects don't design houses." His mouth gentled into a half smile. "Enough about me. When is this wedding going to happen?"

THE NEXT DAY, DAD TOOK the guys golfing, and Mom drove me to New Braunfels to find a wedding gown. I tried on dresses in white, ivory, and candlelight. No matter the color, none of them fit a waistline that no longer belonged just to me. That peanut had grown, and a half-melon sprouted at my waist.

"Try this one." Mom pointed to a gown with a deep-plunge sweetheart neckline.

"A little low, don't you think?"

"We can fix that," she said. "Let's try it on." She nudged me toward the back of the store and shuttled me into the fancy dressing room. She pushed a canopy of ivory tulle over my head. With a tug here and a twist there, she fastened the buttons along my lower back and straightened the lace over each shoulder. "Okay, turn around."

Her face shifted quickly, and her eyes glistened with tears. "My baby. She's so . . ." She hiccupped her next words. ". . . grown-up . . . beautiful."

Mom led me from the dressing room to a stage bordered by three angled mirrors. When I got my first glimpse of the gown, I stood a little straighter, lifting the tulle skirt and twisting to inspect how the keyhole back revealed just enough skin without looking trashy. Pregnancy had provided me with boobs to fill it out, and the skirt bloomed above my waist, disguising the bun baking in my oven.

As Mom and I carried the giant bag out of the store, we passed a row of bridesmaids' gowns. "Have you thought about asking Della?" she asked.

I shrugged. "She doesn't like Caleb. I'm not sure she'll even come to the wedding."

"I think you're underestimating her. In a sense, she's losing you to Caleb. Even though it's not intentional, you've hurt her feelings."

Has she ever given a second thought to mine?

❦

DURING THE HOUR-LONG DRIVE back to Fredericksburg, I considered what Mom had said. Della and I had been like sisters since kindergarten. It would be a shame to drop our friendship. Maybe it was time to mend our rift? When we arrived home, I called her, and she agreed to meet me at the ice cream shop on Main.

"LONG TIME, NO SEE." DELLA gave me an icy side-hug. She looked like the old her. It was too soon to say if her attitude toward Caleb had changed.

I had prepared, even rehearsed, how I'd tell her about the wedding. I expected her to be surprised, even shocked, but I believed she'd want me to be happy. *We're best friends, right?*

Wrong, apparently.

"You can't marry him," she told me. "He's sleaze. I can't stand by and let you do this."

There goes my maid of honor.

"He's my baby's father." *A minor detail.*

Leaning across the table, she snarled, "He took advantage of you that night. You can't marry him. Are you stupid, Sissie?"

Double ouch.

She kept talking. When she took a breath, I interrupted, "We've always been best friends, and I don't want that to change. Even if you don't agree with my decision—"

"It's not *your* decision. Your dad and Caleb are running the show." After a long pause, her mouth pulled to one side. "I hate seeing what they're doing to you. Don't cry."

"You hurt my feelings."

"It hurts my feelings to see my best friend flushing her life down the toilet. Once you two are . . . I can't even say it." She pretended to shiver. "Just wait. You'll see where I'm coming from, eventually. And I'll be here when you do."

"What about now?"

"I told you, already. I can't stand by and watch you do this. He's going to hurt you, and you know it."

I stood with tears in my eyes and sadness in my heart. Then I turned around and walked away from the best friend I'd ever known.

BEFORE OUR JULY WEDDING, Mom's seamstress, Hortencia, monitored my measurements as closely as the gynecologist monitored my baby. Each week, she'd add a pin here or let out a seam there. I hoped we'd have enough fabric to cover the curves popping up on my body.

Mom was a wedding-planning dynamo. Within a few weeks, she brought it all together, from cake tastings to embossed invitations. She'd even managed to convince a few of her friends to host a bridal shower.

My guest list for the shower was short. I was surprised when a handful of school friends had showed up. A few came with their mothers. They watched me open gifts like they were unsure what someone our age would do with a three-speed blender or an All-Clad roasting pan.

That was the day I met Caleb's mom. When she walked into the shower, I assumed she was another one of Mom's bridge friends until Mom pulled me aside.

"Martha Dietrich." Mom said it like a code to take cover. "Over there."

A petite woman in a dark pantsuit, Martha's frosted hair was cut in an asymmetrical bob, showing off the tackiest red earrings I'd ever seen—somewhere between Christmas ornaments and fishing lures.

I walked over to her. "Mrs. Dietrich, I'm Sissie. Thanks for coming."

"I can't stay long. Wanted to drop this off." She handed me an envelope.

I introduced her to Mom, but Martha didn't have much to say.

"I'll put this with the other gifts." Mom took Martha's card from me.

"Don't leave that laying around," Martha told her. "It's got money inside."

"Alright. I'll place it somewhere safe." With that, Mom left us to talk.

"It's so good to finally meet you," I said.

She frowned.

"Would you like some coffee? Or punch?" I pointed to the dining room.

"I can't stay."

I stood there uneasily. *Do I hug her? Shake her hand? Leave her alone?*

Her wobbly hand grasped my arm. "You're a pretty girl. Caleb's lucky to have you." A slight smile formed. "We'll have plenty of time to get to know one another. Go on, now. Enjoy your party." With that, she turned toward the door and walked out.

A little while later, Della and her mother slipped in while I was opening gifts, and Della edged over beside me.

"Want me to get rid of this wrapping?" she asked.

I shrugged. "Sure. Thanks." *Is this her apology?*

"I can write down the gifts if you want a break," Della told my cousin Jenn, who was writing ceaselessly.

Jenn shook her head. "I got it."

"Thanks, anyway," I said.

Della stood behind me, every so often commenting on a beautifully wrapped gift. When all the gifts were opened, she told me they were leaving. "I guess I'll see you at the wedding," she said.

The shower was a nice reminder I wasn't alone, but the big prize came afterward, when our little peanut had begun churning inside me, a delicious experience.

TWO WEEKS LATER, CALEB'S PARENTS hosted our rehearsal dinner. Martha wore a tasteful black dress and the same, gaudy earrings. *Note to self: Buy her a pair of earrings for Christmas.*

My mom buzzed around the room, welcoming out-of-town guests, while Martha buzzed on something else. Primed on her medications, she floated through the evening on an ocean of gin and tonics.

Mom and Dad overwhelmed us with their wedding gift: a three-bedroom, two-bath Victorian off Main Street with white clapboard siding, paned windows, and a roomy front porch. "It's a house you can fill with babies," Mom said.

"Eh," Martha murmured.

The yin to Martha's yang, Pike hooted at the news. Wearing his ear-to-ear grin and holding a glass of Glenfiddich scotch, he toasted to our future and announced their gift—a four-night honeymoon at an all-inclusive resort in Mexico.

After we thanked him, he added, "Now, if you have a boy, you have to name him Pike," at which Dad asked the hundred-thousand-dollar question: "Is that your real name?"

Pike shared his endearingly authentic "huk-huk" laugh before he said, "Funny story—a real hoot!"

"Do tell." Dad smiled along.

"When I was a wee cowboy in my mom's belly, I wiggled and bucked like Red Rock." He laughed, but the rest of us waited for the punchline. "Red Rock? The bull that took Lane Frost from us." He lifted one finger toward the skies. "Rest in peace, Bad to the Bone." He explained, "That was his nickname. Anyway, where was I?"

"Red Rock?" Mom prompted.

"Right. Right. Daddy figgered they wouldn't be traveling after I came along, so he took Mom on a road trip. All over the US— from sea to shining sea. They went fishing up in Michigan with the cousins, and he caught a bucketful of pike on Houghton Lake." He took another sip of his scotch. "End of the day, they drove back to the cabin, and the whole way, those fish just flipped and flopped inside that cooler in the trunk of their Oldsmobile." He laughed. "Thomas, you ever lay eyes on pike?"

"You'd be the only one."

"Huk-huk." Pike pointed a finger at Dad. "They're wild. Make a ruckus. To hear Daddy tell it, my momma grabbed her belly and said, 'Those fish are twisting around like our bundle o' joy.' Well, Daddy got an idea, then and there."

"You're shitting me," Dad mumbled.

"Shit you not," Pike said in an oddly subdued voice. "That's how I became Pike Jameson Dietrich."

"Fascinating." Dad took a sip of his drink and winked at my brother.

"What were they going to name you if they had a girl?" Mom asked.

Dad breathed out. "Let me guess. Carp?"

Eight

A number of guests asked me how I was feeling or joked about the lack of sleep to come. We hadn't fooled anyone with the hurried wedding.

My heart swelled when Della and her parents appeared in front of me at the reception.

"You're gorgeous in this dress," she said, pulling at the skirt.

"It hides a lot," I glanced down.

"Didn't imagine your hair could get any longer and thicker. It's gorgeous."

"Prenatal vitamins."

Behind me, Caleb wrapped a hand around my waist. "Hey, Della."

Della pulled back and nodded coolly before stepping out of the line. She reappeared for a quick hug after I tossed the bouquet. And that was all she wrote.

WAS IT MY DREAM WEDDING? Probably not. Probably wasn't the one my mom dreamed of, either. All told, however, it was the love-liest event Mom could arrange on our abbreviated timeline.

Mexico was nice, too. Without morning sickness to restrict my appetite, I ate like a little piggy the whole time. We entertained ourselves with other activities, too. It was our honeymoon, after all.

On the last morning, we snuggled in bed, talking about what life would be like when we returned. I'd start decorating our new house, and Caleb would help me set up a nursery.

In a dead stop, he went silent, and his face filled with worry.

"What's wrong?" I asked.

"Sis, you've got to help me when the baby gets here. I'm nervous about taking care of it—never been around a baby before."

"We'll figure it out together."

"Just know . . . I'll do my best. And if I screw up, just tell me, okay?"

"Sure." *Like I have a clue how to do it?*

OUR GROWN-UP LIVES BEGAN as soon as we returned to Fredericksburg. Caleb returned to his job, and I cracked the books for my GED.

My belly swelled to the size of a miniature watermelon. I exchanged my normal clothes for maternity wear. Clothes weren't all—Dad traded in my sporty Cabriolet for a reliable family-friendly Ford Explorer.

Fall arrived, and everyone went back to school except me. Sure, I ran into my former classmates at restaurants and the movie theater, but marriage and pregnancy put space between us. I was an outsider now.

Caleb embraced his job—going in early, staying late. While I admired his work ethic, I hadn't anticipated this second wave of loneliness that came as he proved himself to his bosses.

I would've lost my mind if not for my online GED program. Hell bent to prove myself, I endeavored to complete the program before our baby arrived.

My body had other ideas. Besides swollen feet and blood pressure spikes, the doctor identified too much protein in my urine and ordered bed rest. My mom became my warden while Caleb worked, and she enforced doctor's orders to the letter. Feet up. No walking except to use the ladies'. No reading unless it was a shamelessly soppy romance. And absolutely no talking unless it was to discuss said trashy romance novel or baby names. End of story.

Caleb and I spent the Friday evening of my thirty-second week apart. While he celebrated the end of an important project with some coworkers, I spent it with Jennifer Garner. To be precise, Jennifer appeared on the TV in my bedroom in *13 Going on 30*. Right before Jennifer's character makes it right with her childhood love, a spasm wrenched my lower belly.

Unlike Braxton Hicks contractions, these pains nearly jerked me off my bed. I reached for my phone, barely able to press the buttons.

Calls to Caleb went to voicemail, so I called my parents. They arrived in minutes, and Dad, balancing me in his arms like I might break, carried me outside and placed me in the backseat beside Mom.

From there, time became like a car with an easy gas pedal and sensitive brakes—the minutes passed in erratic stops and starts. In agony and bleeding—there was so much blood, and it left me with only disjointed recollections of my arrival at the hospital.

I'd never seen my father as desperate as he was that night. "Help my daughter," he pleaded with them, his voice quavering, when we burst through the emergency room doors. Those doctors and nurses must've been convinced, because after they checked me over, their faces looked like Dad's. Someone mentioned a "hemorrhage due to an abruption," and a swirl of activity followed.

With my parents trailing along, a woman pointed to a clipboard and rattled off a list of complications. Time stopped outside the surgical suite. Mom and Dad kissed me and said they loved me.

"What about my baby?" I asked.

"Baby will go to NICU," a nurse explained. "Your parents can follow along, if it's okay with you?"

"You'll go with the baby?" I asked, locking eyes with Mom.

"Of course." Mom's hand fell away from mine as they pushed me toward a set of metal doors.

"Find Caleb," I yelled to her.

Inside was a blur. The doctor mentioned my uterus and how he had to take the baby out early. Then he waved to a masked woman. "This nice anesthesiologist will help you nap while we work."

That nice anesthesiologist-lady put magic in my IV, and my body melted into the thin mattress. Then I counted backward from one hundred.

"One hundred, ninety-nine, ninety-eight, ninety-seven, ninety . . ."

I WOKE IN A FUZZY, antiseptic world, surrounded by beeping monitors and a woman in a paper shower cap.

"I'm Trisha, your nurse," she said.

"Where's my . . ." I couldn't pull the words from my foggy brain.

"You're in SI so we can keep a close eye on you."

"SI?"

"Surgical ICU."

"Where's my baby?" My voice was raspy, and my throat hurt. I tried to lift my head.

"Don't get up." She touched my shoulder. "Your baby's in NICU."

Nurses came and went. Each told me to rest. It seemed as though falling asleep was a sure bet to be awakened by the next one who had come to check blood pressure, administer medications, or hook me up to a greedy breast pump.

At some point, my doctor arrived, telling me, "You have a pretty little girl."

I have a girl. A pretty little girl. "Can I see her?"

"Soon. You've been through a lot of surgery. We need to keep you up here for a while."

He explained the bleeding and what happened in the operating room. My stupor made his explanations clunky, although one word was clear. Hysterectomy.

I woke to Pike's voice.

"She's waking up," he said in a loud whisper. "Son, get on over there."

"Sissie?" Caleb appeared over me.

"Did you see our baby?" I asked, my throat raw from the anesthesia.

Caleb nodded, and a whiff of beer hit my nose. "She's teeny, Sissie. They've got her hooked up to wires and—"

"Is she gonna make it?"

"Sure, she will," Pike answered over him. "She's small, but strong as hell. You should hear her scream."

I swallowed. "Pike, can I talk to Caleb? Alone?" It was a struggle to push the words out.

"Why, sure. I'll just go say hello to the nurses." He waggled his brows and ducked out the door.

Caleb leaned over me. "How's it going?"

"Where were you?"

"Man, I'm sorry, Sis. I came home, and you weren't there."

"We were supposed to do this together."

"I know. Scared the hell out of me when they said they had to cut into you."

"Yeah." I breathed out. "Scared me, too."

He pushed my hair from my face. "Sis, I love you. And I love our baby."

Nine

Mom and Dad only left my room to go downstairs for meals or when the nursing staff changed my dressings. Their company was reassuring, especially since I was too fragile to travel to the NICU to see my baby. *My baby.*

Pike came around, too, although I was beginning to think he was coming around to check out the nurses more than to check on me.

Caleb came before and after work and sometimes at lunch, too. It wasn't as if he could actually do anything to help me or the baby, so we agreed it made sense for him to keep his usual schedule at work.

On the fourth day, my world changed for the better: the doctor transferred me to the labor and delivery floor. I didn't care about the new room—I wanted to see my still-unnamed baby.

While Mom and Dad moved my things, a nurse wheeled me to the NICU. We passed the newborn nursery, where giant six- to eight-pound infants slept, wiggled, and squeaked in their swaddles, but my baby wasn't there. A little farther along, we reached a locked door.

My nurse picked up a phone located near it to announce, "Mrs. Dietrich is here."

The lock clicked open, and we entered the softly lit, hushed neonatal unit. The air was thick with hopeful tension. We spoke in whispers, like a normal conversational tone might rip a hole in the building.

My ICU nurse wished me well and handed me off to a perky blonde in light blue scrubs. "I'm Meghann, the nurse who's been taking care of your little girl." She nodded to the ICU nurse. "I'll take it from here," she said, and started pushing me to an area with lockers and handwashing sinks. She had a bright smile, and her ponytail bounced when she moved.

I thought I knew how to wash my hands, but Meghann taught me to scrub from the tips of my fingers all the way up to my elbows using a special soap, a fingernail cleaner, and a soft-bristled disposable brush. Then she helped me pull on a paper gown to protect my baby from any heebie-jeebies that might be lingering on my nightgown.

Holding my elbow, she led me past a nursing station on the left, and then to a row of rooms where curtains could be drawn for privacy. Some were dark and empty. Others held miniature cribs and clear plastic isolettes.

"This is a minimal-stimulation setting. Our babies require quiet. For the most part, they need to be left alone," Meghann said in a near-whisper. She gestured to a tiny being beneath a warmer. "Here's your girl."

My girl wore a white onesie. A striped knit hat covered her head. Wires vined over her papery skin, and her legs were bent in froglike right angles.

"Baby Girl Dietrich" was written on the whiteboard above her, and under it was an ongoing list of her daily weight in grams. She'd started at 1,918 grams but dropped to 1,690.

Alarm sliced through my anesthetized senses. "She's losing weight?"

"Most babies do. She probably picked up extra fluid during birth. It's normal."

"She's so tiny." Ugly tears clouded my view. "What can we do?"

"We gave her your colostrum, and we blended formula with the milk you pumped. Keep pumping that liquid gold, and she'll pick up the weight."

"Why does she have these?" I gestured to tubing around her nose.

Meghann explained the wires on her chest, the pulse oximetry, and the patch on her skin (there to monitor her temperature, apparently). Clear tabs formed what looked like a tiny electrical plug poking into my baby's nostrils. "This gives her an added burst of oxygen, and that's her feeding tube." She gestured to the brown tube sprouting from one nostril.

"Can I touch her?"

Meghann nodded. "If her breathing or heart rate changes dramatically, we'll pull back." She pointed to an overhead monitor tracking her vital signs.

"How long will she be here?"

"Can't say. We've had six-pounders stay for a month, and ones tinier than yours that stayed for three or more."

"She looks like a doll." I inspected her translucent eyelids and touched her cottony-soft leg—unblemished and perfect. "Can I hold her?"

"Let's see how she handles being touched, first. Neonates are sensitive to touch and noise. Any stimulation can affect their breathing and heart rate."

My baby laid before me, and I couldn't pick her up. *I feel more disconnected than ever.*

"Does she have a name?" Meghann asked.

"I want to name her Lindsey, or Sarah." I shrugged. "My husband wants to name her Layla. From the Eric Clapton song?"

"Pretty."

"If you listen to the words, Layla's not a nice girl. She plays this guy and breaks his heart." I glanced at her nametag. "I like your name. Meghann." I let the name rest on my tongue. "Do you know what it means?"

The baby wiggled, creating a change on the monitor overhead.

I jerked my hand away from her leg.

Looking at the monitor, Meghann said, "She's okay. You can touch her."

Fearful of upsetting her delicate balance, I brushed her arm lightly.

"Ever hear of a book called *The Thornbirds*?" Meghann asked.

"No."

"It's where my Mom got my name. She read the book before she had me. It's about an Australian girl named Meghann. When I was twelve, we rented the movie."

"Why's it called *Thornbirds*?"

"This crazy bird flies all over the world looking for the perfect thorn. That part's not great—when he finds it, he impales himself. But before he dies, he sings the sweetest song anybody's heard. Sounds tragic, but it's actually a pretty good story."

"What does Meghann have to do with the bird?"

"Well." Her mouth twisted to one side. "She loves this priest, and they only get one chance to be together. I guess their love is like that bird's chance to sing the perfect song. It could've been worse." She gave a small shrug. "Mom's a consummate reader. She could've named me Lolita." Meghann removed the infant's knit cap. "There. You can see her better."

"I thought she'd have more hair on her head, like I did when I was little." I gazed at her like she was a rare painting. "Pictured her more like babies on TV."

"Give her some time. She was supposed to bake for six more weeks. She'll get there." Meghann replaced the knitted cap and cocked her head to the side. "Should we try to hold her?" She widened her eyes encouragingly.

Fear raced down my spine. "She's so tiny. I'm afraid I'll hurt her."

"Babies need their mommas. Get comfortable." She gestured to the gliding rocker beside the bed. "I'll place her in your arms."

After settling the baby in my arms and arranging the wires and the oxygen tubing, Meghann took a step back. "Support her head, here. I'll leave you two to get acquainted, but I'll be right outside if you need me."

I exhaled to calm my nerves, but it was no use. An anxious wave zipped through me. *Surely she's not leaving me alone with this baby?*

Surely, she was.

"Um, would you mind sticking around?" I said, catching her before she got far.

"Just a sec." She stepped out and returned with a chair.

The baby moved an arm to her face, and I took hold of it, mapping it with my eyes. "She's hairy," I said. "And her skin's so dark."

"Extra hair is normal. Jaundice causes the skin color. We've had her under the bili lights, and she's lightened up."

"Has she been up here all by herself since I had her?"

"We're here. Your husband and your parents have been by. Oh, and yesterday, your husband brought his mom and dad to meet her."

His mom? That's something. "We haven't been married very long." I hoped she'd get the message. "It's kinda crazy."

She nodded sympathetically. "Marriage is stressful, especially when you're expecting."

"Do you have kids?" I ran a finger along the baby's leg.

"Two."

"She'll be my only one. They gave me a hysterectomy." I paused. How old are yours?"

Meghann's face turned solemn for a moment, but she quickly reshuffled it into a smile. "Tanner's three and Katie's six months, and they are wild. My husband's a firefighter, so my mom keeps them when we're both working. Don't know what I'd do without her."

"My mom's been the best through this," I told her.

"Moms are incredible—the way they love us through all the stuff we put them through."

"Yeah, I was pregnant before we got married." I laughed weakly. "Guess you could tell? Anyway, Mom planned the wedding and has helped us every step of the way. Pretty sure this isn't how she expected me to end up."

"End up?" Meghann shook her head. "You're just beginning."

"Finishing school and going to college aren't gonna work now."

"Don't say that."

I can't even bend over to tie my shoes right now, let alone think about going to college. What would I do? Stick the kid in my backpack with my books?

"They have online classes," she said, as if reading my mind.

"Yeah. I took some for my GED. I had almost finished before I had to go on bed rest."

"Bet you'll get it done." She winked.

We sat in the near silence of muffled mechanical bleats tracking the baby's pulse. The beats ushered in a surge of postpartum emotion, and I worried I might drop her. "Can you take her?"

Meghann's swift hands stole the infant from my grasp. She placed her back in her crib. "Time for a diaper change, if you feel like sticking around."

"Alright."

She helped me stand and drew four plastic gloves from a box anchored to the wall. Once we pulled on the gloves, she passed me a miniature diaper.

I stared at the diaper like she'd handed me a scalpel and asked me to perform brain surgery. "I'm afraid I'll break her."

"You're her mom. You won't break her."

I unfastened the old diaper. The baby wriggled and twisted her neck. Her face contorted in a breath-holding wind-up. Blue-faced, she delivered an angry kick, and dread thudded in my chest.

"I made her mad."

"You haven't seen mad yet. Just wait until the wet wipe hits her bottom." Meghann eased a disposable wipe into my hand.

"Maybe you should take over?" My voice splintered.

"I don't have any magic. She'll do the same for me."

With a reluctant nod, I gave it another try. As Meghann predicted, the squeak immediately pitched to a punishing, primal squeal.

"Don't cry, baby. It's almost over," I told her. "Not trying to hurt you. Please don't cry. I don't want to make you sad. See? I'm almost done." I pulled the tabs around a waist no wider than my hand. "We're done now. Don't cry." I peeled off my gloves and rubbed her belly. In seconds, her crying weakened to whimpering hiccups.

Meghann searched my teary face and helped me to the rocker. "Good job, Mom."

Mom? She's talking to me. I am someone's mom.

"I think I know what you ladies need." Meghann wrapped the baby in a receiving blanket, tucking the edges around her like a burrito, and put her in my arms again. "Try this." She handed me a blue pacifier—smaller than any I'd ever seen.

I grazed the baby's lips with it. Like a fish coming up for bait, she opened her mouth, inviting it to pop inside.

"Look at her go." Meghann's voice was reassuring. "Preemies are notorious for being slow to suck. She's catching on. Soon, we'll have her nursing like a pro."

Finally, I did something right. "Is there a chance she won't make it?" I asked.

"Babies declare their futures," she said cautiously. "We can give them what we *think* they need, and they can turn in either direction without warning. But so far, so good."

"You think?"

"Well, you heard her scream. She's got power in those lungs. Smart girl—saving it to get mad, like when we change her or when she's hungry."

"Saving it for when it's important, like that bird in your mom's book?"

"Let's keep her away from thorns." Meghann offered a wry grin.

For the first time since I had arrived at the hospital, I laughed. My abdomen ached. But when that baby settled in my arms, it was like she belonged there. "How's it going, sweet baby?" I sniffled. "Baby." I shook my head. "Can't believe we haven't named you."

"During our childbirth classes, everybody else had their baby names but us," I admitted.

"I believe you have to see them first. Once they get a name, they're stuck with it."

"Tell me about it. Sissie?"

"Cute."

"My real name's Priscilla, but my big brother couldn't say it right. Don't think they thought how it'd sound when I grew up." I shook my head. "I would've liked Priscilla."

"You can go by Priscilla now."

I shrugged.

Meghann squinted at the baby's face. "Tell us your name, little girl."

"I like Meghann." I stroked her tiny paws and ran a hand over her soft, fuzzy skin. "We could call her 'Meg', for short." I dropped my head for another look. "Tell me, baby. Are you a 'Meg'?"

MY BABY DIDN'T INDICATE AN opinion about the name, but that time with her sent me back to my hospital room with fresh fortitude. From then on, I confronted the stingy milk-extracting machine head-on, even if it did make my boobs feel like they'd been run over. If that milk would help my baby, I'd suffer through it.

The nurses let Caleb and me feed our baby over the next few days, pushing the milky fluid through a syringe into her feeding tube. We didn't care that we couldn't use a bottle or nurse her, so long as we got to participate in her care.

During one of the evening feedings, Meghann popped into the room. "How's the name coming?"

Caleb raised one brow. "I like Layla."

"She's not a Layla." I shot him a dismissive glance.

"Uh-oh." Meghann laughed, saying, "I'll leave you two to talk," while she walked away.

"She's not a Sarah," he said, holding tight to his grudge against "elementary-school-Sarah"—who, apparently, had left him with a fat lip and a detention after a playground confrontation.

"What about Meg?"

"Meg." He rubbed his chin.

"Like, 'I'm here to pick up my daughter, Meg,'" I say—"or, when she has a bad dream, 'It'll be alright, Meg.' And when a guy asks to marry her, you can say—"

"You're not good enough for my Meg." Caleb's face burst with pride. "Yeah, I like it."

I gulped a breath. "She's a Meg, then?"

"Maybe. Where'd you get it?"

"It's from a book." I explained as if I had read *The Thornbirds* myself, leaving out the bird's doomed fate.

"Meg what?" Caleb asked when I was done.

"Meghann Elisabeth Dietrich."

"She'll need three sheets of paper to write her name." He threw in a wink. "But I like it a lot—especially, if we can call her 'Meg.'"

"Meg?" I whispered. "Your parents are here."

She squirmed and gave a slight smile.

"She smiled!" I pointed to her tiny mouth.

"My mom said babies do that when they're gassy," Caleb said.

"She's not gassy." I frowned at him. "She's smiling because she likes her name. Isn't that right, Meg?"

Ten

The next day, a nurse appeared in my room. "NI called. Dr. Gerald is doing an eval on your baby, so they're not going to have you come for her two o'clock feeding."

Disappointment replaced my anticipation. "What came up?" I asked.

"They didn't say, just asked us to let you know. I'll call down there and see what I can find out."

My mind twisted with worry for Meg. *Was it too much to expect a baby so small to survive this big world?*

The nurse returned, explaining, "Her oxygen saturation levels dropped, but she's doing okay now."

"Can I see her?"

"Not till five." She said it kindly enough, although I felt no less cheated out of time with my daughter.

WHEN FIVE DREW CLOSER, I walked to NICU, scrubbed, and gowned—and discovered, upon entering the NICU, that Meg had received an upgrade in her accommodations: a clear plastic box, accessible only through two round openings. A mask covered most of her face, and she was tethered to the bed with new wires and tubing.

"Her O_2 sats dropped, again, so we switched her to a CPAP mask," a doctor explained, but heck if I knew what all those letters meant. He must've caught on to my confusion, because he added, "It sends forceful shots of air, so Meg can reserve her energy."

"I thought she was doing better."

"Every day's different with these babies. When her numbers improve, we'll see about taking her off."

I searched his face. "It's breathing *for* her?"

"Not completely. You might say it does the heavy lifting while her body gets stronger."

"Should we move her to a bigger hospital, like the one in San Antonio?"

He shook his head. "Moving her will add to her stress. She's had a busy week. Needs time to bounce back from all the commotion she's been through after she was born."

THAT EVENING, AS SOON AS the second hand struck 7:50, I trudged toward NICU for Meg's eight o'clock feeding.

Now, a white mask covered Meg's eyes under the blue neon glow of a bili light.

An unfamiliar nurse stood over Meg's bed. She introduced herself as Ximena, and she had a staid face, wore gold-rimmed reading glasses, and pulled her silver hair into a punishing twist at the nape of her neck.

"How is she?" I asked, irritated that we couldn't have our favorite nurse, Meghann, during such a crucial time.

"About the same."

"No better?"

"Same is what we want. Worse is bad." She stepped away from us.

My baby, so helpless and tiny, needed a pep talk. It was all I could do. "Meg, you have to get stronger, so you can sing beautiful songs like that thornbird. Except you'll sing thousands of songs. You'll sing and laugh and play."

I thought back to the days after I learned I was pregnant when I had wished I could make this baby disappear. My baby's life hung in the balance, and I wanted nothing more than to see her become healthy so I could raise her with Caleb.

"I'm sorry, baby. I want you. I want you so much, and I'm not leaving this hospital without you. Please, Meg. Show them how strong you are."

Meg squirmed a little, and I read her movement as agreement.

Helpless, I dropped to the floor. My bony knees met the tile, and I flattened a hand on Meg's plastic box and closed my eyes, whispering as the CPAP machine buzzed nearby, "God, I'm sorry. Please give me a chance to give her what she needs. I promise to make a family out of our mess. I promise, if you'll make her healthy, I'll give her everything I've got. Caleb and I will give her all the love we have to give. Amen."

Ximena announced her appearance behind me with a cough and helped me stand. "This girl's a fighter. Keep praying, and she'll make it out of here with you."

❧

WHEN I RETURNED TO MY room on the L&D floor, I heard Caleb bark a swear. I pushed the door open and was met with a furious Della glowering at my husband.

At once, she and Caleb turned toward me.

"What happened?" I asked.

Della tossed a thumb at Caleb. "He needs to get his priorities straight."

"She needs to mind her own business," Caleb said.

She stepped closer. "My mom said he wasn't even here when you had the baby." Her words shot an angry pulse into the air.

I stopped and met Caleb's gaze. He was my partner now, the man who would raise Meg with me. Della wasn't a part of our family. What happened wasn't her business.

"This guy can't raise a kid," she said.

"We're married and have a baby together," I told her firmly.

Della's teary eyes vacillated between Caleb and me. Finally, she shoved a gift at me. "Here. Hope your baby gets better. Have a nice life."

She darted from the room without looking back.

Caleb shook his head. "Sissie, I tried to be polite, but she won't give me a shot. She hates me. You sure you want to be friends with her?"

Am I? The space Della put between Caleb and me presented a challenge—threatening the peaceful family I'd promised to build with Caleb, the one my baby deserved. This wasn't the time to worry about making Della happy. If God fulfilled his part of our agreement, Meg would require my full attention.

❧

MEG SWEPT INTO THIS WORLD like a meteor, and for a while we weren't sure she'd survive the landing. But our girl determined her future, just like our favorite nurse said she would. Soon, she had gained weight like a little champ and finally graduated from the NICU. She had my round brown eyes and Caleb's straight-line nose, and she quickly became the love of our lives.

Mom was right—most of the time, babies smell like heaven. But raising babies wasn't for the faint of heart. My limited experience with babies at the church nursery hadn't prepared me to take a baby home. I'd had no freaking idea how hard those moms had it when no one was around to help. Meg filled my days and nights with diapers, feedings, and exhaustion.

Caleb was a hands-on father, but he couldn't be around all the time. Thankfully, my mom picked up wherever she saw an opportunity. After Caleb left for the office on weekdays, she appeared with willing arms, allowing me to shower or catch up on sleep.

By the second week, I had the hang of nursing—until my breasts swelled into hard, fiery melons. *Welcome to motherhood, Sissie Dietrich. Congratulations! You've won a wicked case of mastitis.* A week of pumping and dumping while taking antibiotics brought me back to the world of the living—just in time for my next challenge.

Without warning, Meg became a burpy, spit-uppy, unhappy girl who refused to sleep more than an hour at a time. One night, as I walked around the house tearfully holding our crying baby—away from our bedroom, since Caleb had a big meeting the following day—I pleaded, "Meg, please stop crying," I switched to holding her like a football—a position that delivered slight relief. But exhaustion still pulled me down like an anchor. Frustration prickled my chest, and patience was replaced with resentment.

What have I done? Trading one night for all the things I took for granted. Sleeping. Driving too fast. Playing music too loudly. Laughing. Dancing. Looking forward to college, parties, my wedding.

In less than a year, life as I knew it had vanished. *And now this is my freaking reality—walking around the house with a baby who refuses to stop wiggling, crying, and screaming.* I dropped to the edge of the sofa, my head and chest bobbing in a measured rhythm to prevent Meg from exploding into screams. "This is so hard," I said into the darkness.

"Hey," Caleb rounded the corner, pushing the back of his hands over his eyes.

"Go back to bed. We're fine," I lied.

"Let me take her," he said. One hand rubbed my back. The other smoothed the hair over Meg's head.

"You have work in the morning."

"Here." He reached for her, relieving my drained arms. "Go to bed." He pulled her into the crook of his neck and bounced in a convulsive rhythm. "Go on."

I dragged myself to our bed.

I woke to sunlight and whispers.

Down the hall, Caleb was saying in a caring tone, "There you go." I turned the corner to see my freshly showered husband wiping foamy drool from Meg's mouth. He glanced up at me. "Showered in the guest bath. Holding out to wake you until the last minute before I had to leave."

"How'd you keep her quiet?"

"I dragged her car seat into the bathroom. She stayed there while I showered."

"Just need to dress, and I'll be out of your hair. You okay?"

"Yeah," I said. "Did you get any sleep?"

"Yeah. That couch your parents got us is pretty comfortable." He shrugged off any inconvenience with the pride, earned after a night of accomplishing what I couldn't—quieting our fussy daughter. *Does he have the magic touch?*

MEG'S INTERMITTENT COLIC CONTINUED, and most nights, I managed alone since Caleb was expected in the office for early morning meetings. He'd check on me, offering to take a shift. Just knowing he was there when I was drowning made all the difference.

Fatherhood softened Caleb's rough edges and fortified his devotion to our family. He made every effort to attend Meg's pediatric appointments, always with questions about developmental milestones. His presence was especially helpful when those appointments involved immunizations to soothe Meg and console her crying mother.

The doctor predicted our "little squirt" would catch up to her peers. Knowing that, we didn't get rattled when she fell below the average percentiles in every physical category. What she lacked in size, she made up for in cuteness and spunk.

Mom and Dad kept a standing date with all that cuteness, translating to a weekly date night for us. Every Friday evening, they pushed us out of the house for their "Grandma and Grandpa time," allowing Caleb and me to connect. Creating a loving environment for our daughter helped us to discover our own brand of love.

Those days of walking out of the house with a credit card in my back pocket were over. I didn't carry a purse, but what amounted to a small piece of luggage to transport everything from diapers to pacifiers, from a change of clothes in case she barfed or pooped. And don't get me started on the stroller and car seat. Sometimes, I had to remind myself not to forget the baby.

Despite my love for Meg, motherhood made me feel like an oddity. My person wasn't my own. I smelled like baby spit-up, and even after I lost my pregnancy weight, my jeans no longer fit right.

One afternoon, I lifted Meg into my baby pack and pulled the diaper bag over my shoulder, and we walked to my favorite boutique on Main Street. By the time we arrived, Meg had fallen asleep.

Inside the store, a few of my former classmates hovered around a jewelry display. At first, I didn't recognize Ava Russo. She was a brunette when I last saw her. Now, she was rocking a Britney Spears' look. We'd always gotten along okay, although after hearing her talk about some of our classmates, I sensed she had solid mean girl potential.

Ava leaned into her friends and then, all at once, they turned to face me.

"Sissie," Ava said, not moving away from the display. "How's it going?"

I probably should've said, "Good," and kept walking. Instead, I walked right over to them.

"Hey." I glanced at one of the other girls who held a pair of hoops from the display. "Those would look great on you, Crystal. Especially when you put your hair up like that."

Ava gave a little chuckle. "Is that your baby?"

Grinning at the mention of Meg, I bent to one side so they could see her sleeping in the pack. "This is Meg."

At first, they looked like I had just unveiled an alien, and one of the girls seemed especially uncomfortable.

I decided to be the adult and break the ice, asking about our choir teacher, who they were dating, and which colleges they were considering.

Their answers were brief, and then Ava asked, "How is it? Being someone's mother?"

Detecting some snarkiness, I didn't answer for a second. *Take the high road, Sissie.*

"Pretty great," I said, tipping my head toward my baby.

Crystal took a slow step toward us for a closer look. "She's cute. Does she talk?"

Not even teething.

"Not quite." I suppressed a laugh.

"How's is it? Being married?" Ava asked, tossing a glance at her friends.

When I didn't answer for a long moment, Crystal explained, "I think she means . . . like, is it strange waking up in the same bed with a guy every morning?"

"It would be weirder waking up in the same bed with a different one every morning," I laughed at the picture in my head.

A woman walked over. "Can I help you ladies?"

"No, we were just looking," Crystal said.

"You can help me," I said. "I haven't been shopping since before." I pointed to Meg.

"What are you looking for?"

"First, some new jeans. My old ones don't fit the same." When I turned back to the girls, all three looked like they'd just heard a good joke.

You, Sissie. You're their joke.

The salesclerk introduced herself as Nancy, and from the way she moved around the place, I began wondering if she was the owner. "I have some new items in the back that I worried wouldn't fit most of my customers. You know, most young women don't have your height and figure to carry off these looks, but you? I may need you to model for my next print ad. You are gorgeous!"

"It was good seeing you," I said, following Nancy to a rack of clothes.

Walking back to the house, I bristled at how the girls treated me. Then I remembered it wasn't that long ago, I'd seen the world like them, in black and white until I became the walking billboard for teenage pregnancy—the girl you don't want to be, the one to learn from so you don't make her the same mistake. Being that girl was isolating and, at times, scary. I could only hope a day might come when I wouldn't stick out anymore.

$\approx$

My mother called my sad days, "the baby blues." She said they came from post-pregnancy hormone changes, but I disagreed. Don't get me wrong—I loved my baby, but staying home with a tiny human who ate, slept, cried, and did nothing more became mind-numbing.

Caleb encouraged me to return to my GED coursework, but even that was a solitary experience. I was desperate to speak to another human, preferably one over the age of three months.

Then, like a stroke of magic, Meg hit that age when she'd actually produce meaningful reactions. Her ticklish feet guaranteed solid-gold, hiccup-filled-giggles. She watched our mouths move when we spoke and jutted out her tongue, producing chirps and squeals.

She also fell into a feeding-rocking-napping routine that enabled me to return to my online classes to satisfy requirements for my GED.

Caleb, meanwhile, was satisfied with his career trajectory. All those sixty-hour weeks rewarded him with a promotion less than a year after he began. By the time Meg was able to push herself up on her knees, her father and I had forgotten our rocky beginning. I loved Caleb, especially for the way he loved Meg.

Firmly planted on Austin Street, we were the Dietrich family.

Part Two

Eleven

Our first summer with Meg flew by. I savored every moment with her, spending countless hours rocking on the wide wicker swing Caleb and my father had mounted on the front porch. When Mom outfitted it with a blue-and-white-striped cushion and fluffy floral pillows, it became my favorite spot in or out of our house.

Even on rainy days, Meg and I rocked to the rhythmic patter on the porch's roof. On sunny days, I pointed out the cardinals and blue jays that visited the redbud tree in the yard. I loved our time on that swing.

Meg grew faster than the weeds along the fence line behind our house, blabbering and holding on to the furniture as she motored around us. It was all going too fast.

Meg wasn't the only one stretching her wings. Della was preparing for her big move to the Texas State dorms, and she asked me to lunch before she left. Hoping she'd appreciate my point of view, I agreed.

A few days later, the three of us—Della, Meg, and I—met at the Sunset Grille. Della hugged me and looked at Meg with wonder. "She's so cute, Sissie. Like your mini-me." She'd brought a Beanie Baby lamb for Meg, and Meg loved it. She kept sticking the fluffy toy in her mouth while she gurgled her undecipherable language.

"Can I hold her?" Della asked.

I nodded, but warned her, "Since she hit eight months, she's become clingy. Don't take it personal if she's scared. It's normal at her age." I handed her off and hoped for the best.

Meg furrowed her brows and locked eyes on me, but after a minute, she took to Della.

"Looks like she rubbed against a helium balloon," Della joked. "Is it supposed to do that?" Della pointed to Meg's thin, brown, standing-on-end hair.

"Mom said it'll lay flat when it comes in."

"Glad she looks like you."

What? I was taken aback, and the cheer fell from my voice. "She looks like both of us."

"I just mean, she's a girl, so it's better she looks like you."

That's not what you meant.

Della pivoted back to Meg. "Look at those smooshy, gooshy, chunky cheeks."

The waitress took our order, Della's first.

"I'll have a Diet Coke," Della said, "a small house salad, no cheese or croutons, and instead of dressing, I'll just have a few lemon wedges and salt."

I ordered a cheeseburger and fries with ice water and a chocolate milkshake.

"Dang, hungry?" Della asked.

"As long as I'm nursing that baby, I can eat to my heart's desire." It was mostly true now that I went up a size in my jeans, but I didn't need to share that minor detail.

Della pulled Meg's hands to help her to a wobbly standing position, like a chubby marionette doll. "Look how strong you are."

Our food came, and I put Meg in a highchair.

"Tell me about your roommate," I said, putting on a brave front.

"We only talked on the phone, but she seems alright. I'm nervous about living with a stranger. Living with you would've been perfect. We just go together, ya know?"

I did, although it didn't seem that way now. While she rattled on about matching bed linens and showering in the coed dorms, my interest in her life on campus faded.

"When you turn one," Della said to Meg. "I want to come to your birthday party."

Della and Caleb in the same room? Not on my watch. "We're not going to have a big party. Just our parents."

"Oh, alright."

"You won't have time, anyway, not with school and all those cute guys."

Della resumed her baby-talk, "Tell your momma, Meg. Girls rule and boys drool. No silly boy's gonna keep me from seeing you or your mom. Isn't that right?" She nuzzled Meg's neck and inspired a rousing, bubbly laugh.

Message received.

"Meg, don't you let her just sit around all day. Make her go to school."

"You think I sit around all day?" I asked.

"I'm just kidding around, Sis." She gave an inauthentic laugh.

"I finished my GED, and I'm going to take a couple distance-learning classes."

"What are you going to school for?"

"I don't know yet." I waved to our server. "Can we get our ticket?"

"Here," Della pushed cash at me.

I pushed it back. "I'll get it. Caleb got a promotion."

Della thanked me, seemingly unimpressed with Caleb's accomplishment.

With Meg on my hip, I traipsed to the car.

Della followed, seeming more sentimental than I remembered. "Sure wish you were going with me," she said.

I almost said, "Me, too," but saying so would betray Meg and the life I was building with Caleb. Meg had determined her future, and she had determined mine, too. Different than I had imagined, but no less wonderful.

"Are you gonna be okay?" Della asked.

Meg chattered, "Bah, bah, bah, bah," and I turned to look at her.

"Bah, bah, bah." I tapped Meg on the nose. My chest filled with overwhelming joy, and my mouth bent into a smile. "We're exactly where we're supposed to be."

⚜

OCCASIONALLY, DELLA MAILED A NOTE or a card, mentioning ski trips and her business classes. Some included photos of her with college friends whose names she'd list on the back of the pictures. These glimpses into her college life only put more space between us.

But when Meg was sick or especially whiny or if Caleb came home in a bad mood, I'd think about those pictures and wonder what my life would be like if I had left with her that night in San Marcos. On good days, I carried guilt for having considered a life without Meg and Caleb.

For what it was worth, Caleb and I were happier than Della could ever acknowledge. The second he walked through the door each evening, he reached for Meg. He fed her and held an open towel at the end of bath time. And at bedtime, he loved rocking her to sleep.

He became a caring husband, too. Even in those early days after I accepted my fate, I didn't expect the good to outweigh the bad. I wouldn't ever tell Caleb, but I went into our marriage cautiously optimistic, even expecting him to slip up. It took some time before I gave him my whole heart. Once we got settled into our home with our baby, though, I recognized his desire to be a dedicated father and husband.

When Meg turned one, we celebrated with a family-only party. Mom and Dad brought a cake. Pike brought a numbed Grandma Martha and a motorized Barbie car wrapped in a giant red ribbon. *For a one-year-old. What should we expect for her first Christmas? Her own apartment and a pair of Jimmy Choos?*

With only a few weeks before the winter holidays, I addressed my concerns with Caleb. "Before it's too late, you have to talk to your parents and ask them to back off on the gifts."

"She's their only grandchild," he protested.

"She's my parents' only grandchild, too. You don't see them buying her a car. Besides, these toys are taking over our house. Our living room looks like Toys "R" Us."

"Your brother will have kids someday. Meg is all my parents can ever expect to have."

Oh, right. I'm barren.

I let his comment simmer. The thought of not having more babies pained me. I couldn't physically produce a child, but that didn't mean we couldn't give Meg a sibling.

"We could adopt," I muttered, testing the waters.

"Mmm." He lifted a shoulder. "Who said I wanted more kids?"

His question put a crack in my optimism about our marriage. Sure, Meg's unexpected appearance had brought us together, but in my mind, committing to more children would truly mean our marriage was solid.

Until then, I poured myself into motherhood—making sure our daughter was always clean and well dressed, taking her on walks, and reading to her. Caleb would soon see—I was made for this.

❧

MONTHS LATER, MEG HAD FALLEN asleep in Caleb's arms one evening, and he rose to carry her to bed. I followed them into the nursery, and he whispered, "Her bunny?"

I retrieved the bunny from the window seat and passed it to him, observing with wonder. The man could barely fasten a watch on his wrist without dropping it, yet he changed Meg's diaper, redressed her in a flowery sleep sack, and placed her in the crib without eliciting more than a soft whine. When he was done, he set the bunny beside her.

"Just look at her. She's so big now. When you said you were pregnant, I thought my life was over." His smile grew, and he turned to look at me. "My life began with her."

A love story in reverse: first came the baby carriage, then came love—a love discounted by the situation that brought us together. I wanted to be his first choice. I wanted him to love me wholly. I wanted him to wrap me in his arms and say, "Let's adopt some babies."

As the months passed, I prompted him with encouraging messages: "You're such a good dad. A shame we don't have more." But no amount of compliments bent his will.

When Meg turned two, I pressed him, "What happens when Meg is grown up?"

"We'll be fine." He shrugged.

We *were* fine, if the word translated into "stuck in our ways." Caleb worked, golfed, and traveled for business, leaving me as a single mother the majority of the time. I made a handful of friends from my volunteer positions at Meg's nursery school, but none would I consider especially close—nothing like the friendship I had with Della.

After college, Della landed a position with a Big Four accounting firm in Dallas, putting her on a trajectory that didn't leave much time to return to the Hill Country. She returned when her mother experienced a bad COPD spell or her father's heart gave him trouble.

Soon, Della's trips included a boyfriend, Jared Betancourt, a CPA who managed his family's ranching operation south of the DFW metro. The guy handled Della like fragile china and listened to her like she knew the secret of life. Caleb guessed it would only be a matter of time before she crushed him like a bug. I wasn't so sure he was wrong.

Meg began first grade a few months before Fredericksburg's famed annual Oktoberfest celebration, where tourists flocked to the center of town to sway to polka music, drink from authentic beer steins, and revel in the town's collective heritage. Even six-year-old Meg had grown to love it, donning a dirndl and join her friends at the Kinderpark.

That year, Della and Jared surprised me when she said they were driving in for the celebration, but she blew my mind when she invited Caleb and me to meet them there.

THERE HAD BEEN MANY CHANGES for all of us over the years, and I'd hoped the years had brought understanding and tolerance. Since we'd last spent time together, Della had scrapped her hot rollers and hair spray. Her ivory skin glowed against the curtain of straight, dark hair that met her shoulders—and a glimmery rock shone from her left hand.

"You're engaged?" I asked excitedly.

"Not exactly." She looked away. "We already had a trip planned with some friends, so we just . . . did it when we were in Nevis."

"You're married?"

"Yes!"

"Did your parents get to go?"

"They're in rough shape, and I couldn't drag my mom through a bustling airport. She requires that oxygen tank all the time now. Honestly, I think they were relieved not to have to plan a big wedding. We persuaded some friends to come along."

"Erin and Joe," Jared said, like I should know who they were.

Della shook her head. "She doesn't know them." She looked at me. "Our best friends . . . in Dallas, you know?"

An uncomfortable spray of jealousy washed over me. Our lives had taken us in different directions—Della to new places, meeting new people, while I was stuck in the same place she'd left me.

"Anyway, my parents will have lots of time to see us now," she said. "I'm taking over the family business."

"We're moving here," Jared said, placing a hand on her back.

My eyes widened. "When does this happen?"

"As soon as we find a house." The polka music ramped up, forcing us to shout to hear each other. Della put her hands over her ears. "Can we get out of here? Go to your place?"

I nodded, eager to hear more. But we couldn't take off until I pulled Meg from her friends in the Kinderpark. *This ought to be fun.*

Della followed me to the Kinderpark to retrieve my departure-averse daughter. Reading Meg's frustration, she teased her with, "Aunt Della's so excited to see you. I brought you a surprise!"

Della's affection for my daughter warmed my heart and prompted me to recalibrate my expectations.

⚘←

AT HOME, WHILE THE MEN enjoyed a glass of whiskey and cigars on the back patio, Della and I went into the den.

Della pulled Meg close to help her with the origami kit she had brought while she filled me in on her upcoming move. Della, who once told me she'd never return to Fredericksburg, was now jazzed. "This will be a blast, Sissie. You and me again. You know?"

Nodding along, I read my old friend like a new book, soaking up her mannerisms—the way she waved her left hand around in a circle when she asked, "You know?" and jerked her head back every once in a while so her hair fell away from her face.

"Didn't want to say too much in front of Jared, but we're bringing his son here, too."

"He has a son?"

She squinted. "I told you. Didn't I? Maybe not. Anyway, he's in first grade. The ex is a hot mess, so Jared thought the move would give the kid a break. So . . ." She slapped her thighs. "Looks like I'll be spinning plates between work and all that. He'll spend one weekend a month in Lampasas with his mother, and the rest of the time, he's all ours." She rolled her eyes and turned to Meg. "When he gets here, we'll introduce you."

"Della couldn't wait to see you, Sissie," Jared said as the men joined us in the den.

"She's been talking about putting together a trip for the four of us. Maybe skiing or Mexico?" Jared added.

Caleb tossed me his *what the hell* expression.

I couldn't do anything more than nod and smile.

Twelve

After the new year, the Betancourts found a home just outside of town, and Jared's son, Weston, enrolled in kindergarten at Meg's school.

When hunting season came around, Jared hauled Caleb to his family's hunting lease in Comanche County for a weekend of bow hunting. In turn, I repaid the favor—nothing fancy, just a good old girls weekend at a cute little house on Austin Street.

On Saturday night, I arranged a babysitter for Meg and treated Della to a four-course dinner at one of Fredericksburg's finest restaurants, Cabernet. We might have been more than a bit tipsy walking back to the house, but the night was young, and though I did have to pay the sitter, I didn't have to drive the girl home.

First things first—I checked in on my baby girl, who was well into her dreams by the time I dropped a kiss on her forehead. Second, I opened a bottle of wine about ten minutes after I'd learned Della had cracked the seal on a bottle of Tito's finest. We changed into our pajamas and took both to the front porch.

The bugs were long gone, but there was a chill in the air. I grabbed two quilts out of the linen closet, and Della began razzing me about the boys I'd gone out with in school. "Remember when you made out with . . . what was his name? With the braces?"

A giggle bled into my shushing. "The neighbors'll hear you."

"What was his name?" she asked.

"Jason Daschel. He moved our sophomore year."

"Too bad that didn't work out. You might've avoided—"

"Really?"

She pulled her hair over her eyes. "Sorry." She ducked her head and sipped whatever had landed in her glass. "Don't take this the wrong way, but people in your situation who get married because . . . don't usually make it this long. How'd you pull it off?"

I frowned at her as I gauged her sincerity.

"I saw y'all the other night. After all this time, you actually like each other. How'd you turn one terrible night into a solid marriage?"

I think there's a compliment somewhere in her question. "Time, a steady supply of babysitters, and lots of Westerns." I lost control of a silly laugh and adjusted my posture. "Caleb likes Westerns." I lifted my glass. "And I like Sam Elliott."

"The moustache?"

"That voice—I can be scrubbing out the vegetable crisper, but if I hear that voice, I am putty in Caleb's hands."

"That's how it is?"

"Uh-huh. Damn straight." I lifted my glass.

"Sissie, I'll never understand what goes on inside that head of yours."

ALL THAT FUN AND GAMES came to roost the next morning when Meg shook us awake.

"Meg, if you don't let Aunt Della sleep, I may squash you like a bug," Della said.

"No, you won't. You love me." Meg edged onto the swing.

"It's too early," I said.

"Mom," Meg grunted indignantly. "Wake! Up!"

"Whoa, little filly," Della twanged. "You'd best listen to your ma, or I reckon she'll force us to watch spaghetti Westerns till your pa comes back to the ranch." She giggled to herself. "Or should she come home with Aunt Della and give you two time to—"

"Stop it." I gave her a playful punch on the shoulder.

OUR MEN SAID THEY'D HAD a decent hunting trip, giving me reason to believe we might've moved past our old contentions.

Two weeks later, Della shot me a text—"WE'RE EXPECTING!"

"That's awesome," I wrote back. "Let's celebrate!"

She didn't respond, and I could only assume she was preoccupied taking over her dad's business. I sent her a few more texts—asking how she felt, if she needed anything.

Her responses were brief, usually a cheerful emoticon, confirming my suspicion about her busy schedule. What little time we'd spent together since they moved to Fredericksburg had left me hungry for more.

CALEB'S HARD WORK EARNED HIM another promotion. This one would require twice as much travel. It would also fund the home renovation he had drawn up one night after finishing off a bottle of wine.

He complained that our house was tiny. I found it cozy. He complained about our one-bay garage. I didn't mind parking under the carport. He argued the remodel would increase resale value. I had no interest in selling the house. But I didn't fight him on the remodel.

At the end of many a long workday, Caleb now met with our contractor to review the garage redesign, sometimes over a few beers. The meetings often prevented him from attending some of Meg's volleyball games. These were not our finest days as a couple.

Della opened satellite offices in San Antonio and Kerrville and refused my offer to throw her a baby shower. "I have to give every spare minute launching these offices before the baby arrives," she said. "We'll be fine. Jared's setting up the nursery for us."

A few days later, she called me. "Can you come to my parents' house?" Her voice was heavy with sadness, so I jumped into my car and drove straight there.

I found a few cars in the driveway and strangers in the living room. One directed me to the master bedroom where Della and her father framed each side of her mother's hospital bed.

Decades of sitting in the family's real estate office with a phone in one hand and a cigarette in the other had taken their toll. Della held her mother's hand, and I held Della when COPD robbed the woman of her last breath.

THROUGH THE FUNERAL AND THE following days, I remained by Della's side. A certain tenderness grew between us, and her behavior indicated she'd recalibrated her respect for family time. She delegated management of her offices so she could allocate more time to Jared and Weston.

I was thrilled when she carved out an hour a week to volunteer at Gillespie Primary, allowing us to reconnect while cutting laminated pictures for classroom bulletin boards, organizing supplies, and making copies.

After the agents at her office surprised her with a shower, I helped her put away all the gifts she'd received.

"Della, we've come a long way," I said.

"It takes some of us extra time to grow up." She pulled a receiving blanket to her chest.

Is this an apology? "Fault goes both ways," I said, eyeing the baby giraffe wallpaper.

"What do you mean?" she asked.

What do *I mean, and why do I feel like I'm standing in quicksand?* Finally, I told her, "You and Caleb."

"That's what I meant. Caleb's grown up."

"Della, all due respect, but you didn't just poke the bear—you chased him down first. You see that, right?"

"I don't," she said flatly. "Caleb didn't treat you well." She sighed and set the blanket on the changing table. "You were only sixteen, but he was old enough to know he'd taken advantage of a young girl. Can you imagine if a guy did that to Meg?"

I broke eye contact.

"Let's not do this. We're solid again," she said.

"If we're solid, then why can't you stop with the accusations?"

Her hand fell to the small of her back. "I'm tired. Can we circle back to this later?"

"Sure," I said, feeling she'd just slammed a window closed . . . on my fingers.

IN FEBRUARY, DELLA DELIVERED a healthy, eight-pound, six-ounce baby girl.

Carrying a basket of snacks, lotions, and magazines, I paid a visit to Della's hospital room and introduced myself to Josephine Castro Betancourt.

"Love that you named her after your mom," I said.

"We're calling her Josie. Want to hold her?"

"Do I ever!" I washed my hands and accepted Josie in my arms. Her head was covered in long tufts of dark hair, and she melted into my chest like she belonged there. I took in her sweet, milky scent. "I miss this."

"You could adopt."

That's a topic best left on Austin Street. I stared down at Josie, cupping her head in my hand. "We're good with Meg. Besides, those teen years are right around the corner."

"Ours weren't so bad, were they? Seems like yesterday when you and I were driving to San Marcos." She laughed.

I bristled inside, keeping my eyes on the infant.

"Some memories, huh?"

"Don't remember too much about that weekend—fortunate, huh?" I glanced upward.

The humor left her face. "Ever considered hypnosis?"

I yanked my eyes away from the baby. *Is she kidding?*

"I've seen people on TV recall traumatic events. Might settle what happened that night."

My heart raced as I searched for words that wouldn't destroy this beautiful moment with my best friend's new daughter. With a small shrug, I returned Josie to Della's arms. "I've already stayed too long. Meg's waiting for me to pick her up."

Part Three

Thirteen

The next years took our family in a hundred directions as Meg entered junior high school and explored activities, from ballet to archery before returning to her first love: volleyball, where she landed a spot on a club volleyball team as an ace setter.

Each activity obligated me to man concession stands, peddle raffle tickets, and make snacks. You name it, I did it—at least twice.

While my world rotated around Meg, Caleb dragged himself to an office he'd once treasured.

Voyce's stodgy management style became increasingly limiting—rejecting casual Fridays, micromanaging itinerantly, and avoiding modern performance initiatives like Six Sigma. Morale was in the dumpster. But having sunk all that money in our remodel, Caleb was hesitant to consider a career change.

Then, after a contentious debate between Voyce's board of directors and two Voyce grandsons, a company-wide renaissance offered hope. With renewed enthusiasm, Caleb jumped on the innovation rollercoaster.

Hands and feet in the car at all times, Voyce employees. Could be a bumpy ride.

Caleb carried the day's frustrations home each night, chucking them at us like grenades.

A FEW MONTHS BEFORE HER thirteenth birthday, Meg began leaving notes and pictures of puppies around the house. There was no doubt what she wanted. This discussion had become a well-traveled road, one I'd hoped we wouldn't revisit.

Caleb was allergic. We weren't getting a dog.

Meg didn't give up. She checked out library books and searched the internet for hypoallergenic breeds.

Her timing couldn't have been worse.

The new team at Voyce delivered far more complications than efficiencies for Caleb. His emotions had reached DEFCON-5. From the top down, Voyce had restyled workspaces, restructured budgets, and realigned travel schedules. Events like team-building retreats and workforce improvement brainstorming sessions bled into weekends and evenings.

Caleb almost surrendered his management position after learning about the last mandate: managers were required to attend at least four sessions with an on-site counseling team. Voyce's rationale: "Healthy emotions deliver healthier results."

"This is bullshit. I'm being bossed around by a hippie-dippy kid wearing a hemp necklace who thinks he's at Google," Caleb spat as I cooked dinner. "They replaced our chairs with giant plastic balls. Do you know what it's like to sit on a three-foot-tall purple ball?"

I started to laugh but caught myself when I saw his gaze darken.

"I'm tired of being pushed around," he said. "Enough is enough."

Just then, the kitchen door swung open, and Meg appeared holding a book. "I found the perfect one, Dad."

Caleb didn't look her way.

"See?" Anticipation bubbled around Meg as she pushed the book at him. "This is a Portuguese Water Dog. He's so, so cute," she squealed.

"Hmm," he mumbled.

"Dad? Dad?"

He flashed a look at me.

"Look, this breed won't make you sneeze." She held up the book. "Pleeease," she begged, sounding younger than her age.

"Dammit," he breathed out.

"See? This kind . . ."

His cheeks reddened. His eyes widened. His hand shoved the book from the table. "NO DOGS."

Meg's eyes followed the book to the floor.

"Meghann Elizabeth," Caleb said, drawing her teary eyes to his. "I mean it. I don't want to hear another word about a damned dog."

She looked eviscerated. "Dad?" her voice was a squeak.

"I'm not hungry." Caleb left the table.

I dropped the spoon in my hand and leaned over my daughter, whose hopes had been crushed to broken glass. "Meg, how about we look at it after dinner?"

She shook her head, tears streaming down her face. "No. I don't want to ever look at a dog. Ever again." Her shoulders shook as I pulled her close. "Dad was so mean."

"Honey, he's had a bad day at work, and he took it out on you. I'm sorry."

"I told him I'd do everything, even clean up its poop."

"I know, honey. I know. Things will get better soon."

A boldfaced lie. Truth was, I didn't even know how bad it was already, let alone how much worse it would get.

❧

CALEB'S RESPONSE TO MEG'S REQUEST for a dog offered a peek into his psyche. The peaceful home life we enjoyed during our early marriage had been the closest thing to normal Caleb had ever experienced. His work boosted his esteem in those early years, but the new Voyce Brothers weren't appeased by extra hours. According to Caleb, they wanted his soul.

I had to wonder if they had taken a piece of it when stinging comments and pity parties became commonplace. "Who'd think I was a football captain?" he'd mention as he dressed, noting how his slender frame had settled into the rounded torso of middle age.

His hairline retreated, so he let those bangs grow longer, borrowing my hairspray to keep them from falling in his face. And at night, he mourned his youth with his new friends, Jack and Coke. They were better listeners than his wife.

Lord knows, I tried. Every evening, while making dinner, I'd listen and nod while Caleb tossed back drinks and vented. The conversations always began with, "Did I tell you?"

After that, I could imagine no force strong enough to extinguish his oncoming rant. Even Meg's chipper interruptions couldn't break his concentration.

"Dad, I aced my algebra test," Meg said one evening.

While I gushed, Caleb tossed out, "Good job," then immediately followed up with, "Did I tell you these kids don't even wear socks to work?"

"No." I offered a sympathetic smile to our daughter.

"Did I tell you David Voyce set up an incentive for riding a bike to work?"

"Cool," Meg replied.

He snarled. "That idiot can risk his life riding to work beside eighteen-wheelers going ninety, but I'm not doing it. Kid thinks he's Mr. Athlete. He should've seen me in the day."

Caleb's drink-fueled diatribes included various other work-related grievances, including lackluster appreciation of his work and the unfairness of lost opportunities.

Playing the part of the sympathetic wife and the cheerful mom to an emotive teen left little room for me to address my own tangle of resentment—until, one day, while Meg was at a friend's house and I was washing dishes, I lost it.

"Today, this stupid woman," Caleb began, his words like hot forks stabbing my ears. "These idiots . . ."

I funneled my hot anger into a dirty skillet, scrubbing until my knuckles bled. Meanwhile, Caleb kept talking. *Not talking. Batshit crazy complaining. About everything.*

I lifted a hand in surrender, but his voice droned on until I said, "Caleb."

"This guy auditing my expense report has the gall to—"

"Caleb."

He didn't skip a beat. "My report isn't lined out correctly."

"CALEB!"

Suddenly, he noticed I was in the room.

"I can't do this anymore," I said.

"Do what?"

I paused. *How best to tell him his rants are making me physically ill? Go slow. Be gentle.* "I'm sorry you aren't happy, but I can't do this with you every night. It's not healthy for our family."

"Jesus. If I can't vent to my wife, then, what?" he spat out.

"Not venting. Exploding and spraying it on us."

"Alright."

Alright? He took that well. Why didn't I do this earlier?

He blew out a weary breath and smacked both hands on the table. "You got something to say? Let's hear it."

This is why.

"What, Sissie? You're trying to . . . what? Run a division? Pay for travel volleyball leagues and private coaching lessons and whatever else the kid wants? What's my reward? A guilt trip for telling my wife about my goddamned day!"

That escalated quickly. I spun around. "Caleb, settle down. I understand what you're going through—"

"You don't know jack shit what I'm going through." His anger wasn't new, but in ten years, I'd never heard such venom drip from his lips. He took to his feet, and his icy stare shook me to my core.

"Caleb, you're scaring me."

"Am I? 'Cause I could say the same about you. One day, you're this sweet girl. Now, you nag when I need to talk about my shitty job." He got louder with each world. "The same . . . shitty . . . job your dad *pushed* me into."

"I'm sorry," I said quietly. "Dad was helping you. Us. We didn't have many options."

"I had options. Plenty of them." He kicked the chair from behind him. "Plenty. Till you came along."

"This wasn't my plan, either."

"Sure took to the lifestyle." He waved a hand at our Wolf range. "Gourmet kitchen. Landscapers to plant your hibiscus or whatever the hell they are. You have no problem spending the money I make."

"If you hate your job so much, let's look for another one."

"You don't get it. They're looking for a reason to can my ass." He turned away from me and refilled the bourbon that had evaporated from his glass over the span of a half hour.

"Maybe we should lay off the . . ." I tipped my head toward the bottle.

"Maybe, WE—" He threw his glass into the sink. Ice, glass, and bourbon splashed into the air. "—should get off my ASS!" He shoved open the side door and walked out.

Fourteen

That night rendered our marriage into an unrecognizable form. Our conversations became largely transactional. When Caleb was having a particularly bad day, he'd toss a sweet nothing at me in the vein of, "You're so damn stupid. Why do I keep coming home to you?"

One afternoon, I stopped at a boutique owned by the mother of one of Meg's friends. I passed my credit card to the clerk.

The machine beeped, and she frowned. "Your card's not going through."

It was the only card Caleb shared with me, so I called him. *Big mistake.*

Disdain dripped from his voice, "I told you to *ask* before you use the Amex. What are you buying?"

"A shirt." My gaze shifted to the store owner, now standing behind the clerk, wearing a polite smile.

"I can't deal with this now," Caleb said. "I have a job."

The line went dead.

Shit. Now what? I grasped for an explanation. "Someone tried to commit fraud on this card." I slid it into a slot in my wallet. "Sorry, but it's probably for the best. I have three just like it." I glanced at the crisp white blouse the clerk had already folded and wrapped in tissue paper.

She and the owner nodded in unison, and I disappeared as quickly as I could.

THE DREAD IN MY BELLY grew heavier as the afternoon dragged on. Despite my self-doubt, a small voice broke through. *You're an adult. You don't need permission to buy a shirt.*

Guilt etched at my voice of reason. So, that evening I tried a different tact with Caleb. I began preparing beef stroganoff—one of Caleb's favorites.

When he came home, Caleb didn't mention the call. He just poured a drink and slipped into the den. Maybe an hour later, he returned to the kitchen. Assuming the savory aromas had drawn him, my mood lightened—until he refilled his glass without asking what I was cooking and disappeared again.

Thirty minutes later, Meg led him into the kitchen. "You're going to love what Mom made," she told him.

"Hmm," he muttered. He sank into his chair and surveying his plate. "Hmm," he repeated.

Across the table, Meg's orthodontic hardware amplified her bright smile. "This looks great, Mom.

"Thanks."

Caleb leaned toward Meg. "Your mom knows she's in trouble." He chuckled at her, and her brow line bent in confusion.

"Your crazy mother." He shook his head and pushed a fork into the pile of saucy noodles.

"Didn't listen when I told her we got new credit cards. Tried to use the old one." With a mocking laugh, he added, "You know how she never pays attention."

Meg's eyes fell gently to her plate. After a long pause, she tried to break the tension. "Today, in history, I think I was the only one who had actually read the chapter."

"Way to go," I said.

She finished eating in record time and cleared her plate. "I'll be in my room finishing my homework."

I began loading the dishwasher while Caleb refilled his plate. "Caleb, I didn't know you canceled the American Express."

"Not canceled. We got another set of cards. I told you last week."

"I didn't get a new card."

"You probably lost it."

"Caleb, I would remember you handing me a credit card. I've never lost one."

"Kudos for competence," he said sarcastically and sipped his drink. His face neutralized. "Maybe I'll increase your allowance."

Later, when I undressed for bed, a new Amex was on my dresser.

CALEB'S MOOD CHANGES BECAME DIZZYING, making intimacy impossible. When the rare opportunity presented itself, he'd kiss me, and I'd respond as warmly as I could. All too often, though, he abbreviated the kissing part, handling me with rough hands and rougher words.

The last time, I swore it would be the last time.

"Come on." He kissed me and pressed my shoulders down. "Do me. On your knees."

I laughed a little, hoping he was kidding around. "Caleb."

"Come on. You never do it. Give me your mouth."

The pressure on my shoulders and a wash of embarrassment pulled me to the ground.

"Unzip my pants," he said. "Take it out. Come on."

"Caleb. Not like this. You're scaring me."

"Scaring you." He chuffed. "You should be scared I don't find another woman. You never knew how to make a man happy."

"Then tell me."

"Shouldn't have to." He became frustrated. "Just get up."

He wouldn't face me. "Go back to whatever it was you were doing. I'm not in the mood anymore."

His rejection was disheartening, and our relationship grew cooler over the next few years. I welcomed Meg's frenetic activities, consoling myself in Meg's company. Maybe she didn't need me, but I sure as hell needed her. Short of following her to college, I didn't have a plan for my life after she left us.

Until then, I donned my best poker face, pretending to be oblivious to Caleb's emotional fluctuations. Inside, the burden of carrying the lightness weakened my bones and crushed my spirit. I just hoped our family looked normal from the outside.

Jesus, I'm more like my mother than I ever wanted to admit.

※

Eventually, Caleb's mood improved. I didn't question why. Cushioned by our daughter's presence, a platonic tone replaced the touchiness that had been plaguing our marriage.

I suppose I shouldn't have expected a miracle on our fifteenth anniversary, which fell on another volleyball weekend. *Who needs Paris when you can spend your anniversary in a muggy high school gym watching your daughter bump, set, and spike a volleyball?*

The ref blew the final whistle on the last match, and we slipped into a caravan of volleyball families to a pizza joint.

"Care if I stay at Jordan's tonight?" Meg asked me as she sipped her soda.

"Sure," I said, jolted by the possibility this presented. *A night alone with my husband on our anniversary?*

While Caleb handled our ticket, a faint reminder of our happier days came to mind, spawning a thread of hope. Our relationship had been all over the map these last five years, but we were still together. Perhaps tonight was our opportunity to reconnect.

※

At home, while Meg packed a bag, Caleb stopped into the bathroom where I was preparing to shower. "I'm taking her to her friend's," he said. "Want to watch a movie when I get back?" He cocked his head to the side, and his mouth eased into a smile.

"Sure," I answered quickly, attaching meaning to his invitation. We'd passed the point of candles and lingerie, but I hoped some measure of romance was still possible for us.

After a hurried shower, I applied lotion to my smoothly shaved legs. A low-cut V-neck T-shirt exposed just enough cleavage. I spritzed on perfume, tiptoed into the den, and took a seat beside Caleb on one of the leather sofas. His head was angled over his laptop; a glass of whiskey sat next to him on the end table.

"Happy anniversary." I pushed a card and a small gift box toward him.

"What's this?" He looked at the box like a dead fish. "You didn't tell me we were doing gifts."

"Something little I thought you'd like."

"Hmm. Okay."

"Open it."

He didn't bother closing the laptop before ripping into the card with a shrug. He peeled the paper from the box and removed the money clip.

"Look on the back."

One eyebrow pitched up when he read the inscription out loud: "Love always, Sissie." His eyes shifted to me. "That's sweet. Thanks." He patted my hand. "I didn't think we were doing gifts. Next time, let me know ahead, and I'll come prepared."

Something inside me deflated. *I wasn't expecting magic, but a card would've been nice.*

❧

SINCE MEG WAS A TODDLER, we'd made a habit of stopping by Pike and Martha's house on Sundays to keep the reclusive Martha engaged with her granddaughter. While Meg and Martha chatted, Caleb read the paper or answered emails on his phone. I was always a bit restless and the house begged for some attention, so I used the time to run a load of wash, empty a dishwasher, or restock the kitchen with groceries when Pike was out of town.

Toward the end of September, we made our usual rounds. Pike had gone boating with friends on Lake LBJ and Martha didn't come to the door, so Caleb used his key to enter the house.

Martha was curled up in her recliner, looking particularly . . . well, discarded. She resembled Phyllis Diller with her unkempt hair. Beside her, on an end table, a bowl of bran flakes had congealed. Her eyes held a deadened look, and her decelerated gestures suggested she'd dipped into the Percocet or started off the morning with a Xanax.

Meg told her about a recent volleyball game while I went to work on the house and created a grocery list of depleted items. Pike didn't mind shopping when he knew what was needed, and I didn't mind leaving a list for him.

A half hour later, Caleb nudged me to wrap it up.

At home, Caleb was changing his clothes to meet a buddy at the club's driving range when the landline rang.

A few minutes later, he yelled from the hallway, his voice desperate.

When I reached him, his face was white; his eyes, glassy. "My dad . . . he's gone."

⚘

PIKE'S HEART ATTACK OCCURRED IN an artery called "the widow-maker." Should've called it "the troublemaker" for the ruckus that followed.

Caleb waded through the shock of losing his father and best friend while attempting to keep his mother upright—not an easy feat for anyone.

Pike's viewing was a testament to the breadth of the friends and business acquaintances he'd made throughout his sixty-two years. Wreaths and sprays packed the funeral home with colorful banners that read, "With Sympathy" and "With Love and Fond Memories." A few—"For Making Me Smile," for instance—raised some eyebrows.

Pike's charisma and quick wit had made him a natural charmer, so it wasn't surprising that attractive women of a certain age came from near and far to pay their respects. One even flew in from Kentucky.

My mother lent a hand with host duties—directing guests to sign the book, offering coffee, and pointing out trays of cookies she'd arranged. *Only Kathleen Klein, the hostess with the mostest, turns a viewing into a social hour.*

"Quite the showing," Mom whispered at one point, her interest piqued. "I'd heard the man knew how to make friends with the ladies, but—"

I shushed her. "Let's be here for Martha."

She lifted her arms. "What would you have me do? Hand her a pair of blinders so she doesn't have to see her husband's mistresses?"

"Stop it." I gently elbowed her, and we moved to the door of the viewing room to greet the line of mourners trailing into the room. Pike's jovial nature and folksy personality could be overwhelming, and, when I first met him, he'd annoyed me with his cocky affability. But, as time went on, he'd grown on me. Dinner theater had nothing on Pike Dietrich. Who cared if his facts were correct? He'd spun fascinating tales. He'd made us laugh—God, could he make us laugh. Even my stodgy dad had loosened up around him. Pike had been a bright light in our famly—a bona fide hoot. And for his part, he'd loved everyone he met—maybe too much, if that were possible.

For whatever reason, he and Martha had stuck together, living separate lives. And now that separation was final. Pike's goofy laugh had been silenced, and the world seemed broken.

The funeral director missed the mark arranging Pike—mouth closed with a subtle, smirklike grin. Pike wasn't Pike unless all thirty-two shiny white teeth were on display.

Then again, I guess he's run out of reasons to smile.

The same could be said for Martha, who thanked mourners with indirect nods from the velvety green chair in a corner of the viewing room.

"I've got to return a few calls, but I'll do it in the car," Caleb said, stepping outside.

I'd like to think an angel pulled him away to save him from witnessing what came next.

Fifteen

Caleb didn't share many details about his dad's last outing, but Mom's bridge club, garden society, and bunko group awarded her with a treasure trove of delicious tidbits—the most scandalous was the identity of the sailing mate who'd been rocking Pike's boat for years.

A glistening mist surrounded the woman as she strutted into the funeral home. And strut she did, wielding those five-inch gold pumps like she was born with them. Loose, honey-colored curls fell over her shoulders, and she wore a creamy, winter-white Chanel suit. She whispered, "Excuse me," a dozen times as she bypassed the line and stopped squarely in front of me.

"You must be the daughter-in-law?" she twanged in a whisper. "Sissie, I feel like I know you . . . from pictures on Pikey's phone."

Pikey? Oh, sweet Jesus.

"How nice," Mom said.

"He told me you're a saint," the woman said.

A prickle ran up my backbone and I narrowed my eyes a bit. *Did Pikey know something I don't?*

"And, lord, he was just so dang proud of that granddaughter. Meg this and Meg that. Is that her, over there?" She pointed to Meg, who was sitting with a friend she'd bribed to come along.

"Have we met?" I asked as gently as I could.

"I only wish." She pressed a hand over mine. Her jewelry was cold, and a French-manicured nail bit into my hand. "Fiona Stowers.

129

Pikey and I were . . ." Her lips turned inward in that way women do to refresh their lip color. "Friends." The word was heavy with meaning.

Ding, ding, ding . . . Ladies and gents, she DOES exist.

Mom cleared her throat, and I introduced them. Mom took great satisfaction in meeting the woman behind the stories she'd heard over the years. Fiona wasn't just Pike's friend, she was a former Miss Austin, former Dallas Cowboys Cheerleader, and former senator's wife.

By golly, there she was, bigger than life with her model looks, extra-long lashes, and a vivid persona—much like her—*cough*—friend "Pikey."

Grasping for words, I asked, "How are you?"

"Oh, honey, you're so sweet to ask. Losing him is like losing all the fun in the world."

Tears glistened in her eyes, without leaving a smudge of mascara. "We were lucky to know him. Am I right?" Her mouth formed a sad smile.

"Yes. He was a good man."

"Very good." Pulling a silk handkerchief to her face, she gestured to the casket. "May I?"

Who am I to say? I glanced to Mom and stepped back, indicating she could pass.

Fiona didn't so much as glance at Martha, still fixed in that chair.

Those in line ahead of her retreated, inviting her to advance. *Do they know?*

With inexplicable subtlety, Fiona nodded her thanks and touched the casket. Then she pulled back her curls and bent over the coffin. With a hand on Pike's chest, she whispered only God knew what in Pike's ear. She stood back to take a long look at him, then adjusted the handkerchief in his suit pocket.

"Psst." Mom jerked her eyes toward Martha, now sitting bolt upright.

My mother-in-law's face shifted with awareness, and her mouth twisted to one side. Then she took to her feet, her gaze trained on Fiona.

I see formal introductions won't be necessary.

The whispering hum of mourners fell silent as Martha crossed the room and set her stubby, unmanicured hand on the corner of that shiny mahogany casket.

Fiona met her gaze, and an eerie stillness held until Martha lifted her head a tad higher and said in velvety voice, one I'd never heard before and haven't heard since, "He screwed you. He came home to me. That's love."

If that's love, count me out.

Martha didn't blink; Fiona rearranged her stance, gave a solemn nod, walked to the door, and glided out of the building with beauty pageant finesse.

Face drawn and visibly spent, Martha dropped into her chair, having staked her claim on her highest treasure: Pike's love.

Caleb didn't flinch when I told him what had happened. He just said he didn't want to talk about Fiona and asked that we not mention her name again.

THE NEXT DAY, OUR FAMILY moved as a unit, bracing Martha at the funeral as Pike's friends praised him as a husband and father.

The service ended, but Caleb's grieving had only just begun. It was impossible not to notice the pain in his eyes, the weariness in his movements, or the uneven pitch of his voice.

He had fallen into a hole so dark and deep that not even Meg could tease him out. She invited him to take walks, tried to distract him with stories about school, tempted him with the latest superhero movie, and asked me to make his favorite foods. She did her level best.

I'd like to think Caleb tried, too. His hurt was immeasurable, and it warped into a bizarre sullenness that threatened to consume him.

A few weeks later, I thought we might have turned a corner. After Martha asked him to take Pike's gold Porsche 911 for the fifth time, he finally agreed.

On the way, we dropped Meg off at a slumber party. At Martha's house, I pulled into the driveway and switched off the car.

"I'll take it from here," he said, suggesting I didn't need to bother with getting out of the car. "I need some time. Don't worry about making dinner for me."

❧

WHILE CALEB SPENT TIME WITH his mom, I drove to Burger Burger for a juicy cheeseburger, salty fries, and a smooth strawberry milkshake.

Once I changed into a T-shirt and a pair of well-worn flannel pajama pants, I scuffed into the den in my slippers. The gods were on my side: a *Law & Order: SVU* marathon was on TV—the perfect accompaniment to a greasy dinner, balm to my wearied spirit.

At ten, I texted Caleb, "Checking in. You okay?" I followed up at eleven: "I'm assuming you and your mom are still talking. Give her my best. I'm going to bed soon. Love you."

He didn't respond to either message.

At midnight, I moved to our bedroom and said a short prayer for Caleb's safety and the safety of others on the road with him.

Sleep wouldn't come. No matter what restful scene I visualized, from swaying on a hammock beneath the live oaks to resting on a beach as the ocean lapped the shore, my eyes opened every eighteen minutes. Not ten, not fifteen—every eighteen minutes, starting with 12:48, then 1:14, then 1:32 shining in blocky, blue numbers from the LED clock on Caleb's nightstand. A disruptive stillness filled our bedroom.

At 2:44 a.m., an engine roared into the driveway and splashed light through our bedroom windows. I braced myself and played possum.

Caleb's feet bent the creaky floorboards as he wandered down the hall to his office. The door closed—then silence.

A while later, the creaking along the floorboards resumed. Then the mattress shifted as he sat at the foot of our bed.

"Sissie? Are you awake?"

"Yeah." I sat up. "Couldn't sleep. Worried about you."

"We should talk."

I flicked on the lamp, blinking while my eyes adjusted to the brightness. Before me, Caleb wore a disturbingly frozen expression.

"Sissie, I'm moving out."

I stared at him dumbly.

"Did you hear me?"

Disbelief dulled my responses. Finally, I eked out, "Yes," stopping short of asking why. I'd endured months of his erratic mood swings. Asking for a reason bordered on self-flagellation.

"Don't worry about money. I'll take care of you and Meg. But I've got to live for me before it's too late. I'm going to stay with my mom for now, figure some things out." There was an unnerving number of I's in his manifesto.

Don't react, Sissie. He just lost his father. Give him time. He'll be back.

I told him I understood while he tossed items into a bag he kept half-packed in the closet for work trips.

"Thanks for not being pissed at me," he said before slipping out the door.

Who said I wasn't?

THAT PORSCHE'S MOTOR REVVED BEFORE ripping out of our driveway, and I realized Caleb expected me to make sense of his absence to our daughter. I didn't go back to sleep. My mind churned as I considered what to tell her when I picked her up from the slumber party.

By the time I pulled up to her friend's house the next morning, any understanding I had for Caleb's rationale had metastasized into full-on fury.

Meg climbed into my car, sleep crusted in her eyes and a pink heart, drawn in marker, on her left hand.

Choose well, Momma. Your words will become etched into her being.

Taking it slow, I reminded her of her father's profound loss—a loss so devastating that it required him to set aside "alone time" to clear his head.

She bit her lip and nodded.

This is too easy. Way too easy.

Then the other shoe dropped.

"So . . ." She turned to me.

Caleb might be the one who left, but *I* had just broken her heart. *Some wives have all the luck.*

"When is he coming home?" she asked.

"I'm not sure. But we'll give him some time. Just know, we'll always be a family." I hoped I was telling her the truth.

WEEKS PASSED, AND CALEB CALLED to announce he'd purchased a house nearby.

My stomach slammed to the ground. *What happened to staying with your mom? Your mom, who needs you to get through this difficult time? What the hell's going on?* So many questions zoomed through my head.

"You can tell Meg," I spat out. "I'm not doing it."

"That's fine." He said it like I'd asked him to carry in the groceries.

"Not fine. She feels your absence to the bone. You may miss your dad, but you seem to overlook how Meg misses you."

"Sissie, leaving isn't about Dad."

Bam. Boulder to my chest.

"Losing him was my wake-up call. Like I told you, I've got to live my life before it's too late."

He did tell me, I realized. *I just chose to hear another message.*

"We aren't happy together," he said. "I'm doing you a favor."

It doesn't feel like a favor. It feels like being put out with the trash.

"Meg has been devastated," I said.

"She knows I love her."

"Really? Maybe you should come around and tell her that yourself. I'm done trying to make you look like a decent human."

"You don't need to speak for me."

"Someone does."

"Don't talk to me like that. Meg's well loved."

"Good fathers don't just pick up and leave because they're not satisfied with their lives."

I slammed down the phone.

Sixteen

Maybe it was out of anger—or vengeance—but I called Della right away and unloaded. Apparently, I was late to the party. She had heard. Caleb had spoken to Jared at the club.

Of course he had. Apparently, I was the only one in this god-forsaken town who didn't have their finger on the pulse of my husband's romantic escapades.

To her credit, she didn't jump at the chance to rip Caleb a new one. Instead, she tried to build me up. "You're smart and strong. You'll manage just fine."

"I moved from my parents' house to this one. I've never been alone before."

"You're not alone—you have Meg. And me."

⚜

In time, Meg adjusted to going back and forth between our home and her father's two-bedroom post-war bungalow.

His absence was reminiscent of the business trips he took on alternating weeks. I guess I had become used to it over the years. Without the interruption of helping him unpack, doing his laundry, and repacking for another business trip, my days were free to consider a life without him.

Caleb was right about one thing: we *should* live while we had the chance. *Who knows what I might become?*

His work travel ramped up, and when he wasn't roaming the country, we carried on much as a married couple would—co-parenting our daughter and even sharing meals, going to movies, and talking about our days with one another.

Then I called to ask if he'd like me to book a room for Meg's next volleyball tournament.

"From now on, please email me about stuff like this," he said in a businesslike tone.

"Am I calling at a bad time?"

"No, but . . . we should probably talk to your dad. Get him to help us with the paperwork."

You want me to ask my dad to handle our divorce?

"Make a clean break, wouldn't you say?"

I can't think of anything to say.

THE FOLLOWING MORNING, AFTER MEG left for school, I called my dad at his office.

"Thomas Klein," he answered after his receptionist put me through.

"Dad?"

"Pardon?"

"Dad, it's me. Your daughter. Your only daughter."

"Right. How are you?"

"Oh, I've been better, but I suspect your golf partner's already filled you in," I said, nervously poking Papa bear.

He didn't respond.

"Can you take care of my divorce?"

"Yes, honey, I'll handle it."

"Dad, could you handle it in a way that puts my interest and the interests of your granddaughter ahead of your cheating son-in-law?"

"Sissie, what are you talking about?"

"Dad, I already know about Caleb's piece on the side at Voyce. We don't need to belabor the subject. Will you promise me to put my interests first?"

"Of course. Honey, your mother and I are here for you, no matter what."

"Love you, Dad."

"Love you, too."

NOW THAT MY DIVORCE WAS underway, I had way too much time on my hands. Della asked me to help with a project at the elementary school. I didn't even have a child there, but I didn't mind. It gave me something other than Caleb to think about.

The night she asked me to accompany her to the PTO meeting, I had almost bugged out. She insisted, arguing the benefits of getting out of the house, and offered to pick me up.

She came right from work, still wearing a suit jacket, matching copper dress pants, and heels.

"Crap, Del. I look like your maid." I gestured to my white cotton blouse and jeans.

"Don't worry about it."

"Says the woman who owns a pair of Jimmy Choos."

"Five."

"Is that a brand?"

"Five pairs of Jimmy Choos, and I'm not even ashamed." She laughed. "Come on." She gestured toward the door. "Meet the other moms. It'll take your mind off what's-his-name."

"Ha, ha. For all I know, one of those women is dating my husband."

Her face was tight with worry. "Well . . ." She hesitated. "Probably better you heard this from me."

There's a million-dollar conversation starter.

"Jared ran into Caleb at card night—at the club?"

"How do these guys have so much free time?"

She shrugged it off. "Jared said the liquor was flowing. Caleb was bragging about some ex-girlfriend from high school who's moving back to town."

"Did he get a name?" I asked, remembering some of those nights when he and Jack Daniels discussed their glory days—football games, keggers with the guys, and a former girlfriend he said all the guys wanted.

Della hesitated.

"Lark Lovejoy," I asked.

Della's wide eyes provided my answer. "How did you know?"

"Her name's come up over the years." With a dramatic flair, I echoed Caleb's words: "All the guys would've married her if they'd only had the chance."

"She's baaaack."

"Probably why he left."

"I'm sorry. Caleb might not have been my first choice for you, but I wanted him to make you happy."

Della cared, but I wondered if she took satisfaction in Caleb rejecting me. "I'm fine." I cleared my expression and held up my purse. "Shall we go to that meeting?"

"If you feel like it?" she asked, wincing.

"Beats sitting around here having you give me that I-told-you-so look."

"It was a he-was-never-good-enough-for-you look."

"Yeah, I got that message, too. Sixteen years ago."

"Yeah, well." Della's mouth clicked.

I motioned to the door.

The meeting was held at Bianca Jarboe's home, and it was unlike other PTO meetings I'd attended where the hostess had served bottled water and store-bought cookies. This one featured a charcuterie tray, cut fruit and veggies, petit fours, iced tea—peach and plain—and white wine.

In what looked more like a cocktail hour than a parent meeting, women swirled around the house, chatting and laughing. I was in no mood to do either. I should've stayed home. I was terrible company.

While Della mingled, I tucked myself into a corner of the kitchen and flipped through the Ree Drummond cookbook I found on the counter. The words and pictures couldn't break past the thoughts weighing heavily on me, but I kept my head down in the hopes it would send a message: I wasn't in the mood to chat.

Naively, I believed Caleb and I had discovered a sweet spot between peaceful separation and healthy co-parenting. One week, the three of us were sitting at the same table, teasing each other over bowls of chili. The next, Caleb was asking me to communicate by email and finalize the divorce.

I refocused on the cookbook. It threaded appealing recipes between sunlit photos of the copper-haired chef, her family, and the rolling plains surrounding their home. The Pioneer Woman made her simple life look glorious.

Caleb on a tractor? Meg feeding the livestock? Me whipping up lemon blueberry pancakes? Is living off the land the secret sauce?

Who was I kidding? Caleb wouldn't even let us have a dog.

Della's voice interrupted my prairie contemplation. "I'm sorry I dragged you to this."

"It's good for me to get out for a little while." I pasted on a smile.

"That's the spirit."

Just then, I exchanged smiles with a woman standing nearby. She stepped toward us, and I introduced myself. Before she had the chance to say her name, Della blurted out, "You're Lark Lovejoy."

"I am," she said. She had a cute giggle and bouncing blond curls. "This is my first PTO meeting. Everyone's so friendly." She gestured to the groups of women chattering around the house.

Lark was petite, wore no makeup, and lit up the room with her smile. I wanted to hate her almost as much as I wanted to know her.

"How nice." Behind Della's wry grin, I detected trouble.

Lord, help us all.

"We've heard about the elusive Lark," Della said.

No stopping her now.

"Elusive?" Lark chuckled.

Poor lamb.

"Good golly! Sounds like you're talking about a nature video." Lark's voice dropped to a theatrical whisper, "The hunter has finally located the elusive—"

"Cougar?" Della interrupted. She never could resist the temptation of pulling that one thread capable of unraveling an entire sweater.

"Hardly." Lark snorted a laugh. Even that was cute.

Della quirked her brow suspiciously.

Buckle up.

But before another nasty word could leave my friend's lips, Lark took a tiny step forward and squinted at her.

That little husband stealer's dumb like a fox, my dad would say.

"You seem to know me, but we haven't been introduced."

"This is Della Betancourt," I said from my perch in the corner.

"I'm Sissie's best friend," Della added. "Listen, Lark . . ."

"What am I missing?" Lark glanced at me before shifting her gaze back to Della. "You say my name like a dirty word."

Della gestured to me. "Sissie . . . Dietrich? Doesn't ring a bell?" Della's voice pitched up an octave, and she sloped her head with indignation. "Dietrich? As in, your high school boyfriend?"

Lark batted her hands like Della had just pepper sprayed her. "Wait. Caleb Dietrich?" Her face relaxed into a smile.

"Caleb Dietrich." Della sounded like a DA from *Law & Order: SVU.*

Lark threw her head back. "Oh my gosh. There's a blast from the past."

"I'll bet." Della gave me a knowing look.

I hate that look, by the way.

"You're Caleb's wife?" She bent toward me. "How cool."

So cool. Let's braid each other's hair and swap stories about my husband.

Pulling the pin from her next verbal grenade, Della threw out, "They're separated."

"Oh." Lark's face sobered, and she shifted her gaze to me. "Sorry to hear that." *If I didn't know better, I'd think she pitied me.*

Della lifted a finger. "Haven't you and Caleb reconnected?"

Lark looked genuinely confused. "Not recently." She laughed. "Let's see . . . last time I saw him was . . . when? Our ten-year reunion?"

Oh, yeah. Remember it well. Caleb attended the reunion while I stayed home with our chicken pox–riddled child.

"Since your reunion? Really?" Della demanded.

"Really." Lark shot me an *is-this-lady-for-real* expression.

"Interesting. Caleb's been giddy as a schoolgirl since he heard you moved back here." Della spoke like she'd been in the room to hear Caleb brag. "Made it sound like you and he were . . ." She rocked her head back and forth.

Deeper confusion colored Lark's face. "Haven't seen hide nor hair of him. Matter of fact, this is my first"—she flung out finger quotes—"night out since I moved back to Fredericksburg." Her eyes dropped to me. "Living with my parents and kids—*la vida loca,* right? Why'd you think I was involved with Caleb?"

She was asking me, but Della jumped ahead to toss this woman against the ropes. "How would you feel if *your husband* couldn't keep from wetting his pants every time someone mentioned his ex-girlfriend?"

What, exactly, was Caleb sharing with Jared?

"Well." Lark swallowed and wobbled her head like Della had a minute earlier. "My husband passed away."

"I'm sorry for your loss," I said.

Lark nodded. "Thank you. I—"

"Do you know how many times Sissie heard him go on about the perfect Lark Lovejoy? How'd that go, Sis? 'Lark was the one . . .'"

"'The one all the guys remember,'" I mumbled and went back to biting the inside of my cheek.

Della bobbed her head. "My personal favorite was, 'Any of the guys would've married Lark if she'd just come back to Fredericksburg after college.' Now you're back, and he wants a divorce. Convenient."

Lark covered her mouth. "What the . . . ?"

"Must be nice, being someone's fantasy girl, hmm?" Della asked.

"We barely dated in high school. Hardly serious."

"He was serious about you." Della made a sucking noise through her teeth.

"I can't even . . ." Arms crossed over her chest, Lark turned to me. "Do you have children?"

"Just one." I nodded. "A daughter in high school."

Lark glanced around the room. "Is this a combined meeting with the high school?"

"No. I still volunteer at Gillespie every once in a while."

"That's generous of you. Look, I'm sorry you're going through this."

"I'll survive."

"Yeah, she will," Della said. "Her daddy's Thomas Klein. The divorce lawyer? When he's done ripping Caleb a new one, the jerk won't have two crumbs left to spend on the next woman."

Not exactly, considering my dad and Caleb have a standing tee time.

Lark's blue eyes landed on Della. "I'll bet Sissie's grateful you have her back. Friends are important during a separation—especially when you can't tell what you're up against."

"No doubt," Della said.

"Don't waste all that fire on me. I have no designs on him, or anyone else." Her concerned eyes met my gaze. "I'm sorry Caleb spoke about me like that to you."

"I'm sorry about . . ." I shot a glance at Della.

"Don't apologize for me," Della said.

"Della, please."

Della breathed out. "Can't be too careful."

"Right." Lark lowered her voice to a whisper to tell me, "I'm not your enemy." She stood. "Well, it was nice meeting both of you." Then she walked away.

"What *was* that?" I asked.

"Thought she should know you weren't anyone she wanted to mess with."

"She said she wasn't interested in Caleb."

"What would *you* say if you were fooling around with a married man, and his wife was standing in front of you?"

"I think I believe her."

"Sis. C'mon."

"Della, I appreciate your support, but that . . ." I tipped my head toward Lark. "*That* was too much."

CAN'T SAY I WAS SURPRISED when I heard Caleb was dating. *He is Pike's son, after all.*

The week after Della's block party, she called me. "This neighbor of mine works at Voyce, and she said Caleb's dating an analyst from one of the East Coast offices."

I was pretty sure she'd gone digging, but the facts were what they were. "Thanks for letting me know," was all I could say. I was relieved when it wasn't Lark.

If I had any doubt about Lark's denials, my suspicions were put to bed after Caleb went full-on stalker, following Lark around the Oktoberfest venue. This time, I didn't need to hear it from Della. My parents were there, witnessing Caleb binge-drinking and picking fights with Lark's beefy boyfriend.

Shocking Lark doesn't run when she sees the Dietrichs around town!

In fact, she didn't appear to avoid me at all. She'd even put me in touch with Julia, a counselor friend in Houston. Julia worked at a domestic violence shelter but agreed to speak to me remotely during her off-time so I might avoid becoming fodder for small-town gossip. Julia had this way of asking questions that led me to a deeper understanding without being told what to think. Our talks gave me the confidence to negotiate the ground rules for my divorce from Caleb and to consider my future as a single mother.

One January evening, after taking Meg to dinner, Caleb followed her into the house as he had on occasion when she wanted to show him something in her room. This time, however, Meg went to her room, leaving Caleb in the kitchen.

"Sissie, can we talk?"

Oh, how I hate those words. "Want to sit?" I waved at the breakfast table.

He nodded and sat in his usual spot at the end of the table.

"My dad said you and he talked about the visitation schedule," I said. "Whatever's best for Meg is best for me. But we need to talk about the big ones like Christmas and—"

"Sis, can I come home?"

My blood ran cold. Months earlier, I would've crawled over razor wire to have him come back. Now, the prospect of returning to a life marked with unpredictable emotional outbursts and mood swings renewed a familiar dread. "What about the divorce?" I asked.

"Cancel it."

"And what about your girlfriend?"

His eyes popped. "Where'd you hear—"

"We live in Fredericksburg. Please."

"It's over."

"What about your house?"

"I'll sell it. Sissie, Meg wants us together. We're all she has."

"Caleb, you were terribly unhappy."

"I was." He fidgeted with a napkin ring. "Remember those counseling sessions Voyce made me attend? They got me though Dad's death. And they got me to a doctor who put me on a medicine that evens out my highs and lows. All that helps, but I need my family."

"Are you sure?" *Am I sure I'm willing risk going back to that life?*

"I'm sorry for putting you through hell. It's been a rocky road getting here, but I'm ready to be the husband and father you and Meg deserve."

Caleb's revelation knocked the wind out of me. He was making promises to be a better father and a gentler husband. *Could I deny my daughter an unbroken family?*

With a few stipulations, I agreed. The following Saturday, Caleb borrowed my Tahoe, packed his house, and moved home. That night, we ordered pizza, and the three of us curled up together on the sofa to watch *Lilo & Stitch*, one of Meg's favorites. Once again, the Dietrichs were back together on Austin Street.

Part Four

Seventeen

It seemed that while we'd been apart, my husband had worked through his work-related frustration. The same hippie-dippy initiatives that had driven him to drink became his salvation. Those mandated therapy sessions he'd resisted so strenuously were now a lifeline for him.

According to Caleb, those sessions hadn't just made him a better manager. They'd helped helped him define the sources of his anger. As we walked around the neighborhood one afternoon, he peeled back the curtain for me.

"I held a whole lotta resentment for my mom not being around. Not just her. I thought Dad walked on water, and I wanted him to give me the attention he handed out to complete strangers." He snickered. "At least, I thought they were complete strangers. I want Meg to have everything I missed."

"You've been a pretty great father," I said.

"When you got pregnant, I thought . . . I don't know . . . it was like a sign. Like, if I just got married and took care of you and our baby, everything would snap into place. I'd have this normal life."

"Normal?" I snickered. "What's that?"

He laughed. "Losing Dad, I thought I'd lost my rock. Kinda forgot I had you."

If I ever cross paths with that therapist from Voyce, I thought, *I'll give her a big hug.* She'd saved our family.

I didn't mention my calls with Julia, Lark's therapist friend. I didn't think Caleb would take too kindly to me talking to a domestic violence counselor. Also, I relished the privacy of my calls with Julia, taking comfort knowing she was always just a phone call away.

When I told Julia about Caleb's return, she said she supported my decision, so long as I protected Meg and myself. We continued to talk, and I found the counseling helped me navigate other relationship potholes.

When I'd told her about Della's penchant for doling out opinions, and she asked, "How does it feel when Della tells you what to do?"

"I know she cares and wants the best for us," I said.

"Uh-huh. How does it make you feel?"

"Trapped," I admitted. "Between her and Caleb."

"Before Caleb, what did your relationship look like?" Julia asked.

"We were kids. I guess I went along with whatever she wanted. She wanted me to go to Texas State so we could room together. My parents wanted me to go to UT. I fought hard and won." I laughed and tried out my best game show host voice: "'Tell Sissie what she's won, Steve!' 'You've won an all-expenses-paid life of domesticity. The kid. The husband. The house. And, just for playing, we're including all the problems, too.'"

Julia laughed. "If only you had a sense of humor, I might be able to help you."

"What else can I do but laugh?" I took a long breath. "Anyway, that might've been the last argument I won with my parents. After a trip to the campus, I got pregnant. No more decisions for me."

"Sounds as if you didn't feel free to choose for yourself," Julia observed. "How about now?"

"Now, things are better, especially since Caleb's counseling."

"You didn't answer my question. Do you feel comfortable making choices for yourself?"

"Nothing left to choose. Meg's happy, looking at colleges. And Caleb and I are doing alright."

"You allowed Caleb to return because you assumed it was in your daughter's best interest. How do you feel about that one?"

"Good."

"Since he's moved back into the house, do you feel safe around him?"

"I'd be lying if I said I was completely relaxed when he's close by. But he doesn't yell anymore."

"How about intimacy?"

"We haven't slept together yet. I mean, we've literally slept together in the same bed, but he hasn't even tried to, you know."

"What would you do if those old behaviors returned?"

"Which one?"

"Say he tried to force you into sex?"

"He really hasn't even tried anything."

"Alright. But if he were to become forceful?"

"I'd probably go to Della's."

"With the tension between you and Della, should you consider other friends?"

What friends? Damn, this is embarrassing. "I have people from church, PTO, volleyball, but I don't really have real friends besides Della," I said. "You don't invite people around when your husband's self-destructing on a regular basis."

"Now that Caleb's in a healthier space, would you be comfortable opening the door to new friends?"

"I have Lark," I said slowly, registering Julia's connection to Lark. They were the best of friends. "She doesn't know everything I've told you."

"Nor will she. What's said here, stays here."

"I mean, when you asked if I had other friends, she came to mind. She doesn't know the extent of what went on between Caleb and me. She might be confused if I showed up on her doorstep, although I suspect she'd tell me to come on in."

"She would."

"Meg babysits for her kids every once in a while. I've gone over there with her, too. Not to help, just to love on Lark's baby."

"Ah, baby Georgia. I've got to see her before she's all grown up," Julia said.

"Lark's something else. She's a tough cookie, but also so sweet."

"She's good like that." Julia laughed. "You're right. She's tough. You should've seen her taking care of those boys while her first husband was sick. That tiny woman is a well of strength."

"You'd never know what she went through, the way she's always smiling."

"Don't let her sunny disposition fool you. She has her moments. We all do."

"I guess," I said. "Anyway, since she bought that winery, she's a busy little bee."

"What if you reached out to Lark? Tell her you realize she's busy and ask if you can share a safe word, just in case you need to decompress. That way, she'd recognize your call or text if Caleb's behavior made you uncomfortable."

"I really think Caleb's mellowed out."

"Fair enough. He's mellowed out. Would it hurt to have a safety net in place?"

"No. And Lark *would* probably be better. If Della thought I were in trouble, she'd show up carrying a twelve-gauge shotgun with Caleb's name on it."

"Ah, back to Della," Julia said. "She sure injects tension in your life."

"She wants to take care of me. But sometimes when she stands up for me, it hurts."

"Hurts more than it helps, or just plain hurts?" Julia asked, her voice serious.

"Both."

"People can intend to help us, but their help can feel a lot like control. It can knock healthy, functional relationships into—"

"Dysfunction?"

"You've been paying attention. Here's what I want you to do. Before we talk again, start thinking about activities or hobbies you'd like to try. Don't worry if they aren't interesting to Meg or Caleb or Della."

"Okay." *Glad she can't see me rolling my eyes.*

"One more thing—I'd like you to pay attention during inter-actions with Della. How does she respond when you disagree?"

To her face? Would I dare?

MY OPPORTUNITY CAME THE FOLLOWING weekend when Jared had taken the children to Dallas to visit his family and Della invited me over on Saturday morning for coffee.

I wouldn't have been surprised if she already knew about Caleb's homecoming, but I decided to tell her anyway. And I prepared to make one thing clear: it wasn't up for discussion.

Carrying our mugs to the wide porch on the back of Della's house, we watched her children's empty swings sway in the fall breeze.

"Took the whole weekend off," Della said. "I just needed some time for myself." She sipped her coffee. "Let's dart off to San Antonio for a spa weekend soon."

"Sure," I said, halfheartedly.

While she went on about mud wraps and massages, I wasn't ready to leave my newly repaired family this soon.

"What's the latest with Shithead?" she asked coolly.

No time like the present. "He moved back into the house."

She set her mug down with a thud. Her mouth tilted in a half-smiling, half-grimacing expression.

"Don't get flustered. Meg deserves a home with both parents."

"You are kidding me."

A jarring chord rang in my chest, one I had ignored for too damn long.

"You were finally getting away from him. Finally getting a chance to be whoever you wanted to be."

Or who you want me to be?

"I'm saying this because I care about you," she said.

There goes that chord again.

"Sissie, I can't allow you to do this. You deserve better. Listen, I think—"

"You're *like* family," I said, remembering Julia's advice and permitting myself to give voice to that warning sound rising from my belly, "but Caleb and Meg *are* my family. I made the decision to allow Caleb back into my home."

"At least let me try to talk you out of this before it's too late," Della said.

"My decision's made. Don't look at me like I've let you down." I sighed loudly. "I'm so tired of trying to mold myself around what everyone else expects of me. Dammit, I've been carrying those expectations around for years, and it's breaking my back."

"Hold on, here." She threw her hands up. "Any high expectations I've had for you are about making your life better."

"I don't need you to make it better."

"Lest you forget, I know too much. I'm the one who picked you up the morning after he took advantage of you."

"Another topic that's off limits."

Her face was inches from mine. "Sissie, c'mon."

I stood, blinking away a tear. "I'm going home so we can let this conversation air out."

"I'm only trying to take care of you."

I set my mug on the table. "I have a mother. Be my friend." I left her house feeling weary, sentimental, and strangely empowered. *Making decisions isn't so bad.*

WHILE I WAS IN DECISION-MAKING mode, I called Lark. After I caught her up on Caleb's return, I shared Julia's recommendation. "I don't think it'll ever happen, but Julia recommended I have a safety net, a place to go if . . . if Caleb became upset, or, God forbid, violent. Honestly, he's rarely escalated to a point where he scared me, but—"

"You don't have to explain," Lark said. "Of course. Any time. I'll come to you, and you and Meg are always welcome here."

"Oh, and . . ." *Here goes nothing.* "Julia recommended a safe word?" I closed my eyes, feeling silly.

"Got one in mind?"

"I have no idea."

I heard one of Lark's boys trying to get her attention. "Hang on, Sissie." Muffled voices, and then she was talking to me again. "Alright, I'm back. Charlie couldn't reach the Pop Tarts."

"How about Pop Tarts? As the safe word?"

"Works for me," Lark said.

I'll never see a box of those toaster pastries the same way again.

FOR THE NEXT YEAR, CALEB and I fell into a loving, largely platonic marriage, eliminating the necessity for a safe word. He became healthier, physically and mentally. He rarely drank alcohol, he exercised, and he met with his therapist at Voyce regularly. For what it was worth, Caleb Dietrich had returned to us as a new man.

Eighteen

At the beginning of Meg's senior year, she hung up her volley-ball jersey to channel her energy toward studying for college entrance exams. She'd always been at the top of her class, and she had her eye on a university in Virginia.

One afternoon, while I prepared dinner, she slumped over a once-pristine silvery MacBook now defaced by stickers of Rosie the Riveter and Ruth Bader Ginsberg. "Argh. These questions. What do they even *mean*?"

"I thought you were happy with the essays you wrote."

"This is for the Texas application."

"Can't send the same one?"

"I wish."

I waved a bottle of olive oil over raw green beans and glanced over at her. *When did she get those serious cheekbones? Those full lips? When did she take her dark hair out of those braids and begin looking like a grown woman?*

"Mom?" Meg waved a hand, catching me lost in thought.

I shook my head. "Yeah. What's the prompt?"

"I just told you." She blew out a hard breath. "I can't think of one stupid challenge that affected my"—she squinted at the laptop's screen—"'personal growth or academic achievement.' Who writes this crap, anyway?"

"They want to get to know the real you."

"The real me wouldn't talk like that. Besides, I'm in the top 10 percent of my class. I do a ton of extracurriculars. Now they want me to wax poetic?"

I crinkled my brow. "Wax poetic?"

"My English teacher says it." Meg returned her gaze to the computer. "Anyway, challenges?"

"You've had challenges. Like, when . . ." I thought about Caleb moving out. *Too personal.* Instead, I threw out, "Remember the first time you tried out for volleyball? You didn't make the A-team, but you practiced and earned a spot the next year."

Meg made a face. "I've got nada, because you guys made life too easy for me."

"Fine. We'll kick you out of the house for a month. Will that help?"

She rolled her eyes. "You'd miss me too much." She reached across the island, picked up one of the green beans, and bit into it with a crunch. "What if I took a gap year?"

Our eyes locked. *A gap year opens the door to ambition-averting variables, like getting pregnant and skipping college altogether.* I knew she knew what I was thinking.

"Whitney Reinhart's taking one. She's backpacking around Europe. She's gonna sleep in yurts and see the world."

"You aren't Whitney Reinhart."

"Dad was cool with it. Said it sounded fun." Meg shrugged.

Hear! Hear! The retired party boy has spoken.

"You're going to college, and you're going next fall." My eyes settled on the back of her laptop. She'd added a new sticker, although I couldn't make out the words. I recognized the line from *The Handmaid's Tale*—"Don't let the bastards grind you down." My lip twitched with the beginning of a smile. *Oh yeah. My baby's gonna shake the world.*

"Just because *you* didn't go to college doesn't mean I have to go right away. I've got my entire life ahead of me."

Ouch. A wave of shame shoved me out of my easy mood.

"Gah, Mom. I'm just messing with you." She cocked her head to the side. "You really think I'd skip college? To do what? Become somebody's housewife? Worked too hard for *that*."

My cheeks grew hot. *That's been my life since I was her age.* But amid my mortification, Meg's comment delivered a glimmer of relief.

I fidgeted with the green beans and avoided her eyes to lighten the intensity. "Baby girl, I want you to have the moon and the stars—"

"Everything you gave up when you had me?" Meg asked.

"*You* are my moon and my stars."

Meg pushed away from her seat and wrapped her arms around me. Her lankiness didn't allow for the yielding sensation of the soft cuddles we'd shared when she was younger. I tried to drop a kiss on her forehead, but she twisted away from me to pull her keys from her backpack.

"Where are you going?"

"Class council meeting." She shoved her laptop and cell phone into the green Patagonia backpack she'd carried since sophomore year. "Save me some dinner. Love you." She threw the side door open.

"Love you, too," I said, as my moon and stars zipped out of the driveway.

A WEEK LATER, CALEB FLEW to Maryland for work, leaving me solo while my moon and stars babysat Lark's three children. Much as I would've loved to have enjoyed one-on-one time with my daughter that weekend, I didn't begrudge Lark for asking her. After all she'd endured before moving back to Fredericksburg, Lark proved her strength when she bought a defunct winery, married a younger man, and became pregnant—not necessarily in that order.

Won't catch me throwing stones.

So while Meg babysat, I spent Friday evening with Lady Clairol, dying my grays.

Just after I finished rinsing, Meg called my phone.

"Mom? I think I ate some bad grocery store sushi. Jamie's had to help me with the other kids because I can't stop going to the bathroom."

"Oh, Lord. I'll be right over."

"I'll text you the code to the gate."

The braless, pantless woman in the bathroom mirror had no business leaving the house, but duty called. I slipped on the requisite clothes, toed into my sneakers, tacked my wet hair into a ponytail, and grabbed the Zofran pills from our last food poisoning incident, before dashing out the door.

I DROVE AS FAST AS I dared to the winery and punched in the code Meg had sent me. The gate hummed open, I drove onto the winery property. Past the winemaking buildings, I took the narrow gravel road to the Gifford's home, surrounded by acres of grapevines.

Lark's second grader, Jamie, answered the door, his sable eyes pinched with worry. "Hi Mrs. Dietrich!" He wiped his chin. "Are you here to help?"

"That bad?" I asked, stepping into the house.

"Real bad."

Meg greeted me with a moan from the sofa. Sweat beaded on her pallid forehead. "Georgia's asleep upstairs."

"I'll check on Georgia. Here." I passed her the nausea medicine. "Let this dissolve under your tongue."

Upstairs, fourteen-month-old Georgia slept in her crib. Her gentle snore made me long to hold her.

I walked downstairs where six-year-old Charlie stood over Meg, patting her head.

"How about we let Meg sleep? Wanna play a game in the kitchen?" I asked.

Charlie perked up. "Chutes and Ladders?"

"Ehhh." Jamie was less enthused, but after some thought, he agreed. "Okay. C'mon, Charlie."

Charlie pulled the game box from a bookshelf in the living room and carried it into the kitchen.

ONE SPIRITED GAME LATER, Charlie raised his arms overhead in triumph.

Jamie rolled his eyes. "It's a kid game, Charlie."

"I'll be right back," I said.

I checked on Meg. She was sleeping soundly, so I returned to the kitchen.

"Hi," Charlie said from his lone perch at the island.

"Where's your brother?"

"Doesn't want to play anymore." With an elbow on the table, Charlie propped a hand on one of his full cheeks. "Said it's a kid game."

"Well . . . you are kids." I winked at him.

"Doesn't like kid games."

"We can play."

The doorbell rang, and Charlie peeled out of the kitchen.

"Let an adult answer the door," I called, chasing after him.

"Who is it?" Jamie asked.

"Someone who has the code to the main gate." I peered through a side window.

Charlie shrugged. "Does it look like a bad guy?"

"Maybe."

He slinked around the corner, and Jamie pulled the door open.

"Jamie," I said, but it was too late.

"It's just Uncle Harlan," he said.

"*Just* Uncle Harlan," the man said in a voice I could've sworn belonged to Sam Elliott. When he stepped inside, I might have swooned a little.

"This is Mrs. Dietrich," Jamie said. "She's our babysitter's mom."

He crossed into the foyer. Taller than me, he had a solid build and smelled like pine trees and spice—and maybe a hint of puppy breath?

"Nice to meet you." He reached out a hand, and I offered mine. Something awakened in me when we touched.

I pointed to his face. "You have . . . eyes."

His jaw twitched. "I do?"

"I mean . . . you have Lark's eyes."

He cocked his head to the side.

"You two have those pretty blue . . ."

"Uh-huh." His mouth crooked into an amused grin.

I'm an idiot. A certified, nonverbal idiot. Get it together, already.

"You two have the same eyes," I said, unable to stop now. "They're nice eyes."

Nice eyes? Who says that?

"They belong to our dad," he said. "Lark and I take turns borrowing them."

"He-he-he-he-he," I chortled—too loudly. Too late, I covered my mouth.

Harlan jerked his head back like my laughing hurt his ears.

"Hope I didn't wake Georgia."

"Or Meg?" Jamie added.

Not to worry, kid. She's out for the count.

Harlan took in the lay of the land. "If you want to take your daughter home, I'll handle these mongrels." At least, I think that's what he said. I was too distracted by that manly voice to hear things properly.

"Couldn't wake her if I tried," I gestured behind me.

Brows raised, he put a hand on Jamie's shoulder.

"Stomach thing," I explained.

"Ew." He jerked back. "Bug going around?"

"She thinks it was grocery store sushi."

"Gotcha. Well, hope you don't mind me hanging out here until my parents get home? They're flying back from New Mexico. They weren't expecting me, and the house is locked."

My therapist did say I should make new friends. Did Lark tell me she had a brother?

I tapped Jamie's shoulder. "Could you come with me for a sec?"

Jamie shrugged and followed me into the kitchen.

I whispered, "Your uncle . . ."

Jamie waited.

"Did your mom know he was coming?"

He shrugged. "I dunno."

I bit my lip, searching for words that wouldn't scare the boy. "Is he a nice man?"

"Yeah." Jamie's face brightened. "He's cool. He has a gun that can shoot a can from a mile away."

You're not helping, kid. "Does he have a lot of guns?"

"Prob'ly. He lives in the wilderness all by himself."

Oh, joy. The Unabomber's in the house.

Jamie went into a circuitous description of Uncle Harlan's nature experiences—catching fish, scaring away bears, and climbing trees. When the kid took a breath, I interrupted, "Honey, what I'm asking is if your mom would be okay with him being here with us?"

"She likes him." Jamie worked his mouth. "She calls him her stinky brother." His shoulders rose. "I don't think he really smells that bad, though."

I laughed. "Think she's kidding around?"

"Prob'ly."

"Mom!" Meg shrieked.

I nearly tripped over Jamie when I took off through the narrow hall, past the foyer, and into the living room.

"Give her to me!" Meg yelled. She had the remote control in her hand and was waving it over her head. I could almost see cartoon stars floating over her dazed expression. "I'll throw it!"

"Simmer down," Harlan said, chuckling, and I saw that he was holding the baby—hence Meg's ire. "What're you gonna do with that—mute me to death?" He patted his teary niece's back.

"Meg, he's Lark's brother." I pulled the remote from her hand. "It's alright."

"Huh?" She kept her serial killer stare locked on him.

"Uncle Harlan?" Charlie called from the staircase landing.

Harlan pivoted and jogged up the stairs.

"Go back to sleep," I instructed Meg, helping her back to the couch. "I've got this under control." I covered her with a crocheted blanket I found in a basket beside the couch.

I followed the children's voices upstairs to Georgia's room, where they provided me with an impromptu viewing of *Three Men and a Baby*: all three males in the room standing next to a changing table with a fussy Georgia squirming on it.

Harlan lobbed his head toward an opened package of Huggies on the chest of drawers. "Jamie, hand me a clean diaper."

"Yeah, but Uncle Harlan, Mom always does the wipie first cause she gets stinky."

"I'm the king of stinky, remember? Hand me the wipes."

Amusing as it was to watch these three try to change a diaper, it wasn't fair to Georgia. "Need a hand?" I stepped into the room.

"Ah, we'll get it," Harlan said, picking wipes out of a plastic box in Jamie's hands. "Atta girl," he said, sweetening his voice. "Uncle Harlan's got you."

That has a ring to it.

"Push the tapes really hard. Sometimes, she pulls them off." Jamie pointed at the diaper.

Harlan gave a generous nod. "Thank you, Jamie. I can do this. I've diapered all three of your little hineys."

Jamie and Charlie laughed.

While he threaded pink leggings on her chunky legs, Harlan's gaze drifted to me. "Hey, sorry about all that racket. Not sure which of us was more scared. Your girl's got a heck of a pair of lungs. Poor Georgie over here didn't know what was happening."

"Sorry, sweet girl." I ran a hand over her brown curls.

Harlan lifted her from the table and helped her to the floor.

Charlie ran between us. "Uncle Harlan, wanna see my room?"

"I'll take her," I said, lifting Georgia.

Charlie's blond curls bounced as he led his uncle out of the room. I nuzzled the baby in my arms. "Just us girls for now, Georgia."

WE PLAYED TWO MORE GAMES of Chutes and Ladders. After Harlan won both, we tag-teamed the kids' dinner. I sliced apples and celery sticks. Harlan tossed pizza rolls in the oven. Then, he cleaned up the kitchen while I gave Georgia her bath. Soon, I heard him down the hall, ordering the boys into the shower.

Under Jamie's direction, Harlan managed the boys' bedtime rituals while I read to Georgia and rocked her, teasing her damp brown curls around my fingertips. Her binky rose and fell against her lips as she sucked on it. A hint of Baby Magic shampoo sent warmth through my chest. *Man, I miss these days.*

The boys resisted going to bed until Harlan made them a deal: one more wrestling match, and then they'd hang it up for the night. Surprisingly, they kept their end of the deal, and we didn't have to do much in the way of coaxing to get them into bed.

"That wasn't so bad," I said as Harlan and I walked downstairs.

"They're great kids."

"Absolutely," I agreed.

"Want something to eat?" he asked.

"Maybe in a bit. Need to check on Meg. I gave her another dose of Zofran before I fed the kids."

"I'll be in the kitchen." He tipped his head and walked away.

Meg was right where I'd left her, sawing logs, so I poked my head in the kitchen just seconds later.

"Hungry?" Harlan opened the fridge.

"A little." I had snacked on the celery sticks the boys left on their plates.

He stepped back, balancing a hodgepodge of items in his arms—cheese, butter, fresh spinach. "Thought I'd make myself an omelet. Want one?"

"Can I help?"

"Keep me company?"

Nineteen

I took a seat on a barstool at the island and watched Harlan remove milk and another cache of vegetables from the crisper. He grabbed a beer from the door and held it up. "Want one?"

"Probably shouldn't, since I'm babysitting."

"Your daughter's babysitting. You're pinch hitting." He set two beers on the counter and popped off the lids. "Technically, you're company. Our mom taught us to treat company right." He slid a bottle of Shiner Bock across the stone counter.

"Thanks. Your mom was Meg's fourth grade teacher."

"She taught most of the kids who grew up here." He started chopping a bell pepper.

For a second, I forgot where I was. *A handsome man is making me dinner while my daughter is knocked out in the living room.*

"Who's older? You or Lark?"

"Who do you think?"

A gray patch played at his hairline and wrinkles folded handsomely around the outer edge of each eye, but why ruin his night? "Twins?"

"I'm eleven years older." He glanced up from the cutting board and shot me that beguilingly crooked smile. "I'm fifty-one."

I took a sip of the beer, enjoying the way the bubbles rolled along my tongue.

"You?" he asked.

"Thirty-four."

His eyes bounced up from the cutting board. "You're not old enough to have a teenager."

"She was a surprise."

"Gotcha. Her dad around?"

"Travels a lot."

"Must be difficult. Having her go back and forth between you two?"

"Oh, we're still married."

He frowned and glanced at my left hand.

Not exactly a "no ring on my hand, no slob on my couch" situation. I laughed to myself. "I took off my ring to color my hair. Then Meg called."

He pursed his lips and cracked the first of many eggs, dropping the contents of each one in a bowl with flawless precision.

"Cook a lot?" I asked.

"Not too many restaurants where I live." He waved with his beer and took a sip.

"Jamie said you live in the forest?"

"Hmm. Yeah, I'm a regular forest dweller. Actually, a forest ranger. Got some unexpected time off. You know how the president's on a tear about this wall? He closed shop until Congress pays more attention to him."

"Sorry."

"It's alright. Probably needed a break." Harlan whisked the egg mixture and poured oil into the hot skillet. "Plus, Lark's been getting after me to help her with their website."

"Probably none of my business, but do people get paid when they close the parks?"

"No, ma'am. They . . . *we* do not." He pushed the chopped peppers and mushrooms into the skillet, quieting the crackling onions. "Everybody hurts when it happens. Last time they shut us down I hung around, expecting it to end after a day or two. Went on for more than a month."

"What'd you do?"

"Fished. A lot. So much I'm pretty sure the guys recognized my lure and jumped on my hook because they felt sorry for me."

I frowned. "Guys?"

"Trout," he said over his shoulder, stirring the vegetables. "Catch and release."

"Does it get lonely?"

"It can. When I worked in Idaho, on the Snake . . ." He glanced back at me. "It came in waves—groups came to raft and fish, then winter came. It got real quiet."

Fish, snakes—I don't care, just keep talking. I nodded encouragingly.

"If I wanted to get in my truck and drive, I could snow ski," he said.

"Skiing might be fun?"

He chuckled. "Kind of. Learned after college. Put a little kid in skis? They fly all over the mountain. A tall guy like me? It's ugly." His torso wavered back and forth like that cowboy in *Toy Story*.

"Jamie said you worked in Colorado, but you said—"

He nodded. "Moved to Colorado a year ago. They reorganized and gave me three options: South Dakota Badlands, Yellowstone, or the Uncompahgre Peak in Colorado. It was an easy choice."

He swirled the vegetables. An Aggie class ring sparkled on his right hand; I noticed none on his left. A flush crept up my neck.

I'm married. Look away. "Better check on my girl." I edged toward the hall.

"Let me know if she's hungry. We've got plenty more eggs."

Meg couldn't have slept more soundly if I had slipped her a mickey.

Returning to the kitchen, I began unloading the dishwasher. With a mesh strainer in hand, I flitted through the kitchen, searching for the right cabinet.

"That one," Harlan gestured.

On my way back to the dishwasher, our hands bumped, and I tugged mine away.

He shot me a smoldering glance.

I was no expert but—gun to my head? Harlan had mastered the smolder.

A pleasant sensation bubbled up in my chest, and I backed away from him, without regard to the dishwasher door that was hanging open. My ankle hit the metal door, and I shifted toward the island, missing it completely.

"Whoah," I breathed out, falling backward. "Ow!" My elbow crashed against the tile floor.

Harlan shoved the omelet pan off the burner, killed the gas, and dropped to my side.

I shot a *go-to-hell* look at the dishwasher door.

"Don't get mad at an innocent appliance. It wasn't personal." He held my elbow with care. "Let me see."

"I'm sure it's fine." It hurt like the dickens.

"Stay put." All those aromas put on hold, he rummaged through the cabinets for a plastic bag, which he proceeded to fill with ice. "Here." He cupped it around my elbow and cocked his head at me with such kindness, I couldn't look away.

"Thanks."

"Let's get you to your feet." He planted me in a chair, closed the dishwasher, and resumed his cooking duties. A few short minutes later, he slid a plate in front of me.

"Looks fantastic." My stomach growled as the savory scent of the mushroom and cheese mixture wafted up to my nose. My right arm too sore to extend it, I lifted my fork with my left and clumsily cut a piece the size of my fist.

"Need a hand?" He dropped his fork and stood.

Flushing, I leaned back, and he cut my omelet into bite-size pieces.

"You were a pro up there with Georgia," I said. "Do you have children?"

"Just a niece and nephews."

"Are you married?"

Carrying his plate, he shook his head and sat beside me.

"Girlfriend?" I asked, my eyes on my plate.

"Nope."

I lifted my head as he stuck a forkful of cheesy eggs in his mouth. "Boyfriend?"

"Uh, no." He tipped his beer to his lips. "Lived with a woman for years if that counts. Never married."

"She didn't fold your socks the right way?"

He swallowed another bite. "Didn't feel right. If I wasn't all-in, it wasn't fair to her." He laughed. "A year after we split, she was married and pregnant. I've run into her over the years. Got the ring and the babies. Seemed happy enough."

Men. "*Give a girl a ring and a baby, she'll have no complaints.*"

He gestured with his knife. "It was good while we were together. All said, we both ended up in the right spot. Saw her last Christmas when I was here. We talked about our old times. When we walked away from each other, I knew I'd done the right thing."

"Like that old song? Where the couple broke up and ran into each other years later on Christmas Eve?"

He frowned, clearly coming up blank.

"We used to sing it in high school choir—Christmas Eve, this woman drops her purse in the grocery store, and the guy who picks it up is her old boyfriend. They talk about old times and go their separate ways. I think it's James Taylor?" *Come on, dude. At least, pretend you remember it.* "You have to have heard it. It ends with this Kenny G version of *Auld Lang Syne.*"

He lifted his head and mumbled, "Fogelberg," around a mouth full of food.

"What?"

"Not what—who. It's a Dan Fogelberg song, not James Taylor. You're talking about the one where he walks home in the rain?"

"That's it."

He lifted a brow. "Never was sure about her—"

"Your ex?" I asked.

"The chick in the song. It's snowing, then it's raining. She's got the car. He's walking. Why not offer him a ride?"

"She was afraid her husband would get mad," I said, all too reflexively.

He punched out his lower lip and nodded. "Maybe so."

"Don't give up. You'll meet the right woman one of these days, and you'll just know."

One brow pitched up, and I tried not to stare into those shockingly blue eyes.

"You will. It'll be a full-on, heart-squeeze, bees-swarming-in-the-belly jolt to your senses." *Like I've read about in romance novels—thank you, Kristan Higgins.*

He gave a small laugh. "If you say so."

So much for talking romance. "What do you catch on those lakes?"

"I fly fish so, it's usually on a river. There's a difference between what I catch and what I like to catch, but brook trout is my favorite."

"Why's that?" *Like I care about trout? Just keep talking.*

"Their colors—yellow flecks that shimmer beneath the surface of the water. Stronger than a bull when you're bringing 'em in. Feisty suckers." He laughed, then he got quiet and stared ahead, like he could almost see one. "When you release 'em, it's spiritual. You've got this gorgeous creature wiggling in your hand." His fingers bent like they were holding a fish. "Remove the hook, drop him into the water, and he speeds away."

"Mmm."

"I see you're impressed," he said dryly.

Meg stumbled into the kitchen. "You're still here?"

"Hey, honey." I glanced at my nearly empty plate. "Want some?"

She frowned, looking anything but good. "May never eat again."

"How do you feel?" I asked her as she sat beside me.

"Better." She drew her knees into her chest. "Mom, you don't have to stay."

"I don't mind," I told her.

Harlan's eyes went small staring at his phone's screen. "Parents are on their way home, so I'll clean this up and get out of your hair."

Meg waved a hand. "Leave it. I don't have anything else to do."

He stood and carried his plate to the sink. "Won't take long." In the ensuing minutes, he cleaned the kitchen, took out the trash, and refilled the improvised ice pack quelling my swollen elbow.

"I can take it from here," Meg said, taking the ice pack from him.

While Meg pressed the pack to my elbow, I stole a last glance. This man was a mix of burly and gentle. Outdoorsy and domestic. Experienced and innocent. Demanding and compromising. He was like a book I didn't know I wanted to read, but once I cracked open the cover, temptation pulled at me to keep turning those pages.

Twenty

I stayed with Meg until the following morning. The elbow was sore, but it was nothing Advil couldn't temper.

On my way home, I picked up groceries and swung by Martha's house. The front door was open, and *Forensic Files* blasted from the television.

From her recliner, Martha mumbled something I couldn't make out over the ear-bleeding TV noise.

"Whaaaat?" I asked.

"Can't find the remote," she hollered back.

I walked to the set and manually lowered the volume. "Have you eaten today?"

She scanned the room as if the answer might drift by. "Eh?"

"Are you hungry?"

"No, I had . . ." Her head tilted toward a bowl of popcorn debris on an end table.

I warmed a bowl of soup, but Martha barely threw it a glance as I delivered it.

By the time I had put away her laundry, she'd eaten just three crackers. "Not hungry," she said, glancing wistfully at the cold soup.

My pleasure.

At home, I deposited a pair of shoes in Meg's room that she had left in the den. Before stepping back out into the hall, I stopped to admire the four-by-four bulletin board that hung over her white wooden desk, which was overwhelmed by photos of her with friends. I picked up a faded blue composition book. It held notes from her college prep classes and her short-hand responses to the essay prompts.

"How do you expect college to change you?" was one prompt.

Below it, Meg had scratched out, "I'm 17. Mom was 17 when she had me. When I leave, who will keep my parents together? Stressful. Sometimes overwhelming."

My hand quivered, tracing Meg's inky loops and swirling cursive. *When she leaves?* Those words bit into my skin. I slapped the notebook closed and left the room.

ᔕᕮ

A FEW HOURS LATER, MEG returned home, sticking around long enough to grab her backpack. She had an ACT study group, followed by dinner with friends. She didn't return home until nearly ten.

"Where's Dad?" she asked when she found me alone.

"I was about to check on him."

He answered on the fourth ring.

"Running late?" I asked.

"Just landed. Spent at least two hours with a dead phone on the Atlanta tarmac."

"I wondered what happened, because, you know, we talked about dinner?" *But the carrot sticks in the fridge were great. Thanks for asking.*

"Got an upgrade to first class, so they fed me some gravy-covered rubber chicken, but I can pick up food for you on the way home." Our house was over an hour away from the San Antonio airport.

"I snacked, and you're probably exhausted. Just come on home."

ᔕᕮ

THE FOLLOWING MORNING, I SET out muffins for breakfast while Caleb tapped his finger on the counter, impatiently waiting for the Keurig to dispense his coffee. He glanced at me, then took a second look.

"What'd you do?" He pointed to my arm. "The bruise?"

"I was helping Meg at Lark's house. Tripped over the dishwasher door." I lifted a shoulder, unconcerned, then ran my other hand over my hideously purple skin. The residual pain renewed the memory and started a lightness buzzing in my chest.

"Damn." Caleb frowned. "Did you break anything?"

"I . . . *we* put ice on it. It's sore, but nothing serious."

"Wasn't talking about you. I meant, did you break their dishwasher?"

"No."

"Need to be more careful." He gave a short laugh and pulled his stainless Voyce-branded Yeti from the machine.

"Got it." *Thanks for your heartfelt concern.*

He sniffed at the basket of muffins and picked up the soft-sided briefcase he carried everywhere. Meg and I jokingly called it his tumor. "Let you know about dinner."

Dinner? Oh! As in, let you know if I'll be there. Nice.

The side door closed and a minute later, the Porsche throttled past the kitchen window and left our driveway.

Another day in paradise.

⚘

LARK CALLED LATER THAT MORNING. "Hey, girlie. Sorry my stinky brother popped in on Meg this weekend. He said you were around to help out. Thanks."

"It was fine. Actually, he cooked dinner for me. Cleaned up, too."

"Mom trained him well."

"How was San Antone?" I asked.

"Nice. Stayed in a suite at the Saint Anthony. It was bliss."

"Sounds lovely."

We chatted about the kids before her youngest began crying and she had to run.

Must be nice to be in demand. Maybe I should get a hobby— something that would make me more interesting? I sipped my second cup of coffee at the breakfast table and considered Julia's homework. *I haven't played tennis in over a decade. I have no interest in painting or needlepoint. Travel can't happen until Meg leaves.*

Unable to sit still, I pushed away from the table. The next thing I knew, I was in my car. Ten miles away in Johnson City, I pulled over at the Johnson Settlement Historical Park, where the former president's grandparents had begun their ranching businesses.

On the other side of the towering live oaks, highway sounds disappeared. Two longhorns, a mom and her baby, swatted flies with their tails, unconcerned by my presence. I hiked along the dirt path leading to one of the Johnson family homesteads, a dog-trot log cabin.

I stopped to read a plaque. "In 1937, the Johnsons' eldest son, Lyndon, launched his first campaign for Congress, and his ascent to the US presidency, from the east porch."

Must be nice to know where you want to go.

My mother had signaled her choice of colleges for me (Thee University of Texas), what I'd study (education or fashion marketing), and which sorority I'd rush (Chi Omega). *Well, I sure showed her. Jesus.*

Meandering back to my car, I considered how I had raised my daughter. For seventeen years, I'd done everything possible to steer her away from making my mistakes. And so far, my work proved successful.

But maybe I'd failed her in another way. Meg was my everything, just like I'd been for my mom. And I knew, from experience, that being someone's everything was as fun as dragging a suitcase of bowling balls up to a fourth-floor walk-up.

Julia's onto something. I need to get my own life.

On the way home, I pulled through the gates at Lark's winery, LL Cellars, and parked near the front doors of the stucco- and stone-covered event center.

"Yoo-hoo," I announced myself as I opened one of the glass doors.

"Back here," came Lark's voice.

I zigzagged past an office, a cavernous open room, down a hall past a darkened kitchen. At last, I reached the office at the rear of the building. But I didn't see anyone inside. "Hello?"

"About time," Lark said from beneath a desk. Her head popped up, and she barked out a laugh. "Oh, God. I'm sorry. Thought you were my computer help."

"Sorry for showing up like this. Do you have a minute? I'm having a hard time."

She shot me a sympathetic look. "Aw, come with me." She dropped the cord and led me to that large room filled with empty tables and chairs. She gestured to a table. "Have a seat. Caleb?" she asked.

"No. Me." I told her about Meg's notebook and my lack of brag-worthy success.

She shook her head. "Meg is an amazing young woman *because* of you. Be proud."

"I am, but . . ." I shook my head. "What am I'm supposed to be when she's off to college?"

Lark sat back in her chair, probably wondering what she'd done to deserve my kind of crazy on her busy workday.

"My mom had all these ideas who I'd become—before I had Meg." I threw my hands up. "Obviously, those zoomed out the window. I don't want my expectations to weigh her down."

She snickered. "My mom wanted me to become a lawyer."

"Which you did."

"I wanted to make wine."

"You did that, too."

"Not right away. Took a long time getting here."

"Lark, I didn't become *anything*. When I was young, I thought about becoming a nurse—the kind who takes care of tiny babies. You know what babies I took care of? One Meghann Dietrich. Next fall, what'll I do? Wait for her to have babies? When I die, you know what my obituary will say? 'Sissie Dietrich lived a normal life, screwed it up, and raised Meg.' That's all I've got."

"It's not too late. Send Meg to college and become a nurse if that's what you want."

"I'd need a four-year college, and Caleb—"

"Have you and Caleb talked about what your life will look like when she's gone?"

A tear dropped on my cheek; I laughed and wiped it away. "You sound like Julia."

"I'll take that as a compliment. Tell you what—take a breath. Enjoy the rest of this school year with your baby girl. When she's on her way, you'll have nothing but time to decide what comes next."

I nodded several times and wiped my eyes.

"Lark?" a deep voice hollered from the hall.

My palms grew sweaty.

"There's my computer help." Lark pointed a finger into the air.

"Sorry I interrupted you," I said.

"Can't interrupt what hasn't started." She patted my shoulder.

"Where you at?" the man yelled.

"In here!" She rolled her eyes. "You remember my stinky brother?"

My chest became tight, and I didn't move from my chair.

Harlan came around the corner. His brows shot up, and his mouth curved into a smile. "Hey, Sissie."

My heart tapped my ribs at the sound of him saying my name.

"Have I been replaced?" he asked.

"Maybe." Lark laughed. "Sissie, you know anything about Wi-Fi networks?"

"I can barely plug in my toaster."

He responded with a grin.

Lark's cell phone rang, and she frowned. "Gotta take this. Be right back."

"Park still closed?" I asked.

"Yep. Wyatt's training for a wounded warrior event, so Lark's put me to work. Gives me time to get acquainted with my new niece and my nephews."

"They're sweet kids."

"Agree. How's Meg?"

"She's great." I smiled, maybe a bit too proudly.

"And the elbow?" He glanced at my arm.

"It was touch and go for a while, but looks like I'm gonna live."

He flattened a hand over his chest. "Whew. Glad to hear it."

"Sorry if I interrupted y'all."

"You didn't. Won't take me long to do what she needs, but"—he leaned in close enough that his breath brushed my face—"don't tell Lark. I've convinced her it'll take hours."

"Secret's safe with me."

"Thanks, partner." He gave me a fist bump. "Did your husband get back from . . . where was he?"

"Baltimore. His flight ran late on Sunday. Bad weather in Atlanta."

"Really?" He pursed his lips in thought. "Huh."

"He's leaving again in a couple days." I sighed.

"Keeps logging miles like that, you two can fly around the world."

I gave a wry laugh. *As if.*

Lark returned. And it became obvious she and Harlan had work to do so as much as it pained me, I excused myself, leaving them to their work.

Twenty-One

I had decided I would come up with some hobbies for Julia's list if it killed me. My self-imposed week of introspection delivered mostly zilch.

Like clockwork, Caleb packed his travel bag on Thursday morning for a conference. He always complained about going to conferences, with all their schmoozing reps and stale conversations, but it was part of the job.

Wouldn't mind a few stale conversations and a change of scenery.

On Saturday, Meg finished her college essays and joined her girlfriends for a sleepover. Backpack on her back and pillow under her left arm, she couldn't leave fast enough, excited about watching movies over pizza and raw cookie dough (cue the foodborne illness warnings).

I retreated to the den. Nothing but news on the television, I turned it to music and opened up my computer to google Baltimore restaurants. *If I ever get there with Caleb, I'd be ready.* He'd complained about the barebones efficiency apartment his company provided, but it didn't sound so bad. *Maybe a woman's touch is just what it needs?*

Until then, it was Netflix for me.

Around ten, I checked on my girl. "Hey, honey. Did I call at a bad time?"

"No. What's going on?"

I sighed. "Quiet around here. Just wanted to hear your voice before I called it a night."

"How sweet." I heard a commotion of voices in the background. "Mom, Eliza's mom made piña colada milkshakes. Don't worry—she made them without alcohol." One of the girls spoke to her. "I've got to run. Chloe wants me to ride with her to pick up her phone at her house."

"Alright. Be careful."

"Will do. I love you, Mom."

"Love you right back."

I hung up and restarted my show. Before the episode ended, the doorbell rang, and I could only assume Meg was stopping to get something on her way back. The doorbell rang again. *Silly girl— must've left her key behind.*

I tabbed on a switch and amber light poured over the porch, illuminating two uniformed figures. I peered through the wide shutters. Two cars parked along the street—one was a police car with its lights off.

Meg went out with Chloe. Helpless panic poured into my bloodstream.

The bell rang again, and I turned back to the door. Two sharp knocks sent alarm looping around my spine. I spun around, leaned my forehead against the wood, and whispered, "Jesus, please tell me she's safe."

Seventeen years of handholding and wish-making stopped on a dime. My lungs were bloated with fright. I turned the deadbolt, and its click sent a gut-clenching warning into the air. *God, please.*

"Priscilla Dietrich?" a woman called from outside.

I dragged the door open, unable to denote anything but visual fragments in the dim light.

"Ma'am? I'm Lieutenant Maywood," the woman said, flashing a laminated ID. Her matronly bun couldn't obscure her youthful face—she couldn't have been more than twenty-five. She gestured to the man beside her. "This is Captain Welker."

"Sean Welker, ma'am." He raised a hand in greeting.

Staring at them, all I could manage was a faint, "Okay."

"Might be best if we spoke inside," Welker said.

Worry congealed around me, slowing my movements. I led them into our rarely used formal living room. Maywood's brows shot up at the yellow accent chairs across from the navy plaid sofa.

My mind went to Meg, how she had asked, "Why'd we buy SpongeBob chairs?" when those chairs were delivered. *Please let me hear her voice again.*

"Mind if we sit down?" Maywood asked, carrying a tablet in one hand.

I waved toward the chairs and dropped to the sofa. Finding my voice, I asked, "Where is she?"

The officers exchanged looks.

"My daughter? Where is she?"

Maywood ran a finger over the bridge of her nose, then threw a glance at her partner. "When did you last speak with her?"

"Twenty, thirty minutes ago. She told me they might run around the corner to her friend's house."

"We can send a car to look for her." Maywood glanced at Welker for confirmation, and he waved a hand.

My heart slapped my chest, like it knew what I hadn't.

"Ma'am." Welker leaned forward, elbows on his knees. "Would you like for us to wait until she can be here with you?"

"Why?"

"To talk about . . ." His head cocked to the side. "Is Caleb Dietrich your husband?"

"Yes." Fresh scenarios raced through my brain. *Driving drunk? Gambling?* "What has he done?"

Welker cleared his throat. "We're sorry to have to tell you this. A little before noon, a helicopter carrying your husband went down outside of Atlantic City. There were no survivors."

I shook my head. "You've got the wrong guy. He's in Baltimore." Unease drained from my body.

Maywood turned her tablet toward me and pointed to an image of Caleb's driver's license. "Is this him?"

"That's his license, but he wasn't in Atlantic City. We talked this morning. He had trade shows all day. He told me how much he hates them—all the glad-handing? Caleb's a total workaholic." I sighed. "On the bright side, he enjoys what he does."

"Ma'am," Welker's familiar tone was unsettling. "It's possible Caleb wasn't at a—"

"I helped him pack."

"The NTSB checks these things out before they bring in local authorities."

None of this made sense. "Caleb would be the last man on this earth to skip out on work to hop into a helicopter. He was in Maryland, not Atlantic City."

"Maryland and New Jersey aren't that far apart," Welker drawled.

"He would've told me." *Wouldn't he?* My mouth opened to defend my husband. No sound came.

"Not trying to point fingers, ma'am," Welker said. "Just getting to know the landscape. If there's something you'd like to share with us—"

"Is there a question in there?" I asked, but his insinuation was already poking around my brain's dormant strata—occasional hang-ups on the landline, late work meetings, calls he took outside . . .

Welker held up a hand. "Now, ma'am, we're not implying anything. Just trying to collect information to help the folks in Jersey conduct their investigation."

"Caleb didn't—" I stopped myself. *Why does defending him come so naturally? It's not like I owe him anything.* But what about Meg? She shouldn't have to suffer embarrassment if Caleb was dishonest with us. "Caleb's not a liar," I blurted out.

Welker took a step forward. "How long've you been married?"

"Almost eighteen years."

"Long time. Couples married that long can find themselves in . . . precarious situations one time or another," he said slowly.

My eyes narrowed. "Are you speaking from experience?"

"No, ma'am." He wiped his upper lip. "Stick with me here. Let's say coworkers attend the same conference." He lifted a shoulder. "They get tired of all that glad-handing you mentioned. One says, 'Let's check out the scenery, take a break,' and they jump on a train to Jersey?"

Coworkers? Plural? "Who else was on this helicopter?"

"The pilot and another passenger. Until families are notified, that's all we can share."

I stared at him, willing him to crack. Instead, he stood. "I'll make some calls, ask for more details."

I excused myself to locate my phone. When I returned, Maywood asked for a glass of water and followed me to the kitchen.

"How about some coffee?" I asked.

"Yes, please."

I stuck a pod in the Keurig while the officer perused family photos on a bookshelf.

"How do you take it?"

"Black." She gestured to a photo of a three-year-old Meg wearing bunny-ears and holding an Easter basket. "This your daughter?"

I pushed the mug toward her and looked at the photo again. *I'd give my right arm to return to that day and hear Meg giggle like she did when I put that headband on her head.* "She's seventeen now."

"Has she spoken to her father?"

"I don't know." I pulled my phone from the counter. *Really, Sissie? What will you say? "Have you talked to your father, the police are here"?* The longer the other officer was gone, the stronger my suspicions grew.

Who could I call to help me make sense of this?

I scrolled my messages and stopped at a Betty White meme Lark had sent. Beneath my "ha-ha" response, I typed, "Pop tarts."

"Do you have other children?" Maywood asked.

I hit send and turned around.

"Just Meg." My heart skipped when I said her name.

Maywood sipped her coffee. Her hair, pulled into that tight bun, and the sturdy black belt and boxy uniform on her body neutralized her gender, though a touch of mascara added a hint of femininity to her young face. Any other day, she might've been one of Meg's friends, lounging in nylon shorts and running shoes and talking about boys.

But she wasn't here to talk about boys. She was here on official business, the kind of business she'd probably waited for in our sleepy town. Now she'd prove herself—get noticed by her captain, or whoever.

Except the poor lamb's big break wasn't real. It couldn't be.

"Hello," Lark called from outside the kitchen.

"In here," I yelled.

Lark shot into the kitchen. "Are you alright?"

"I'm fine. I'm sorry to worry you. I just needed . . ." My mouth tightened around my words. "Someone."

"Okay." Lark turned to the officer and introduced herself.

"A helicopter crashed in New Jersey, and they think Caleb was on it. But it's not him." I dropped my gaze to the floor. "I don't *think* it's him. I mean, he's in Baltimore. It doesn't make sense."

"Sissie?"

Dad? I ran from the kitchen.

He was standing in the living room and running a hand over his disheveled gray hair, his face more drawn than usual. "I'm sorry," his hands were quick to reach for me. "Where's Meg?"

"At a friend's house," I said. "What're you doing here?"

He pulled back, and his expression turned all business. "I got a call about Caleb."

"That's why they're here." I pointed toward the door. "It must be a mistake. He was in Baltimore."

Dad's lip quivered. "I'm sorry, Sissie. It's him. Caleb was on that helicopter."

Twenty-Two

L ark and I rocked on the front porch while Dad and the officers spoke inside. "Does Voyce even have an office in New Jersey?" I asked.

"Maybe so." Lark patted my hand.

The late hour didn't prevent my neighbors from trickling out of their homes to investigate the police presence as more officers arrived.

"Let's take you inside," Lark said. "I'll run interference."

From the dining room window, I observed pajama-clad neighbors lingering on porches and along the sidewalk, as if it were a nightly ritual to stargaze in their bathrobes and slippers.

Suddenly, my home wasn't mine. Someone had turned on the overhead lighting, leaving the perfectly good lamps—the ones that offered ambiance and shaded imperfections—unused. Officers were jotting notes onto notepads and typing into their phones. Their steady buzz teased the ear while revealing nothing.

Phrases like "helicopter tour service" and "debris field" floated around me, but my father managed to answer the officers' questions, leaving me to process Caleb's omission. *Doubt I would've ignored his mention of a helicopter ride.*

In the din, Welker hooked my attention when he mentioned the other—female—passenger.

"What is her name?" I asked Welker. "The woman with my husband?"

Welker turned to my father.

"He's not asking. I am. What is her name?" My voice turned stubborn, and Dad planted a hand on my shoulder.

"There was a pilot, your husband, and the woman," Welker said in a single breath.

"I asked the woman's name."

"NTSB hasn't notified family yet, so we can't release names."

"But you have it?"

"Sissie," Dad said in a corrective tone.

"Who was with him?" When no one answered, I turned around to Dad. "You know, don't you?"

Dad offered a slight nod.

"We need to talk." I stood, summoning my father to follow me to Caleb's home office.

When he stepped inside, I closed the door behind him.

"Sit down," he said.

"I don't want to sit down. I want you to tell me. Who was with Caleb?"

"It's not that simple. He had a . . . special friend."

"What the hell does that mean? Like Pike's special friend?"

"I'm sorry."

"Why won't they tell me anything, but they're telling you about Caleb's special friend?"

"Sissie, don't do this now."

Scars that held us together through eighteen years began to tear open, resulting in a hot, reddened wound that couldn't hold my anger another minute. "You knew he was screwing around and didn't tell me."

He put a finger to his lips.

"Don't shush me in *my* house. I'll bet you knew he was dead before me, too."

He didn't answer, a pretty good indication I was onto something.

I grabbed my hair like I might pull it out at the roots and released a powerful scream. "You know what's worse than Caleb betraying me? Finding out my father did."

There was a knock, and I ground out, "Not now."

"Sissie?" Lark opened the door slightly. "It's Meg."

I stared into my father's eyes. "This conversation isn't over."

Lark stood in the hall, holding my phone. "It's been blowing up. I wouldn't interrupt, but some are from Meg." She pushed the phone into view.

Among the many messages, the last caught my eye: "REINA HARRIS SAID THE POLICE ARE AT OUR HOUSE. Why aren't you answering your phone? I'm coming home."

"Shit," I said. "She's coming here."

Behind me, Dad said, "Tell her to stay put."

You're the last person who should give me orders right now. "I'll handle it," I snapped back at him and followed Lark down the hall.

"Might be better to tell her now, before she catches it from friends," Lark said.

I stepped into the living room as the front door flew open. Della rushed across the room, arms wide. "It's going to be alright." She rubbed my outer arms like I was cold, winking at whoever was behind me.

Dad. He called her. Of course.

"Honey, we'll get you through this. Where's Meg?" She craned her neck to take in the room—and, before I could answer, pulled on a fake smile and pulled her chin in tight. "What's Lark doing here?"

"Meg's on her way."

"Okay, want me to get rid of everyone who's not family?" Della winked.

"Don't do anything." It was all too much to have to deal with Della's antagonism.

"Mom?" Meg's voice came from the kitchen—she always entered the house through the side door off the driveway. Wearing heart-patterned jammie pants, an old volleyball tournament T-shirt, and slippers, she scanned the room. Her cheeks flushed, and her dark eyes bulged at the sight of the cops, my dad, Della, and Lark all being gathered there.

"Come here, baby," I held out a hand and she made a slow walk to me. "It's your dad."

Before I said another word, her eyes became glassy. "Where's Dad?"

"There was an accident. He's gone, baby."

She let out a small squeal. "I want to see him. Where is he?"

Meg's words demanded that I make Caleb materialize, but all I could do was hold her squirming body to mine. For a moment, everyone else disappeared. My dad and his secrets. Della and her jealousy. Caleb and his cheating, deceitful ways. It was just Meg and me, together.

Then we disentangled and Meg stared up at me, the emptiness in her face begging me to carry her away and hold her forever. "What happened?" she asked in a whisper.

"He was on a helicopter."

"A helicopter?" She shook her head. "How? I want to see him." Her chest heaved with desperation. "I . . . need . . . to see . . . my dad."

"I don't know the details yet." I ran a hand over her lopsided top knot, imagining how it must've bounced as she laughed with her friends earlier tonight. She fell into my arms, her words mostly unintelligible into my shoulder, but I understood the important ones—her father was gone.

❧

MEG REMAINED GLUED TO ME. Mom and Della hung around my house, offering coffee, sleeping pills, and companionship to whom-ever wandered inside.

Mom orchestrated Dad's appearances at our house, which was fortunate since I couldn't be in the same room with him without my pulse sprouting into a drumbeat.

"A time and a place," Mom had always said.

I'd focus on Meg now. When the time was right, I'd get my answers from Dad.

❧

DAD HAD, AT LEAST, DONE me one big favor: he'd escorted the police to Martha's house and then waited until her brother arrived to sit with her. *It's the least he could do.*

The next morning, a man from the NTSB arrived. He wore a navy windbreaker with an embroidered eagle on the pocket. I held my breath, praying he was there to tell us they had made a mistake. My gaze hooked on his clean-shaven head, alight with the morning sun shining into the room, as Mom ushered him into the house.

The man had barely introduced himself as Grant Bradley before Meg started asking questions.

"What happened to my dad?" she began.

Grant's soft-spoken tone was both comforting and off-putting. I wondered if they taught that—a quiet gentility to temper details of a family member's last seconds.

"Before we get into details, I'd like you to know how sorry we are for your loss. As a member of the National Transportation Safety Board, I am here to assist your family and answer your questions."

Meg started to talk. I placed my hand on her arm. "Let him speak," I said quietly.

"We'll step in as liaisons between you and the flight operator. Following the mechanical investigation, there may be claims or litigation. We'll transfer relevant documents to the appropriate representatives." His dark, hound-dog eyes met mine. "We can coordinate counseling and local survivor support resources for your family."

"When can I see my father?" Meg asked.

"Your father's remains should be returned within a couple weeks, following the investigation."

"You think somebody did this to him on purpose?" she asked.

"Any flight-related accident prompts an investigation. Investigators look at everything. Foul play, weather, health events, or mechanical errors. The full report can take weeks, or months," Grant said calmly.

"When can we plan a service?" I asked.

"The remains have been taken to the local coroner's office. Personal belongings will be catalogued."

Meg's jaw clenched. "I want to see my dad."

Grant's mouth went tight. "I can assure you, you don't." He shot me a pitying expression. "The aircraft caught fire upon impact."

"Oh, God," Meg cried. "Did he suffer, or did he die right away?"

"Most helicopters don't have flight data recorders. You know? Like black boxes?" he said.

"Uh-huh," I said, watching the man's lips move robotically. The man must repeat these explanations several times a year. *Does he think about what to eat for dinner or his kid's last soccer game while he recites these details to families like mine?*

"The coroner's report will provide more specifics, but my best guess? It was immediate." He sighed. "I'm sorry."

"Who were the others?" Meg asked.

He swallowed. "There was the pilot and another passenger."

"Do we know them?" Meg asked him and turned to me. "Is it someone from his work?"

He looked a question to me.

"Please. I'm not a kid," she said.

"Please tell her," I said, digging my nails into my palms.

"Around two on Saturday, the helicopter left Maryland's Middle River Airport." He put up a finger and swiped at his phone and displayed a map. "Here it is. At approximately 2:30 p.m. Eastern Standard Time, the pilot reported a mechanical problem. Almost immediately, he lost altitude and failed to respond to controllers. The craft fell into rough terrain seven miles east of the Absecon Lighthouse."

Twenty-Three

Caleb had always enjoyed brandishing his flair for things big and small. He bought his socks at Walmart but carried a Mont Blanc pen. When we separated, he bought a tiny house and updated it with a jetted tub and a wall of shower jets—perfect for a born-again bachelor. He couldn't park his father's used Porsche in our old-fashioned garage. He needed LED lighting and an acrylic floor. And when it came time for him to leave this life, he disappeared into a ball of fire.

I could get past his screwing around. People survive divorces every day. He didn't have to climb into that helicopter and leave Meg fatherless.

I tried to keep it together. Meg deserved one loving, breathing parent. She didn't need a tornadic mother spilling profanities—no matter how well deserved—on her father's memory.

Privately, a part of me hoped he *had* suffered. Another part hoped they were wrong—that Caleb had merely taken a platonic flight with a coworker. I wanted him to be innocent, and to be remembered as a man who wouldn't let his family hurt this way.

DAD CAME AROUND ME ONLY when Meg was around, using her as a buffer. He knew darn well I wouldn't dig into my husband's secrets around my daughter.

Day by day, unanswered questions threatened to upend my self-control. Finally, I couldn't take it anymore.

"Dad," I said, interrupting Mom's chatter about Brent's work schedule. "Let's talk."

Dad's head jerked forward.

"In the office." I gestured and walked ahead of him without looking back. Inside, door closed, I crossed my arms over my chest. "What did Caleb do?"

"From what the police said, it was a sightseeing tour."

"Cut the crap, Dad." I hoped my expression indicated my lack of patience.

"His friend?" he asked.

A wry laugh burst from my lips. "It's a start." I waved my hand in a "be my guest" gesture.

"Honey, Caleb's like a wild horse—always had a side we couldn't break."

A horse's ass is more accurate. My laugh became diabolical. "Just perfect. You were covering for him?"

"What do you want me to say?"

"The truth."

"He cared about you and Meg."

"If he cared, he wouldn't have been in a helicopter with . . . what is her name?"

"Faith."

I screwed my eyes shut with disbelief. "Faith, huh? Funny name for a whore."

Dad wiped his brow.

"Mom?" Meg called from the hallway.

"This isn't over," I said, jutting a finger at him.

"Fine." Dad held his palms out to me.

"Not fine. Unfuckingbelievable."

I slammed the door behind me.

"What's wrong?" Meg asked, eyes wide.

"Nothing." My phone, still on silent, vibrated in my pocket, and I pulled it into view. "It's your uncle," I said, and accepted the call as I strode toward my bedroom.

"How're you doing?" Brent asked.

I shut the door tight and said, as quietly as I was able, "Our father's been in cahoots with my lying husband, so how do you think I am?"

"Cahoots? Aren't you a little too young to use that word?"

"I'm pissed."

"I can tell. Anything I can do?"

"Doubtful."

"I was planning to fly out there for services. I'll come sooner if you need backup."

"I'd hate to put you out." *And suffer the guilt for causing the inconvenience. Your time is so much more valuable than mine—everyone's made that clear my whole life.*

"Mom?" Meg knocked on the door. "Can I come in?"

"Hang on," I called—then, to Brent, said, "I've got to run."

"K. Let me know when you need me there."

I just did.

THE NEXT MORNING, MOM SHOWED up alone. We sipped coffee and read the paper while the *Today Show* hummed in the background. When the show shifted to local news, a reporter from the San Antonio affiliate said, "Hill Country man killed in Saturday night's New Jersey helicopter crash." A picture of the scorched ground appeared in the background. "A spokesperson from the NTSB confirmed the names of three victims: Pilot Gene Felton, fifty-eight, from Nassau County, New York; passenger Caleb Dietrich, forty-one, from Fredericksburg, Texas; and passenger Faith Willets, thirty-five, a resident of Lutherville, Maryland. The owner of the sightseeing helicopter declined comment." She shifted to another camera and her face lightened. "This afternoon, the San Antonio Spurs will grant a wish to—"

I paused the television and rewound the segment.

When the reporter said, "Faith Willets," I left Mom at the table, repeating "Willets," until I reached the office and opened Facebook on the computer.

My jumpy fingertips hit all the wrong keys. I slapped the delete button repeatedly and tried again. Finally—saying each letter as I poked the keyboard, "F-a-i-t-h space W-i-l-l-e-t-s"—I succeeded in typing correctly and hit the return key.

Two profiles appeared. The first Faith Willets had cough-medicine red hair and held an overweight gray cat. "Cat lady Faith," a retired schoolteacher from Arizona, enjoyed gardening and taking pictures of Smokey, her portly fur baby.

The second profile had a cartoonish avatar of a blond woman with rosy cheeks and pink lips. She'd set her privacy settings so only those on her approved friends' list could view her photos and timeline. Even her friends' list was hidden. *Crap!*

Then I clicked the "About" tab and it opened. *Eureka.*

Faith was "in a relationship" and worked for VBI.

VBI. Voyce Brothers Industries.

Part Five

Twenty-Four

A t first, Grant Bradley's calls stopped me cold and sent panic racing through my body. I'd soon learn it was customary for NTSB officials to contact the surviving families frequently, informing them of the investigation's progress. Eventually, I saved his number in my phone as "Crashman" and began screening those calls. Once sent to voicemail, I could take my sweet time to learn no news is no news without an uncomfortable conversation.

Until the NTSB completed its investigation, we attempted to continue our normal lives—a joke when you're awaiting the return of remains. Though a final determination had yet to be made, all indications pointed to pilot error. Meanwhile, Grant said we'd hear from a grief counselor. Although I thanked him, I couldn't even think about talking to anyone outside my family besides, perhaps, Julia. Meg, however, might need their help.

I encouraged Meg to join her classmates for her school's Senior Workday on Saturday morning, where the kids earned volunteer hours cleaning closets, painting stripes in the parking lot, and whatever else the teachers could find to keep them occupied for a full day.

All alone at the house, I carried my coffee to the front porch to contemplate the memorial service. To date, my ideas lacked respect for the dead, so I'd been keeping them to myself.

Lark's Sequoia pulled up, and I started to stand—until I noticed Harlan behind the wheel. I gave a quick wave and dropped back into the swing. My battered and bruised heart came to life, and his little feet pulsed nervous energy through my veins.

He parked on the street and stepped out of the car. "Morning!"

"MORNING." I BARELY GOT THE word out. I was confused by my excitement—*Not the time or the place*—but that heart ignored me, dusted off his sad little self with a whistle, and threw a fist in the air, punching my system with a friskiness I hadn't enjoyed since high school. A flush heated my skin, and I tried not to stare.

Harlan carried a foil-covered pan up the three steps leading to our porch. "Interrupting anything?"

"Nope." I straightened my shoulders and got to my feet, and a smile jumped onto my face.

"Lark made cinnamon rolls—our Mom's recipe. She's busy with the kids, so here I am."

Here you are, indeed. "Want to come in?"

He nodded.

As I led him toward the kitchen, a delicious scent reached my nose. He saw the look on my face and grinned.

"They're still warm." He lifted the foil to reveal cinnamon rolls bigger than my hand, bathed in creamy frosting.

"Want to split one?" I asked. "I mean, they're just so big. I couldn't finish one on my own." *Could you sound lamer?*

His mouth edged up on one side. "Wouldn't turn you down."

Oh, boy. He flashed a grin that spelled capital T-R-O-U-B-L-E.

He set the pan on the island, and I removed two glasses from the cabinet and orange juice from the fridge.

"Plates?" He held out his big hands, and I wondered how they'd feel covering mine. "Sissie?"

I shook the thought away. "Upper cabinet, left of the window."

Undeterred by a strange kitchen, he ferreted through drawers and produced forks and napkins before joining me as naturally as if he'd plopped down at my breakfast table a hundred times before.

It was both strange and comfortable, as if the universe had shaken everything loose and I'd fallen into the correct place.

"Hope I'm not being too forward," he said. "I was sad to hear about your husband. How are you and your daughter doing?"

I had just stuffed a hunk of doughy sweetness in my mouth so I just nodded.

"Yeah, dumb question. Shouldn't be asking you that." His head dropped over his plate.

I swallowed and took a sip of juice. "Thanks for asking. It was a shock. He was in Maryland for business." I tipped my head and shot a dubious look at him. With air quotes, I repeated, "For business."

"Eeemm."

"Left behind oodles of surprises. He and his"—more air quotes—"'friend' were taking a joyride around Atlantic City. Nothing like having your husband's affair garner coast-to-coast news coverage."

"I'm sorry."

"He'd messed around before, but I guess I thought he had embraced clean living."

"Don't get guys like that. Just get a divorce if you want to play around."

Guilt niggled at me. "He tried. We were separated for a while, but when it looked like we were on our way to finalize it, he back-pedaled for Meg."

"I see."

"You know, I tried to make it work. Wanted her to have every-thing I didn't—to travel, learn, be unafraid to raise her voice or say, 'No, I won't do that,' and not feel she had to explain herself."

"Don't need a husband to do that."

"I suppose I wanted her to have the whole package—a mom and a dad. We were friends, and . . . I made peace not having the fireworks and la-di-da."

"'La-di-da.'" He chuckled. "New one on me."

"I just mean, getting married so young. Probably expecting too much to think you can force love and all that. We tried."

"What did Yoda say about trying?" He squinted at the ceiling, then dropped his gaze to me.

Those eyes were electric; I couldn't look away.

"I'm no expert," he said, "but I always thought it should happen without trying so hard. Gotta give you props. Most people would be too selfish to suck it up that long, even for their kid. Maybe the next time, you'll get your happily ever after." He gestured at my mostly untouched roll with his fork. "Gonna get cold if you don't eat it."

I carved myself a forkful and took a bite, savoring the blend of butter, heavy cream, and sugar. "Hey, did I see on the news that the parks have reopened?"

"You did." He leaned back and stretched his long arms overhead. The man was lanky, but not gawky. Long legs and arms, but solid like he'd earned those muscles chopping wood.

"When are you headed back?" I asked.

"Not sure I want to go back. Got weeks of vacation piled up. Figured I'd take 'em while I decide what's next."

"Mother Nature run her course?"

"Love *her*. It's her old man I have a problem with." Even his grimace was handsome.

"Old man?"

"Government can't leave our parks alone—downsizing staff, changing regulations, letting folks come in and drill, log, whatever. Hell, they're gonna let people bait and shoot young bears, little ones still toddling around with their moms." He held out a hand at his waist, indicating their size. "Little."

My heart covered its cartoony eyes with its stick-figure hands.

"That's what happens when folks don't get out of their offices and see how the circle of life works. They make legislation that kills a bug, thinking, 'People don't like bugs, so who cares?' They don't stop to appreciate that bug they eliminated is the same one that used to eat another one that spread tree diseases that took out entire forests." He carried our empty glasses to the sink and rinsed them.

"I'll get that," I said, taking a bite of my roll.

"Nah." His mouth did that half smile thing that made little lines appear at the edge of those gorgeous blue eyes. He wiped the glasses with the towel beside the sink. "Care if I steal one more?"

"Be my guest."

He dished it out and returned to the table. "Lark said you have an older brother?"

"Brent. He's three years older."

He shook his head. "Too young for me to have known in school."

"Being so far apart in age, do you and Lark feel like you're from two different families?"

"It was like that when we were younger. Mom and Dad had me fresh out of high school. Then Vietnam sent home a different man. Dad needed time to sort it all out, get right again, if you know what I mean? And when they finally decided to have another one, it took longer than they expected. They'd given up when Lark came around."

"Must've been weird, going from an only child to having this baby around?"

"It was cool. That runt brought new life into our family."

"She's a mighty runt." I rose from the table.

"Won't argue." He smiled at me. "She thinks you're pretty special, Sissie."

"It's mutual. When I found out about Caleb, I called her first. She has a way of being there without overwhelming me."

"She's helped me through my share of rough patches. We're like this." He braided two fingers.

"Must be nice. My brother and I couldn't be more different. He's the overachiever who did everything perfect. I'm the family screw-up."

He did a 360. "Doesn't look like you screwed up."

My chest rose as I took a heaving breath. "Math wasn't my strong suit." At his narrowed eyes, I explained, marking each on my fingertips, "Let's see. Sixteen plus alcohol, plus sex, minus birth control, equals Meg."

"That's called life. And I'd say yours turned out alright—I mean, minus recent happenings. Don't beat yourself up. People don't get pregnant by themselves. Caleb?" His name sounded so strange coming out of Harlan's mouth. "He was there, too."

"Ah, Caleb. All his trips to Maryland—at least, that's where he said he'd gone. I saw that woman's Facebook page. Says she worked at his company, and she's"—I leaned in and lowered my voice to a whisper—"in a relationship.'"

"From the news, it sounded like a work thing. You sure there weren't other company folks on different helicopters? Companies do that sort of thing to thank their employees."

Have I assumed too much?

"Then again . . . you said he'd done this before?"

I nodded.

"When someone shows you who they are, believe them."

"Is that a Harlan original?"

He shook his head. "Maya Angelou. Saw her on *Oprah*."

"Didn't take you to be in Oprah's book club."

"Lots of time to read in the mountains."

Handsome, kind, and well read. Nice.

"Anyway, I'm sorry."

His sincerity was palpable. "Thanks." We sat in silence for a long moment, then a random laugh bubbled up in my throat.

"What's so funny?" He carried our plates to the sink.

"Caleb said Lark stole his heart in high school. You know, 'the one who got away'? She moved back when we were separated. He went whole hog after her. Talked about her around town like they had all but chosen the rings."

His voice hardened. "Shouldn't speak of the dead like this, but Caleb was a jerk to her."

"Took a while before I got that side of the story." I nodded. "Lark and I hadn't met until a PTO meeting. It was so embarrassing—my friend accused her of being a cougar for chasing after Caleb." I shook my head. "Della, my friend? She had my back but not the complete picture." My eyes dropped. "I'm rambling."

"Probably healthy to vent while Meg's away."

"Just hope her father doesn't have any more surprises. Not that I'd have any way to find out if he did."

He lifted a finger. "Actually . . ."

I blinked a few times, awaiting his explanation.

"Look, I wouldn't do this unless I was asked. But if you wanted, I might be able to look into his computer for you. I'm a retired IT geek. Give me a circuit board and some keys, and I'm MacGyver."

"Secret superpower?"

"Eh, not so secret. Before the forest service, I owned my own company. Sold it to a not-so-little four-letter company . . . in Austin?"

"Good for you. Think you could find out what was going on in Maryland, or New Jersey, or wherever?"

He leaned closer. "I do. But before I do any digging—are you sure you're ready to face what I might uncover?"

"Knowledge is power."

"Agree, but it might bring along more chaos than you're ready for—especially so soon after losing him."

"When Caleb fooled around before, I sniffed around his computer. So he changed the way our computer worked, making it where I could only get into my own section of it. Everything else was password protected, but I couldn't have his password. He said it was required by Voyce. After that, I couldn't even see the Gmail account where we got our bill notices. Could you help me get into that one, too, so I can see if we owe anyone?"

"Mmm." He wavered. "Digging into his account might be considered illegal."

"It's my computer, and we used to share the account."

"If he used it for work, there could be an intellectual property issue."

"He logged onto Voyce's computers, but that computer belongs to us. I'm not asking you to break into the mainframe at Voyce Brothers. What if a *Dateline* predator was contacting Meg?"

"You think Meg's been exchanging emails with a child predator?" He cocked his head to the side.

"She could be. I won't know if you don't help me."

"If Meg can get into her account, why not ask her?"

"I wouldn't want her to know I was looking. She's a minor. A child."

Without lifting his head, that brow pitched up again. "Am I looking for scoop on Meg or Caleb?"

"If, while you're helping me protect my daughter, you discover information about my husband on *my* home computer, all the better."

His eyes drifted to the ceiling and his head gave a small shake that I interpreted as, "I shouldn't get involved, but what the hell?"

I smiled grimly. "Thanks. I'm done being the last to know."

Twenty-Five

There was something very James Bond about the way Harlan made quick work of removing the hard drive, a rectangular sliver of the box housed beneath a 24-inch flat-screen monitor.

He held it into view. "Shouldn't take too long."

Down the hall came the click-click of heels.

"Expecting anyone?" he asked.

Della appeared in the doorway. Her mere presence charged the air with scrutiny. "Saw Lark's car outside and assumed you were accepting company. The front door was open." She pushed her silky hair back, her eyes scouring every square inch of that office.

Did you put a tracking device on Lark's car to notify you if it came within twenty yards of my house, Della? "This is Lark's brother, Harlan," I said. "He's visiting from Colorado."

He stood to offer his hand.

"Della Betancourt." She gave his hand a solid shake and stared as he returned to the computer's keyboard.

"He's helping me with a computer problem," I said.

"All you had to do was ask, Sis. Jared's a computer guru."

"Got everything I need," Harlan said. "I'll call when I . . . when it's . . . *fixed*. Nice meeting you. I'll let myself out." He flashed a quick smile and disappeared.

Della was still gawking at the computer when my phone rang and Crashman appeared on the screen.

"Need to get that?" she asked.

I shook my head and punched a button on the side of my phone, sending the call to voicemail.

"What's wrong with your computer?"

"Can't access our old email account," I said. "Who knows what bills are coming due?"

"How'd *he* get involved?" she asked.

"He brought cinnamon rolls—want one?"

"Eech. All those carbs."

"What do you have against carbs?"

"Since Josie destroyed my metabolism." She moved to the windows and peered out as Harlan pulled away.

I moved toward the door. "What brought you to my end of town?"

She followed me. "Meeting with the owners of that ginormous house on Quaker. I think I'm getting the listing." She sighed. "Had a few minutes to check in on you."

After a spell of bland small talk, she left for her meeting. She seemed a little wounded—but I'd survived our encounter with my self-respect intact.

❧

ON SUNDAY, MEG AND I drove to Martha's house. The front door was unlocked, and we found Martha sleeping in the recliner.

"Martha, when did you last eat?" I asked.

With a small shrug, she mumbled, "When can we see him?"

"Martha, even when . . . we won't be able to see him—not like before. He'll be cremated, remember?"

She didn't respond, just fell into a puddle of tears, mourning her only child. On my knees, I patted her leg, trying to soothe her.

After some urging, Martha agreed to eat, and Meg warmed a can of soup. We stuck around while she showered and dressed. I cleaned up the house while we waited. As I organized her nightstand, I found a pile of photos of Caleb as a baby and Caleb with his parents. Those photos showed the family's early days, before their marriage was shaken by Martha's surgeries and addiction. In a way, she'd lost Pike twice—to another woman . . . or, women—and to death. Losing Caleb now only compounded her grief.

Before we left, the priest at St. Barnabas's stopped by the house. Fluent in the Dietrich family history, Father Daniel had been Martha's spiritual support after Pike was laid to rest. He prayed with us and promised to give special attention to Martha as she walked through the next days—earning himself, in my book, a special place in heaven.

As luck would have it, Crashman's message delivered a real update: the investigation was over.

When I returned his call, he told me, "The pilot reported a mechanical problem at 2:30 p.m. Eastern Standard Time. Witnesses reported a hard landing seven miles east of Absecon. NTSB has determined an in-flight separation of the tail rotor occurred." He read the report without offering extemporaneous opinions. "Your husband's remains will be returned, and we'll share the reports with whoever you designate so that you may pursue remuneration."

I thought I'd feel a sense of satisfaction with an explanation, but the details he shared brought to life the terror my husband must've experienced prior to impact.

Two days later, Caleb's remains arrived, and Meg, Martha, Father Daniel, and I met at the funeral home. Martha requested that we lay his ashes to rest beside Pike's in the courtyard at the church. Meg compiled photos for a slideshow. I contacted Caleb's friends to speak at the service.

On the way home, I looked at my girl. "You were great with your grandma. Those were difficult decisions. Not sure I could've done it without you."

"You're stronger than you think." Her gaze fell to her phone. "Diego's headed to the house. He's bringing my books."

"Thought you had your books."

"Not all of them."

"We just left the funeral home. Can't he get them to you later?"

"*Mom*." She pushed back in her seat and rolled her head to one side. "Maybe I want to think about something other than death." *Amen*.

By Thursday, the house was bustling with extended family. Brent stayed at our parents' house and came around during the day. Dad made himself scarce. All too conveniently, an urgent client matter was demanding his attention.

The night before the memorial, Meg slept in my bed, and both of us managed to sleep through the night—until 5:00 a.m., that is, when I woke up and couldn't go back to sleep. After thirty minutes of trying, I got up, showered, and picked up the house in preparation for the post-memorial crowd.

When I went back to the bedroom to wake Meg, she wasn't there. I found her in our home office, sitting on the floor, sifting through a pile of papers in her lap. Her eyes were red, and the stony look on her face shouted betrayal.

"Meg?" I sat down next to her.

"Dad has a house in Maryland." She thrust a US Bank mortgage statement at me. Above "8209 South Delaney Lutherville, MD 21093," was Caleb's name.

"It's probably one of the Voyce Brothers' properties," I said.

"Doubt it."

"You don't know—"

"Mom." She slapped the paper, pointing to the original transaction date. "Wasn't that long ago, he was leaving us." Her mouth pinched into a tight band.

I wanted to smack him for lying. After a deep breath, I said, calmly, "He wasn't leaving us."

"Open your eyes, Mom. He—"

"If he was leaving, he was leaving me. Not you." I scooted closer to her and wiped the tears from her cheeks. "Whatever this is . . ." I gestured to the papers on the floor. "We can't fix it now. I need you to be with me today. It's going to take everything we've got to get your grandma through the service."

"Who's gonna get *us* through today?"

"We're gonna do it together." I took her round face in my hands. "And after everyone leaves, we'll deal with this."

About the time we pulled ourselves together, I spied a black Town Car in front of the house. I opened the front door and found Caleb's uncle Wilmer standing outside.

"Ready?" he asked me gently.

"Where's Martha?" I asked.

"In the car." He ran a hand over his slicked white hair. "Best to leave her be."

Won't get an argument out of me.

§≪

DUANE WOOLDRIDGE TUGGED ON HIS tie and cleared his throat. Before a couple hundred people at the Episcopal church, the lights over the lectern illuminated his blond hair and golf-tanned face. "Caleb Dietrich was my best friend in high school, and we stayed friends—at least, up until last week. Like to think we'll catch up again. That Caleb was a wild man." He gave a nervous chuckle. "He could make you laugh at the craziest sh . . . stuff. Man, I can't talk about the trouble we got into together at State. But I'll tell you this much—I hope there won't be boys like us when Meg gets there."

He drew laughs from that. He went on to speak about Caleb's kindness and talents—his willingness to share a twelve-pack, how he knew all the words to "Friends in Low Places," and his ability to talk his way out of speeding tickets. "Sometimes all in the same night." Duane's eyes glistened with the memories. "Kid you not, the man had a heart of gold."

Surely you've used up all the clichés now, Duane.

"He'd give you the shirt off his back."

Spoke too soon.

He looked directly at Meg. "Your dad's face lit up whenever he talked about you. That man loved you with everything that he had. Don't ever forget that."

Meg nodded and wiped a tear from her cheek.

"Sissie, there's some stuff going on we don't understand, but you'll see in the end: Caleb was a good man who loved with his entire heart."

But who did he love? That was a different matter.

"Anyhow." Duane wiped an eye. "I'm grateful he crossed my path." He lifted an imaginary beer. "Here's to you, man."

I gripped Meg's hand for luck, and we exchanged a glance. "You can do it," I whispered.

She grabbed the back of the pew and rose to her feet.

Now almost a grown woman, Meg was still my baby girl. My heart dropped with each step she took toward the podium. She was so brave.

"I'm Meg Dietrich, Caleb's daughter." Her voice was meek as she lowered the microphone. "I want to thank you for coming today, and for being a friend to my family. It means a lot to my mom and me to see so many people who loved him. Duane's right—Dad had a big heart. Sometimes, it led him into trouble . . ." Her mouth bent to one side. "But I want to talk about the good times." A smile rose with her eyes. "Dad was funny and smart. He always told me I could do anything. He taught me to play golf. When I was bored, he taught me how to play tennis. Not that long ago, I dragged him out onto the court." Her brows rose. "I showed him. Beat him in two games." She paused. "When we got home, he beat me at a video game. He showed me."

A collective laugh softened the tension in the church, and my heart ached watching my baby girl invite outsiders into the relationship she shared with her father.

"Dad wasn't perfect. None of us are. But he gave me the strength to get through times like this. Ironic, isn't it?" The church became completely silent but for her sigh. "I can't think too much about what it'll be like not to see him in the stands at graduation in May, or, like, in a million years from now, when I get married, not having him to walk with me. We talked about taking a big trip after graduation. He wanted Ireland. I wanted—"

A child whined from the back of the church.

"Australia." Her chin quavered. "He didn't think we should—"

The whine matured into a cry, then a squeal that stole everyone's attention. Meg dropped her head and wiped her eyes. The cry softened, and after a thirty-second pause, I nodded for her to continue.

She inhaled sharply and increased her volume to compensate when the noise returned. Against the backdrop of the child's crying, Meg hurried through anecdotes of her first day of school, when her father taught her to ride a bike, and how he was a master at grilling hamburgers. Her gaze locked on mine. "Thanks for celebrating my dad's life with me and my mom and grandma." She looked up. "I love you, Dad."

She returned to the pew beside me, and Father Daniel pointed to a screen. Accompanied by a soundtrack Duane provided, Meg's slideshow lit up the church. Beginning with Caleb's baby pictures, the slides traced his life while Aerosmith, AC/DC, Garth Brooks, the Beastie Boys, and Alan Jackson played. I could only imagine what the priest thought of AC/DC playing within those hallowed halls.

Father Daniel returned to the pulpit while the music wound down. There would be no silence, however. Not until someone removed that child in the back.

Meg tapped my leg. "Whose kid is that?"

I shrugged and shook my head, then pointed to the front of the room to redirect her attention to the priest.

Father Daniel lifted the brass box containing Caleb's ashes and instructed everyone to follow him to the courtyard.

Uncle Wilmer escorted Martha ahead of us, and we stood over Pike's resting place. Beside it, a paver had been removed, exposing a square metal box about ten inches below the earth.

Father Daniel said a prayer while he placed Caleb's ashes in the ground, then he crossed himself, closed the lid, and covered the space with a paver. His work complete, he stood and addressed the crowd: "The Dietrich family asked me to invite each of you to join them as they remember Caleb at their home following the service. Now, let us pray." He raised his hands to the sky. "Lord, we humbly ask that you watch over this family in the days to come, as those days won't be easy without Caleb in their earthly lives. Amen."

Martha wavered, literally swaying, as a breeze tossed leaves over Caleb and Pike's stones. On each side of her, Uncle Wilmer and my dad hooked her elbows, supporting her like balustrades, and guided her back to the Town Car.

Brent rode with us, filling the silence with comments about the beautiful flowers and the number of mourners.

Martha's only words, "He was loved," filled the space around us like thick smoke, obscuring the unsavory memories. All we could see or hear was the sadness of a mother losing her only child.

I thought the nightmare was nearly over—that taking care of Meg and the business associated with Caleb's death would be the worst of it. But Caleb had left one more surprise for us.

Twenty-Six

M y mother's older sister, Mardi, and her husband, Ray, had flown in the night before the memorial.

The McGrath sisters couldn't have been more different. Aunt Mardi was a more conservative, less demure version of Marilyn Monroe next to my mom's skittish Jackie O. Aunt Mardi was fearless, her skin tanned from a recent bicycling trip around Tuscany. She wore her bottle-blond hair in a short, angled style, and stood a good four inches over my mother—likely where I inherited my height.

"Honey, come here." Aunt Mardi pulled me aside. "Meg's speech just took my breath away." She ran a hand over her wrinkled neckline and leaned into me. "This can be overwhelming," she whispered. "When you've had enough of your mother, just signal. I'll get the happy hostess out of here so you can unwind." She squeezed my arm before walking away.

A smile pulled at my face. Aside from her physical appearance, Aunt Mardi didn't much care what people thought of her. Mom said she was too loud, too bold, too risky. Over the years, I'd gathered from Aunt Mardi's expressions that she held opinions about my mom's deference to my dad. I wouldn't go so far as to say Aunt Mardi wore the pants in her family, but I wasn't surprised to see her—with many a wave of her supernaturally toned arms—ordering Uncle Ray to set out folding chairs, take purses to the guest bedroom, and deliver coffee to the early birds.

Uncle Ray governed the entryway like a bouncer at a senior citizens' center. He was bustling around nonstop, directing guests to open chairs and delivering plates of crudités to rickety-kneed old women. Tall as Aunt Mardi, his wavy silver hair was a bit too long for a man his age. I suspected Aunt Mardi had prescribed the style. He didn't seem to mind. From the way he looked at her, he would've let her cut it into a Mohawk if it tickled her fancy.

Dad wasn't as helpful. He carried himself like a host, thanking guests for coming.

Lark appeared next to me in the living room. "You making it okay?"

"Didn't think so many people would show," I said.

A group of chattering women from Voyce came through the door, and I lost my nerve for playing the role of grieving wife. I pulled Lark into the kitchen. "Not sure I can do this."

She touched my hand. "Want some advice?"

"Drink wine?"

"That's one way to manage. Here's my take, straight from the widowhood manual. Stick to, 'Thanks for coming,' or 'It was good to see you again.' Nod along to the random stories. And creepers show up at these things, so don't feel obligated to hug everyone."

"Okay." I took in a deep breath.

"When you've had enough, just excuse yourself. Hide out in the restroom and lock the door. Let me know which one you plan to use, and I'll stash snacks and your choice of adult beverage."

"Master bath? Cream puffs?"

"Got it." She winked and gave me a playful push toward the door. "Off with you, now."

As soon as I walked into the living room, Della grabbed my arm. "Sissie, what can I do?"

"You're doing it. Being here for us."

"My heart imploded when Meg spoke."

"Mine, too."

"Although I wanted to strangle that brat for interrupting."

"Ah, it's okay."

"It's not. Who brings a toddler to a memorial service?"

I gestured toward the door. "Her?" I waved at a petite woman, too old to be the mother of the child in her care. My dad moved across the room to speak to her, and I figured she worked at his office. I wouldn't have been surprised if Dad was giving her a talking-down for bringing the kid to Caleb's service.

"Who's that?"

"Couldn't say. Honestly, I don't have a clue who most of these people are."

Hours of nodding and thanking and hugging left my mind and body exhausted. When nearly everyone had left, my parents, looking worn out themselves, drove Uncle Wilmer and a wrung-out Martha home.

Brent didn't leave with them. Instead, he joined the few of us left in the kitchen.

"You don't have to babysit me," I told him.

"Trying to get rid of me?" he asked as he loaded coffee cups back into their rental boxes.

"No, I . . . never mind. Thanks for helping."

"You're welcome," he said, with a touch of sarcasm—a touch I didn't have the patience to address.

"Where's Meg?"

"She and her friends carried what was left of the cream puffs to your patio." Brent cocked his head to one side. "You've had a hell of a day." His hand brushed my arm. "Sorry."

"Thanks." I'd take whatever he could offer.

"One more," Della announced, carrying an empty pitcher to the sink. "Unless you want me to stay, I should probably get home."

"Your baby needs you more than me. Go tuck Josie into bed."

"If you say so. Call, and I'll be here in a flash."

Faster, if Lark comes first.

As Della darted through the side door to the driveway, Brent angled his head in the same direction. "Some things never change."

"Della?" *Shot in the dark.*

"Feisty and bossy as ever," he said.

"Feisty? Bossy? Next you'll say 'bitchy.'"

"Wouldn't dare." He chuckled.

"I'll bet." I pulled the pitcher he was drying from his hands.

"So this Jared? How does that work?"

Often wondered myself, not that I'd tell you. I shrugged. "They balance each other. She does her thing, and he has selective hearing."

A welcome ray of sunshine blasted into my kitchen. "I think this is the last of them," Lark said, holding out two glasses.

I took the glasses and Brent leaned against the island. "Did that lady with the toddler finally leave?" he asked.

"Nope," Lark said.

Brent raised an eyebrow. "Should we offer her a doggy bag?"

Lark giggled.

"I think she works for Dad," I mused. "She had John cornered for a half hour."

"John Morales?" Lark asked.

"That's the one." He was Dad's partner at the law firm.

Brent worked his mouth like he was letting our words roll around in that big head of his, then said, "I'll be right back," and strode out of the kitchen.

"Mom." Meg shoved her head through the side door. "Running up to the school with Bree for the last of the volleyball game against Kerrville." Her words came at me like bullets, too fast to stop and impossible to examine. Her head disappeared just as fast.

"And . . . she's gone." I blinked a few times at Lark.

"She's handling things well, all considered," Lark said. "How's her mom?"

"Tired, and it's only . . ." I lifted my phone. "Four thirty. Your boys must be champing at the bit to get out of here."

"Wyatt took them home hours ago."

"Thought Charlie had been awful quiet." I grinned at her.

"Right, Charlie." She laughed. "My force of nature."

"A sweet one. What'd you do with Georgia?"

"Georgia Grace is bonding with Uncle Harlan." She glanced at her watch. "By now, she's probably taught him to braid My Little Pony's mane. And he's loving every minute of it. He loves my kids." Her eyes crept up to mine. "Said he enjoyed getting to know you better, too."

"You sent those cinnamon rolls. He looked hungry."

"Very charitable to share, Sissie," she said.

Damn, Lark. You've got my number.

"Merely mentioned I was making them for you, and he was all about delivering them."

My cheeks grew hot. "Don't tell him I told you—he said you were busy with the kids."

"Did he, now?" She rolled her head back and forth. "You know. Might be early in . . . what happens next in your life, but . . ."

"But what?" *Don't keep me hanging.*

"You might keep my stinky brother on your radar, because you're squarely in the middle of his." She winked at me.

I smiled giddily, feeling only a tiny bit guilty for doing so on the same day we put my husband to rest. Then something occurred to me. "Does he do this a lot?"

"Chase women?" she asked.

I braced for her response.

"Hell, no. Harlan's the pickiest man I've ever known. He doesn't go gaga over a woman unless she's pretty special."

"So, I should probably take his . . . interest . . . with a grain of salt?"

"No," Lark said immediately, then covered her mouth regretfully.

"What?"

She removed the hand. "I'm afraid I'll freak you out."

"Freak away. What's the story?"

Lark swallowed. "Harlan is already gaga over you. He's of the school of 'when I know, I know,' and it's clear you've snagged the poor, defenseless man."

I snorted. "Defenseless, huh?"

"My brother is nobody's fool. He's methodical to a fault. *And* he believes that love, like all else in his life, should exceed normal expectations. He had a multimillion-dollar business, but it didn't make his heart happy. He had a sweet girlfriend, but she wasn't his"—her hands made air quotes—"'soul mate.' Spontaneity's alright, so long as it produces magic."

Am I complicated enough for your seemingly simple brother? "Might be too sophisticated for me."

"Don't misunderstand me. He knows what he's looking for. Once he thinks he's found it, God help the target of his desire."

Desire. I felt a tingle go through my body.

The kitchen door swung open with a flourish, and Brent's face, painted with distraction, appeared. "Where's Meg?" he asked hurriedly, avoiding my eyes.

"At school," I said, wishing he hadn't returned. I wanted to hear more about Harlan.

Brent pulled a Shiner Bock from the fridge and plopped on the barstool beside me. "How can you listen to them talk about Caleb like he was a saint?"

I frowned, hoping to shut him up.

"Come on," Brent said, looking at Lark. "She went to high school with him." Their eyes met in an evocative glance. "She knows."

"Caleb had a good side," Lark said, charitably.

"He was a human train wreck." He pointed to me. "Lucky he didn't take you and Meg down with him."

My emotions were raw, and my politeness had worn thin. Brent's piety cracked clean through what remained. I stood up, stalked around the island, and stood so I was facing my brother squarely. "I screwed up—getting knocked up, marrying him. You know it. I know it. It's over. Can you give it a fucking break now?"

His head jerked back. "You . . . *you* never screwed up."

"Bullshit," I hissed.

"Don't be pissed at me. Caleb lied. Caleb screwed around. You've never been anything but honest. You gave everything to your daughter. You are—"

"What?" I demanded. "A saint?"

"Yes. You're a goddamned—"

"Don't say it. Sticking it out with a man who doesn't love you doesn't make you a saint. It makes you a damned fool."

Brent slapped his beer down on the granite counter. "Sissie, stop. Stop listening to Mom and Dad."

"Should I let you talk in private?" Lark asked, backpedaling toward the door.

"Sorry, Lark," I said, remembering my manners. "Sure, could you give us a moment?"

"Of course." She pushed through the door and disappeared.

I shook my head. I walked around the island, stopped beside my brother. Then I took a gulp of his beer. "Ahh." I closed my eyes for a second. "Forgot how refreshing a cold beer tastes."

"I'll get one for you," Brent said.

"I want this one."

"Fine. Have it. Tell me when you're ready for another." He grinned, and I nodded. "When that woman leaves, get some rest, will you?"

"What woman?" I asked.

"The one in the den? With the kid?"

I felt my forehead crinkle. I finished off that beer in record time, then set the empty bottle on the stone counter. "Who knows? Maybe Caleb had an affair with Miss Maryland." My voice became louder. "My husband probably had a wild affair with a tall, skinny blond with big boobs, just like his daddy taught him. Give me a couple years, Brent. You'll find me curled up in a recliner, watching game shows, like Martha."

Brent scratched his nose. Whatever he was about it say, I could tell it wouldn't come easily—and wouldn't make me feel any better.

Words bring understanding. They clarify, elucidate, amplify. When put in coherent order, they can make enemies, divide countries, reunify lovers. Brent threw a hand over his mouth like doing that might help him hold back whatever he was trying not to say.

"Brent—why do you look like that? What is it?" I asked.

An unnatural stillness surrounded us. A bad feeling sent my pulse racing.

"Sissie, you should sit." His words fell against my pounding ears.

"No. No sitting. I'm a stander. Standing. Here. Um." I rubbed my forehead. "Words are hard today."

Brent pulled out a bar stool and twisted his hand in a circle. "Please. Sissie."

I slapped my hands down at my sides. "You got it. Sissie. Your unbelievably sad little sister who's firmly planted in Fuckupville. And you don't have to tell me about Caleb anymore. Caleb and Faith." I mock-laughed. "A relationship for the ages—that ended in a ball of flames." I shook my head. "Don't judge me. I'm so tired, and—"

"God damn, Sissie," he snapped, loudly enough that it scared me a little. "Will you let me talk?"

I took a seat on that barstool.

"I want you to consider which of Caleb's friends would fly all the way across the country to pay their respects."

I squinted at him.

"Schlepping an infant."

"I never met half the people in my house today."

"Did you meet the kid in the den?"

"Not exactly," I said. "But we all heard him loud and clear at the church."

Brent stared down at me. "A woman named Theresa." He pointed behind me. "Is camped out in your den with that kid. Says she wants to talk to Meg. Also"—he held up his index finger—"a point I'd caution you not to overlook: the crier's name is 'PJ.' Theresa said it's a family name."

I blanched. "Short for?"

"Pike Jameson."

Twenty-Seven

Pike Jameson Dietrich has a love child.

"The man's been dead for, what, three, four years?" My brain refused to complete the simplest math, but even in my numbed state I couldn't ignore the obvious. "That kid can't be much older, if even that. There's got to be another reason he's carrying Pike's name."

Brent gaped like he expected me to pull a rabbit from a hat.

I frowned at him. "What?"

"Pike Jameson?" he asked.

"My best guess? She and Pike had an affair, and now she's dragging a grandson carrying Pike's name to Texas to rub it in Martha's face. Class act. Will you tell them the party's over and send them on their way?"

"Did you hear me? She wants to talk to *Meg*," Brent said. "Sissie. She said the kid's Meg's brother."

My stomach slammed to the floor.

"Sorry to interrupt," Lark said from behind me. "Anything I can do before I leave?"

"Yes," I managed to get out.

"What's up?" she asked, rounding the island.

"The woman with the kid? In the den?" Brent began.

"She told Brent the boy is Meg's brother," I finished.

Lark's blue eyes bugged out and shifted to Brent.

"True," Brent said.

"Okay, well . . ." Lark frowned like she was considering what I'd said. Then, speaking more to herself than me, she said, "The boy does resemble Caleb. But that could be a coincidence."

"Is it also a coincidence that he's named after Caleb's father?" Brent asked.

"If the kid's Caleb's, who's the woman?" Lark said.

"Theresa," Brent answered. "A family friend who keeps the boy when his parents travel."

"Parents, plural?" My volume was rising. "What the hell?"

Lark put a hand on her hip. "Sissie?" she hesitated until our eyes met. "Totally your call, but—I could introduce myself as your attorney . . . or, Meg's attorney? If she's here to make a claim on Caleb's estate, we can set the tone, so she knows it's not a free-for-all."

While my shocked mind processed the identity of the child in my den, Lark and Brent left me in the dust, discussing common-law marriages and child support.

A sudden silence filled the kitchen, and I realized they were both staring at me. "Is that alright?" Brent asked. "If Lark talks to her?"

"As your attorney," Lark clarified.

"Sure. Why not?" I said—a bit too flippantly, I realized as soon as the words left my lips.

"Are you sure?" Lark asked.

I tried to sound clearer. "Yes. Please talk to her. And tell her you're our attorney."

When she walked out, Brent put an arm around me. "I won't leave you until we get this straight."

WE WAITED. EVERY SO OFTEN, Brent stepped out of the kitchen and attempted to capture bits of Lark's conversation with Theresa.

"Eavesdropping would be a hell of a lot easier if that kid would stop jabbering," he reported after the second try.

Lark returned with a terrifyingly expressionless face.

"What?" Brent asked impatiently.

"Apparently, PJ doesn't have any family except Meg and Martha."

"Meg is *my* family," I said, thrusting a finger at Lark.

"Easy," Brent said. "She's just the messenger."

"What do they want?" I asked.

"Doesn't sound like money's what they're after. The woman's name is Theresa Doorly. She said Caleb's attorney took care of all their travel arrangements—soup to nuts, from flights to meals while they're here."

"His attorney?" I asked.

"John Morales," Lark said flatly.

"Dad's partner is overseeing the care of Caleb's . . ." I swallowed, the word "son" stuck in my throat.

"His mother was with Caleb on that helicopter," Lark said. "He's an orphan now. Without other family, he's depending upon Meg or Martha to step up and raise him."

"No effing way." At Lark's straight face, I added, "There's someone else. There has to be a cousin or someone who can take him."

Lark pressed her lips together and gave a slight shake of her head. "No. I told her Meg wouldn't be available to speak to her today, and she took the child back to their motel. I gathered her information, told her we can meet after I've had a chance to review the matter with John."

"Brent, when Dad finds out—"

"Dad has to know," Brent said. "John wouldn't be involved, otherwise."

Fury heated my chest as a whole mess of expletives threatened to bust out of me like a smoking, cursing volcano. I guess I was too busy being pissed to notice Meg's 4Runner snaking up the driveway, because suddenly the side door was creaking open and there she was, complaining about being hungry.

"Can we order Chinese?" she asked, not looking like a young woman who'd eulogized her father earlier that day. "I know there's tons of food around here, but it's funeral food." She wrinkled her nose.

"Chinese works for me," Brent said.

"Love you, Uncle Brent," she said, shining a broad smile at him. We were about to ruin that beautiful smile.

"Want to hang out with us and eat Chinese?" she asked Lark.

"I'll hang out for a while."

"Come here." Brent pulled out another barstool and put an arm around Meg as she lowered herself into it. "I've got something to tell you, okay?"

Meg's brow furrowed. She nodded.

"Remember the kid at the service making all the noise? He's . . . related to you." Brent shot a hard breath from his lips. "He's your brother."

"Half-brother," I corrected.

Meg laughed. "Quit screwing with me. I've had kind of a crappy day. Can we get food?" She faced Brent. "Did Mom tell you about my dad's house in Maryland? I found papers. He was going to leave us."

"He was going to leave *me*, not us," I corrected.

"She's in denial," Meg said.

Attempting to telegraph my desperation, my eyes flew to my brother, then to Lark.

"Your uncle's not kidding, Meg," Lark said. "The woman who brought the baby to the service? She said his mom was with your dad on that helicopter. And . . . she said she brought him here so he could live with his family."

"Sure he's really Dad's kid?"

"He has your grandfather's name," Lark said.

"Pike?" Meg chuckled. "Poor kid."

I rolled my eyes. "Goes by PJ."

"Dad had a kid with another lady?" Meg's face sobered.

Brent gave a solemn nod.

"Dad had a kid with someone else. What a clusterfu—"

"Meg."

Her voice ratcheted up, "Mom, it is! Bad enough he was with some other chick, but a kid, too? Is this why he has a house back there?"

Brent raised a brow—confused by Meg's question, but I didn't explain.

"I don't know, baby." I smoothed her hair. "I'm as confused as you. They want you or your grandmother to take him. But that's not going to happen. We're getting a good lawyer and—"

"Grandma Martha? With a kid?" Meg wiped her nose. "Get Grandpa Thom to tell them to take him somewhere else?"

Brent edged closer. "Grandpa's partner represents them."

Confusion crossed Meg's face.

"It's gonna be okay. That's why Lark's here. She's getting to the bottom of it," I said. "Whatever problems your dad left behind . . . they're not yours to sort out. I give my word."

No way in hell will I allow Meg to give up her dreams to raise Caleb's bastard child.

Twenty-Eight

I woke the next morning to my girl snuggled in beside me. It seemed she was done clinging to her father's pillow.

Brent came over around nine, and we talked over coffee while Meg slept in—the child deserved an escape after learning her father hadn't just left this world but left it in the company of the woman with whom he'd created a secret family.

"Crap." I lifted an envelope. "Forgot to give this to Father Daniel before he left yesterday."

"Need me to run it to the church?" Brent offered.

"No. I'd like to tell him what's happening. We might need him around when Martha finds out she's a grandma again."

Brent breathed out a rueful laugh. "Better start the prayer chain now."

"Want to ride along?" I asked.

"I have emails to comb through. I'll stick around so Meg doesn't wake up to an empty house."

"Thanks, Brent. It's nice having you around."

While it lasts.

⚘

Unlike the previous morning, the parking lot at St. Barnabas was nearly empty. I went inside, past the nave, the main part of

226

the Episcopal church, and wound through the building toward the administrative offices, where I hoped to find Father Daniel. As I neared the children's chapel, a child's voice leached into the corridor.

I walked over and peeked in.

Father Daniel stood on the small altar, his arms outreached in prayer for the three parishioners seated at the front of the chapel. At "Amen," he gave a gentle nod and waved for me to enter. I dropped into the last row of miniaturized pews at the rear of the twenty-row-deep youth sanctuary and, looking forward, recognized John Morales.

John held up a hand in greeting, then turned back to the altar.

A low hum vibrated around me, working its way into my veins, warning me to climb out of that tiny chair. One by one, the pieces began to tumble into place as I scanned the seats beside him. *I'll be damned.* John was sitting beside Theresa and a squirming tawny-haired toddler.

"We commend to you our sister Faith, who was reborn by water and the Spirit of the Holy Baptism," Father Daniel read from the Book of Common Prayer I'd come to know well. This wasn't a routine Episcopal mass, but one for Caleb's baby momma, Faith Willets.

Closing my eyes in a prayerful ruse, I collected my muddled thoughts, tried to clear the wash of jealousy filling my limbs. A priest shouldn't play favorites, but surely Father Daniel could've declined.

Now that Father Daniel hadn't just seen me but also invited me to join them, I couldn't escape. A part of me didn't want to. Stuck in this back-row seat, I became privy to an unfiltered view into Caleb's other life.

After reading from the Gospel and reciting the prayers, Father Daniel raised his head. "Theresa would like to speak."

"Do I have to stand?" the woman asked through the tissue she held to her face.

"You can speak from there."

She glanced at John, then looked down at PJ. "Faith always cared about others, always put herself last."

Oh, really?

"All her life she helped others. She became a counselor to listen to people's problems and guide them through difficult situations. She celebrated when they found their way. Only thing that made her happier than her job was PJ." Theresa gazed at the boy with a grandmotherly smile, then turned around and met my eyes.

I froze, a baffling stew of emotions bubbling in my chest.

Theresa threw a glance at Father Daniel, then returned her gaze to me. "Growing up, Faith never had it easy, but she never gave up on herself or anyone else. When Caleb came into her office, he didn't think he needed help."

Faith was his therapist?

Theresa continued, "She saw something in him."

A meal ticket?

"She saw a man in pain. She was determined to help him sort through the unresolved issues he'd had since childhood that were affecting his relationships."

While she spoke, the boy pulled at the hem of her skirt. Whatever his age, he really was too young to grasp the occasion.

Can we skip to the part where Faith counsels Caleb right into her bed?

Tears congested Theresa's voice. "Like everything else in Faith's life, things didn't happen in the order she would've liked, but they happened." She gave a slight shrug. "She never meant to hurt anyone. Getting along without her won't be easy." She grasped PJ's hand. "Will it, buddy?"

PJ whined. He'd sat through enough.

You and me both, little man.

"We will . . ." Anguish overpowered her weak voice. "Never . . . for . . . get . . . her." Theresa gasped out the last word, then squeezed a tissue over her face.

A crushing silence followed.

After what seemed like a lifetime, Father Daniel began speaking, but his voice faded behind the insistent pulse thumping against my eardrums. I lifted my gaze to the crucifix featuring our Savior, arms outstretched.

Come on, Jesus. You can't expect me to sit through this and feel sorry for this woman?

Jesus's expression had changed. Imagined or divine, his expression said, "Don't try to make sense of it. Stay put. I've got you."

I sure hope so.

A crushing silence followed.

Father Daniel cleared his throat and offered a prayer for Faith and Caleb, asking for special consideration for their son. "Amen," he finished, and then he lifted a box identical to the one we'd chosen for Caleb's ashes and invited us to follow him to the courtyard.

Apparently, I hadn't tortured myself enough, so I followed the processional, assuming two and a half mourners following a priest counted as a sacred rite.

My husband's mistress had found her final resting place in my hometown. And Miss Faith Willets wasn't being laid willy-nilly in any old spot. She was being placed smack in the middle of the Dietrich family section.

Let no woman put asunder?

That hussy nabbed the spot above Caleb—in life and in death, she got top billing.

Reciting the same language he'd used for Caleb, Father Daniel set Faith's remains in the open space.

Theresa put a pink rose in PJ's chubby hand and gestured for him to set it on the box. "Give this to your momma," she said.

He inspected the rose. "Momma?" Searching for her to no avail, he frowned at Theresa.

"See?" Theresa kissed the top of one of the roses and set it down. "For your momma."

He kissed his flower.

"Tell her, 'I love you,'" she instructed.

Apparently, the boy was too young to perform on command. He leaned into Theresa, laid a slobbery kiss on her cheek, and mumbled something I supposed could've been "Lub you." Then he rubbed his face with the back of a hand.

Theresa placed another flower over the box while Father Daniel knelt beside PJ.

PJ grabbed at one of the brightly colored sashes adorning Father Daniel's purple vestments. Then, he pulled at his own khaki pants, making them look like knickers, revealing navy socks, plump shins, and scuffed hiking boots.

A pang of guilt arrived. Meg at least had Caleb's debris trail to sort through. This innocent child had nothing. My view of him became feathery as tears filled my eyes.

Thomas and Father Daniel turned their attention on Theresa. While they spoke, PJ squinted past me at the church preschool's playground.

Pointing at the banana slide, PJ took off on his squat legs without regard to the balance and height he'd need to navigate the concrete steps. He fell with a thud, and without thinking, I raced to him and scooped him from the concrete and carried him to Theresa.

In a breath-holding pocket of silence, my heart galloped in anticipation of the shriek to come. And come it did, in fierce waves. Unanticipated tears coated my face as the mini stranger clutched my blouse. I rocked and patted him while he rested his head on my shoulder, his presence both strange and familiar. I had to wonder if, on some level, he recognized the mother in me, even if I wasn't his own.

"You're okay, little man," I told him.

"I'll take him," Theresa said, reaching out.

"Eeeh," he whined, unwilling to release his grip on me.

His touch brought a strange consolation. "I don't mind," I said, half expecting her to rip the child out of my arms.

"Alright," she said, turning to share an appreciative smile with Father Daniel.

PJ's chest shook as I bounced him, and his hands tightened around my shirt, inspiring old emotions—nostalgic touches of soft skin, untamed expressions, that side-to-side soothing dance engrained in post-pregnancy DNA that cements a woman into parenthood. Apparently, it never goes away.

His cries diminished, and his small hands touched my face. Comfort went both ways.

"Did those mean old steps jump in your way?" I asked.

He took a deep breath, and his entire body shivered with his exhalation. He couldn't understand who I was or why he was there. But his needy grasp bore testament to the unbearable ache of his mother's absence.

He glanced up at me with caramel eyes I knew too well. *Those eyes, the slant of his nose, that russet hair—you are Caleb's son, through and through.*

"Here." Theresa put out her arms. This time, PJ leaned into her. "Thank you," she said to me, running a freckled hand over the boy's thin hair. "So brave, going off on your own," she said in a grandmotherly voice.

PJ pointed toward the playground.

"You're not going to let me off the hook without taking you over there, are you?" Theresa asked PJ. "It wouldn't hurt for you to burn off some steam after sitting so long in church."

"If you have business to discuss"—I nodded to where John and Father Daniel were standing—"I don't mind."

"Our business is done." In what seemed like an afterthought, she looked at me. "But you're welcome to come along with us."

I took the opportunity to pass along my card to Father Daniel, then glanced at my phone—no calls or texts, no excuses not to stay longer. Besides, what could it hurt to learn more about these relative strangers threatening my daughter's future?

§➤

THE EQUIPMENT WAS SET ON a layer of mulch to soften the falls of its users but not easy to walk upon in pumps, as Theresa would learn in her first few steps.

"I'm in sneakers," I said. "I can take him."

"If you're sure you don't mind, I'll just watch from right here." She pointed to an adjacent bench.

"Ready, buddy?" I escorted him to the equipment and followed his movements as he attempted to push himself up through the yellow-tunneled slide from the bottom. He only made it a couple feet before rolling on his back and sliding back into my grasp with a Chiclet-toothed smile. A small wonder that smile remained, considering how much he had lost. Meg's world was broken in half, but she still had one parent. PJ had none.

"How old is he?" I called to Theresa.

"Seventeen . . ." She looked at the sky, her lips moving silently. "Eighteen months tomorrow."

I turned back to him, adjusting my words to a child that age. "You're big for your age." Meanwhile, like a rubber band, my mind snapped backward. *What lies crossed Caleb's lips eighteen months ago? And nine months before that?*

My phone vibrated in my back pocket. I pulled it out and looked at the screen. Brent.

"Hello," I answered, breathless after catching PJ at the base of the slide.

"Where are you?" he asked.

"At the church."

"Uh-gan! Uh-gan!" PJ urged.

"Are those kids?"

"I'm at the church playground," I amended. "Ran into a little boy named PJ—"

"What the hell?" Brent asked.

"Ran into him, them, at his mother's service. Accidentally stumbled into it." I lifted PJ onto the slide. "Where's Meg?"

"In the shower. What are you doing there?" he asked.

"Tell you later."

"Don't do that to me," he barked.

"Be home soon." I ended the call and shoved the phone in my pocket.

"Everything alright at home?" Theresa called to me.

Oh yeah, just peachy. "Meg's wondering where I've been. Better head home. But I think PJ's not gonna be too happy with me."

"I'll bet I can tease him away." Theresa lifted a packaged snack from her bag. "PJ, want some?"

He nodded insistently, and I carried him back to the bench.

"Thanks for playing with me, bud."

He didn't respond; his attention was locked on his fruit snacks.

Taking Theresa's nervous smile as permission to leave, I crossed the grassy lawns to the parking lot.

The pieces of my life I thought were certain—my marriage, my family, my identity as a wife and mother—had swirled into a mist I no longer recognized. *How did holding the boy for minutes blur my view of Faith from a home-wrecker to a mother?*

My anger toward Caleb remained, but my resentment toward his child had dissipated. I felt a strange kinship with Theresa and a physical longing to hold PJ in my arms.

I drove away, leaving behind the rage I had earlier and carrying an ache to hold the best of what Caleb had left behind.

Twenty-Nine

Meg set her coffee on the table and rose to her feet when I walked into the kitchen. "They were at *our* church? That's so wrong."

Echoing my previous opinion, the words took on an air of selfishness coming from her mouth.

It was my turn to lead by example. I cocked my head to the side. "That church doesn't belong to us. They have a right to pray, too." How could I defend my anger toward two people who couldn't defend themselves? "You know, I've thought about this. If things were different—if he *had* divorced me and remarried? You might have become friends with . . ." I swallowed the bad taste in my throat. "Faith."

"I would've hated both of them."

"Maybe at first." Brent, surprisingly, jumped in. "Easy to hate a stranger. Not so easy when you get to know someone, especially someone who is loved by one of your parents."

High road or not, that one burned a little.

"Didn't get the chance, because my dad kept a whole other life from me." She waved a hand, knocking her mug over. A layer of milky coffee spread over the table in every direction.

I jumped up for a towel, while Brent, armed with good intentions, hung in there. "Meg, your dad may have sucked as a husband, but he loved you." His voice wavered. "And I'm afraid you're going to be upset when I say this, but it should be said. He probably loved that kid, too."

Tears clung to Meg's long lashes. Watching Caleb's betrayal blister our daughter's innocence made my heart hurt.

Dammit, Caleb. Couldn't you just learn to use a damned condom?

§←

AFTER MEG RETREATED TO HER room for some quiet time, Brent left to drive some of our out-of-town family to San Antonio to catch their flights. I took advantage of the breathing space and went to see Lark at the winery.

Wyatt gave me a warm smile when I walked in. "Hey, Sissie. She's upstairs." He pointed to a lofted section overlooking the bottling machinery.

Lark sat before a laptop at the old library table she used as a desk. Behind her, invoices and sticky notes littered a bulletin board. "I've pulled cases to review, and they look promising."

I filled her in on my visit to the church and my time with PJ. "He said he didn't want more kids. I'd brought up adoption. He wouldn't even let us have a dog, yet he had this whole other family?"

Lark's hand went to her mouth, and she cleared her throat. "Funny you should mention a dog. John told me he's having Caleb's dog shipped here. Until they find a home for him, they'll keep him at the kennel off the highway, by the Williams' peach orchard. He said they're hoping the dog can stay with the boy."

"Back up. We couldn't get Meg a dog because Caleb was 'too allergic.'" I ground out the words. "Unbelievable."

Harlan's head popped through the door. "Hey, Sissie."

Wyatt appeared behind him, waving to Lark. "Can I borrow you for a minute?"

"Be right back," she said.

Harlan pulled a matching spindle chair from the corner, turned it backward, and straddled it beside me. "Anything I can do?"

His deep voice shot my pulse into a pleasant uptick. "I wish," I said. "Want a dog?"

"I might. What kind?"

"Who knows? Besides the extra child and secret mistress, I just found out my husband had a dog, too."

"Lark said the boy was a handful at the memorial. Dog might be easier to handle?"

"That kid can't help any of this." Talking about PJ made me hungry to hold him again.

"Anyway, if Meg gets a dog, it'll be one she wants. Not her dad's leftovers."

"Gotcha." He pursed his lips in thought. "Glad you stopped by. I opened that hard drive."

"Do I want to know?"

"Nothing too shocking. Lark's got me tied up today. Swing by your place tomorrow?"

"It's better if we're not around my daughter."

"Till they call me back to Colorado, Lark's got me set up in an apartment down the hall." He gestured behind him. "Spoken for most of tomorrow, but I'm free early evening. Text me if you can come by." He picked up a pen and scratched out his phone number on a sticky note.

Lark's footsteps announced her return.

He raised a finger and touched my arm. "Back to it."

"Bye," I said, enjoying the warmth spreading across my chest.

"Shut the door behind you, please." Lark paused, waiting for privacy. "Sorry about that. Is he giving you a hard time?"

"Just talking."

"Oh yeah?" She winked. After a pause, she blinked hard. "Where were we?"

"Finding a home for a boy and his dog."

§←

On Sunday, Brent returned to Chicago. Uncle Wilmer offered to stick around longer, so I didn't make my usual trip to Martha's place. I was hoping to spend some quiet time with my daughter, but she went to a friend's house to catch up on homework, so I found myself unexpectedly alone.

As the sun fell, my reflexes anticipated Caleb's return, as had been the status quo every other Sunday following his Maryland "work trips." I lifted my phone, half expecting a text about a missed flight when a stifling quiet followed me.

I retrieved Harlan's number and typed out a message.

SISSIE: *It's Sissie. Am I catching you at a bad time?*
HARLAN: *Not at all. Can you come by tonight?*
SISSIE: *What works for you?*
HARLAN: *An hour?*
SISSIE: *See you then.*

He supplied the instructions to open the gates at the winery. I had them from the night I helped Meg babysit, but I thanked him anyway and rushed to my closet to get ready.

"Don't you dare look at me like I'm doing something wrong," I said to the wall of dark suits along Caleb's side.

I changed into my dark jeans and an oversize white blouse, adding a pair of diamond studs and a spritz of perfume. Flats filled almost every shoe cubby. They'd been the go-to for a woman who didn't dare threaten her husband's manliness with her height.

Not anymore, though. Tonight I'm pulling out the black heels I haven't worn in years.

Since I turned fifteen and had to dance shoulders to nose with Paul McCaslin, my height had led to apologies. Young men were all about sexy long legs—until they stood toe-to-toe with them, that is, and then, not so much.

"No man likes standing beside an Amazon woman at the company Christmas party," Caleb always insisted. "Put on a pair of those flats, will ya?"

No one likes putting a lying, cheating, good-for-nothing jackass in the ground, either, but sometimes a woman's got to suck it up, buttercup.

I was pleased with myself for hiding those heels in the back of the closet instead of tossing them into the Goodwill bin. A quick dusting, and they cleaned up like new. A once-over in the mirror showcased the mocking glimmer on my left hand.

Time's up on that one, baby. I licked my finger and slipped off that tired ring. *We are officially ready to roll.*

My phone rang before I reached my car.

"Mom?" Meg said breathlessly. "Before you say no, hear me out. Tomorrow's alternative schedule, so we don't have to be at school until ten."

"What about it?"

"Can I stay the night?"

Normally, I wouldn't entertain the thought on a school night. But nothing was normal anymore.

"Are Eliza's parents okay with it?" I asked.

"Yeah," she said with "duh" in her voice. "Her mom's even making pancakes for breakfast."

"Can't beat that. Don't stay up too late."

"We won't! You're the best, Mom. Love you."

"Love you too, baby." I dropped the phone in my bag and climbed into my car.

Thirty

"Open Sesame," I said, punching in the code at the winery's gates. Harlan was waiting for me on a narrow porch outside the mechanical barn. He greeted me with a sideways hug. His hair was wet, and he smelled of lemony soap.

Inside the dark mechanical barn, digitized screens on the metal tanks offered dim light. He led me up the stairs and past Lark's office to a suite similar to what I'd seen at those extended-stay hotels.

"Nice place." I surveyed the efficiency kitchen, sitting area, and bedroom.

"Gives me some privacy. Can only stay with the parents for so long."

A table for two and a denim-covered loveseat separated the area containing a queen bed and chest of drawers. The overhead lights were off, but two lamps and George Strait on a portable speaker created a pleasant ambiance.

"Want a drink?" he asked.

"Do I need a drink before you tell me what you found?"

His mouth twisted, and he gave a sniff. "How about a glass of wine?"

With my nod, he poured two glasses of a red blend and gestured for me to join him at the table. A dozen tabs were open on his laptop screen—invoices for utilities, property taxes, and repairs, mostly.

Without skipping a beat, Harlan confirmed the purchase of a home on the East Coast almost two years ago.

When Faith was expecting PJ.

"You okay?" Harlan dipped his head to meet my eyes.

"No surprises yet," I said stiffly.

"Don't forget—I'm just the messenger."

I smiled at him and sipped the last of my wine, probably too eagerly. Harlan took note. While he refilled my glass, I walked around. "Is there a restroom?"

He pointed around the corner.

Don't have to go, but I would like to know more about you.

The bathroom was impeccably neat—sink wiped clean, mirror Windex-shiny. I flushed the toilet and washed my hands for good measure, careful to leave the chrome faucet spotless like I'd found it.

When I emerged, Harlan nodded to the wine on the table.

"Thanks," I said, but didn't pick up the glass.

His brows pitched up, and he tilted his head to the side. "What's up?"

"Nothing." Thoughts were bouncing around my head, but few related to Caleb or that hard drive. "You sure there's not a special lady in those mountains?"

"There's a badger who's constantly pregnant, but I hardly know her." He displayed his palms.

"Hard to believe you don't have women swooning over you."

"Swooning women?" He rumpled his face.

"Shouldn't be difficult for a handsome guy."

"Thanks." He blushed and took three measured steps toward me.

"Tall, and that deep voice—you're really attractive." *You've said too much. No more wine and no more talking, woman!*

His next slow step brought him close enough to touch. "Since that afternoon at Lark's—whenever I see you, it kills me not to stare." His fingertips traced the length of my arm and pushed my hair off my shoulders. "Can't explain it, but I can't stop thinking about you."

I couldn't tame the stupid grin taking over my face.

His head dropped dangerously close, hovering, and then his lips touched mine—but barely. It was innocent enough, just a hint of a kiss. *Is this me getting even with Caleb?*

Once more.

Nope, Caleb doesn't have a damned thing to do with it. Off with you now, guilt. A man is looking at me as no man ever has before, and I intend to enjoy every toe-curling second.

Harlan's thumb grazed my bottom lip and take-me-now-or-lose-me-forever raw longing set my skin on fire. Despite my wobbly knees, I managed the few short steps to the bed.

A shadow of whiskers raked my neck as Harlan laid a path of kisses along my collarbone. His skin was so hot, I felt it through our clothes—during the brief time they remained on.

He made quick work of my blouse's buttons, pushing it over my shoulders. Air blew from an overhead vent, shocking my skin like an admonition, a threat to my courage. *Oh no, you don't.* I reached for the blanket and pulled it over my body.

Harlan's chin turned to the side appraisingly. *Is that shock or interest on his face?* His kiss answered my question, and I closed my eyes. Intimacy pushed away words like right or wrong, leaving only what could be seen, heard, and tasted.

Color rose on Harlan's face, and he cupped my shoulders with his strong hands. His tongue brushed mine slowly as if asking to be invited to do more.

Beneath the blanket, Harlan pulled me to him. I pushed his long-sleeved T-shirt over his head and gripped his muscled shoulders.

"Mmm . . ." Even his moan was low-pitched. He lifted my chin. "You sure about this?"

I met his gaze and gave him what I hoped was a seductive nod.

He pulled at his belt until it became loose, and the buckle pinged against the wood floor. Soon, we'd peeled away all the layers keeping us apart. His hands traced me intimately and his tongue teased my breasts before moving lower. I rolled over onto him, kissing him with such intensity I thought I might explode.

"Hang on." Breaking the current between us, he retrieved his wallet from the nightstand and removed a foil packet.

"Okay?" he asked.

I pulled him closer, whispering, "I told you, yes."

With that, he rolled on the condom, an image I hoped never to forget.

He eased himself inside me, and I let out a teasing groan. His skin was deliciously warm, and my body pressed itself to him with delight.

Harlan let himself go, and I pulled him tighter, passion overtaking my will.

I drank in every breath until we were done, lying together in a daze.

"Be right back." He slipped into the bathroom.

When he returned, he curled up beside me, and I rested a thigh over one of his. He brushed a gentle hand over my shoulders and back, turning shamelessly every so often to smell my hair or kiss my face. At some point, he laid back and closed his eyes, but his grin didn't melt.

"It's not the best time for me to ask this, I know, but . . ." He grazed my thigh with his knuckle. "What happens next?"

I perched myself on an elbow. Meeting his gaze felt like a deliciously terrifying commitment; goose bumps rose on my skin.

"Oh, shit," he breathed out. "I scared you. Should've kept my trap shut."

"No, tell me what you meant."

"I want to keep seeing you." He kissed me, hard. "Not the best time for you, but when life settles, I'd like to see where we can take this."

AT FIRST LIGHT, WYATT'S VOICE rang out downstairs.

"Dammit," Harlan grumbled sleepily. "Wyatt."

I bolted upright, grabbing frantically for my clothes.

"He won't come in."

My eyes roved the room but stopped short when they met Harlan's easy smile. After recalibrating with a breath, I returned the look. "Not used to doing this."

"We're adults." He moved to the edge of the bed.

I tossed my head back and forth. "Yeah, but . . ." I gestured to my half-naked body, and self-consciousness folded my smile.

"Come here." He held out his arms, and I crept toward him. He pulled my hips to him and gave me a lingering stare, his eyes puffy with sleep. "Don't want you to go."

"I don't want to leave you, but . . ."

We heard Wyatt talking to someone downstairs. I pulled on my clothes and returned to his side. I could've stayed there all day had my phone not pinged with a text.

LARK: *Can you meet today?*

"It's your sister." I laughed. "She wants to meet today."

"Tell her to pop over, but warn her to knock before entering," he said, pulling me to him.

I resisted, my eyes on the phone as Lark and I exchanged messages. "Meeting her back here in a few hours. Need to go home and shower up."

"Lunch?" he asked.

"Maybe." I bit the side of my cheek. "Can I let you know?"

"Of course." He sat up and started pulling on his jeans. "Come here." He pushed my hair off my eyes and gathered me to him for a lingering kiss. "Walk you out?" he asked.

"Better not."

"Ashamed of me?"

"No! But . . ."

"I understand." His hands didn't leave me.

After another kiss, I stepped away from him and out the door. *Clunk. Clunk. Clunk.* Those heels seemed determined to broadcast my departure no matter how softly I stepped.

"Howdy." Wyatt met me at the bottom of the staircase.

"Hi. I was just . . ." I gestured to the stairs.

Wyatt waved a hand, a gesture telling me he didn't require an explanation. "No worries. Have a good one."

AT HOME, I NOTICED THAt my blouse was hanging long on one side. I scuttled into my bedroom to get a better look at the mismatched buttons, hoping Wyatt hadn't noticed.

A few minutes later, beneath the shower's spray, I ran a hand through my hair. A strand caught on my left earring. My hand rose to my right ear. Nothing.

I switched off the water and searched the tile floor. Nothing. In between drying my hair and dressing, I searched for it. I traced my path through the house. I returned to my car. Each time, I came up empty-handed.

The doorbell rang, and I ran to the front of the house.

"Hi, honey." Mom sashayed inside. "You didn't answer your phone."

"I have a meeting about Caleb's other family today. I assume Brent filled you in?"

"Actually, your father told me." She took a seat in one of the yellow chairs and folded her hands in her lap, pretty as a pie supper.

I sat on the sofa, combing her prim, blank face for answers. "What did he tell you?"

"Well . . ." Mom said around a sympathetic smile. "Last year, Caleb spoke to him." Her pitch rose apologetically. "Now, your father only got involved to protect you and Meg. Caleb needed advice about a divorce. You know your father. He wasn't going to let that woman, or her boy, take a dime from you and Meg."

I stared at the wall. *Don't look shocked and don't lose your composure.* I had to unravel Dad's part in Caleb's deception.

"I know this is upsetting." She said. "You want some tea, honey?"

I needed answers, so I swallowed the gnarled ball of angry rising in my throat and squared my expression. Dad had shared Caleb's secrets with her—I was sure of it. But getting her to unlock them would require methods I found unappealing.

With a touch of syrupy southern lady and an air of indifference, I nodded. "Know what? Tea would do the trick."

She climbed out of her chair, and I followed her into the kitchen. While she located and filled a teapot, I rattled on about how much I appreciated her support. She beamed as she poured the water over the bag and dipped it in and out of the mug until it reached a satisfying shade.

"Here you are." She passed me the cup and lifted an identical one to her lips.

"So, Dad was protecting me?" I watched her over the rim of my mug.

"With every cell in his body."

"And keeping Faith and their child a secret was to protect Meg, too?"

Mom winced. "Poor Meg would have to learn about them soon enough."

"When was that supposed to happen?"

The corner of her mouth quirked downward. "Honey, Meg was bound to figure it out. It was only a matter of time. Caleb was leaving after her graduation."

"So when Meg left for college—"

"She was already planning to attend one of those East Coast schools, and he'd be in Maryland. They'd still be close."

The words emerged from her mouth gently, but they hit me like a battering ram. *Don't react, Sissie. Just nod along.*

"Mmm." I nodded. "I'm grateful Dad went the extra mile for us."

"I'm so glad you understand."

"He must've moved mountains to keep this under wraps."

"You know your father." She lifted a shoulder, then breathed out a huff. "His family comes first. He sat John down and made things perfectly clear. John would handle the divorce and anything that pertained to the woman and her child."

How generous. "And you, Mom?" I asked as gently as I could.

"Me, what?" She took a dainty sip of her tea.

"How did you manage to keep all this inside?"

Another long sigh. "Wasn't easy. My heart just broke some days when I thought about my daughter getting a divorce."

It was absolutely killing me not to scream, but I had one more question. "How long have you known?"

"Honey, that doesn't matter."

I squinted at her. "It sort of does . . . to me."

"Don't do this, honey. What's done is done."

She's onto me. Dammit, all. Might as well give up the charade. "No, really. How many times did you sit beside me knowing my husband was making a fool of me with another woman?"

She didn't answer.

"How many times were you with Meg knowing her father was breaking up our family?"

Mom opened her mouth like a gasping fish, and it took a long while for her words to materialize. "There was no use ruining Meg's last year of high school."

"What about me? Finding out my life with him was a complete lie?"

"You still have a family."

Without the words to convey my anger, my voice came out as a growl, "Where's Dad?"

"At home. He wasn't feeling well, so he's not going into the office until this afternoon."

I lifted my phone, and she frowned.

"Don't bother him right now. Wait until he's in better spirits."

"I'll give him better spirits," I said as I punched the keys.

I didn't waste a beat when Dad answered.

"So, Caleb was planning to divorce me when Meg graduated?"

"Um . . ."

"And you covered for him? Let John take care of his mistress and kid? What about me, Dad?"

A series of bumps and bounces came from the other side of the line. Then, silence.

"Dad?" I said through my teeth, meeting Mom's eyes. "Dad?" I shook my phone at Mom. "He thinks he can just hang up on me? I'm going over there. The lying stops today."

Part Six

Thirty-One

A fire-breathing dragon wouldn't have had a thing on me when I jerked my car into my parent's driveway. After all these years, Sissie Klein was ready to unleash a rebellion years in the making.

Dad let Mom control what he saw as the unimportant facets of my life, only jumping in when he felt so called. Sissie needs a homecoming dress? Kathleen's her girl. Sissie gets pregnant? Better call in the big guns. Thomas must lay down the hammer and show these little ladies how it's going to go down.

It had taken thirty-four years and two colossal complications for me to get here, but it finally hit me—I had the power to push back—and now this woman was ready to push with every cell of her body. It was my turn to lay down the law to the all-powerful Thomas Klein.

My parents' doorbell sounded out an abbreviated version of "Für Elise," adding to my mounting irritation.

"Ding dong, asshole," I said under my breath and punched the button again. "Answer, already," I yelled.

Dad didn't answer. I called the landline and his cell phone and only got more of the same. But when I spied through the garage door's windows, I spotted his truck.

That chicken's hiding from me.

Fury clouded my senses, and it took an excruciating minute to remember the piece of metal dangling from my key ring. With a twist and a push, I was in.

Hot damn. Let's do this.

"Yoo-hoo," I called without an ounce of congeniality.

The rose-scented living room was empty. I followed the voices of the 24-hour news channel that droned from the wall-mounted TV in the great room. I lifted the remote and snapped it off.

That'll get his attention.

Nothing. No, "God damn, who's messing with my TV?" No, "Who's there." Only silence.

Something splintered inside me, a warning. Things were off. Way off.

"Dad?" My voice cracked. I cleared my throat and stepped into the kitchen. "Dad?"

That morning's copy of *The Fredericksburg Standard* was folded in half and sitting beside a half-empty coffee mug on the table.

"I know you're here," I said in an uncharacteristically gruff tone. "I'll stay as long as it takes for you to come out and face me like a man."

Surely I've poked the bear enough now?

I snaked from the great room, through the dining room, and into the master bedroom. From there, I stepped onto their patio and was met by a brilliant red cardinal perched on the back of a wicker chair. It pointed its orange beak at me, and I shot it a dirty look. "Eff you, bird. Where's my dad?"

It fluttered away.

I returned to the house, startled when the glass door quaked closed behind me. "Dammit." My nerves were as raw as hamburger and my patience was zilch. "Where the hell are you?" I growled, marching into the kitchen.

"Ehh . . ."

The deep moan stopped me mid-stride. I rounded the island and found him—splayed out in front of the refrigerator, body contorted awkwardly, his face lax, his mouth open, and his eyes exaggerated wide.

I dropped to the tile, and he managed a faint whimper, although his words were unintelligible. His eyes pleaded for help.

I pushed a folded towel under his head and tapped 9-1-1 on my phone, my fury temporarily forgotten. "Hang with me, Dad. Help is coming."

"I TOLD YOU HE WASN'T feeling well." Mom said in a heated whisper as a nurse passed us in the cardiac care unit. "You shouldn't have upset him."

"I didn't do anything to him," I said through my teeth. "I found him like that."

"Klein family?" A man in scrubs gestured for us to follow him into a private waiting room. Once inside, he explained, "I'm Dr. Carter, the hospitalist caring for Mr. Klein."

Mom held out her thin hand. "Kathleen. This is our daughter, Sissie, and our son's on the way."

"Brent's coming?" I said.

"Of course." She cut her eyes toward the doctor. "He's an architect in Chicago."

"Oh," the doctor said, pushing a lock of black hair over his exposed scalp. "Mrs. Klein, your husband suffered a stroke in the left hemisphere of his brain, affecting his right-side functions."

Mom's questions were exhausting and elicited what soon became a familiar refrain: "Until he is stable, we won't know."

When the doctor left, Mom glared at me like I'd intentionally caused the stroke. "I need to call Brent," she snapped before walking down the hall to contact her favorite child.

I hovered outside Dad's room. After shooting a text to Lark to let her know about Dad and cancel our meeting, I considered calling Meg. There wasn't anything she could do, so why yank her away from school after she'd missed so many days already?

Mom came down the hall, bleary-eyed and walking like someone had knocked the wind out of her. I hooked her elbow and walked with her.

"Sissie?"

"Yes?"

She stopped walking and looked up at me. Her hand floated over my head like a halo. "You are . . ." She took in what might've been a painful breath for the way she bit her lower lip.

Pay attention. These may be the words you'll recall on her deathbed.

"You are in serious need of a color job." She pulled a gray strand plumb out of my scalp.

"Ouch!"

"Quit frowning. Those lines stick to you." She shook her head and passed through the door of Dad's room.

I followed her, averting my eyes from Dad's face. The room's simple furnishings and sterile scent neutralized all that had come before, leaving us to focus on a man who, at least for now, could not speak for himself.

"Hey, Grandma." It came as a shock when Meg appeared in the room.

"How'd you know?" I asked.

Meg glanced at Mom. "Grandma called."

Why am I surprised?

Mom's frustration with me was palpable. I was the horrible daughter who was responsible for my father's stroke.

Meg rested her head on my lap and peeled the plastic from a candy bar while I combed her hair with my fingertips. "A cardinal was on your grandparents' patio today," I told her.

"Aren't they supposed to be lucky?"

I sighed. "You'd think, but here we are."

Meg pushed a nougaty piece of her candy bar to my mouth. "It *was* lucky. If you hadn't gone over there, no one would've known he'd fallen."

Your grandma doesn't see it that way. My phone rang. Seeing it was Harlan, I nudged Meg. "Gonna take this outside, sweetie."

She lifted her head to free me, and I slipped out into the hall.

"Got a minute?" Harlan asked as soon as I answered my phone.

"I'm at the hospital with—"

"Your dad. I heard."

"Small town."

"Pretty much. Sorry to bug you now, but I wanted to let you know—I'm heading back to the mountains tomorrow. Seems I wasn't the only one who wasn't ready to jump when they opened the parks. Can't leave them uncovered."

My breath caught, "O-Oh."

"I was hoping to see you before I leave, but it doesn't sound like it's gonna work out."

My mind swirled with competing priorities. "I'd love that, but yeah . . . we should stay here with Mom."

"Right. I understand. You take care of yourself . . . and your daughter, your family." He paused for a few seconds. "And I really enjoyed our time together."

I felt a blush creep over my skin. "So did I."

Meg twisted around to look at me.

"Well, I appreciate your help with everything. Safe travels."

"Who was that?" Meg asked.

"Nobody," I mouthed back.

Just then, a nurse appeared and explained the strict visiting hours. Only one of us could stay with him.

Mom, of course, claimed that privilege.

Once we were back at home, I texted Harlan.

SISSIE: *Change of plans. They only let one person stay at night, so I'm home.*
HARLAN: *Can I bring dinner?*
SISSIE: *Cooking again?*
HARLAN: *Let me rephrase. Can I treat for pizza?*
SISSIE: *Meg will be here.*
HARLAN: *I'll share.*
SISSIE: *She's been through a lot. Can we keep things platonic around her?*
HARLAN: *Of course. What kind of guy do you think I am?*
SISSIE: *A gentleman?*
HARLAN: *What's with the question mark? I am a gentleman.*
SISSIE: *See you in an hour?*

As I showered and dressed, I told myself not to look too long or smile like a lovestruck fool around Harlan. Meg needed me, heart and soul.

The doorbell rang and Meg's bedroom door flew open. "Mom! Somebody's here!"

"I got it."

"Hey," Harlan said, wearing boots, jeans, and an untucked, collared white shirt. He sneaked a quick kiss as he leaned in for a hug. "Do you have any idea how beautiful you are?" he whispered, his lips close to my ear.

His proximity and that deep voice only reignited my appetite for him, but I straightened my face and took a step back. "Meg's in her room."

"How convenient." He winked.

"Who was it?" Meg asked from the hall.

"Harlan," I said, flashing a big smile at him. "Lark's brother."

"What's he want?"

"He's treating for pizza," Harlan answered.

She walked into the living room. "Oh . . . kay." Her eyes combed the space between Harlan and me. "Didn't know we were doing this," she sang in a whisper.

I put a hand on my waist. "Starving. Haven't had anything since morning coffee."

"Meg." Harlan nodded to her. "What kind of pizza do you like?"

She stared at him for a moment, then shrugged. "I'll pull up Peppy's on my laptop."

"Peppy's okay?" I asked.

"Sure." He watched Meg disappear into the kitchen, then swiveled back to me. "You look great." His smile accentuated his crow's feet. "How's your dad?"

I raised a shoulder. "He's in the doghouse with me."

"While he's in the hospital?" Harlan gave me a confounded glance. "Remind me not to get in *your* doghouse."

"Well." I inhaled deep, then blew the breath out loudly. "Don't conspire with my husband to cover up his secret family, and you'll be just fine."

With a salute and a smile, he asked, "How about them Bears?" pulled me close, and dropped a kiss on my collarbone. "Rrrrr," he rumbled, and the vibration of his voice bubbled across my skin.

"Remember our deal." I glanced at the flimsy door separating us from the kitchen. "Meg's in there. Come on."

His brows rose and his mouth twisted flirtatiously. "Yes, ma'am."

"Twenty-one bucks—twenty-five with the tip," Meg said as we entered the kitchen. "Hope you like Canadian bacon and pineapple."

He shrugged. "I'm usually a pepperoni guy, but I'll try it."

"Pepperoni's too greasy," Meg said, spinning away from the island. "Be in my room. Holler when it gets here."

"Will do," I said, opening an overhead cabinet. "Want something to drink?" I asked Harlan.

"Whatever you're having," he said.

"Scotch?"

"I thought you were going to offer me a beer, but . . ."

"Did I mention how shitty my day was?" I dropped ice into each of two lowball glasses I set on the counter.

"Scotch it is." He poured from Caleb's last bottle of Glenfiddich, one he had rarely enjoyed since moving back into the house. At least, he saved something good for me.

I would've invited Harlan to the front porch, but there was no use putting our relationship on display for the neighbors. Instead, we sat on the sofa, and I filled him in on the events surrounding Dad's stroke.

"I'm real sorry." Harlan gave my knee a squeeze. "Hope he bounces back soon."

"Me too. Don't get me wrong—I'm still ticked at him. But I never would've wished anything like this on him."

"I know you wouldn't." He lifted his drink, and we clinked glasses. He winced as he swallowed. "Ahh."

I took a hefty swallow and coughed. "Uh-huh. Forgot how strong this stuff is."

"Easy, girl."

His words felt like velvet on my skin, and that was before he laid an earth-shattering kiss on my lips. I knew I should stop him, but I couldn't deny myself. He made me feel like more than somebody's wife or mother, and it was a nice change.

Car lights flashed in front of the house, and I stood. "We're friends. Got it?"

"Oh, I got it alright." He ran a hand over his hair, flattening the mess I'd made of it.

Thirty-Two

I opened the door to Brent. "I left like five messages. Ever look at your phone?"

"Mom said she filled you in." I stepped back as he dropped his bag at my feet. "You look like you just came back from battle."

His hair was uncharacteristically uncombed and standing up in spots. "Had to fly standby, then got caught in San Antonio traffic." He waved a finger at my head, then took a sniff. "You drinking scotch?"

"Yeah," I said. "I'm a big girl, remember?"

Harlan cleared his throat and raised a hand. "Hey."

I introduced them, then plowed on, "We ordered pizza, and Harlan came by to tell me what he found on Caleb's hard drive."

The part about the hard drive was news to Harlan. He frowned and cocked his head to the side.

"What'd you find?" Brent asked. "Lemme guess: the freak was into bestiality."

"Your mother would be so disappointed hearing you talk like that," I said.

"*Your* mother would agree about *your* husband's freakishness. Hid a woman, a kid, and a dog. Wouldn't put bestiality past that jerk."

"Shh. That jerk is somebody's father—somebody who's in this house."

"She can't hear me," he whispered through his clenched teeth. "That asshole treated you like—"

"Is the pizza here?" Meg appeared at the mouth of the hallway. "Uncle Brent?"

Harlan's sturdy shoulders folded inward slightly, and he appeared at my side. "Seems like it might be best for me to take off."

"No," I said quickly. "Stay put. Please."

The doorbell rang, and Meg's eyes lifted to Harlan. "How should I pay the pizza guy?"

Harlan peeled two twenties from his billfold, but I put a hand over his to stop him. "You're not paying to feed my family." I pointed down the hall. "Meg, my purse is in the bedroom."

"Sissie, that"—Brent gestured to the door—"is not the pizza man."

I opened the front door. "Father Daniel." I wasn't sure how to process this surprise visit. "We're, uh, having pizza delivered—are you hungry?"

He shook his head. "Had a late lunch. Can I bother you for a minute?"

"Sure."

Taking in the others in the room, he added, "In private?"

I led him to the office and closed the door.

"Sissie, I got your thank-you note and the generous check in the mail." He glanced at his hands. "Your check was returned for insufficient funds. I don't want this to be a burden on you and Meg, and I doubt you've had time to balance a checkbook in recent weeks, but I thought I should let you know as soon as possible in case there were others outstanding."

My brain felt like it was inside a pressure cooker. I had been so dumb when it came to business. Caleb earned the money. Caleb paid the bills. I wasn't even sure how to log into our bank's site.

Father Daniel left as the pizza guy arrived.

"Wait," I interrupted Meg before she handed my debit card to the pizza guy.

"What's wrong?" she asked, looking hurt.

"I'm overdrawn," I said quietly. I felt the tips of my ears burning.

"I got it," Harlan said, removing that billfold from his back pocket again as he walked onto the porch. He handed the pizza guy the money and hefted the box. "Where to?" he asked me.

I signaled in the direction of the formal dining room, and Meg fetched paper plates and napkins.

As she returned, Brent tapped my elbow. "Need some help?"

"Huh?"

He rubbed his thumb and middle finger together, the international symbol for cash.

I turned to Harlan. "Any chance you could find my online banking login somewhere in that hard drive?"

"You got into Dad's computer?" Meg asked.

"I asked him to do it." I held up a hand. "I don't even know how to access our bills, Meg."

She frowned and asked Harlan, "When are you going back to . . ."

"Colorado? Tomorrow." When he finished his slice of pizza, Harlan folded his napkin over his plate and cleared his throat. "I'd better go, let y'all enjoy your family time. Lark needs me at the house." He moved toward the door. "Good to see y'all."

I followed him outside. "You don't have to leave so soon."

"I don't need to be in the middle of your business. My timing is shit."

I felt my face slump. "I hoped we'd get time together. Sorry."

"Not your fault. No time for a proper good-bye. I'll be back."

"You better."

He ran a finger over my chin. "Take care of your family." He kissed my cheek and squeezed my hand before he drove away.

MY FEET DIDN'T CLEAR THE threshold before Meg went on the attack. Arms crossed, jaw jutted forward, her eyes bulged with distrust. "What was *that*?" She looked like a bull about to charge.

"I saw him kiss you."

"Meg, please."

Brent chewed on his pizza slice, gawking at Meg and me.

"Tell me you haven't been making out with Lark's brother."

I didn't respond.

Meg inched closer. "He's old, Mom. Gross."

"He's not . . . old. Or gross." *Am I sixteen, defending him to my friends?*

"Tell her, Uncle Brent. He's *way* old."

"How old is old?" Brent squeezed his brows together.

"Not that old," I said. "A few years older than you."

"How many's a few?"

"Not helping, Brent."

"How many, Mom?" Meg demanded.

"He's fifty-one."

Brent grinned. "Explains why she's not coloring her hair anymore."

Meg stared at my hair. "He's right. Are you're growing it gray to make him feel better?"

"Why is everyone in this godforsaken family obsessed with a few gray hairs?" I complained.

"It's true, isn't it?"

"Actually, no. Since we lost your dad, people have been delivering groceries right and left. I just haven't had made it to Kroger."

"Well, tell us what to get so you don't end up looking old like him." Meg jutted out her chin and crossed those bony arms again.

Brent laughed, and I gave him my evil death stare.

"Seriously, Mom, do you like him?" Meg asked.

I touched her cheek. "I'm not going to lie to you. Harlan's timing isn't great, but—"

"We just lost Dad." She plopped into the chair by Brent. "I'm gonna vomit. Mom's macking with an old man." Her voice carried an ounce of humor and a pound of sarcasm.

Brent finished off his slice, nodding politely, as Meg ranted about her whorish mother. He wiped his hands thoroughly and tossed the napkin onto his paper plate. Then he sat a little straighter and cut her off.

"Meg? Your mom's a grown woman. From the second she knew she was going to have you, she's put you first. Time and again, she's taken the backseat so you would have a nice house with two married parents. You're not blind. You know how much of herself she sacrificed." Brent tapped the table. "About damn time to cut her some slack, don't you think?"

Meg shot him a look of disbelief. "You and Mom start getting along, and right away you two decide to gang up on me?"

"Your mom isn't doing anything wrong. I'm not gonna skate on by while you pin her down for enjoying herself for a change. Don't expect her to spend the rest of her days mourning a man who was scheming to divorce her and marry PJ's mother? Show her a little respect, will you?"

I was confused by his sudden protectiveness. "I can manage."

"*Manage* me?" If Meg's eyes had rolled any farther back into her head, she would've stared down into her spinal cord. "What . . . ever!" She spun out of the kitchen.

I took small relief in the fact that she looked more pissed off than tearful. "God help me." I dropped into a chair.

"I tried to . . ." Brent lifted his palms.

"This isn't one of those times." I gave a short laugh.

"One of those . . . what?"

I pushed my hair out of my face. "One of those Brent-drops-into-town-and-fixes-everything-before-he-catches-his-flight-home times. But it's fine. I know you mean well."

A line creased his forehead. "Wait. You don't get to do that—insult me, then say I mean well, end of conversation. You want to throw it? Hit me while you're hot."

"Besides being our parent's favorite child, with your perfect life—"

"Haven't we talked this into the ground? I'm not apologizing for a life well lived."

"You fly in and it's like, 'Here comes hero Brent to save the day. Just don't expect him to be around for dinner. He's got a big life in Chicago.'" I waved to no one. "If anyone forgets the towering level of your eminence, Mom beats them senseless with stories of your buildings, your famous friends, your—"

"That's not fair. After you had Meg, all I heard was, 'Meg did this, and Sissie did that. Why don't you settle down and have kids, like your sister?' No one cared what I did."

"Are you kidding me?" I raked my hands through my hair. "Living in your shadow is exhausting."

"When were you *ever* in my shadow?"

"My entire life. God, Brent, they changed my name because you had a lisp—"

"Will you listen to yourself? If I had a lisp, would Sissie be any easier to pronounce than Priscilla? 'Thithie,' or 'Prithilla'?"

I felt a giggle bubble up. "Say again?"

"Prithilla. Prithilla Klein."

We both laughed.

"Your nickname isn't my fault." Brent shook his head. "Mom just thought 'Sissie' sounded cute. You probably don't remember, but she tried to get you to call me 'Bubba.' Yeah. Can you imagine? 'Meet your architect, Bubba Klein'?" He chuckled, then grew sober. "When you found out about Meg, I told Dad we could manage without Caleb. I offered to come home to talk you out of it before it was too late. He said you were in love."

I barked out a laugh. "I was sixteen and getting a load of 'kids need married parents' every time I mentioned doing it myself."

"And, here we are," Brent said, snickering.

We sat together without speaking for a long moment; then I asked, "Did you know about Faith?"

"Last summer, when I came in for the Fourth of July, Dad said he didn't expect you to stay married after Meg graduated. I could tell something was up. Caleb had lost weight, was on his phone every time I turned around . . . no one told me anything concrete, but I had a pretty good idea."

"Huh. Didn't see it."

"Dad told me to leave it alone because he had Caleb"—he made air quotes—"handled."

"If 'handled' means helping him hide his secret family and make plans to divorce his daughter, then, by golly, Thomas Klein took care of business."

"I'm sorry."

"Me, too." I held out my hand, and he took it. "When Caleb left a few years ago, it took a while, but I pulled myself together. And right when I was ready to do it on my own, there he was, standing in our kitchen, full of his sorry promises."

He huffed a sigh. "I pried bits and pieces out of Mom, got the picture. The kid? The dog?" He jerked his chin to one side. "He certainly had a pair on him."

I couldn't argue.

"Enough about him." Brent stood. "Let's get to work on your finances before you bounce another check."

Thirty-Three

Lark arranged a meeting with Theresa and John two days later. Sensing another storm coming, I put on a mind-centering pot of hot tea that morning and pulled Meg outside for some front porch sitting.

Honk! A car horn drew our eyes to the SUV pulling into the driveway. *Della.* My stomach twisted with new verve. *Not today, Satan. Not today.*

She cut the engine and got out. "How are my girls?" she asked, nearing the porch.

Meg scooted to the edge of the swing, making room for her. "Sit down."

Della dropped between us, arms spread over the back of the swing. To her credit, she seemed genuinely worried about my dad.

Meg delivered the golden goose, filling Della in on the meeting we'd be attending that afternoon.

"My calendar's clear this afternoon. Let me drive you," Della said.

"No need," I said. "I can drive a car just fine."

Della's face shifted quickly, and Meg slapped my arm. "Mom, don't be rude. She's trying to show us moral support."

"That's really nice of you, Del, but this is only an information-gathering meeting. They'll probably keep us there for hours going over boring legal papers."

Looking like I had insulted her, Della put a hand over her chest. "There's nowhere else I'd rather be than by your side." She cupped my hand, then one of Meg's. "But I don't want to get in the way."

"Alright," I said—submitting, as usual.

Della nodded, and Meg bebopped to her room to get ready. She emerged in slim-cut jeans, a loose floral blouse, and Birkenstocks. Her freshly brushed ponytail and clean face made her appear as young as she was. It was a look that said, "I'm too darn young to raise a child."

§⟵

WHEN DELLA SLID HER SUV into a spot in the parking lot of my father's law offices, she looked at me. "What's your plan?"

I stared back, stupefied.

"You need a plan before you go in there," she spoke like she'd been through something like this a hundred times before. "Otherwise, they'll just roll right over you."

Thanks for the vote of confidence, old friend. I pulled myself together, hoping to look like I had half a clue. "I told you. We're collecting information. Nothing to be decided today."

"Sissie." She pointed at the building. "Look where we are. You're not meeting this woman for tea and crumpets."

"Lark will be here. We're supposed to stay quiet unless she directs us to jump in."

Della formed a silent "O" with her mouth, followed by a "K."

On the way in, Della's heels slapped the pavement, and a chill ran down my spine. The back of my shirt stuck to my skin, and my hands became so clammy I had to grip the handle on the door twice before I managed to pull it open. Della's presence could only make things worse.

Whether as a result of our circumstances or from the receptionist's oddly chilly welcome, I didn't feel I belonged—odd, because I'd entered that office hundreds of times over the years.

Lark smiled as we entered, and I watched Meg pull out a chair. I could only imagine how anxious she felt. She was too young to be there, defending her right to be a normal teenager.

"You look great." Lark's gaze traveled down the table. "Didn't expect to see you, Della."

Della's hair stirred around her face. "They needed moral support," she said, as if we had implored her to come. *That's Della—her train often leaves the station before I hear the whistle.*

Since I'd last visited that conference room, the dark wood paneling had been painted Nimbus gray, same as Mom and Dad's guest bath at home. All the fresh paint in the world couldn't suppress the scent of years of cigarette smoke, dusty books, and coffee from worming its way to the surface—a reminder that Dad, even when he was in the hospital, was in charge.

Meg and I sat on each side of Lark, and Della made herself comfortable in the leather chair to my right. She removed a pen and a yellow legal pad from her Coach bag to document the proceedings. *And I didn't even have to ask her.*

PJ's voice trickled down the hall, exciting and terrifying me. A few seconds later, he burst into the room, followed by John and Theresa.

John wore a white shirt and red tie beneath a gray suit—no points for imagination. His hair, whether by birth or by bottle, was crow black and combed away from his expansive forehead. I couldn't believe he had agreed to represent Caleb's mistress and child. *So much for a home-court advantage.*

To his left, Theresa looked like a schoolteacher in a long denim skirt, brown Dansko clogs, and a red cardigan. She wore her gray-streaked auburn hair twisted into a bun at the back of her head.

PJ, outfitted in a long-sleeve blue T-shirt, a pair of denim overalls with a yellow dump truck on the front pocket, and high-top tennis shoes, wiggled into Theresa's lap as soon as she sat down. A rashy circle surrounded his mouth where a pacifier had been. He grunted and shot a hand over the table to reach for a pen in front of John.

"Hands to yourself, please." Theresa ran a hand over his. "How about this?" She shook a few Cheerios from a green-lidded plastic bowl in her hand, and his eyes lit up.

He bent his chubby forefinger and thumb toward her hand.

Do you remember me? I met his eyes, and he lifted one to show me. "Yummy?" I asked.

Meg's aloofness faded. "Hi, PJ," she said warmly.

My Spidey senses chimed. I winked at PJ, communicating telepathically, *You're cute, kid, but you're not upending my girl's life. Got it?*

Theresa made small talk with Meg like they were old friends. "Your father always bragged about you."

"Oh." Meg sent a nervous glance my way before answering, "Thanks."

I thought I was smiling until she cocked her head at me. "Mom? Are you alright?"

"Sure." I thought I was convincing.

She covered her mouth with a hand and whispered, "Close your mouth."

"I'm sorry about your dad," Theresa said. "This has been a horrible time for all of us. I got to know your dad pretty well these last couple years. He wanted you and PJ to be close."

Meg's nod was barely perceptible.

"Maybe he should've told them himself," Della blurted out.

Lark blinked a warning.

Theresa fished around in a canvas shopping bag and pulled out a photo album. "This might fill in the gaps." The book's cover displayed cheerful red and yellow ribbons stretched over a navy-and-cream-striped background. From what I could see, the pages threatened to burst with hope and happiness; it was not the sort of book one would use to catalogue evidence of a deceitful husband.

Meg's hand hovered over it, hesitating to open it.

"Go ahead," I said as her eyes met mine. I swallowed, feigning courage, but I couldn't hide the dramatic rise and fall of my chest as terror shot through my veins.

Meg flipped the page, and I avoided looking inside. Once we saw these photos, we couldn't return to the safety of the darkness.

Della shot out of her chair to stand behind us. The first page slapped me with a photo of my husband's sunlit hands wrapped around another woman's swollen belly. Above the photo, artfully scripted letters stuck to the page, announcing, "We're expecting!"

Meg turned the page with one hand, squeezing my leg beneath the table with the other. Then she pushed back her chair and burst from the room.

I rushed after her and herded her into my father's office, darkened by heavy faux suede drapes. She dropped into one of the chairs reserved for Dad's clients, crying, and I passed a tissue box from the cherrywood credenza behind the desk.

"You don't have to look at those pictures," I said. "You don't have to do anything. Let's just go home. John'll figure out the details."

"I'm all he's got." The burden of her father's misdeeds was palpable in her slumped posture. Ever so slowly, her gaze floated upward. "He's my brother. If Dad had left us first and told me, I would've been in those pictures."

My heart tugged me down at the notion of Caleb's new family separating me from my daughter. She was right. If our separation had finalized to a divorce, there would've been angry tears, but Meg would've settled into our family's changed form, likely complaining how weird it was to have to spend holidays with her dad's new wife and kid.

But that wasn't how it worked out. Instead, Caleb climbed into that helicopter and a fresh hell was created for our daughter.

Meg wiped her eyes with tissues. "Dad loved those people like I thought he loved us," she cried.

"He loved you just as much," I said. *I think he did.* I lifted a round amber paperweight and shifted it from hand to hand, contemplating a wind-up and a toss through the picture window opposite Dad's desk. *Too late to punish Dad or Caleb. Give her the right words—make her feel like she mattered.* "Your dad had so much love, he couldn't stop with just one family, so he went out and started another. Not saying it was right, and it doesn't mean he loved the first one any less. He just had to do something with all that love before he spontaneously combusted."

Meg's lip trembled. "Not funny."

"What?"

She couldn't contain the laugh rumbling in her chest. "Dad *did* spontaneously combust. Sort of."

"Meghann Elizabeth Dietrich. That is dark, even for you." We shared a laugh. "Baby, we have to believe what we've seen. Without a doubt, he loved you."

"And PJ."

I nodded a few times. "And PJ."

"Where do we go now, Mom?"

"We could walk home, but Lark and the rest of them won't take too kindly to us leaving them in there with Della."

She laughed. "They might tape her mouth shut."

I shook my head. "Wouldn't stop her."

"If we don't take him?"

I shrugged. "John and Theresa—they'll find him a home."

"What if Grandma and Grandpa made you give me away? Wouldn't you always wonder if you'd given me to bad people?"

"That's different. PJ isn't your baby."

"But I have to make the same choice—to take care of a kid I didn't plan on having or give him to people I don't know."

"To be fair, you don't know him, either."

"It was the same with you and me."

"It's not the same. I carried you in my body."

"He's my family, our family. We can't give him away."

Her words hollowed me out. Seventeen years of "You can do anything you put your mind to" and "Use your big girl voice" and "Don't let anyone tell you who to be," and what did I get? An assertive young woman poised to make world-shaking, life-limiting decisions.

I had one last shot. "What about college?"

"I'll go to college."

Like I did?

"What if we did it together?" Meg asked. "Like you'd be the mom and all, but I would help. With everything."

"Meg, they're not going to let us—"

"If they did, would you?"

"Meg—"

"You love babies. I know you can't have more kids—didn't you want more?"

I gave a slight nod.

"There you go—instant kid who just happens to have a really cool sister." She smiled. "It's simple."

I practically choked. "How is any of this simple?"

"I used a Dr. Seuss quote in one of my essays, 'Sometimes the questions are hard, but the answers are simple.' This is one of those times. PJ's family—our family."

There was a knock, and Lark poked her head through the door. "Sorry to interrupt. Are you coming back, or should I ask if we can reschedule?"

"We're coming." Meg stood. "Before we go back, Mom and I were talking . . ."

Lark's head bobbed, and her eyes widened while Meg very cheerfully explained her idea.

"How do you feel about this?" Lark looked at me.

"Don't see what it would hurt to ask," I said.

"Sure. Sure." She seemed to be thinking and talking simultaneously.

"Can we agree not to commit to anything until we can regroup?" I asked.

Meg bypassed Lark's presence. "Mom? Even if you decide not to take him, if I do, will you stand by me?"

"I'll stand by you no matter what," I promised. "But please. Don't make any promises until you and I can talk it over."

Thirty-Four

Lark presented a "broad strokes" version of Meg's idea to the group—Meg and I would share the legal and parental responsibilities for PJ, enabling her to attend college as planned.

Theresa's expression relaxed. "I'm open to it." She stood and lifted PJ. "He needs a diaper change. Excuse us."

Lark took advantage of the break to address the financial snags caused by Voyce Brothers' complicated post-mortem salary payout with us. Upon Faith's death, the legal department discovered discrepancies in Caleb's survivorship declarations in anticipation of our separation. He had crafted two versions of his will, pre- and post-divorce. The man was nothing if not thorough.

Meg appeared bored and pulled that photo album into view again. She paused at candids of her father painting a nursery.

Neither of us was prepared for the next page.

At the top of the page, Caleb stood beside Faith's hospital bed. A blue surgical mask covered his rosy, round cheeks, and he was handling a goo-covered baby beneath blinding lights. In the next photo, he held the squirmy creature near Faith's weary face.

He made it for his birth. And photos, too? A baby born into the world with loving parents, plus photos—who'da thunk it?

A sigh escaped, and I clapped a hand over my mouth.

Della's quiet spell expired. She stood behind me and she huffed at the photo. "In the names of God, Jesus, and Mary."

"It's okay," I whispered.

Della waved at the book when Theresa returned. "This isn't fair to them."

I put a hand on Della's arm. "Stop."

"Did it occur to you that Sissie was married to him while"—Della threw her head back, sticking her sharp tongue against the side of her cheek, then twisted a hand at the book—"all this was happening."

"Actually, he was separated when they became a couple," Theresa said.

The band holding me together cinched tighter. "How long ago?"

"Three years." Theresa's voice was raspy.

"Three years, and he didn't have the courtesy to break it off with this family before starting that one?" Della gestured at PJ, who was cluelessly shoving another Cheerio into his mouth.

"Stop." I lifted a hand to silence her.

Meg's expression mirrored my own. "Aunt Della."

"Father of the year," she said, dropping into the chair beside me. "I hate to sound mean, but—"

"If you don't like sounding mean, then be quiet," I whispered.

Her head jerked back like I'd slapped her. She threw her arms into the air. "Fine. I'll be quiet over here."

"Sorry," I said automatically.

"It's hard for all of us." Theresa caught a stray Cheerio falling from PJ's hand. Her affection for the boy was as evident as the exhaustion on her face. She hadn't signed up as a full-time caregiver for a rowdy toddler.

"There really isn't any other family?" I asked. "No cousins? Aunts? Uncles?"

Theresa shook her head. "That's why she spelled out specific plans in her will. She had lost her own parents at a young age, so planning for the inevitable was a priority. It was important to Caleb, too. It's the reason he specified Meg and Martha by name."

"Doesn't it seem odd to you? Passing along a child to a sibling who never knew he existed?"

"I wouldn't call it odd." Theresa shrugged. "Experience handed Faith a warning, and she heeded it by making preparations."

John cleared his throat. "There's a house in Maryland," John said. "If Meg wants it—"

"I don't." Meg frowned.

"Then it will be liquidated, and the funds will be split between the children."

While Lark and John discussed the various insurance policies between Caleb and Faith, I patted my girl's back. "Hang in there. We'll get through this."

"This sucks," she whispered.

Theresa shot me a mournful look. "I'm sorry for both of you. You two deserve some time to process all of this. He said you might attend college out on the East Coast?"

Meg's brows rose in question.

"You'll get there," Theresa said warmly.

With PJ in tow?

"John?" Della began. "How did you ever pull this over on Thomas?"

A fair question.

"Actually, Caleb and Thomas made arrangements before they brought me online. Thom didn't want to be so closely involved, so he asked me to manage Caleb's af—"

"Affairs?" Della took advantage of John's abrupt silence. "A real gentlemen's agreement." She sneered. "How do you lawyers sleep at night?"

It was aimed at John, but it was a dig at Lark, too. I threw her a nasty look. "Would you like to step out?" I mouthed.

It would've taken a team of Clydesdales team to pull her from that room. She made the sign of a lock and key over her mouth and stopped talking.

With a sweet giggle, PJ touched his nose. "Nodes," he said.

Meg laughed with him. "That's right!"

"Meg, you didn't know about PJ, but he knew about you." Theresa pulled another book from her bag.

Not another walk down Caleb's East Coast memory lane.

The yellow-covered book was small enough to fit in Theresa's hand. PJ's face bloomed with excitement when he saw it, and he reached for the laminated cardboard pages.

"Who's that?" Theresa asked.

"Daaaah-da," PJ answered.

"That's right. Who's that?"

"Maaaah-ma."

"And, who's this?"

"Mug." He lifted a bent finger from the book and pointed across the table and giggled. "Mu-u-u-u-g."

"That's right," Theresa said.

The striking evidence of Caleb and Faith's unrestrained joy sent jealousy snaking through me. In a sudden surge of possessiveness, I wrapped an arm around my daughter.

There would be no satisfying resolution. I would always be on the outside of a family Caleb had created with Faith. Meg might not have known it at the time, but Caleb had integrated her into that family, too.

Caleb's betrayal went deeper than infidelity. He had conspired to keep Meg in his life, even as he conspired to cut me out of it.

As the surviving parent who hadn't lied or cheated on my family, Meg should've been my reward. But Caleb seemed to be winning the battle from beyond the grave.

John stepped out of the room, and I caught Lark's attention. "Can we step out?"

She followed me to the hall.

"Theresa's nice," I said, "but she's a glorified babysitter. Who is she to say where the kid goes?"

"Faith's will designated Theresa as interim custodian until PJ landed with family." Lark shrugged. "Better for the child."

"Not mine." I folded my arms. "John knows Meg's going to college next fall. Why didn't he cut this off at the pass? I can't believe my dad would've let Meg get saddled with his kid."

"Look." Lark's gaze shifted behind us. "As far as John is

concerned, PJ could sleep in the same kennel they're keeping that dog in so long as he thought both were warm, safe, and got two meals a day. It's just business to him."

"Shit, I forgot all about that dog. I forgot to tell Meg."

"No one's mentioned it yet. Break it to her when you get her home."

BACK IN THE CONFERENCE ROOM, everyone at the table looked like they'd been watching paint dry for hours—and we were just getting started.

John looked at Meg. "If you take him, you and PJ will have access to Faith's life insurance policies and the proceeds of her 401(k). It's a substantial amount." Head still bent toward the papers on the table, he raised a brow as if to gauge our interest in the money. "We anticipate a generous accident settlement, likely three times the amount of the trust." His dark eyes rolled up to me. "Sissie, you and Meg can expect to collect similar settlements."

"So if Mom and I take PJ, Mom won't have to use her own money to pay for babysitters and food and stuff?"

"Correct," John said.

I scrutinized Theresa. "You and PJ are close. Faith never considered you as a guardian?"

Theresa closed her eyes for a beat. "My health isn't good. At some point, this cancer's going to take me. He shouldn't lose another parent."

I took in a breath of dense, bitter air. My eyes crossed the table and met Theresa's. I mouthed, "I'm sorry."

"It's an ongoing situation. Most days, I can take care of myself. But when I have him . . ." Theresa ran a hand over his thin hair and smiled at him. "It's almost too much."

"You've had him since it happened, right?" Meg asked. "You must be exhausted."

Theresa nodded. "He's energetic."

"Let me take him." Meg's eyes shifted to me. "Just for a day."

What happened to no commitments until we can talk, Meg?

"Might give us a chance to wrap up some estate matters," John said.

"Is that alright with you?" Theresa asked, eyes on me.

"Of course," I said, but the words left my throat raw.

"PJ, want to hang out?" Meg asked.

PJ grinned at her.

She turned to the yellow photo book. "We can read your book." She turned a page and pointed to a picture of a round-bellied retriever licking PJ's face. "Who's this?"

"Woof-woof." PJ's eyes searched the room.

Lark put a hand to her forehead.

"That's Finn," Theresa said.

"Dad had a dog?" Irritation striped Meg's face.

"They got it for PJ," Theresa said.

"Her father wouldn't let us have a dog," I explained.

Theresa's mouth thinned. "Finn's a sweet boy . . . if you want him?"

"If she wants a dog, she'll pick it out herself. She doesn't need *his* leftovers," Della said.

Sounds vaguely familiar, and yet so much uglier coming out of your mouth.

She wasn't done. She always had more to say. "Wow. Pawning off a kid *and* the dog, John?"

Theresa squirmed a little and rolled her chair away from the table. PJ leaned into her shoulder, and she patted his head. "Better get back to the motel. Past naptime. Can we touch base tomorrow?"

"Why don't you let us take him now?" Meg asked.

Theresa didn't have to think about it. "He's tuckered out. Wouldn't be fun for either of you. Let's talk tomorrow."

While she packed PJ's toys and the photo albums, John asked me, "How do you want to introduce him to Martha?"

"How about cupcakes and a piñata?" Della looked even more pleased with her quip when I snort-laughed.

"No, no," I said, carrying on the joke. "Someone could get hurt swinging that stick."

"How about a petting zoo?" Meg said.

Theresa bent to pick up a toy that had just fallen out of PJ's bag. "Fireworks?" She lifted her gaze and winked at us. "Too much?"

"Fireworks are perfect," Lark quipped, adding, "Let us know how it turns out, John."

Thirty-Five

Meg was almost giddy as we walked to the car. "Having a brother will be fun."

My stomach clenched. *Fun isn't the word.*

She must've read my expression, because she pulled me close. "We're gonna be okay. I promise."

We climbed into Della's car. She turned the key and cold air blasted out the vents, creating a welcome white noise.

"Where to?" Della asked.

"Home. I'm spent," I said, rubbing my forehead.

"Cheer up, Mom," Meg chirped. "It's not like anybody's asking you to raise your secret brother."

Not sure you're getting the magnitude of this situation, "Mug."

"Aunt Della, did Mom tell you I caught her macking with a boy?" Meg practically sang.

Della's ruby fingernails fell from the gear knob, and she quieted the AC. "Pardon?"

"Mom's fling. She's getting back at Dad."

What's that saying about children being seen and not heard?

"Spill it." Della's face begged for details, and for a split second, we were sixteen again, sitting in the McDonald's parking lot.

I blinked away the memory. This time, I did want to talk—I could go on all day about Harlan—but I restrained myself because of Meg. I stalled, sorting out how much to "spill."

"Boyfriend, huh?" Della asked.

"He's too old to call a boyfriend," I said.

"Yeah, he is," Meg said with a heavy dose of sarcasm. "Real old."

I flashed her a warning look.

"Old, but nice," she amended.

"Is that what the gray hair is about?" Della asked.

I pulled at a strand of hair self-consciously.

"Harlan Lovejoy?"

"How'd you know?" I asked.

"He was there when I stopped by the other day."

"Where was I?" Meg asked.

I didn't answer.

"Jumping right in there." Della faced forward, her head bobbing.

I tensed. "I'm not jumping into anything."

Della turned toward Meg. "What do you think?"

She shrugged. "Mom deserves to go crazy with a dozen guys to get back at Dad."

The image struck me as one unfit for . . . well, for any of us to envision.

At home, Meg disappeared to her room, leaving Della and me to talk on the porch. I prepared myself for a good old-fashioned Della Betancourt grilling.

She wasted no time. "So, Harlan Lovejoy's your crypt-keeping lover boy?"

"Stop. You've seen him. He's middle-aged."

My mind went to the next sentence. *Middle-aged and . . . no. You can't talk about his chiseled abs, and you certainly can't discuss his strong shoulders, and by no means can you mention how your toes curl when his breath hits your cheek.*

Della worked her mouth as she considered the damage, studying my face.

I wiped both sides of my mouth for drool.

"Uh-oh. You are smitten."

I couldn't curb my smile. "Smitten's not bad." *Smitten's damn good*.

"How far has your lovefest gone?"

I shrugged.

"Kissing?"

Another shrug.

"Making out?"

Another shrug.

"Don't make me work through the bases, Sissie."

"Not nice to kiss and tell."

"Bullshit. How far?"

"Let's just say, when he's up to bat, you can kiss that ball good-bye." I reached a hand to the sky.

"Grand slam?"

Now more than my chest became warm, and I couldn't face her.

"Oh my gosh. A four-bagger?"

"Gross. I don't even want to know what that means."

"Get your mind out of the gutter. It's a baseball term."

"When did you become a baseball expert?"

"Weston started coach pitch."

"Aw. Maybe I can make it to one of his games one of these days."

She snorted. "If Meg gets stuck with that kid, you might as well camp out at the ballpark. You'll watch plenty, Grandma Sissie." She knocked me in the ribs with a playful jab.

Della, the great joy stealer, strikes again!

LARK CALLED A FEW HOURS later. "Whelp." She breathed out a sigh. "Just hung up with John."

I braced myself for the next gut punch. "And?"

"He asked me to make sure you were okay after today. Said he hopes you'll understand Caleb didn't tell you he was leaving because he didn't want to ruin Meg's senior year. You know, I used to think John was the progressive one in your dad's practice."

"Obviously, he takes us for hysterical women, fanning their vapors."

"The only feminist in that office was the office manager, and they ran her off." She gave a humorless laugh. "Anyway, with the two wills, John is hoping you'll allow them to execute the new one. We could fight to enforce the old one to prove your point, but I doubt you'll end up with more money."

"Hardly worth proving a point to a dead man, is it? What can we do to shut this down quickly? I'm not as worried about finances as the boy."

"There's always Martha?"

I snorted. "If Caleb thought leaving a toddler with Martha was any kind of possibility, he must have been out of his ever-loving mind." I paused. "Guess that much goes without saying."

She sighed. "So, how's your dad?"

"Haven't heard. With all that's happened, Brent's handling things with them."

"Can I say something to you as your friend, not your lawyer?"

"Of course," I said quietly.

"If my dad pulled a stunt like this, I'd be running barefoot up to that hospital to quiz him. I wouldn't do anything until I got answers."

"Brent said he's still nonverbal. And I'm not sure I could face him right now without screaming."

"To be fair, even the best parents stomp all over their kids' toes trying to help them. Misdirected or not, parents do what we do out of love."

"Dad could've shown his love without helping Caleb make me his fool."

"I hear ya, but . . ."

"What are you getting at?"

"Your dad just had a significant stroke. If he doesn't . . . make it, you might regret not talking to him about this before he was gone."

I grunted in frustration.

"Well, food for thought," she said quickly. "You've had a long day. Get some rest. We'll chat tomorrow."

A few minutes later, my phone pinged with a text from Brent: "Don't wait up for me. Sending Mom home to sleep in her own bed. She looked awful. I'm staying here tonight."

He was a better man than me, that was for sure.

Meg and I tucked in early that night, too tired for words. Thoughts shuffled around in my head—the scrapbook, the baby, the lies, Dad's stroke, and that ever-loving dog. Tired as I was, sleep wouldn't come. Eventually, I gave up, pulled on a pair of jeans and a sweatshirt, left a note for Meg, and sneaked to my car.

I drove to the hospital on reflexes. I hadn't thought through what I might say, or what I hoped to accomplish calling on my father in the middle of the night. I drove and sat at red lights, staring into the void when no cars crossed the empty streets, never once tempted to turn around. I had a stash of words piling up. Dad's stroke, be damned. All I needed to do was open my mouth and let them flow, give it all back to him with the delicacy he'd afforded me when he watched my husband's steaming pile of lies fall squarely in my lap.

I could've been driving to the dry cleaners. My hands didn't shake on the steering wheel. My pulse wasn't percussive. My mouth wasn't dry.

I entered that hospital like an old pro—like I'd been there a hundred times.

The lighted halls proved empty but for the occasional nurse parked beside a computer on a rolling cart. When I passed the nurses' station, a man glanced up and gave me a look like I didn't belong.

He's right. You don't.

"Can I help you?" he asked.

"Checking in on my dad—Thomas Klein?"

He cut the awkwardness short with a quick nod, and I traversed the next thirty feet of tile giving myself a silent pep talk: *Open the valve and let 'er rip, girl. You can do this.*

I entered the CCU. Dim lights shone through the opaque sliding glass doors that formed a U-shape around a centrally located nurses' station, where a few nurses spoke in hushed voices. When they noticed me, they stopped talking.

Act like you know what you're doing. I gestured toward Dad's room, and a nurse nodded.

With a deep breath, I peeled back the glass door. The chair next to the bed was empty; I assumed Brent must've gone to the bathroom.

"Dad?" I whispered and dropped my hand to the foot of the bed. The blanket moved, and a woman's voice moaned.

Oh, shit. This is not my Dad. Not sure which of us was more frightened. "I'm sorry," I whispered, backpedaling out of the room. I rushed to the nurses' station. "Did you move my dad? Thomas Klein?"

The man frowned and turned to the woman beside him.

"Are you family?" the woman asked.

"Yes, his daughter."

"He moved upstairs a couple nights ago. I think he's on four. Lemme check." She tapped at a keyboard and squinted at the screen. "Yep. 418. Take the elevator around the corner."

"Thank you." I made a quick escape, shaken by my wrong-room adventure.

By the time the elevator dinged at the fourth floor, my mental fortitude had all but cratered.

Dad's room was dark but for a dimmed lightbox over his bed; Brent occupied a cot on the floor.

"Hey," Brent whispered and rose to meet me. "What's going on?" I pointed to Dad.

"I'll give you some privacy. His notepad is on the nightstand."

"Huh?"

"If he wakes up, give him the pad so he can communicate." He leaned closer. "Writes with his left hand, so it's hard to read. Be patient." He pulled away and turned toward the door.

I waved to stop him from leaving, but the door clicked shut.

Dad made a sound, something between a moan and "Hmm?"

Without the bravado I had earlier, the little girl in me was drawn to hug him, but the woman in me held back.

This man didn't look, act, or smell like my father. Even in the dark, he was a smudged version of my "old dad," with gray skin, ruffled hair, and a droopy face. His feet protruded from a blanket too short for his body. Oatmeal-colored booties covered his stiffened feet. He was bent toward one side, his slackened expression resembled a balloon after it had been overly inflated, then deflated, and his thin arms looked frail beneath the sleeves of his T-shirt.

"Hi, Dad." It came out cumbersomely, like I was asking him about his golf game in the middle of the night. "Can I get you anything?"

His eyes closed, and I accepted the gesture as "no."

"Mom said you're making progress?"

His expression didn't change.

"Brent's probably driving you crazy. Are they keeping you comfortable?" I was out of small talk, and the big guns I had believed I would unload were now unreachable. Seeing my larger-than-life father like this, slumped and silenced, broke my heart.

You deserve answers. Hand him that notepad.

I fidgeted with the switch on his bed and light bloomed overhead. "I couldn't sleep. There's so much I don't understand." I pushed the notepad into his lap and removed the cap on his marker. "Here."

His left hand grasped the pen inelegantly, and his eyes rose as if I'd asked him to take a note.

"Why didn't you tell me Caleb was leaving?"

What do you want? A simpler question? What did Meg say? Complicated questions? Simple answers? There's no way that's gonna happen.

After a long stare, he scratched out, "Meg."

"You didn't tell to protect Meg. You both wanted to let her finish school—that's what John said. But what about me, Dad? Why didn't I get a say? I might've agreed to stay quiet until she graduated." *Could I really have continued to live with a man who had another family? Probably not. But for now that's my story and I'm sticking to it—for the sake of THIS conversation, anyway.* "Why?"

I leaned over him while he drew out the letters like a kindergartener: "S-o-r-r-y."

"You should've told me."

He tapped the word he'd just drawn.

"You helped dismantle my marriage, Dad."

One side of his face bent into a frown.

"I trust you did whatever you did out of love." It wasn't a question.

Embedded in his Picasso expression was a recognizable thread of remorse.

"It was a miscalculated, totally inappropriate way to show love . . . but it was love."

He nodded once.

"Hiding an affair? A child? A dog? Did you know Caleb even bought a house out there?" I glanced at him. "Of course you did. You *do* know it was wrong, don't you? Helping him lie?"

He tortured himself with shaky movements until the marker fell and his hand touched mine. I took it.

"Dad . . ." I started to tell him he couldn't do this to me again, but the man before me wasn't physically equipped to talk or walk. Intrigue wasn't an option. "You love me, maybe too much?" I smiled at him, considering what I'd do for Meg. *How far would I go to ease pain I perceived coming for her? Would I, could I, go as far as Dad?*

Dad had never shown affection easily. Until recently, I'd never doubted his love. Now, searching his face—strange and disguised by a cruel stroke—my gaze met his dark eyes and they told me what I needed to know most. It was the only story Dad could tell, one of good intentions and remorse.

An odd contentment settled inside me. So far as my father was concerned, I'd become unstuck. There were unanswered questions rolling around in my head, but none of them would be asked that night. And in the end, it was up to me to let those unknowns settle. The details of my father's involvement wouldn't amend Caleb's actions. They wouldn't bring Caleb back. And they wouldn't save Meg from the agony she'd already suffered.

For all that wouldn't be spoken, one thing was left to be said.

"I forgive you," I told him. *Make that two.* "I love you, Dad."

Thirty-Six

D ucking into my car in the hospital's halogen-lit parking lot. I reached for my phone and stared at it, craving companionship. Only one person came to mind.

"Hello." Harlan's croaky voice prompted me to look at the time. *It's 3:22 a.m.!?* "Crap. You're asleep. I'm sorry."

"Ah, it's . . . eh . . . you're fine." He groaned, and I pictured him stretching. In bed. Alone. Wearing. Not a stitch. "Everything okay?"

"It's been a long day."

"Calling it this early? Got a whole new shot at a good one, eh?"

I laughed a little. "If your days ended up like mine, you'd lower those expectations."

"I hear ya." The raspiness in his voice made me want to be there with him.

God, I want to tell him how I feel without sounding desperate. What the hell? I AM desperate. "I miss you." *There. That wasn't so bad.*

"Miss you, too. Miss you like crazy."

His voice, his words, heck, just hearing him *breathe* comforted me, like he'd removed a sad, wet wool cloak from my shoulders.

"Sissie?"

I closed my eyes, pretending to hear his voice in the darkness of his bedroom.

"The whole time Lark was driving me to the airport, I wanted to tell her to turn around."

I imagined how that would've ended up had Meg answered the door. This falling in love thing was new to me. *Can I be there for my daughter and give myself to Harlan?*

"You're sweet," I said. "When life slows down, I'll plan a trip up there." I knew I sounded a bit cold, but I was hoping to put his affections on ice until I managed the crosscurrent of the crises I was busy facing down.

I started the car. "Thanks for waking up to talk to me, Harlan. Go back to sleep."

"Alright. Night, Sissie."

❧

THE NEXT DAY, PJ WOULD meet his grandmother before attending a playdate at our house. Nervous excitement filled the air while we picked up around the house, searching for choke hazards and sharp edges.

Despite my earlier refusal to participate in the introduction, Meg's request trumped John's. It was unlikely Martha would agree to raise him, but who the hell knew what she'd say when faced with a boy resembling her dead son?

Lark picked us up at the house, and I attempted to maintain an everything-is-normal expression in an anything-but-normal situation.

"What if Grandma wants him?" Meg asked from the backseat of Lark's Sequoia.

The hairs on the back of my neck stood up.

"Legally, she has a right," Lark said, cringing.

"Then we're taking him, Mom. Not her."

Lark shot me a questioning look.

"Let's see what happens," I said carefully.

"Shouldn't we just tell Grandma we're probably keeping him?"

"Meg." I turned around in my seat. "We said we'd talk it through. We're not . . . I'm not prepared to say I'll help raise a child I just met."

Meg's pale cheeks reddened. "I'll take him to college on my own if I have to." She redirected to Lark. "I love my grandma, but she can't care for a kid."

"And you can?" I probably should've held my tongue, but I needed her to appreciate the gravity of the moment. "I'm not being argumentative, Meg. Attending school and raising a child at the same time?"

"No one told you how to do it. Look at me."

"I took online classes. I didn't move away to college. I had my mom and your dad. You're talking about doing it alone. I'm not saying I won't help you, but give me a beat to wrap my head around it."

"When we were at the meeting, you acted like you'd take him if they said it was okay. Now, you're sounding like you've changed your mind."

I heaved a long sigh. "Meg, I haven't changed my mind. I need some time to adjust my expectations. Raising another child commits me to . . ." I shook my head at Lark. "Geez, packing lunches, tonsillitis, volunteering at school, being there for games and class parties, and—"

"Fine. Whatever." She blew out a raspberry.

"Meg, I hear what your mom's saying," Lark said gently. "When I found out I was pregnant with Georgia, I was in shock. I had the boys already. Wyatt and I weren't married. And I never thought I'd be able to become pregnant again, so there was that, too. Raising children is thrilling and soul sucking, ecstatic and chaotic. You can rehome a dog. You don't rehome a child."

"I'm not going to rehome him," Meg said.

Lark's voice became gentler. "Honey, I love how freely you are willing to give yourself to your brother. But whether PJ lives with you or your mom, you'll see—once they're yours, they become part of you. When they hurt, you hurt. When they're stressed, so are you. Your friendships, your love life, *you* take second place to your child. Be nice to your mom. She wants to take it slow because she's seen both sides."

"But . . ."

Lark parked her car in front of Martha's house, and bent to face the backseat. "If you were my daughter, I'd pump the brakes, too. I'd want you to have a chance to enjoy the hard-earned opportunities you'll undoubtedly forego with a child."

Meg's smugness faded. She clicked free of her seatbelt and slumped in her seat.

I reached my hand out and squeezed her knee. "Sweet girl, I give you my word—if it's in your best interest and his, and they'll allow it, then I'll do it."

A smile hit her eyes before her mouth. "Love you, Mom. I'm sorry."

"Love you, too, baby girl. Shall we get on with this?"

❧

JOHN ANSWERED MARTHA'S FRONT door. "She's nervous," he mumbled as we passed.

A good sign.

We entered the formal living room, and Lark took in the dated wall-to-wall carpet and furniture upholstered with screaming floral prints in jewel tones. Not a recliner in sight; today, Martha perched on a gold- and cranberry-striped chair.

The doorbell rang and John left the room. He returned seconds later with Theresa, who was carrying PJ in her arms with the level of ease one might carry an entire litter of Saint Bernard puppies.

Martha didn't rise from her chair. She just stared at PJ, nervously pulling at the short gray tendrils framing her face.

Right away, Meg engaged with PJ—took him from Theresa, balanced him on her hip, and carried him over to Martha.

"This is PJ. Say hi, PJ," Meg said softly. "She's our grandma."

"Mug," PJ said.

"He calls me that," Meg said.

"Hmm." Martha appeared unimpressed with her grandson's cuteness.

PJ studied Martha's face, mirroring her frown, and I thought I picked up on the family resemblance.

"Doesn't he look like Dad, Grandma?"

"Red hair. More common these days." She side-eyed the child.

PJ lifted a hand to the gaudy black beads adorning her neck.

"Hi." Martha's hand rose as if to touch him, but then she stopped short, like he might bite. "So much excitement for a baby. Is it too much?" she asked him.

Too much for you, Martha? You can thank your cheating son of a—

"He doesn't have any family except us, Grandma."

That's my girl—wasting no time.

"I heard," Martha muttered.

John cocked his head to the side.

Well, good on you for breaking the news, John.

"And you are?" she asked, pointing to Theresa in the corner of the room.

Until then, I had forgotten she was there.

John introduced them, reminding her, "She's the woman I told you about?"

"I see."

"She's a friend, but we're his family," Meg explained.

"Can't she take him?" Martha asked.

"She's had health problems and can't keep him."

"I have health problems, too," Martha said weakly. "My neck and back. I can barely move. I couldn't lift a child." She turned toward John with impeccable flexibility. "He can stay in Baltimore, can't he?"

Yes, Martha. We'll put the toddler on a red-eye and rent him an apartment.

"Grandma." Meg attempted to pull her attention back to her and PJ. "Mom and I might take care of him."

This spiraled quickly.

"Until they find him a home?" Martha asked.

"Until he goes to college," Meg said.

"Mmm." Martha's head bounced back and her thin brows rose like Meg had slapped her.

"I don't want him to live with strangers. He's my brother."

"Honey, remember our talk?" I asked through my teeth. "About waiting?"

Meg shifted PJ to her other hip, blocking my view of him. "He can hear you," she said, also through her teeth, "and we don't want him to think he's not wanted."

"With school?" Martha asked. "This doesn't make sense."

Meg pulled her lips in and blinked, seemingly in search of patience. In a maternal voice, she said, "Grandma, if we let the questions shock us, we won't see the simple answers when they're right in front of our eyes."

I didn't love the simple answer, but I had to give it to her—she made short work of the explanation. We didn't want the boy to go to Martha, and Meg couldn't live with the guilt associated with giving him to strangers. I desperately wanted my daughter to go to college sans diapers and bottles, to have the experiences that had passed me by when I became pregnant with her. The answer was simple, right before my eyes.

Here we go.

"If it's alright with the law, I am considering raising him as my own, Martha. Meg can go to college like she planned, and her brother will be right here in Fredericksburg."

"You're going to raise the baby Caleb had with . . ." Martha glanced at John. "What's her name?"

"Faith."

She shook her head. "Why would you do that?"

"Because it's best for Meg." My gaze shifted to Theresa. "And PJ."

PJ pressed to leave Meg's arms and investigate his surroundings. He'd barely left Meg's grasp when Martha snapped her fingers at him.

Amazing how those reflexes come back when you need them, Martha.

"Grab him. My house isn't set up for children," Martha ordered.

All eyes went to her.

"He could get hurt."

"He might be ready for a nap," Theresa said. "I can take him back to the motel—"

"Can he nap at our house?" Meg asked.

"Fine with me," I said.

Meg looked at Martha. "Grandma, we can come back later, if you want?"

Martha lifted a noncommittal shoulder, and Meg pulled PJ to her.

"Talk to you later, Martha," I said firmly, and I led the group out of the house.

We followed Theresa to the car to retrieve PJ's car seat. She paused at the car, looking back at Martha's house. "That woman is not interested in PJ. Has she always been like that?"

"*That* was a good visit. You should see her on a bad day," I said.

"Sweet holy Moses, please promise you won't let her take him."

We hardly knew one another, but I sensed Theresa read my expression.

"What was Caleb thinking?" she asked, echoing my thoughts.

Oh, the possibilities.

⤥

ON THE WAY BACK TO our house, Meg said, "That was weird. I expected Grandma to be awkward around him, but not *that* awkward."

"I gave up trying to understand that woman a long time ago." I sighed.

"I thought she'd warm up to him, act like a grandma should."

"Has she ever acted like a regular grandma?" Lark asked, innocently enough.

"Y'know, she used to ask about school and pretend to be interested." She twisted her mouth. "But she wasn't like my other grandma. Not like a normal grandma."

"Normal—what's that, anyway?" Lark joked. "Give her time. She's dealing with—"

"As much as Mom and me?"

She has a point.

LARK FOLLOWED US TO THE house, helping us carry all the PJ-related paraphernalia inside.

"Call if you need anything," she said on her way out the door.

"You have done so much for us, Lark," I said. "Don't know how we'll ever repay you."

"Not to worry. John's getting my bill." Her mouth twisted into a wry grin.

"Double whatever you usually get."

She laughed. "Been so long since I was paid for legal work, I don't know what to charge."

After seeing Lark out, I followed Meg's voice to her room and found her giving PJ the dreaded "tickle torture" Caleb and I had given her. Just like it had worked on her, it delivered the same delicious, belly-shaking baby giggles from PJ.

"Wish we could keep him for the night," Meg said over her shoulder.

"You may change your mind when it gets closer to six." I glanced at my watch.

"Yeah," she said. "You love Theresa, don't you?"

"Meesa," he echoed.

"She's like his grandma. We'll have to stay in touch after she leaves."

"She may end up being the only real grandma he'll know," I added as I bent to pick up PJ's sneakers from the floor—so small and cute.

"What if we made Dad's office into his room? Paint it a happy little-kid color?"

"Maybe so." A hazy image of my daughter's college dorm room fluttered in the distance as PJ's kid-friendly bedroom grew before my eyes. *Not one or the other, Sissie,* I reminded myself. *Both.*

"Oooh, what about a sky blue?" Meg continued.

I lifted a section of my hair. "Think I could color this first?"

She sneered. "PJ, Mom's got an old, old, old boyfriend. If they get married, you can pretend he's your grandpa."

"No one's getting married, and Harlan's not anyone's grandpa."

PJ INJECTED FRESH LIFE INTO our house. Our first episode together felt too brief, but we took away bits of knowledge. He wasn't particularly fond of Goldfish Crackers but couldn't get enough apple juice. He enjoyed playing car—taking a caveman-like walk through the house while making his version of a buzzing sound, something like "mmmmm."

And we had no problem identifying two o'clock, when Theresa warned he'd be ready for a nap, because he rubbed his eyes and melted onto the floor.

While Meg took a call in her room, I carried PJ to mine, toting his book of pictures and his blankie. He snuggled at my side and pointed out his house—a two-story white brick with a narrow strip of lawn. He barked when I turned the page to Finn, the honey-furred retriever, and grinned at the photos of his mama and his dada.

I grinned back at him, hiding the sadness I felt for the losses he couldn't yet comprehend.

Thirty-Seven

Theresa arrived early and seemed pleased seeing PJ in my arms. Meg chatted her up about PJ's most mundane actions, then we discussed an overnight and making a smooth transition when—not if—Theresa left him with us.

Given Meg's insistence that he live with me or fall under her care, one way or another, his place in our home had become a foregone conclusion.

Soon, our family would take the form of a Venn diagram, with divergent circles representing PJ and me overlapped Meg's—the common thread, the heartbeat between us.

The joy of introducing a child into a family was, of course, partially overshadowed by Caleb's death and the death of a woman Meg and I would never meet—but PJ's buoyancy did offset the seismic undulations Meg and I had been enduring since the day those police officers rang our doorbell. Against all odds, we were maintaining our footing—fortunate, considering we were now committing ourselves to raising a child we'd just met.

※

AFTER THERESA AND PJ LEFT, I fell back on my usual coping mechanism: I made a cup of orange spice tea and planted myself on that swing in front of my house.

I set my mug on the small table beside me and closed my eyes to savor the sound of laughter that had just left my home. I would've stayed like that all day if not for the sound of a car door slamming shut, followed by my brother's inappropriately jovial voice calling, "Sissie!"

I opened my eyes, only to see that he was wearing his "I'm about to bail on you" smile.

He mounted the porch and plopped onto the swing with an unpleasant backward shove. "Good news."

I attempted to still myself in preparation for my brother's all-too-familiar exit declaration. "Good for who?" I asked.

"For whom," he corrected with a wink. "Actually, all of us."

"You're springing for a trip to Disneyworld?"

"Maybe next year. Look, they're about to discharge Dad."

I shook my head. "It's too soon."

"Discharging him to rehab. He's ready. They've done all they can at the hospital's unit. But hey, I found him a great place in Chicago."

"Chicago? Why not do it here?"

"It's time to get them out of here. I want them close to me. Mom can stay at my place, and Dad'll stay at the rehab a few blocks from my condo—close enough Mom can walk to see him whenever she wants."

"It snows in Chicago."

"I'll make them wear their shoes and buy a scarf for Mom before I make them walk to the rehab. Damn, cut me a break, will ya? Sis?" His expression changed and the confident spark in his eyes turned pleading. "I can handle this. For once, let me take over. Please."

I narrowed my eyes. "It's already a done deal, isn't it?"

He looked at his hands.

"When are you taking them?"

"Flying out next Monday."

"You can't drag Dad through the San Antonio airport."

"You're right. Called a friend who owes me a favor—he's got a plane."

"Thought of everything, didn't you?" I asked, but I was smiling when I said it.

He touched my hand, and for the first time in our adult lives, my brother had my back.

A long breath poured from my lungs, and I leaned into him. "Thanks. I mean it."

He reached an arm around me. "It's gonna be alright, Sis."

"Hope so."

"What'd you decide to do about the dog?" he asked.

"Shit. Keep forgetting about that damn dog." I tried to come up with a quick solution and gave up. "I don't know. John had it shipped to a kennel here."

"Now *he's* taken care of everything."

"He's sending someone after Caleb's car, too."

Brent shot me a look.

"It's been at the San Antonio airport since the last time he left."

"We could go after it," he suggested. "Might do you some good to get out of here?"

"Can't drive a stick."

"How about the dog? Can you *throw* a stick?"

"Ha. Ha. Got enough to take care of right now, don't you think?"

"Right." He slapped my leg. "Right."

A WHILE AFTER BRENT and I walked into the house, the doorbell rang.

I opened the door to Della and her stepson, Weston.

"Tell her why you're here," Della prompted the second grader.

Weston's eyes fell to the paper in his hand, then rose to me. "Um, I'm selling . . . I mean . . . my baseball team is selling these so we can go to a tournament after Christmas. They're chrys . . . chrys . . . chrys . . ." He glanced to Della. "That word's hard."

"Just say 'mums'—she'll know what you mean."

"Okay." He turned to me. "We're selling mums. You can pick red, yellow, orange, or white."

I wanted to buy two of each to help the kid, but I was still reliant upon Brent. "Can I order now and pay when they come in?"

"We're s'posed to get the money first," Weston said.

To his credit, Brent figured out the source of my reluctance right away. "Weston, can I see that order form?"

"Here," Weston passed it to him.

Brent winked at me and whispered, "I'm going to treat my sister, so don't show her what I'm ordering, okay?"

"How's y'all's dad?" Della asked.

"Better," Brent said.

"He's taking Mom and Dad to Chicago next week for Dad's rehab," I told her. "Giving me a break."

"Wow. Nice of you," she said. "What's Sissie going to do when she doesn't have your parents to chase after?"

"She'll be chasing a two-year-old," Brent said.

I laughed and winked at my brother. "Not quite two."

Della's smile slid like an ice shelf from a warm metal roof. "Sissie, no. Tell me we're not taking Caleb's bastard."

My stomach churned a lifetime of Della's judgment until it became rock hard, too heavy to carry for one more blasted second. Then my eyes dropped to Weston—a boy who was learning to toe her conveniently crooked line.

"However that child arrived on this earth, he is a child of God," Brent said. "I'm proud to tell you, *my* nephew will be Sissie's son before long. I'll ask you politely not to use that term around us again."

Thick silence held us in place. No polite "What he means is . . ." would arrive. No apologies. No cowering. I allowed my stillness to speak, and Della heard.

"We should go now. Weston, tell them 'thank you.'"

"Thanks for buying my flowers," Weston said.

"Good-bye," I said.

Della nodded and followed Weston through the door.

Brent shook his head as the door clicked shut behind them. "How do you keep from telling her to stick it?"

"Old habits die hard." I turned to face him. "I appreciate you sticking up for us. What you said was beautiful."

"And true."

My head bobbed a few times.

"Did I shake you up with all that talk about him being your son?"

"He *is* our family. My son."

Saying that made it real—no takebacks, no returns. PJ would be mine.

BRENT COULDN'T KNOW WHY I treaded gently around her.

Before my life-altering trip to San Marcos, Della and I were two young women who spent weekends drenched in Avril Lavigne's teenage angst, watching *MTV Cribs*, and taking *Cosmo* quizzes.

At sixteen, I worried that surly bouncer outside of Wiggins might call the cops when he inspected our IDs. Della didn't even blink when the man waved us into the smoky bar.

Once inside, we ordered rum and Cokes, speaking in near-shouts over a Missy Elliott song. We acted cool while a band took the stage and played aggressive drum solos and distorted guitar riffs to accompany machismo lyrics about getting her back, getting back at her, or getting behind her back. It was a night I was sure I'd never forget. *Correct-o-mundo on that prediction.*

Hyped up on the pretense of being a college girl and lost in the terrible music, the night was just getting good. I had Caleb's attention, Captain Morgan in my glass, and just enough courage to push back when Della insisted we leave.

The rest, as they say, was history—one Della believed she understood. The events of that night hung between us like a loose thread. I feared Della might pull it one day and unravel my daughter's life.

THE NEXT AFTERNOON, THERESA brought PJ over for the sleepover we'd planned. He was full of raucous energy, toddling around the house, exploring fresh territory. Seeing the world as he saw it was invigorating. I couldn't wait for him to live with us permanently.

After homemade mac and cheese, Meg and her friend Diego parked in the dining room to complete their trig homework while I assumed responsibility for PJ.

I had forgotten how satisfying evenings with a baby could be—playing with cups and bubbles during bath time, the smell of Johnson's baby-soft shampoo, holding a tiny, warm body inside an oversize towel. At bedtime, I held PJ—outfitted in a clean Pull-Up and jammies—on my lap beneath a quilt on the front porch swing, rocking slowly. I could've stayed out there with him all night, but Meg urged me back inside.

I carried him to my bedroom and placed him in the porta-crib Lark had loaned me. He didn't make a peep.

Meg sneaked in behind me. "You are an amazing mom. PJ and I are lucky to have you," she whispered.

I ran my hands over her shoulders. "Always wanted another baby. Who knew?" I chuckled softly.

Yes, again, we were the three Dietrichs—alive and well on Austin Street.

Thirty-Eight

When Theresa arrived the next morning, she appeared poised for a conversation about PJ's handoff.

Brent held PJ and stacked cups at the breakfast table as I gave her a rundown of the previous evening—how much PJ ate (most of his macaroni, a few tiny sprigs of steamed broccoli, and all of his fruit), how many Pull-Ups we used (three), and how long he slept (ten hours).

"You're sure you want to do this," Theresa said.

"Yes," I insisted. "I've thought about it, and I am convinced raising him in the same home as Meg will be best for both of them."

Theresa's mouth relaxed into a smile. "You've raised a healthy, bright young woman. You showed me who you were the day you picked PJ up at the church's playground. You could've shut him out. Instead, you put both children first."

I met Theresa's eyes. "Well, we are family."

"He's like family to me, too. I hope you'll let me stay in touch with him?"

"Of course. Any time you'd like to visit him, you're welcome to stay here."

"You've been too kind. Thank you."

We walked through a schedule for the transition. In the following days, Theresa would return to the East Coast, leaving PJ with us for good. The notion sent my head spinning—especially now, as my parents prepared to leave for Chicago with Brent.

Brent made the awkward car seat transfer while PJ and I kissed good-bye. As Theresa's white rental car pulled out of my driveway, she took a piece of my heart with her.

⚜

"Are you okay with Meg skipping school tomorrow?" Brent asked.

"I don't love the idea, but it'll give you two more time together before you leave."

"You wanna come, too?"

I shook my head. "I can't. Lark's supposed to run some papers by for me to sign. I need to clear out the office, anyway. Maybe even throw some paint on those walls."

Brent whistled. "Look at you, getting after it."

"Yeah, well, what else am I gonna do?"

"Let me know what PJ needs, and I'll get it, plus whatever Meg wants."

"I can't afford—"

"When the insurance comes through, you can pay me back. Until then, we're good."

I nodded, and he pulled me into an embrace.

"We've come a long way, brother," I said, squeezing him tight.

⚜

Eager to hear Harlan's voice, I called him twice, but each time I had to settle for his voicemail.

That evening, I got a text:

HARLAN: *Been a long day & I've got to get up extra early tomorrow, so I'm headed to bed. Sorry I missed talking to you. Will check in tomorrow. LY*

Fearing I'd wake him, I didn't respond. Of late, we'd been playing lots of phone tag. Left to manage with texts, our messages maintained the pulse in our relationship. His interest in my daily activities failed to satisfy the intimacy we'd shared in-person.

God, I miss his touch.

BRENT AND MEG TOOK OFF before the sun came up the next morning, and the growing list in my brain threatened to overflow, so I jumped out of bed early, too.

"This is where it happens, my dear," I told myself, schlepping empty boxes and trash bags to Caleb's office. Brent had drilled open the locked drawers, revealing bills addressed to our home in Fredericksburg and the one in Maryland.

I sorted items into piles I had labeled, "Keep," "Store," "Trash," "John Morales," and "Martha." In an act of self-love, I didn't examine documents associated with Caleb's Maryland address too closely. *I'll keep what peace of mind is left, thank you.*

By the time the school buses had picked up the last child in the neighborhood, I had hauled the bags to the trash pile beside the house and placed the boxes in a corner of the garage for safekeeping. On the way back into the house, a pleasant *ping* signaled a text from Harlan, and I peeled my phone from my sports bra.

HARLAN: *How's life?*
SISSIE: *Quiet. Everyone's gone. Think we could actually talk on the phone?*
HARLAN: *You have no idea how good that sounds. But*

I waited for him to finish his sentence. Despite an intermittent inhale and exhale of the dialogue balloon, however, no words materialized.

SISSIE: *Are you still there?*

A few minutes passed with no response, and I found myself second-guessing his affection for me as angry thoughts clanked in my head.

Stop staring at the phone, Sissie.

I walked into the kitchen and opened the fridge. Bring on the stress eating.

Ice cream. Frozen eggrolls. Leftover mac and cheese. Nothing sounded good. *Harlan's nothing special. Just a man. Everyone has a rebound, he was mine. Too busy to wait around for him. Heck, I'm about to have PJ to worry over.* Bread. Butter. Spray cheese. *Who the heck brought spray cheese into my house?* Cool Whip. Apples. *Stop thinking about that stupid, silly, handsome man.*

There was a knock at the side door. Before I walked over, I checked my quiet phone. Still no response. *Stupid man. Stupid Sissie.*

The face on the other side of the door was neither stupid nor silly. Could've sworn a crisp breeze swept into my house when I pulled the door open. His hair was longer, and a beard and mustache covered his face, but his eyes were as bright as I remembered.

"G'morning."

Oh, and that voice.

Restrain yourself, woman. "I'm sorry. Do I know you?" I teased, squinting and running a hand around his face. "Who's hiding under all that hair?"

Harlan scratched the back of his neck and angled his eyes at me.

I touched his chin. "What's all this?"

"Ah, giving my razor a rest."

He followed me inside, and I told him about Brent taking Meg to San Antonio and my parents' upcoming trip to Chicago. He leaned into my hair and whispered, "So, nobody's here?"

His scruff brushed my face, and my skin grew hot. *Words. Find them.* I blinked a few times and squeaked out, "They'll be home this evening."

He wrapped an arm around my waist and pulled me into him. A pleasant tingle trailed up my spine. "What are you doing here?"

"You asked if we could talk. Here I am."

"I meant on the phone. How did you—?"

"I landed in Austin this morning." He leaned toward me, and that mix of spice and soap hit my senses with a mind-numbing slap. "I have three days off, and there's no one else I'd rather spend 'em with. But if it's not a good time, I'm sure Lark'll put me to work." He gave me that sideways smile, and tiny lines appeared around his eyes.

I cocked my head to the side and dropped my voice. "*I'll* put you to work."

"Alright." His head hovered over me, and a flush crept up my neck. "I see." His thumb brushed my bottom lip and longing overwhelmed my senses.

Harlan and an empty house. Oh, the possibilities.

"God, I missed you." He cupped a hand behind my head.

What are you waiting for?

At last, his kiss landed. My heart raced, and warmth swept through my body. Our breaths grew ragged while his hands tugged me as close as our bodies could stand without melting into one another.

"Nobody but us chickens. Shall we?" I nudged my head backward. He got the hint.

A FEW HOURS LATER, HARLAN rummaged through my fridge, removing Gruyere cheese, butter, sliced ham, and a half-eaten baguette. A half hour later, he'd created the best grilled cheese sandwich I'd ever eaten.

My phone pinged with photos of a crib that converted into a toddler bed from Meg.

"I've got to get that room ready," I told him.

"When does the little guy move in?" he asked around a mouthful of sandwich.

"Assuming nothing goes wrong? Monday."

"What could go wrong?"

"Every time I think this nightmare is all wrapped up, it produces another surprise."

He pushed his empty plate toward the middle of the table. "Okay, what do you say we focus on what we can control. Wanna start with that room?"

"Sure." I took a drink of my iced tea. "Can you help me take down the bookshelves?"

"Give it a whirl."

We traipsed down the hall to the old office, and he scanned the wall of bookshelves. Confusion was evident on his face. "Why are you taking these out?"

"Too dark for a kid's room."

"Nothing a coat of paint won't fix."

"Really hoping to avoid a big project."

He threw me a wink. "Alrighty. Run to Lowe's?"

THE LOWE'S ON MAIN HAD A WALL of paint swatches to choose from—too many choices, I found. Staring at the swatches, I felt a smile creep onto my face.

"What's so funny?" Harlan asked, pointing to my mouth.

"Did Lark ever tell you how we became friends?"

"Sort of . . ."

"One day I stood in this very spot, looking at paint chips to paint the walls of that very room—Caleb's office? Lark walked up to me, and somehow, she knew I was hurting." A heaviness landed on my chest, and my mouth pinched tight. "Without prying, she simply offered to listen. It was when Caleb and I were separated. I told her how Caleb didn't want me to talk about our business around here, and she hooked me up with a friend of hers—a counselor in Houston." I swallowed.

"Julia?"

"You know her?"

"Oh, yeah. Her husband worked with Lark's first husband, James."

"We've never met face to face, but Julia's been a fabulous listener."

He gave a quick nod. "She did that for Lark when James got sick."

"That's what Lark said." I shook my head, releasing images of the darker days before Caleb moved out. "Then Lark moved back here and I couldn't do anything right. In his eyes, she was the perfect woman."

"Eh." He paused. "Did she tell you about the year Caleb took her to homecoming? Annika and I came back for the homecoming game. There was Lark with this giant mum on her shoulder—the kind with all the ribbons and crap hanging off it?" He snickered.

"Uh-huh."

"After the game, Annika and I walked into the dance, figured we'd say hi to our old teachers. There was Lark, playing third wheel with a friend and her date." He gestured with a paint chip.

"Where was Caleb?"

"In the parking lot, drinking with some guys. Finally strode into the school commons and told Lark he was going to a party. Lark passed on the party and came home with us."

"What a jerk."

He cocked a brow. "I wanted to kick his ass." He set the paint chip down and wrapped an arm over my shoulders. "For what it's worth, *you're* the perfect woman."

I flashed a dubious smile.

"*My* perfect woman."

"Stop it," I said, embarrassed by his flattery.

"Have you ever been around someone who just peels it all back? Sees everything—the good and the bad—and makes you feel like all of it's okay?"

I didn't answer.

"No? Nobody ever made you feel safe to be like that?"

I looked down. "No."

"I'm real sorry," he said gruffly. "That's how I feel when I'm around you."

Thirty-Nine

At home, I changed into old clothes while Harlan set off to tape off the bookshelves. We worked in tandem in separate spaces—I tackled the shelves in the garage while Harlan coated the dark walls with soft blue paint and wiped it off, resulting in a marriage of old and new.

He carried paint rags into the garage as I was finishing up my first coats on the shelves. "Where can I toss these?"

I waved to a metal shelf. "We'll let them dry out over there. How are you done already?"

"Told you it wasn't difficult." He inspected my work. "Looking good."

"Can I see?" I asked.

He rolled his hand in a circle, pointing to the door into the house, and we walked inside together.

The thin coat of chalky blue paint had softened the look of the dark wood. It was perfect for a little boy's bedroom.

"Sissie?" a voice called from the vicinity of the kitchen. Lark.

"Back here." I had almost forgotten about signing those papers.

"Hope it's okay I walked right in," she called as she came down the hall. "Your side door was propped open." She stepped into the room and smiled when she saw her brother. "Oh, I almost forgot you were coming today. You came here first. Guess I see where I rank."

I could've sworn Harlan blushed a little.

"I won't take much of your time," she said, lifting a pile of papers. "Only need a few signatures."

"I'm gonna check how those shelves are drying," Harlan said, excusing himself.

Lark pushed a document into view. "This is your agreement for the temporary orders making you the custodial guardian, with Meg as the alternate after she turns eighteen."

"Temporary?"

"In six months, they'll schedule a home visit with a rep from the court, maybe a child psychologist, too. Just a procedure to confirm he's doing well—which he will be, so don't let that worry you—and then you'll go to court to finalize everything. By then, we'll know more about the financial part."

"Sure hope they get this straight soon."

"If you need a loan, we can—"

"Thanks. Brent's helping me. It'll be good to pay him back and pay my own bills."

"When I return these to John, I'll nudge him about Caleb's 401(k) at Voyce. They really should've cut a check by now. What else?"

I lifted my hands.

Harlan returned, placing his hands on my shoulders.

"I'll touch base to confirm the handoff. I've got to run. Y'all have fun doing whatever you're doing," she said slowly.

"Painting. We are painting," Harlan said.

A FEW HOURS LATER, MEG rushed into the house with a big grin on her face. That grin slipped when she saw Harlan. "Oh. You're back."

"He surprised me this morning," I said.

"Great," she said, flatly.

"We painted the bookshelves—they look great," I told her.

"I thought we were getting rid of them."

"Changed my mind. Come, look." I led her to PJ's room.

"Hmm." She tugged me back out of the room, more interested

in showing me what she and Brent bought. "The crib and dresser will be delivered next week."

"This is too much."

"For my nephew?" Brent said.

Harlan's value increased exponentially when he helped unload the car, which was packed to the brim.

I pulled Meg aside. "See? He's not so bad."

Her mouth twisted doubtfully. "It's strange having him around. Like, he just shows up whenever."

"It was a surprise."

"What if you and I had plans?"

"We didn't."

"It's like he thinks you're gonna marry him or something." She huffed a laugh. "No offense, Mom, I know you're not completely clueless, but . . . you need to have"—her head kicked back—"the talk."

"What talk?"

"The FUTAB talk."

"Foot-what?" I shook my head.

"Feet Up, Take A Break." She gave me her "duh, Mom" expression. "Don't wait too long or the poor old guy might freak when you cut him loose."

What if I don't want to cut him loose?

"Got company," Brent hollered as he carried a crib mattress into the house.

Meg took one look at who was making a beeline toward us and disappeared into the house without a backwards glance.

"Moving day?" Della asked.

"Prepping PJ's room," I said.

"Cool," she said, confusing me. "Oh, you've got blue on your nose."

I glanced over at Brent's car, where Harlan and he were talking. "We were painting." I swiped at my nose.

"You and . . . Harlan?" she asked with a false smile.

"Yep." I wiped my forehead. "Been a long while since I've had a little kid in this house." I felt my brows pitch up.

"Buckle up. It's a wild ride." When her laugh died, she paused and looked at Harlan a bit too long. "Is he sticking around?"

"He's still working in Colorado."

She gave an unimpressed, "Hmm," and shifted to me. "How's your dad?"

"Well . . ." I explained the upcoming move to Chicago.

She nodded as I described Brent's plans, but her gaze drifted back to Brent and Harlan. I stopped talking.

"A lot of changes around here." She looked at me again. "Be careful."

"We're good."

"Show me that room," she said.

You mean, "Let's go somewhere I can ask questions?"

"Looks good without the desk." Della gestured to an open wall. "Putting the bed here?"

"Maybe. Haven't really thought it completely through."

"Harlan or PJ?" she mumbled.

"Del. I'm talking about the room."

"Fine. Just don't want to see you rush into a relationship and get hurt." She jerked her head toward the door. "You two getting serious?"

I shrugged.

She stepped toward me, and I steadied myself. *This is my life. Get on board or move on down the road.*

"You've been through so much, Sissie. Don't get caught up in the romance of playing house—especially, now that you've got PJ to consider."

"Playing house?"

"He just happens to show up when you're at a low point, helps you make a home for the kid." She gestured toward the bookshelves. "Then, what?"

"Enjoying each other's company, playing it by ear."

"Never married at fifty-whatever? Doesn't concern you?"

It was tempting to respond, but it wasn't her business.

"I asked around about him. This isn't the first time. He's all about the chase, the wild romance, the sweet gestures—he surprises you, puts his life on hold to help you with your house, tells you everything you ever wanted to hear, and, yes, Sissie. I noticed the voice. I'm not deaf." She laughed to herself. "You have to protect yourself, and your children."

"I am." *Don't react. Don't react. Do not react.*

"He's not Mr. Everything. He's just a guy. One who's identified you as vulnerable. He sweeps in, wins your heart, and then, I hate to say it, he'll drag you down like the last one."

"I was sixteen when I met the last one." I sucked back a breath between my gritted teeth.

"Uh-huh. And now, like I said, you have another child to consider."

"Del, give it a rest. I'm a grown woman."

"One who's made a lotta mistakes. Your way of dealing scares me."

Like the slamming of an iron door, what passed between us was unmistakable—an acknowledgment of the secret that defined our friendship.

"It's been a lotta years, but I'll never forget that morning, Sis. You couldn't remember what happened or if he . . . if you were . . ." She bobbed her head.

I glanced at the open door behind her. "Del, not now." *Or ever, frankly.*

She did not stop. "A few months later, you're this happy teenage wife to a man who treated you like shit, and a mother to his kid."

"What's wrong with you?" I demanded.

"So it's my fault?" She crossed her arms. "All I'm saying is you take 'bloom where you're planted' entirely too far. Take it slow. Find out what you want before you take on more children or men?"

"Mom?" Meg slid into the room, her brows pulled down. "What's going on?"

"Della's just leaving," I said.

Della stared at me for a long moment.

"Right? You were on your way out?"

"If you say so." She breathed out a loud sigh and walked out.

Meg was staring at me. "Mom, what was all that about Dad treating you like shit? And you not remembering. What does that mean?"

I stared at the ceiling. *Thanks, Della.*

"What don't you remember?" She wasn't letting me off the hook.

"Come here." I pulled her down the hall and into my room. When we were seated on the loveseat at the end of my bed, I said, "You know how you were conceived—or, rather, when."

"Knocked-up in high school." She slapped my leg. "Got it. What else should I know?"

"Della and I went to a club that night and met your dad there."

"I know all that."

"I went back with him to this duplex that belonged to one of his friends, but we were the only ones there." I waved my arm to conjure the scene. "Other people were supposed to join us, but they didn't, so we watched a movie and drank too much. I drank too much and couldn't remember everything. Della has always assumed . . ."

"Did Dad date rape you?" Meg's chin quivered; hurt was all over her face.

Technicolor memories of that weekend in San Marcos flooded my mind, but all I wanted was to be here with Meg.

"Mom?"

I blinked a few times, but the pictures only snapped tighter in my mind.

"Did he?" Meg pressed.

"I was sixteen, acting like I was older. I woke up naked and freaked out." My mouth became cottony. I swallowed. *Don't make her question her entire life. Don't lie to her. Just tell her what you know and play it as it lays.*

§≪

"DAD WOULDN'T . . . WOULD HE?" Meg's eyes dug into me, speaking to the consequence of my explanation.

"I was sixteen, hanging out with people who were used to drinking and . . ." I lifted my brows.

"Hooking up?" she asked.

"Yeah."

"So you guys hooked up, and you weren't into it?"

"Actually, according to your dad, I was very into it."

"Gross."

"You asked."

"Fine." Meg waved her hand for me to continue.

"I remember bits and pieces. Not everything." I paused. "I was holding a beer and watching Austin Powers. Then, I woke up . . . well . . . you understand. I was in a place I shouldn't have been, drinking and carrying on with an older boy who was used to doing that sort of thing with college girls." My voice rose. "Which . . ." I pulled in a deep breath. "Is why you must always remember to keep your wits about you. Don't go off alone with a guy you don't know."

"Because they'll take advantage?" It wasn't hypothetical.

"They can." I put up a hand. "That doesn't mean your father did. Meg, what's most important for you to remember is this: you have to be in charge of you. If you're not familiar enough with a person, you shouldn't go off alone with him . . . or her."

"Him, but whatever."

I slapped my legs, hoping my explanation was sufficient.

"Mom, Della said Dad treated you bad."

"He wasn't a gentleman that next morning, I'll give you that." I lifted a shoulder. "He was hung over, and guys take longer to grow up."

"Don't make excuses for him. If he was a jerk, he was a jerk."

She didn't get her bluntness from me.

"So Dad was a jerk who hooked up with a drunk sixteen-year-old, but he didn't rape you." It was a statement, and she nodded as she said it. "I can live with that. Can't change it now."

Since that night seventeen years ago, I had dragged an anchor behind me—riding a fine line between Caleb and Della, a line that intensified when Meg became old enough to understand the implications. What Della believed was insignificant. I had shared the truth as I remembered with Meg, the person who deserved it most.

Meg seemed satisfied with my explanation. Then her expression twisted. "I don't get why Aunt Della's bringing it up after all these years. She really needs to get a life. No wonder Dad didn't like her."

"You noticed?"

"He told me."

Of course he did.

"He said all she did was stick her nose where it didn't belong. I don't think he got to see the times she was nice to you."

And vice versa. Then, again, put oil and water together, and . . . "They brought out the worst in each other. Wasn't easy being her friend and his wife at the same time."

"Glad you chose Dad."

Actually, my *dad chose, but tomato, tomato.*

Those big, trusting eyes met mine. "I'm sorry for making one night mess up the rest of your life."

"I'm not. Not one bit sorry." For a moment, she was little again, needing me to help her understand. A tear hit my cheek as I pulled her into me. "Baby, you *are* my life. You are my life's purpose."

Forty

The next morning, Harlan showed up with a box of warm donuts. "Breakfast—fuel for learning." He craned his neck, scanning the house. "Where's she at?"

"She's in bed. I'm letting her skip again. I know, mother of the year, right? Brent's leaving tomorrow, and PJ's coming tomorrow. Aah, it's a lot."

He looked at the box of donuts with regret.

"Teens like to sleep in. Don't take it personally," I offered. "Coffee?"

"You bet." Harlan bobbed his head a few times and stopped suddenly. "You okay . . . with all this?" He ran a finger over one eyebrow. "Taking on a child is major."

"Yeah, well, it's the right thing to do . . . for both of them. And I always wanted more kids." I gave a small shrug.

He frowned a question I could see he didn't want to ask.

"I hemorrhaged when she was born. They took my . . ." I ran a flat hand in a circular motion across my lower abdomen. "So, she was my miracle baby, my one and only." I sighed loudly. "Caleb didn't want to adopt."

"Ah." More head bobs.

I imagined more questions were bubbling up in his handsome head, but he didn't ask them. Not one. He just tilted his head to one side and offered a sweet grin that told me he was trying to understand.

"How about you? Ever want kids?"

"With the right person."

"You told me about Annika. You were never with anyone else?"

"Sure."

I thought about what Della said. "For how long?"

"Mmm." His gaze rose to the ceiling and his lips twisted. "A year, six months, a couple months. I'm old, Sissie."

"How many would you say? Hundreds?"

"Jesus, who do you think I am? Hundreds . . . sheesh."

"Dozens?"

"In my entire life? Sure."

Jealousy took me by surprise. I'd only been with two men before Harlan. Not men. Boys, really. While Harlan was sampling the women of the world, I'd been stuck in Fredericksburg with Caleb. I wished we'd never gone there, because I couldn't sweep the pictures of Harlan and other women from my mind. I sensed a punchiness overtaking my newly minted joy, and I excused myself to check on Meg.

"Donuts in the kitchen," I called into her room, then turned back down the hall.

Was Della right?

Meg was hot on my heels, entering the kitchen like a bear waking from hibernation in spring. "Where are the donuts?"

"Good morning, Meg," Harlan said.

Her head made a slow roll to him. "Hey."

"They were warm when I got here."

She peeled back the lid on one of the boxes, then looked at Harlan. "How long are you in town?"

"Leave this evening."

Nodding, she stuck half a cherry glazed donut in her mouth.

"If I'm in the way, I can hang out at Lark's today," Harlan said, pushing back his chair.

"Have another donut," I said.

Harlan became fidgety. He walked to the sink and peered through the window. "Your mail comes early."

I shrugged. "Some days."

Meg rose quickly, her words indiscernible. With a donut in her mouth, she zipped through the side door.

Harlan's expression asked for an explanation.

"Watches the mail like a hawk . . . for college acceptance letters."

"This early?"

"A few of her classmates have already locked in early decision." I picked a hunk of donut out of the box.

"You can have a whole one," he said.

"Pacing myself." I shoved the chocolaty dough in my mouth.

"Oh, my God." Meg flew through the kitchen door. She dropped the mail onto the island, but for the envelope she clutched like it held the golden ticket. "Oh, my God. Oh, my God. I'm so nervous." She stood over me at the table.

"Which one?" I asked.

"Richmond."

"Top choice," I mouthed to Harlan and crossed my fingers, although I had mixed feelings about her attending college so far from home.

She unfolded the letter with care and traced the words with her index finger, her lips moving while she read it silently. After a long moment—too long, if you ask me, she turned to face me, her eyes nearly glittery. "Mom. Mom. Mom. Mom. Mom."

I stood to look over her shoulder.

Her voice started faintly, but grew into a near shout as she said, "I got in. I got early admission to Richmond."

My heart rose and fell with the news, and I hugged her. Correction: I tried to hug her while she jumped up and down.

"Congratulations," Harlan said. "A beautiful campus."

"Been there before?" Meg's indifference warmed.

"Yup. A friend of mine grew up there."

A friend of his? Bachelorette number what?

"Am I really okay to go, Mom?"

"Yes, honey. PJ and I will be here to visit during breaks and during the summer. This is good news. Celebrate your hard work—you earned this."

"You've got to make the jump when it's your chance," Harlan said. "Your mom's a smart lady. She'll take care of things back here at the ranch."

He meant well, but I bristled inside, and Meg's expression told me she agreed.

"It's normal to be nervous. We can talk about it more later." I winked at her, hoping to postpone the conversation until we could have it alone.

"I'm gonna shower." She glanced at Harlan. "Thanks for the donuts."

"Welcome." Harlan smiled at her. "Good kid you've got there," he said when she was gone. "Worried about her mom."

"Uh-huh," I answered, standing to clear the table.

"I'll help," he said.

"No. I've got it." I moved to the kitchen sink and stared through the window. Before Harlan showed up at my door, my life had spiraled into double time. The last twenty-four hours had pushed it to warp speed, and I couldn't locate the brake. *With PJ coming into my life, can I afford to invite Harlan into my family?* That Venn diagram popped into my head again—the one with Meg in the middle and PJ and me on either side. Harlan simply didn't fit, yet he claimed he wanted to be there.

"When she goes off to college, maybe I can pitch in where I'm needed—when I'm needed, if I'm needed," he said.

"Thanks."

"You getting nervous about PJ coming this afternoon?" he asked.

"A little."

"I can tell. You sort of went off the flight pattern." He pushed a flattened hand through the air like an airplane.

His words fell like tumblers, breaking through the static. Stacked together, they created an image of a shared future, one I hadn't fully considered until now.

"If you want me around, that is?"

I'd never heard Harlan sound so uncertain. "Oh, yeah." I straightened myself. "Sorry. It's all happening so fast."

"Us, you mean?"

"Everything."

"This kid coming . . . is it putting too big a strain on things? Nobody would blame you for feeling the pressure."

The kid. The man. Caleb's death. Meg. Maybe Della is on to something. Should I take a break to decide what I want?

I took a seat across from him at the table. He seemed relaxed around me and confident in his decisions. Why not? He'd tested his choices out in the world. He'd never gotten a girl pregnant or had to forego college, and he hadn't married his first love because he'd known she wasn't the right person.

Worry roiled inside me, reminding me of Della's admonition. *Have I become his fool? Is this how it is for a woman my age? Should I get used to men who try on women like next season's sport coats? I can fool around, but not at the expense of my daughter. My consent will inform her of my self-worth.*

"This has been fun," I said, "but with PJ coming, I need to find my new normal."

Harlan's mouth slanted into a sideways smile, and he tipped his head a little lower to meet my gaze. "Sissie, did I say something I shouldn't?"

I shook my head. "You've been wonderful to me, and Meg. But I'm barely sure who I am some days. I'm not sure I'm in the right headspace to sink myself into a relationship."

His smile went flat. "Sink. Don't see that word on Valentine's cards anymore."

"I wish I could drop everything and follow you to Colorado or wherever you're going. I've got this family, and I need to hit pause before I lose myself in this thing we have."

"Okay, I'm coming on too strong. You need me to back off. I can do that."

"I just think . . . Now that Caleb's gone, I owe it to myself to decide what I want." I paused and looked through the bay window over his shoulder. "You know those sneakers hanging over the power line at the end of Austin Street?"

"Yeah. Been there for years."

"One of Brent's friends dared the guy to toss 'em up there. And you know the sign in front of the sporting goods shop off the highway? The one that they spray painted with, 'That's drop in, not—'"

"'—drive in,'" he finished with a laugh. "No telling how many times that glass window got broken before they decided to stop replacing the glass and nail up that plywood." One of his brows pitched up, and I suspected he wasn't getting my point.

"You know it was my senior class—the class I *should've* graduated with—that bought that scoreboard they just replaced with the jumbotron?"

He set his coffee mug on the table. "Sissie, what's this all about?"

"Other people did things after high school. I just . . . I just stayed here."

"Looks like here turned out pretty damn good . . . until recently."

"For the most part, I turned a rough situation into what my mom called 'a normal life,' whatever that means."

"One person's normal is another person's dream," he said.

"Or nightmare. You see, I never got to choose what normal meant to me. This is my chance."

"And I'm getting in the way." He leaned back.

"Not in the way." I hated the defeat in his eyes. "You arrived when my world upended."

"Okay . . ." His face twisted, and he squirmed in his seat.

"I like you here. I love you here." I covered my mouth and uncovered it as quickly. "But my whole life has been a series of fits and stops, and each stop has dropped me in a place I didn't want to be. 'Bloom where you're planted, Sissie.' Well, I never had the luxury of planting myself—I was like one of those seeds blowing in the wind, eventually stepped on or blown into a puddle. Never able to manage my life, to steer toward what I wanted. If I don't take a step back now, I'm afraid I never will."

His head bobbed several times. "Here's what I'm gonna do for you."

"You don't need to do anything."

He held up one finger and gentled it to his mouth. "Shh. I'm gonna give you space—as much as you need. If you get where you're going and decide I'm not in the picture, then, alright. But I'm gonna take time for me, too. Trips I've been meaning to take." His smile returned, wrinkling his eyes.

"I'm sorry."

He shook his head. "Can I ask a favor? Not sure if I can go cold turkey. When I leave, can I keep calling you?"

My heart gave a jolt. "Of course. I've become dependent on your texts—they get me through the day," I admitted.

"Yours, too. I mean it. Sissie, I can't turn off the way I feel about you. I love you."

"Harlan, you need to know . . ." My face colored. "I love you, too."

"I know you do. And I hope you know how deep it goes with me, too."

I nodded, reaching for his hand.

"Mom," Meg burst into the kitchen, flashed a scowl at my hand on Harlan's.

"Can you give us a minute?" I asked.

Meg grunted her displeasure.

"Please. Give us a minute." I spoke more firmly this time, making clear it wasn't a request.

She spun around and stomped out.

"I do know." A bizarre lump formed in my throat as I prepared to send this man away—this beautiful, kind man who clearly cared about me, even if I was one of many. I deserved to feel good, and he delivered when I needed it most. "Who knows what I'll do while you're gone. Might go to school? Always wanted to become a nurse."

"Do it. Do it all. When you're ready, I'll be here—assuming you still want me."

"I can't tell you to wait for me," I said, hoping against hope he'd argue.

"You're not. I know what I have to do. And if you need me sooner, I'll just be a call away. Walk me out?" He rose to his feet.

"Now?"

"Now's as good a time as any for you to get on with your own damn life. Don't let anyone tell you otherwise."

Forty-One

Theresa delivered PJ and all that came with him that afternoon. She stuck around for more than an hour talking about Faith—how she liked Shasta daisies and the smell of freshly cut grass, how she hoped PJ might play soccer rather than football, and how she'd sing "You Are My Sunshine" to him each night when she put him to bed—anecdotes I'd rely on to tell PJ about his mother, when he was old enough to hear it.

She cried when we walked her to the car. "I'll miss him," she said, pushing a strand of hair into place.

A breeze blew, suggesting the strand didn't belong there after all.

"We will help him call you, and I'll send pictures often," I told her. "I promise."

Theresa hugged me. "This means more than you could ever imagine. Thank you."

I carried PJ into the house, walking around with him, feeling a bit like I had that first time I was home alone with Meg. "What should we do now?" I asked him.

He wiggled out of my arms to inspect photos on a table in the den. "Dada." He pointed to a frame. "Dada." He giggled. I leaned closer, and he giggled some more. "Dada, Dada, Dada, Dada," he called, running into the hall.

"Thanks, Dada," I said to the ether. "This ought to be a wild ride."

LATER, I UNPACKED THE rest of PJ's clothes. My hand lingered on his tiny shorts, his socks no taller than a juice glass, his T-shirts that held the scent of Downy softener. Faith's memory stuck to each item—most likely, she had been the last to wash and fold most of them. A certain sadness pulled at me, a grief I hadn't entirely processed for this woman I hadn't met. From the photos we had seen, Faith had held nothing but hope and love for her son. Now, I hoped . . . wherever she was . . . she could appreciate a morsel of peace knowing I would attempt to preserve her memory and care for him.

LARK STOPPED BY THE HOUSE to deliver a copy of the completed orders while PJ was asleep. It was a brief visit. There was no mention of Harlan or his departure.

Maybe she was disappointed, or perhaps she was just choosing to avoid appearing like a busybody. Regardless, I was relieved when she left.

I took the thick envelope to the den and studied the papers. Below a section titled

"Cause of Action," PJ's custody was spelled out:

Due to the untimely death of the minor child's custodial parent FAITH MICHELLE WILLETS and his noncustodial parent CALEB LEE DIETRICH, minor child PIKE JAMESON DIETRICH is left with no other living relatives.

I READ OVER ADDITIONAL SECTIONS that discussed the terms of Faith's will, Meg's age, and Martha's inability to assume custody due to "poor health."

I had already signed the last page, so my work was done. I pushed it into the legal-size envelope—and then I noticed another document.

This paper was missing the legalese of the first. It was a type-written document detailing the disposition of Finn. *Sweet Jesus, the dog again?*

In addition to the address and number of the kennel, the letter said that if Caleb's family did not pick up the dog or make other arrangements by the end of the month, the kennel would contact a rescue organization.

I shoved the paper into the envelope and dropped it on the hall table. "Too soon to invite another occupant into our house."

WHEN MEG ARRIVED HOME AFTER school, we woke PJ from his nap and gave him a snack. He was in a good mood, thankfully, so we packed him and a stylish backpack/diaper bag I found in his things and took him to the hospital; I wanted him to meet his Grandpa Thomas before Brent hauled him to Chicago.

"Look who we brought," Meg said when we opened the door to Dad's room.

I half expected Dad to smile, but his expression didn't change. PJ wasn't sure what to think about him; he seemed more interested in the workings of the wheelchair my father was sitting in.

"Looking good," I told him. "I see Mom's been shopping." I touched his shoulder.

His slow turn of the head served as a response. Instead of the wrinkly drawstring jammie pants and Hanes T-shirts he had worn since entering the facility, Dad was wearing navy sweatpants, a long-sleeved Polo, and shiny white sneakers.

"Breeeh," he said.

"Brent did all this?"

"Mmm," he muttered with a nod.

"Well, I see what he's up to. New clothes, private plane rides—that twerp's trying to knock me out of favorite child status."

"Hmm." His mouth sloped upward just a hair.

"Hey, like that smile."

"Hmm." Clearly, he wasn't as impressed with his progress. His good arm pushed the wheel of his chair a few feet to the table beside his bed. He pulled a yellow legal pad and a marker onto his lap, and the marker immediately rolled to the linoleum floor.

"Got it." Retrieving the pen, I bent to face him. "Want me to help you write something?"

"Yeeeeh."

I clicked the marker open and held the pad steady.

He took the pen in his left hand and scrawled, "You're good mom."

"Mom's been pretty great through all this."

He shook his head and pointed at me with his left hand.

"Oh, I haven't been around as much as I should. Everything hit at once, didn't it?"

He wrote, "Proud of you."

"Thanks." I patted his leg. "That means a lot to me."

He added "always" above it.

"I've given you plenty of grief."

His index finger tapped the word "always," and his gaze met mine.

A lump formed in my throat. *This isn't one of those in-case-we-don't-meet-again conversations, is it? I can't manage another loss.* I tried to lighten the mood. "Getting pretty good at writing with that left hand."

He lifted the pen, wrote, "Sorry," and pointed to me again.

"We're going to be okay. All of us."

He wrote, "tried, and "protect." Then he pointed to his chest.

"It's okay, Dad."

He lifted his eyes, searched my face.

"Thanks for trying," I offered.

He returned to the notepad. "Caleb didn't deserve," and pointed at me again.

I shot a sideways glance at Meg. She was busy entertaining PJ. "No, he didn't," I agreed with a laugh. "Dad, I love you, and I know you love me, too."

He dropped the pen and lifted his hand to my hair. "L-l-lo-lo-lo-uh . . ." he exhaled hard. "You."

I fetched his walker and helped him stand up. When he made it to his feet, I leaned into him, careful not to make him bear too much of my weight. "I needed to do this before you leave," I said, and wrapped my arms around him. "Your love always came through, Dad." My heart swelled. In that moment, I was six again, in my daddy's strong arms, and I believed he could do anything.

Brent and Mom arrived, and Mom squealed when she saw PJ.

"PJ," she cooed, "come meet your other grandma."

PJ laughed at her.

"You're the happiest boy." Mom turned to check on Dad. "What do you think?"

He moaned.

"Come here, buddy." Brent scooped PJ into his arms.

Mom steepled her fingers and sighed. "We had much to do before we could leave—picking up prescriptions, dry cleaning, meeting with our neighbor's niece who's going to watch the house for us . . ." She went on and on, visibly excited about their trip to Chicago.

Brent's phone buzzed, and he passed PJ to Meg. "That's the transport vehicle that will take us to the airport. They're downstairs."

We followed along as a nurse pushed Dad's chair to the front of the hospital. Mom climbed into the van's passenger seat while the driver loaded Dad into the back, wheelchair and all.

"Where's your rental car?" I asked.

"Already returned it," Brent said. "Mom and I Ubered to the hospital."

"Okay if we follow you to the airport?" I asked.

"Sounds good." He helped the van's driver arrange the bags and climbed into the van.

We were able to drive onto the tarmac and help Dad onto the plane. For Dad, it was awkward and, at times, even painful, from the look of it. Mom, however, was grinning like she'd won the lottery and bought her own plane.

"Call me when you get them settled?" I asked.

"Stop worrying about them," Brent said. "I've got this. You call me when you get PJ settled in."

"Deal," I said.

❧

THAT NIGHT, BRENT CALLED, EXHAUSTED after checking Dad into the new rehab facility and helping Mom get settled in his guest room.

PJ, meanwhile, learned the lay of the land quickly. He took to his new routine like a champ and, pardon me if I tear up, embraced me as his "mama" in no time. Truth be told, my new moniker produced a warm, guilty feeling whenever I heard it—but my love for him was immediate and intense, and eroded the anger I had carried for his father.

Harlan texted daily and called on occasion, too. He resigned from the Forest Service and put everything he owned in storage. For the foreseeable future, he would be a nomad. He'd saved all that money from selling his business years back, and now he was finally digging into it and letting it fund his travels. First on his list, he'd hike and fish along the Canadian Rockies.

❧

ALL WAS GOOD ON AUSTIN Street until the next Saturday when I began the tedious work of sorting bills and other documents into a plastic file box.

Meg was helping. Every so often, she'd lift one to inspect it, then drop it into the pile. Then she opened the envelope holding the temporary orders.

"Mom." Her voice held an edge. "I thought the dog was adopted already."

"The firm arranged for him to go to a rescue organization." *Damn, will that dog just disappear already?* I fixed my eyes on a city water bill.

"It says we have until the end of the month to claim him."

"And then he goes to the rescue organization." *Keep filing like you're playing Beat the Clock.*

"Except for those pictures, we never got to see him. What if he's great? What if he could be, like, an emotional support dog?" Her voice was insistent.

"Then someone else will make him an emotional support dog." I let out an exhausted breath and met my daughter's pleading gaze. *Bad move.*

And that is how we ended up interrupting a toddler's nap and rushing to the kennel before it closed at noon.

A BELL CLANGED OVER THE door as we entered. Meg rushed ahead of us to the desk, puffed up her chest, and—using her big-girl, all-business voice—said, "Yes, I'm here to see my dad's dog. He died, but—"

"Oh, I'm sorry. Depending on when you brought him in . . ." The woman winced. "He's probably gone already. They pick them up the same day."

"No. The dog didn't die. My dad did."

"Oh, dear." The woman pushed a stray gray hair back into the bun swirled at the back of her head.

"He had a dog who's supposed to be here, in your kennel?"

The woman took a tentative glance at me, then returned her eyes to Meg. "What is"—her voice rose—"*the dog's* name?"

"Um, Finn, I think?" Meg said.

"Our . . . his attorney made the arrangements," I added. "John Morales?"

"Uh-huh. I'll be right back." She slid behind a wall of charts. She returned a minute later, nodding. "The dog is here. Are you here to pick him up?"

Meg looked at me.

"Possibly," I said.

"Well, we don't allow customers to go back to the kennels, but I could have him brought into an exam room, if one is open."

I nodded. "Please."

"I'll be right back."

The woman walked into the lobby, waving for us to follow her. "Most of our boarders don't have visitors," she said in a loud whisper as we passed through the door I could only assume led to the super-secret-exclusive exam rooms.

"Not every day someone's dad dies in a helicopter crash and leaves behind a kid and a dog, so thanks," Meg said dryly.

That's my girl.

She left us in the room and went to fetch Finn. We waited, Meg leaning over the rectangular exam table.

"She's a real peach," I said when I was sure the woman was out of earshot.

"Thought she was going to have a heart attack when I told her about Dad." Meg laughed. "People."

A young man in his early-twenties pushed open the door. He held a leash in a tattooed hand, a golden retriever on its end.

Grumpy PJ's frown disappeared. "Fwinnn," he squealed.

"He's sweet," the guy said. "Everybody here loves this pup. I'll give y'all a few minutes."

Meg knelt to the dog and dug into his fur. The pup pressed his nose to her cheek. "You're sweet, alright." She leaned to one side to sit on her bottom and PJ held out his hands and grunted to join her.

We're not getting out of here any time soon, that's for sure. Damn dog.

"Come here, Mom."

"I'm here."

"No, down here." She patted the floor beside her.

I reluctantly joined her and folded my hands over my lap. That dog looked at me and—I swear—smiled. And it was a genuine, I'm-so-glad-to-make-your acquaintance smile.

This was such a bad idea.

He took a step toward me, dropped his head into my lap, and pushed his back legs to the floor, legs splayed out behind him like a frog.

"He likes you," Meg said.

"You're sweet, Finn . . ." His feathery tail lifted and wagged when I said his name. "But we're already taking in more than a puppy."

Meg rolled her eyes to me. "It's not his fault."

Where have I heard that before?

"Not mine, either." I wiggled backward, and the dog lifted his head. He was a gorgeous golden retriever with eyes as convincing as my daughter's when it came to worming his way into my heart. I crossed my arms over my chest, trying to harden my heart against his charm.

"Come on, guys. PJ, come here."

PJ wasn't leaving. Neither was his stubborn sister. The dog, however, stood and shifted his body so it lined up precisely beside me, as if we might walk out together.

"Not you. Sit down, dog."

He did.

"Mom, he's smart."

"Mmm-mmm."

"Lie down," Meg said.

He did that, too.

"Come on," I said, intending to nudge Meg. Instead, Finn pushed up on his feet and returned to my side. *Show-off.*

"Mom, he'll be a good watch dog when I'm at college," she nearly sang.

I dropped my gaze to my daughter, now kneeling again at my feet . . . and I was toast, golden as the pup. I suddenly realized I wanted him as much as Meg did. "Shoot," I said with a sigh, glancing at my watch. "More errands."

"What? Now?" Confusion washed over Meg's face.

"He'll need a bed and food, won't he?"

Meg shot to her feet and put her hands on my shoulders. "We're taking him?"

"I guess we are."

Meg squealed. "PJ, guess what? We're taking Finn home with us!"

All of us were smiling now, including the dog. With hugs all around, we welcomed him into our family—our new-to-us but slightly used, chaotic, mismatched family. When I saw PJ's huge grin, I felt like any parent feels when they nail the perfect gifts on Christmas morning.

And just like that, we became the Dietrich Four, alive and well on Austin Street.

Forty-Two

That evening, as Meg and I ate pizza for the second time that week, she got a serious look on her face. "Mom, can I ask you something?"

"Uh-huh."

"Did you and Harlan have the conversation?"

"About Furby?"

She nearly spit out her bite of pizza. "FUTAB. Gah."

"Remind me." I gestured with my slice.

"Feet Up. Take a Break."

"Sort of."

"Was it a fight?"

"No. Just not the right time."

"I know he's old and all, but . . ." She dropped her head and stared up at me. "Is he, I don't know, like . . . the one?"

A coldness flashed over me like I'd been caught red-handed. I dropped my gaze.

"I won't be mean about him if he is. I was kind of a brat with him. It just felt like he was always around when it should've been just you and me. Anyway, I'd understand if you wanted him to visit or whatever."

"Might take you up on that," I paused. "Later. For now, he's off to see the world, and I'm going to take some time to decide what I need."

"Whatever." She looked like I had just spoken to her in Swahili. "But if you decide to talk to him again, it's okay with me. I mean, I won't be a brat to him."

"I didn't say we weren't talking anymore. We're just FIZBO'ing for a while."

"FUTAB."

"I give up." I threw my hands up. "We're on a break."

THE FOLLOWING MORNING, I SENT a photo of Finn to Harlan:

SISSIE: *Hey, we got a new roommate. Meg calls him her love muffin.*
HARLAN: *Good-looking dog. I'll take him off your hands if you change your mind.*
SISSIE: *How would you do all that traveling with a love muffin?*
HARLAN: *I'd figure it out. Gotta go—catching a flight to British Columbia. Love you.*
SISSIE: *Have fun.*

I held the phone for a second, my heart leaping forward. *Should I say it back? Wouldn't that undo our agreement? What if he's waiting for me to respond right before he gets on a plane? Didn't go so well for the last guy.*

Eh, what the heck.

SISSIE: *Love you.*

PJ called the dog "Fwin," and soon both of my boys fell into a routine. PJ woke early, eager for hugs and waffles; took afternoon naps; giggled at Finn; and cried when his clumsy waddle resulted in falls, which was a frequent occurrence. His joyous spirit dispelled my resentment for his father. How could I look into PJ's round eyes with resentment, no matter how he'd come to be with us?

PJ injected an energetic force into my life—a spontaneity I hadn't known in years. He was wild compared to how Meg had been and happily averse to being tamed. I credited that to his gender. Despite his tornadic expeditions through our home, however, he landed in my arms at the end of each day for shared stories and snuggles. In no time, we'd twisted our way into each other's hearts.

Creepy as it might sound, PJ filled the void left by Harlan's departure. Often, I was too tired at the end of the day to maintain a phone or text conversation; I frequently found myself apologizing for falling asleep mid-exchange.

My days were spent chasing after PJ, cooking for Meg and her friends, delegating yardwork to a landscaping team, walking the dog, and picking up dry cleaning. In what little free time I had, I climbed through mystery novels and went out for the occasional lunch or coffee with Lark. She navigated around her brother in our conversations, and I regretted not being able to talk freely about him, to ask her who he really was. *Is he the guy Della described? Has he already sampled the women of Banff and Victoria?*

What I knew for sure was that Harlan spent copious amounts of time shopping for postcards. He mailed ones with cute animal pictures to PJ, and ones with historical facts or trivia to Meg. I couldn't have cared less about the pictures. They came from a lodge around the Skeena River where Harlan reported catching, and releasing, seven steelheads. I had to google steelheads to learn they looked like any other fish. By the end of January, cards from Banff, Saskatchewan, Ireland, and Stockholm resided next to PJ's artwork on the refrigerator door, each one reminding me that I had pushed Harlan away.

I'd like to report that I was too busy to care about Harlan's absence, but that would be a lie. Yes, I was busier than ever—but late at night, when the house was quiet, I longed to hear his voice, and each morning, when I entered PJ's room, I treated myself to a glance at those shelves we painted together and wondered if we could've held onto that intensity. *Is Harlan the one who could love me and my mismatched family, too?*

In March, our mailman asked me to sign for a fat packet from the insurance company handling the accident. I signed for it and threw it on the entry table while I read a postcard from Ashland, Nebraska. Harlan had met with curators of a safari park to discuss doing consulting work for them.

At least he's back in the country.

Returning to the other mail, I discovered the insurance company had offered separate six-figure settlements for the three of us, all of them generous. Seeing the numbers put me at ease about Meg's education at an out-of-state school.

I hated to bother Lark, but I had come to trust her opinions—legal and otherwise. When I called, she offered to swing by the house. "If you want, I can bring Georgia for a playdate with PJ?"

"Perfect."

A few hours later, the babies played beside us while we sat on the floor of PJ's room, looking through the papers.

"It's a generous offer," Lark agreed, "but you could ask for more."

I took a deep breath and looked at PJ and Georgia playing together with Finn snoring on the floor behind them. "I'm getting more than I need. Can't we just wrap it up?"

"Sissie, you're going to be paying for everything. It's none of their business what Caleb planned to do. You were married, and you deserve compensation."

"Faith had life insurance, too, right?"

"She does. Probably should've talked more about that before Theresa left."

"This is going to sound naïve, but I trust her."

"Yes and yes," she said, with a wry grin. "You're young, Sissie." She shook her head. "You may decide to travel, go to school, open a business. Let's make sure you're covered for the long haul."

Open a business? You have more faith in my abilities than I do, Lark.

Georgia whimpered as PJ tried to stuff her cloth doll into the back of his plastic yellow dump truck.

"Here, PJ, let's put your bunny in there instead." I passed Georgia her doll, and she clutched it to her chest. "Raising a boy's so different. Meg wanted to love on everything. PJ—doesn't matter if it's one of his lovey animals or a dump truck, he puts it in motion."

"Should've seen Jamie and Charlie when we brought Georgia home. They didn't know what to do with her." She glanced at her daughter. "They figured it out, though, and lord help the boy who breaks her heart one day. They have her back."

"Well, it'll just be PJ and me before long."

Lark got up and crossed the room. Cocking her head toward her daughter, she ran a finger over Georgia's brown curls. Her blue eyes, so much like her brother's, rolled up to me. "What about . . ." Her lips tightened. "Harlan?"

My skin warmed, and a smile curved the edges of my mouth. *God, I can't even think about him without losing myself. Pull it together, woman!* "We talk now and then. He's sowing his oats while I'm finding myself."

"Wouldn't call what he's doing 'sowing oats.' Look, tell me to shut up and I will."

Curiosity gnawed at me. "Go on."

"Sissie, he's got it bad for you. I'm not there to chaperone his travels, but I can assure you, he's not sowing anything."

"But . . ." I held on to my breath. "He's never been married, and, well, look at him. He's successful, handsome, has a nice nest egg. He's the perfect catch, but . . . well, I heard he's more into catch and release."

Lark squeezed her eyes tight, scrutinizing my words. "Harlan's always said he won't marry until he meets the indisputable right person. Sure, he's fooled around along the way—he's a man, duh."

I rolled my eyes in agreement. "Was that how it was with Annika?"

"Oy. Annika." An exhausted expression took over Lark's face. "Sweet girl, but he couldn't force it to work. Boy, did he try. He hated hurting her, but he wasn't doing her a favor by staying there."

"He said he's seen her a few times since ending things. I asked him if it was like that song about the couple who run into each other at the grocery store on Christmas Eve."

"James Taylor?"

"Dan Fogelberg," I answered like an expert. "Anyway, he laughed and . . . basically, said, yeah, he didn't have any regrets. Like the couple in the song."

"They didn't want the same things. Annika's twice married now, has three kids. She'd been with Harlan since high school, and I don't think she ever spent enough time alone to know herself before she jumped into the next relationship."

I'm familiar.

"What you and he have, or had?" She shrugged. "Didn't compare to any relationship he's ever had. It was—"

"Della suggested he did this routinely." Seeing her confusion, I added, "Enjoys the early romance, and when it cools, he's gone."

"Where in . . ." Lark's face turned red, and she threw a glance at the kids. "Earmuffs, kids. Where in the hell did she get that?"

"Said someone who works for her, or . . . I don't know. Someone told her."

"Della makes little effort to hide her feelings about me. Now she's going after my brother? She'd better gird her uptight loins, because I'm going to . . ." She gritted her teeth.

"Wait. Please. Just tell me the truth. I can take it."

"The truth? My brother is totally, completely in love with you. He fell hard the day you answered the door at my house. You know how I know that? My brother—who, by the way, is a good and decent human being—told me so."

My chest became hot, and my heart pounded like a jackhammer.

"You really couldn't tell, Sissie?"

I lifted my palms, and a drizzle hit my cheeks. "I love him too, Lark."

PJ abandoned his truck, toddled over to me, and gripped my leg. "Oh, sweetie, your momma's just fine," Lark told him.

I picked him up. His head fell to my shoulder like he required consolation. "I've got to pull it together. He doesn't need a parent crying over—"

"Harlan's not wishy-washy. When something, or someone, hooks him, he gives 'em his all." Lark shrugged. "In my experience, when you feel it . . ." She patted her chest. ". . . you just know. When Wyatt and I first spent time together, I felt it, but it didn't make sense, so I tried to force those feelings away."

Obviously satisfied with my emotional condition, PJ wiggled to the floor.

Lark jerked her head back and laughed. "There I was, newly widowed, hanging out with a younger guy." She leaned into me. "And Wyatt had his own share of baggage. But hard as I fought my feelings, my heart dang near beat out of control and my palms got sweaty every time I got within twenty feet of him. Like my body was saying, 'Hey, dummy, this is the guy,' to make my mind understand."

I looked over at the kids. PJ had Georgia's doll again. "PJ, that's hers," I said, walking over to replace the doll with a Duplo man. "I guess you're telling me you'd like your own doll?"

I left the kids to play and returned to our conversation. It was clear from the dreamy look in Lark's eyes that she had never left it.

"Wyatt and I didn't make any sense yet made all the sense in the world." She shook her head, and a loving smile seized her face. Then she lifted her hands to my shoulders. "Do what sits right in your heart. You'll know."

"Okay."

"And I want you to know, what happens between you and my stinky brother—good or bad—won't change our friendship."

"Wait, didn't you say you and Wyatt broke up for a while?"

"Sure did. Took a car accident to shake some sense into me. Wyatt was about to move to Kansas. They took me to the hospital and, surprise!" She pointed to Georgia. "If he hadn't still been in town when it happened, I'd probably be raising Miss Priss over here all by myself."

"Hard to admit this—but Della's right. I should take some time for myself. My life's been one accident after another." I closed my eyes for a beat. "Would be nice if I could wrap one crisis before the next hits."

"If you figure that one out, let me know. But don't expect your life to look like a Hallmark movie."

"That's cute how you think my life could be a Hallmark movie." I barked out a laugh. "More like a Lifetime Network cautionary tale."

Forty-Three

Grant Bradley continued to provide updates on behalf of the NTSB to check on us and let me know what documents had been shared with whom. Once we had agreed on a number for the settlement, stories about the arrangement hit the national news.

Our lives didn't change after the check was cashed. The majority of my payout went into long-term investment funds, and the children's money was parked in educational trusts.

While I learned about investing, Harlan hit three other continents in all—South America, Europe, and Oceana, which, I learned, was the home of New Zealand. *Learn something new with every postcard.*

Martha suffered a fall and moved to an assisted living facility where she could maintain her independence, be that what it may. We still visited on Sundays, although I could never quite tell if PJ lifted her spirits or rattled her cage.

By the time the peach trees were blooming, our family had found a new normal. We rocked along like any other chaotic household that included siblings who were over sixteen years apart.

Our hearing to finalize custody had been postponed twice—both times due to John Morales's cardiac procedures. Following a reassuring court-required home check from Child Protective Services, we were confident the hearing was a formality only, so I didn't give it much thought. I had PJ's heart, and he had mine. We were a family.

Meg accepted the spot at the University of Richmond, and the three of us spent her spring break in Chicago with the rest of the family, celebrating Dad's progress and PJ's second birthday. Brent bought the kid so many presents, we had to ship them before we flew home to Texas.

Mom said she might get a condo there, and Dad didn't argue. His speech had improved, but walking was still outside his grasp. He kept trying, though. Had to give it to him, he wasn't a quitter.

Spring in Fredericksburg offered hope and filled us with excitement. PJ's vocabulary grew by leaps and bounds and, thanks to Uncle Brent, he had an embarrassingly large wooden playset to go wild on in the backyard.

Then, on a gorgeous spring day, all that sunshine disappeared.

PJ and I were planting pansies in the flower beds along the front of the house, Finn at our sides. It was the kind of day where you catch yourself closing your eyes to imbibe the sweet scents of the Russian olive trees floating in the air, and the slightest breeze reminds you there's still a while before the summer heat will arrived. If I were one of those hashtag people, I'd have called myself "hashtag blessed" in that moment.

To be clear, I am not one of those people.

As if the day couldn't be more perfect, not one but two of Harlan's postcards had arrived earlier. One displayed a miniature deer and was from the Florida Keys. Mickey Mouse waved from the other card; Harlan had met his nieces and nephews there for spring break. "PJ and Meg would love this place," he wrote on that one. "They say it's the happiest place on earth. That would be true if you three were here with me. Love you."

I held the card to my nose, stupidly hoping to smell the spice of his soap. God, I missed him. As lovely as my life had become, there was a gap in it. *Am I holding that space for Harlan?*

Lately, I'd begun thinking about how he might fit into our lives after Meg left for college. I'd begun thinking about what I'd do for me when she left. *Yes, travel would be fun. And no doubt PJ and I will make frequent trips to Virginia in the coming year. But what about school for me? Why shouldn't I make something of myself?*

Looking on with pride at the work we'd done, I turned a sprinkler on in the flowerbeds. "What do you think, PJ?"

He waved his arms in the air. "Biggy?" he asked, his way of requesting a piggyback ride.

"Let's go," I said, patting my shoulder.

PJ mounted up, and I ran in circles around the front lawn until I thought my heart might give out. With each bounce, harmonious giggles bubbled over my shoulder—and I couldn't get enough. I loved this boy every bit as much as the daughter I'd brought into the world. He was ours now—a lovely fusion of Caleb, Faith, and me.

"Mama," PJ said.

I helped him down to the grass, and I saw that he was pointing to our driveway. A man was approaching our house.

"Mrs. Dietrich?"

"Yes."

"I have a letter for you."

"Huh. The mail lady was just here."

"Please sign the green card." He pushed a pen toward me, pointing to the green card attached to an envelope.

"Did our carrier forget this one?" I asked, providing my signature.

He ripped the card free, leaving two green fasteners stuck to the envelope. "I'm not with the postal service, ma'am. You've been served."

At first, my mind blurred—probably from all the running in circles—but then I remembered the upcoming hearing and my breath caught. I herded PJ and Finn to the porch and pulled PJ into the swing. Oblivious to my panic, he was perfectly content with our new situation; he started pushing his chest forward and back, forcing the swing to respond in kind.

I peeled open the envelope, and my heart began to thud sickly as I read its contents.

Part Seven

Forty-Four

"You are hereby served."

The first line pushed my pulse to a crescendo. So much for our uncomplicated adoption hearing.

"Mmmmm," PJ hummed, pushing and pulling the swing with the weight of his midsection. "Mmmmm."

The movement blurred the words before my eyes. My stomach lurched, and I rose to my feet.

I peeled my phone from my back pocket. "Mom needs a sec, baby," I told PJ as I dialed Lark.

"Hey Sissie," she answered cheerfully.

"I got a letter." I could barely breathe, much less speak. "They're suing me."

"Who?"

"PJ's family. Er, someone saying they're PJ's family. They can't take him from me. Not now." My voice cracked with desperation and a string of tears cascaded over my cheeks.

LARK WASTED NO TIME. SHE swung into my driveway at an angle, curb checked her front tire, jumped out of the driver's seat, and slid onto the swing where I was holding PJ like his life depended on it, crunching the papers in my other hand against his back.

"What . . ." she started to ask, then thought better of it and simply peeled the rumpled papers from my hand and pulled on a pair of finger-spotted reading glasses. "Sure did a number on these." She squinted, then pressed the pages against her legs to flatten them.

"Give me those glasses." I snatched them from her, spit on the lenses, and wiped them on my T-shirt.

"Oh, Georgia gets a hold of them and . . ." She shrugged. Then she covered her mouth and, eyes glued to the pages, asked, "Roxanne Acton?" She turned to me. "Never heard of her before. You?"

"No. Never. You were there—they said he had no other family."

"Okay, so maybe it's a case of mistaken identity. Or someone looking for a child. Or, more likely"—a spindly index finger rose in the air—"for money."

"Shit," I breathed out, then cupped my hands over PJ's ears and echoed Lark's, "Sorry. Earmuffs, baby." I stared down at the papers in Lark's hands. "Can they rip him away from us?"

Lark shed the glasses, pushing them over her wild curls. "I hope not." She angled her head to PJ. "'Cause this guy needs you as much as you need him."

"I'll call John, see if he can handle this so you don't have to—"

"Heck if you will. I was here when we got him, I'll fight right beside you to keep him. Isn't that right, little man?"

She tapped PJ's nose, and his mouth bent into the beginnings of a giggle. "PJ, do you think this is funny? You do. You think this is funny." She reached between us and barely touched him, but the threat of a tickle brought on a full-on belly laugh. "Just wait. I'll show you funny." She stood and pulled him to her, and he shrieked with glee.

We went inside so Lark could call John. She claimed one end of the dining room table, and scratched notes on the back of a Bed Bath & Beyond flyer she'd pulled from her purse as they spoke.

"Alright, you'll call back after you talk to Theresa? Great. Thanks." She set the phone down. "He'll get the scoop for us. Don't worry."

A half hour later, John called.

"I'm gonna put you on speakerphone for Sissie." Lark tapped the screen and set the device on the table between us.

My nerves twisted my stomach into knots as I waited for him to speak.

He cleared his throat. "Sissie, you know Theresa's had her share of health problems with the cancer and such?"

"Yeah."

"So it's important we all agree she has the boy's best interests at heart."

"What's Theresa have to do with this?" I asked. "The papers say Roxanne Whoever—"

"Acton," Lark corrected.

"Right, *Acton*, is the one doing this."

"After Faith's parents divorced, her father remarried and adopted the new wife's daughter, Roxanne. Both girls were teens at the time, so their paths rarely crossed."

"But they said—"

"Let me finish." He paused. "Faith didn't want Roxanne anywhere near PJ. She made that clear to me and to Theresa."

"What's the problem, then?" I asked.

"Roxanne claims she was torn up when she heard about Faith on the news. Her version of their relationship is quite different from Faith's. Get this"—he chuckled as he spoke—"she claims Faith came to her in a dream, begging her to raise PJ."

"Bullshit," Lark whispered. Then, more loudly, "If she saw it on the news, she knows about the settlement."

"Exactly," John agreed. "No mystery what the woman's after— her timing's got gold digger all over it. She's playing up the grieving sister bit because she wants a cut."

"Does Theresa know her?"

"Um . . ." His hesitation grew irritating.

"John?" Lark said. "Does she?"

"Lark, please take me off speakerphone."

Fire snaked across my skin, and I shot a dirty look at the phone.

Listening, Lark nodded every so often, keeping her eyes on me. My heart pounded louder and louder, making it impossible to listen in on anything John was saying. Finally, she dropped the phone on the table.

"Theresa knows her, doesn't she?" I asked.

Lark pinched her mouth tight and gave a singular nod. "Theresa kept a few important bits to herself, it seems."

"Like?"

"Like, she's not a family friend. She's PJ's grandmother." Lark's hand rose. "Before you let it rattle you, listen. She's on our side."

"If she's on our side, she would've told us."

"All along, she wanted PJ placed with you and Meg. She believed the less you knew about their relationship with PJ, the less likely it was that she'd lead Roxanne to PJ."

"Damn her. She should've told us. We would've understood."

"Maybe. Maybe not. Maybe knowing he had family would've changed your mind about taking him? Honestly, Sissie, Theresa made the ultimate sacrifice, handing him to you. She risked never seeing her grandson again—all to shelter him."

"But she said we'd have to give him up to strangers if Meg didn't take him."

"She would've placed him with strangers before allowing him to live with, in John's words, 'grifters.'"

"So much for 'better the devil you know.' Dammit. We were so close to finalizing the adoption. If it hadn't been postponed, he'd be mine, right?"

She nodded. "John has another call with Roxanne's attorney later this afternoon. He said he'd call me. You know, these people did their homework. They knew about Meg going to college in Virginia—probably from social media."

"Friggin' Facebook."

PJ toddled over to me, holding an empty sippy cup. "Mo? Mo?"

"I'll get you more. Come here," I lifted him to my hip, and he stared at me like I had two heads and patted my damp cheeks. Did he know our time together might be careening dangerously close to an end?

THE SIGHT OF MEG'S CAR returning from school sent my heart beating like a drum. *Suck it up, buttercup. It's time for another episode of "How to break your daughter's heart."*

I gave her a moment to set down her things; then I let her in on the whole, ugly mess surrounding PJ's long-lost auntie.

Meg didn't wither. She narrowed her eyes at me. "Nobody's taking him, Mom. We're fighting for my brother."

"Honey, I plan to fight for him, but we should prepare ourselves. The court will weigh this aunt against me, a nonrelative."

"I'm his relative. I'll take over as his parent—at least, on paper."

"They know you're moving to Virginia," I said. "John said they probably got it from social media."

She slumped. "I'm sorry. I was excited."

"No, baby. Don't apologize. You deserve to celebrate."

"I won't go. Simple as that. Or tell them I'm taking him with me. We have to protect him," Meg said without blinking.

But nothing was simple anymore. I feared the normal I had come to love might never return.

Forty-Five

"R oscoe, New York: Trout Town, USA." Harlan's postcard was a welcome diversion.

PJ enjoyed its arrival, too, announcing, "Ffff-ssh," at the photo of a spotted rainbow trout on its front.

"Sorry about recent events," Harlan wrote. "It'll get worked out. Don't give up. Love you."

MEG'S FIXATION ON THE UNIVERSITY of Richmond waned— no second thoughts about the school, only its distance from PJ. She spoke to her school counselor and completed applications to schools in San Antonio. Those schools had already made their choices, however. A few waitlisted her, but none accepted her outright.

I attempted to keep our little family running on optimistic vibes, but each day I became more attached to PJ and more worried for Meg. Would our nightmare ever end?

IT HAD BEEN A GOOD while since Della had set foot on my property, so I wasn't entirely surprised when she appeared at the door bearing gifts in May. "One's for PJ's birthday. The other's an early graduation gift for Meg." She stepped inside without hesitation. "How's it going, being Mrs. Mom again?"

"Had better days."

"Sissie, I'm sorry about what happened with us."

"No offense, but I'm dealing with bigger problems than a friend's broken promise."

"Ouch. I guess I deserved that. Sis, I'm stuck in my own shit-storm." Something strange crossed her gaze—something desolate, even pensive. Her face darkened with dread. "Jared took the kids to his parents'."

"I'm so sorry. What happened?"

"Me working too much. Him not working enough, not doing what makes him happy."

"What's that?"

"Living on his dad's ranch. Farming." She pulled her hands into her body. "Sis, I wasn't made to be a farmer's wife."

"Haven't you had offers to buy your brokerage?"

"All the time. But I can't sell what my dad built." She winced with regret.

"Del, your dad's been gone for a long time. Do you think he'd want you to choose his business over your family?"

She didn't answer.

"Otherwise, are things okay between you and Jared?"

"Yeah. He said he loves me, but he can't be"—she made air quotes—"'just Della's husband' anymore." Without pausing, she turned the limelight on me. "What about you and Harlan? How's that going?"

"We're on a break." This line had become second nature now, and I could say it without blinking. "Taking time for me."

"But you love him?"

"Still do. And before you bash him with whatever your friend told you, let me stop you."

She opened her mouth, snapped it shut, opened it again. "How long you gonna make him wait?"

"As long as it takes." I closed my eyes, wondering if Harlan would want me when this chaos came to its bitter end.

PJ woke from his nap.

"Duty calls," I said. "It was good to see you, Della."

WHILE PJ ENJOYED HIS CHEESE and crackers, I chanced on a real-live voice call with Harlan—and he answered.

"You busy?" I asked.

"Nah. Good to hear your voice. What's up?"

I filled him in on the tidbits we'd learned about Roxanne Acton, the twice-divorced, forty-three-year-old, part-time tanning salon manager who claimed she'd been attempting to reach Theresa for weeks. Ultimately, she'd hired an attorney—the kind who doesn't charge unless his client wins.

"Lark creeped on her social media—said it doesn't project her as the maternal sort. I can't imagine handing him off to someone like that. Can't imagine giving him to *anyone*. Meg offered to stay around here for college. Hate to say it, but that may be our best shot."

"What if you and PJ moved with her?" he asked.

"To Virginia?"

"Why not? You said you've never lived anywhere else. She'll only be there four years. Give it a try."

"Hmm. Maybe so." Just because I said it didn't mean I believed it. "Lark said they wanted PJ and 'full access to any and all material assets of the minor child.' Those words have been tattooed on my brain since she said it."

"She wants money."

"That's what your sister said, too."

"People like that have a price. Just have to find it."

Meg graduated from high school on the third Friday in May, and Brent managed to fly our parents into Fredericksburg for the festivities.

I had seen Lark enter the auditorium. I wasn't surprised she'd want to be there to cheer on my girl. But you could've knocked me over with a feather when she and her family piled into the row above us and trailing at the end was her stinky brother.

When the ceremony ended, we filtered into the common area to wait for the graduates to relish the collective praise of families and friends.

"Thanks for coming, Harlan. Really cool of you to fly in for this," Meg told Harlan before she darted away from us to join her classmates.

FAMILY AND SOME OF MEG'S friends came to our house after the ceremony. We picked up barbecue and enjoyed the mild weather from my back patio.

"Knock-knock," Harlan called from the driveway.

I beckoned him over, and he joined us in the yard.

"I can't believe you're here," I said.

"Couldn't miss it."

"How long are you here?" I asked.

"Leaving on Sunday morning. Red-eye to Barcelona."

"Way to smash my joy."

"Sorry. I knew you'd be doing all of this." His gaze skimmed the patio. "Don't want to be in the way."

Is he in the way? Or precisely where I need him?

Turned out, he was correct. My parents kept pulling my attention, and Dad's condition required that we call it an early night.

Dad's speech had improved, I was relieved to see. He could indicate which foods he wanted, and Mom sliced them into small bites since his swallowing reflexes hadn't fully returned. He was even able to show affection. His "I love you" sounded better to me slurred than it ever had before his stroke.

Early to bed translated into early to rise. Mom and Dad were already back over and drinking coffee in the kitchen when I woke. Meg came home from her overnight party around eight and went to bed to catch up on sleep before her own party later that afternoon.

Harlan showed up a few hours later. "Figured you might need a hand setting up."

While he and I strung a "Congratulations!" banner over the back fence, Meg slunk into the backyard.

"Honey, you need to sleep," I told her.

"I can't sleep. I'm too excited."

Gone was the patent aggravation Meg had demonstrated toward Harlan before. At one point, I even caught them laughing together as they played with PJ—but it was a bittersweet moment. Would this be one of our last good times with the little guy? I couldn't push that thought out of my mind.

When the party began, Dad pushed a walker to the backyard. After helping him onto the patio, Harlan put himself to work refilling drinks and, at times, hovering over my parents to allow me to focus on Meg and PJ.

When it was over, Meg dashed off to attend the parties of her classmates, Brent took my parents back to their house, and Harlan hung around to help me clean up.

After we gave PJ his bath and put him to bed, we crashed on the sofa in the den. Falling asleep in his arms was the perfect end to the perfect day.

❧

"READY FOR YOUR TRIP TO 'Barthelona'?" I said over my cup of coffee the next morning.

"Almost." He explained how he'd meet a friend in San Antonio that afternoon to pick up the hiking gear they'd need. "Someday, you'll have to come along."

"You mean when I'm not pushing a stroller?"

"When you're ready in here." He tapped his head. "PJ's welcome, and we don't need a stroller. We'll get one of those backpacks." He leaned close to PJ's highchair. "You can ride along back here." He gestured to his back. "Sound good?"

PJ smiled, and I could see they'd become fast friends.

Dread crept over me with Harlan's impending departure, and I realized how familiar he and I had become around each other. But I was determined to avoid a gloomy good-bye. I would smile till he was gone, even if it killed me. I needed to hold it together for the upcoming fight for PJ.

Harlan leaned into me, his touch igniting a warmth I couldn't return.

"Until next time?" he asked.

"Until next time," I said.

Forty-Six

The following week, PJ bounced between Meg and me while we prepared for Friday's hearing. After hearing Roxanne was in town, I avoided taking PJ outside—not even to rock him on the front porch. Who knew if she would show up unexpectedly?

Theresa landed in town on Tuesday. She couldn't wait to see her grandson, and I made clear she was welcome to see him—at our house. When she came over, she said she didn't blame me for keeping him on lockdown.

Barely six months had passed since we'd seen her, but she looked different—more tired than before, and her clothes hung loosely over her body. I didn't have the heart to pry into her health issues, although seeing her as Faith's mother, her grief was more evident.

"I'm very sorry I didn't tell you," she told Meg and me. "You didn't know me, and I feared you'd hold my daughter's involvement with Caleb against me and reject PJ."

"Probably," Meg said, flatly.

Seeing her with PJ again, however, brought the entire picture into focus: Theresa's dedication to this child, her willingness to stick around Fredericksburg until we agreed to take him, her readiness to walk away, possibly never to see her grandson again. I couldn't be angry with her. She loved PJ as much as Meg and I did.

I HIRED A FRIEND OF MEG'S to sit with PJ that Friday morning while we adults assembled at the courthouse.

Judge Mackie was a white-haired man with tortoiseshell glasses. Looking solemn in his black robe, he scanned a laptop computer and nodded "hello" as people came and went.

Meg and I sat with Theresa, Lark, and John while the court conducted preliminary business with the ad litem attorney assigned by the court to represent PJ's interests— Molly Hawkins, a perky woman with short, chestnut hair. She sat opposite Roxanne's attorney, Buck Squires, a chunky man in a cheap gray suit and a rumpled tie that only made it midway down his abundant torso.

Roxanne Acton made an impression when she entered the court-room. Strands of unnatural auburn highlights rose from a head of overprocessed bluish-black hair. Her leathery skin recorded the years she'd spent baking in the Florida sun. Sparkly eye shadow and heavy kohl pencil gave her the semblance of a shocked raccoon. A tight purple dress—an item one might wear for a night out dancing rather than a morning in court— clung to her lean body.

Pike Sr. used to have a term for a woman like Roxanne—"Rode hard and put up wet."

In case there was any question, John whispered under his hand, "That's her."

Part of me pitied her: she looked terrified. But the other, stronger part of me, the mama bear, wouldn't allow pity to dismantle the family I was determined to protect.

No sooner than the gavel was thrown, the grieving sister's show began. Her attorney had coached her well. She oohed and aahed over PJ's photos and teared up dramatically when anyone spoke Faith's name. Once, her tears fell in such a torrent that her attorney begged the court for a break to allow the overwrought woman to pull herself together.

When we resumed, the judge asked about Roxanne's experience with children.

"The Lord will take my love for my sister and make me into the mother the boy needs. And, Judge," she said, fidgeting with her hair, "no offense, but the boy needs a grown mother, not a teen."

I'll tell you what that boy doesn't need—a money-grubbing grifter.

Meg's jaw pulsed, and I could only hope she'd settle down before the judge posed questions to her. Her gaze offered little sympathy for the woman threatening to rip her brother away from us.

Theresa took the stand and offered a brief history. "Faith traveled for work. A real details girl. You should've seen the lists she left for me each time she left town." She paused, looking lost in reflection. "After my cancer returned, Faith changed the will to remove my name and add Meg's." Sadness dragged at the corners of her mouth, the pain of her loss as fresh as it must've been that day we saw her at Caleb's memorial. "Roxanne was never a consideration for PJ."

"Alright," said Judge Mackie, "you're gonna have to go through this family tree. How are you and Ms. Acton related?"

"We aren't," Theresa replied.

The judge shook his head.

"Faith's father and I never married. I gave her my maiden name, Willets. She and her dad stayed in contact even after I married my late husband, Ben. Ben stepped in as her father, taking her to the father-daughter dance and attending all her school events. We didn't see much of her biological father, and we saw less of Roxanne."

Unsurprisingly, her explanation only left the judge with more questions.

"Who was Faith's biological father?" Judge Mackie asked.

"Eddie Acton."

He took a note and looked up. "Fine. Tell me your role in delivering the child to Fredericksburg."

Theresa detailed her poor heath and Faith's concerns about PJ's care. Then she glanced at me. "Caleb's father-in-law . . . Sissie's father . . ."

I nodded for her to go on.

Judge Mackie's brows rose, and he scratched out another note.

"Caleb was preparing to divorce Sissie, but he didn't tell Sissie that. He told her father, since he was an attorney."

"Hold on. Hold on." The judge peeled off his glassed and waved them. "Let me get this straight: your daughter shared a child with a married man who conspired with his wife's father to divorce her . . . the legal wife. Did I summarize correctly?"

"Yes, sir."

"And the child in question is now living with the legal wife?"

"Yes, sir."

"And you brought the boy to town?"

"Yes, Judge."

"But the father's family didn't realize you were the boy's grandmother at the time?"

"Yes."

"This is one for the ages." The judge rolled his eyes. He nodded several times, tapping his pen against his notepad, rereading his notes. His head made a slow roll toward Theresa. "You didn't tell Ms. Acton about her sister's death?"

"No, sir. They were estranged. Faith hadn't seen her in probably ten years."

"Face-to-face, but we stayed close in other ways," Roxanne blurted.

"Ms. Acton, you'll get your chance." He shifted to the attorneys. "What does the ad litem attorney say about his current home?"

Molly stood. "I don't have an opinion about the mother's relationship with her sister, but I am prepared to discuss the minor child's living situation." She went on to speak favorably of what she'd seen of our home, and of me and Meg. She reported that he was well-cared-for and healthy. Then she took a seat at the back of the courtroom, and a bailiff instructed John to take her place. Lark nudged us to follow.

After we took our seats beside John, the judge sighed. "Most family court matters can be settled if we can get the parties to communicate. Let's see if we can do that. The ad litem attorney has reported favorably about the child's well-being in his current situation, so it'll take a compelling reason for me to disrupt the arrangement. That said, let's hear why the plaintiff believes she should raise the boy."

Cheap Suit licked his lips. "Meghann Dietrich is his sister. She's a minor, as well. Meghann's mother is PJ's custodian. Priscilla Dietrich has no affiliation with the child other than being married to his deceased father."

"Meg wasn't eighteen when the temporary orders were filed; PJ's grandmother agreed it was best for Sissie to care for him until that time," John returned.

"Who's Sissie?" Cheap Suit asked.

"Priscilla Dietrich, also known as Sissie," John said. "She's caring for both siblings."

"Her name appears nowhere on Faith's will. The grandmother doesn't have the right to name anyone she wants."

"Mr. Squires, I'm sure you'll agree with me when I say this is a most unusual situation," Judge Mackie cut in. "The grandmother has lived near the child. She's helped to care for him since birth. Her efforts to secure him a home should be commended." Just as hope appeared on the horizon, the judge added, "This is not to say the court will yield to her decision."

"Judge?" Theresa's thin voice captured his attention. "I put a great deal of thought into PJ's care." She shifted to Roxanne. "I'm sorry, Roxanne. I want to say this as delicately as possible, but . . . Faith didn't mince words. She didn't want you to have him."

Roxanne's eyes went misty again, and she fanned her long, hot pink fingernails at her face. Her attorney set a reassuring hand on her shoulder and asked the judge if she could address the court.

After swearing on a Bible, she took the hot seat. "I loved my sister. We wanted to spend time together. Her mother kept us apart. She thought I wasn't good enough." Roxanne flashed a rueful look at Theresa. "But we wrote each other letters and talked on the phone sometimes."

"And you last spoke when?" Judge Mackie asked.

Roxanne looked at her attorney and then nodded, like she'd just remembered something. "Not long ago. I mean, not long before the helicopter. She was gonna bring the kid to Florida, to see me and go to the beach. They were real excited. Faith said she'd like to live in Florida, so having her kid there is second best, right?"

No flipping way.

"When was this trip planned?" the judge asked.

"My work schedule's all over the place, so it was sorta up in the air."

"You mention your"—the judge peered down at her—"'unpredictable' work schedule. How would you modify it for the child?"

"They said insurance money ought to come with him. I'll quit my job and stay home with him like the other lady who's watching him now."

Watching him? I'm not his babysitter.

Roxanne pointed to me. "Her."

Theresa whispered to John, and John raised a hand. "May I?" he asked the judge.

"Go ahead."

"Can you describe your sister?" John said.

"Real pretty. Not too tall. Thin."

"Can you tell me about her—her job, what she liked to do, her personality?"

"Her looks were plain, but she was smart. You know? Read books and talked like she could be in charge of a big company or something," Roxanne bragged.

Appearing bored, the judge asked a few questions about Roxanne's job and how long she'd lived in the same place.

Roxanne's attorney asked if he could meet with counsel in the judge's quarters.

Things were either about to get much better or much worse.

As Lark followed John and Roxanne's attorney to a door adjacent to the judge's raised desk, Meg gripped my hand tightly.

"What do you think he wants?" she asked.

I raised my eyebrows and gave her a gentle smile. "It'll be okay," I said, knowing my version of "okay" and hers were on opposite sides of the spectrum.

Roxanne turned to us. "So, you're done with high school?" she asked Meg.

Meg nodded and stared her down.

"Going to college sounds exciting. Bet you'll have all kinds of fun . . . living on your own, going to parties, and all that."

"I'm not into the party scene," Meg snapped. "I just want to get a degree."

"Right. Right. Get that degree and make some money."

Meg eyed the woman suspiciously. "I'll stay here if that's what's best for my brother."

"If we get this taken care of, you'll be able to go wherever you want," Roxanne said.

"How's that?" Meg shot back.

"'Cause I'll be his momma."

⚜

THEY MIGHT HAVE BEEN GONE for ten minutes, but it felt like hours.

I'd heard people say, "You'll never love another child in the same way you love one you've brought into the world," or something like that. Now, I knew they were wrong. Since PJ had come to live with us, I'd fallen for him. My heart ached with visions of his departure.

⚜

COURT RESUMED. THE TENSE FACES of the attorneys and the judge's stoic presence offered little encouragement. Lark took her seat and passed a note to us. I wanted to throw up.

A dollar sign.

I waved a hand to say, "Give it to her," and Lark appeared to comprehend.

She and John spoke in muffled voices. Then she asked if she could address the court.

"Thank you, Judge. I represent Meghann Dietrich, PJ's sister. Not only is she his closest available blood relative, but she and the child have also formed a bond. Separating them now would be devastating for them both."

"I'll stay here," Meg whispered. "Hard questions, simple answers."

I shook my head. "PJ and I will move to Virginia with Meg if he lets him stay with us," I hissed to Lark.

"Sure?" she asked.

I nodded and closed my eyes, dismissing any doubts.

"Judge, may I?" Lark said. With his agreement, she stood. "Meg has a spotless criminal record and has shown to be a responsible adult. She has an outstanding support system, so much so that her mother has agreed to relocate to Richmond, Virginia, to assist her daughter in caring for the child, if that would suit the court."

Meg squeezed my hand, and my veins pumped an icy slush in the silence.

"We'd like to propose a settlement," Lark said.

Lark and John bent over their notes for a moment, then, Lark stood. "Meg and Sissie will serve as co-conservators, affording Roxanne two supervised visits yearly, and for Ms. Acton's trouble, she'll receive a portion of Faith's estate."

The judge nodded and addressed Roxanne's attorney. "Is this something your client would consider?"

The man held up a finger and bent toward Roxanne. Then, he stood. "Judge, would you allow us a break so we can discuss?"

The judge agreed and dismissed the courtroom for an hour.

❧

MY HEART RATE ROSE TO Mach 10 when Roxanne and her attorney returned to the courtroom.

"Judge, my client is willing to consider their offer," Roxanne's attorney said.

Roxanne twisted to face us. "If you really think it's best for him."

You don't want to know what I think, sister. Both relieved and disappointed by her willingness to trade money for a child, a stare was all I could manage.

Her attorney continued, "Since the boy will remain in the same town with his sister, my client will drop her suit and any future claims for custodianship or visitation of the minor child. With regard to her sister's estate, we feel it is only fair that she be reimbursed for her pain and suffering in the amount of $25,000, plus the costs associated with this suit."

"Is this acceptable?" the judge asked Lark.

Meg and I nodded wholeheartedly. We would've given that woman every cent of Faith's estate to keep PJ.

Forty-Seven

I n July, I listed my house for sale and rented a cottage in the heart of Richmond, a half-mile from the Richmond campus.

Moving forward or moving in any direction was in the water. Della's company sold my house, but she wasn't there for it. Like me, she was trying something different. She handed the reins of her company to trusted staff to join Jared and their children on the family's ranch outside of Dallas. In time, I trusted, she'd take to it.

On a warm morning in early August, Meg and I watched the moving truck motor away from Austin Street. We loaded the porch swing into the back of her 4Runner and caravanned over 1,500 miles to our new home, PJ with me and Finn in Meg's car.

PJ was an entertaining traveling companion. Unlike his sister, he enjoyed the music I chose. Somewhere between Little Rock, Arkansas, and Jackson, Tennessee, I tuned in to a radio show featuring hits from the 1980s and '90s.

"Remember that one?" The DJ said in her raspy voice. "Boy, I do. I was ten years old when that one came out. Wouldn't it be wonderful if we could tell our ten-year-old selves how life would turn out? What would you say, listeners?"

Chumbawamba's "Tubthumping" played, and PJ kicked his feet against his car seat.

My mind swirled to Gillespie Primary School—running around at recess with Della, the smell of watercolor paints, the feel of a smooth plastic marker in my hand. I was a sponge, grasping at what

369

my classmates were doing, wearing, saying, not entirely different from my mom, who observed other women's cues to inform her decisions.

When the song ended, the DJ talked about scrunchies and banana clips, and I turned down the volume to hear myself.

"PJ, know what I'd say to my little-girl self?" I glanced into the backseat and he gave me a blank stare. "I suppose I'd tell her not to get too discouraged when she gets knocked down. She's gonna get tons of practice pulling herself up."

I glanced at my reflection in the rearview mirror. My eyes were different. They had a few more well-earned lines and contained a fresh spark of determination.

"Might take that girl a while," I said, "but she'll make it, and it'll be on her terms."

My mind was reeling with the possibilities. PJ looked bored, but I hadn't abandoned my love letter to younger Sissie.

"I'd tell her not to pay so much attention to boys. Oh, brother, could I save her from a heck of a lot of trouble."

PJ didn't know what that would mean for him. Had I avoided those boys—one boy in particular—he and his sister might not exist. I bit my lip as guilt swelled in my chest.

That guilt turned to warmth, and I identified it as sympathy for the girl who'd fought to be heard. Self-love requires an indulgence I hadn't permitted my younger self.

PJ FELL ASLEEP, AND I DIALED Harlan's number. But, I got his voicemail. I didn't leave a message.

Much as I loved the man, our love hadn't brought us between the same state lines in months. Harlan said he missed me, but I suspected the clock was ticking until he met someone who had room in her life for a man with his dedication.

Our new/old house took some getting used to. It was smaller and older than our house in Fredericksburg had been. The AC was prone to freezing up. The pipes clanked when we ran the showers. We learned to walk Finn in the early mornings and spent those humid dog days of summer meeting our neighbors and becoming acquainted with our new city.

In no time, Meg attended new-student orientation and moved into the dorms, a short walk from the house. She was a grown woman, excited about her classes, and I wouldn't have wanted her any different.

When classes began, Meg came over on Saturdays to spend time with PJ and give me some alone time. Truth was, I didn't really need it after PJ snagged a spot in a nursery school adjacent to Virginia Commonwealth, where I had just begun coursework to become a nurse. I studied during naps.

We had juddered into a routine with our full schedules. I began to understand how difficult it was for single parents to work and go to school.

When my boy was asleep, I'd become restless for adult companionship. Lucky for me, there was always room for studying. Anatomy & Physiology almost kicked my butt.

I called Harlan a few times, shoring myself up first to ensure a buoyant conversation. He told me about friends he met on his travels and places he visited. He always found a way to slip it into the conversation how much he missed me.

So much time had passed since Meg's graduation. He was slipping away from me, and it hurt. I had paused our relationship for a season of self-discovery, a season of new motherhood, a season to launch my new life. Months later, I had discovered enough and, frankly, I was bored.

And heartbroken.

᪥

At last, I made a friend at PJ's toddler gymnastic class. Adam, a former book buyer, stayed home to raise his daughter, Alice. His husband, Kyle, an anesthesiologist, was prone to long hours at the hospital. On nights when Kyle was away, Adam cooked dinner for us. While it wasn't as exciting as a date with Harlan, these nights out supplied plenty of the laughs and warmth I craved.

They were from Richmond and welcomed us like family. They were a lovely pair—nerdy-cute Adam was so organized, he could've taught Marie Kondo a thing or two. Kyle had chestnut hair and bottle green eyes and was an amazing listener. Attractive as they were, though, they reminded me of what was missing in my home—a dad for PJ and a partner for me.

When I pictured a partner, Harlan filled my thoughts. Who am I kidding? Harlan filled my thoughts always—when I saw happy couples, at nights after PJ was asleep, when I was studying.

Did I make a mistake pushing him away?

❧

In October, Theresa traveled to Richmond and stayed with us. No longer clouded by false identities or legalities, she was free to exercise adoration for her grandson.

PJ called her "Meesa," a name Theresa and Faith had chosen before he was born. Framed by the truth, I saw their relationship with new eyes. Theresa was always searching for traces of his mother in him. "He may have his father's hair, but he has Faith's hairline," Theresa said to me her first morning there—and then offered up an apologetic smile.

"Show me," I said, encouraging her to recover pieces of her daughter in her grandson.

Theresa hadn't broken up my marriage; she'd cleaned up a mess neither of us had made. And together, we shared a love of the same sweet boy. I considered myself fortunate she was trusting me to raise him. I also appreciated the extraordinary efforts she had taken to protect her grandson. Put in the same situation, who knew what I would've done to protect Meg or her child?

❧

At Thanksgiving, Brent escorted my parents to Richmond. Dad's speech hadn't improved much, but he had graduated to walking with a cane. It was reassuring to see he hadn't given up.

The postcards ceased when Harlan returned to Fredericksburg to celebrate the holiday and stuck around to help Lark at the winery. His texts, however, kept my phone buzzing.

HARLAN: *This town isn't the same without you.*
SISSIE: *I'm sure it's surviving.*
HARLAN: *It's become a sad place—without your smile, the mayor has issued an official period of mourning.*
SISSIE: *You're sweet.*
HARLAN: *I don't want to pressure you, but I sure would love to see your face. Sounds promising.*
SISSIE: *Not sure when I'll get back there.*
HARLAN: *We could meet up somewhere?*
SISSIE: *I can't even think about getting away until finals are over. School is hard.*
HARLAN: *I can always travel to you.*

My chest felt like a glitter bomb had exploded. I stared at the phone's screen, unable to punch out as much as a "k." *Answer him, Sissie.*

SISSIE: *Sure.*
HARLAN: *Maybe after the new year?*
SISSIE: *Sure.*
HARLAN: *I'm pressuring you again. I'm sorry.*
SISSIE: *No, it's fine.*
SISSIE: *I mean, yes.*
HARLAN: *I'm sorry.*

Why's he sorry?
I reread his messages. *Crap. Pull yourself together.*

SISSIE: *No. I'm sorry. I meant, yes, I'd like to see you after the new year. It's been hard, juggling school and PJ. Sometimes, finding time to walk Finn becomes too much.*
HARLAN: *Need help?*
SISSIE: *You have no idea.*

These conversations recurred and reignited the warm banter we had exchanged before I sent Harlan packing. I couldn't see myself flying to Fredericksburg to see him, though. I wasn't even sure I could picture him traveling to Virginia. But I knew I wouldn't refuse if he offered again.

He let me know he planned a return to the Florida Keys in early December. When he sent another postcard of those tiny Key deer, he included, "Maybe the third time will be the charm, and I'll talk you into joining me. Love you."

At night, when PJ was down and Finn lay snoring at my feet, thoughts of Harlan would hit me like a swarm of swallows. I'd consider his deep voice, his bright eyes, and his loving touch, wondering if the timing would ever be right for us. Mostly, though, I resolved to be grateful for what we shared, even if this was how our story ended.

My story wasn't over, anyway. I had made choices that offered love and new experiences. Someday, I might find myself on the giving end of one of those newborn Isolettes in an NICU where I might share my experience with a scared young girl. But before that could happen, I had many semesters ahead of me.

Forty-Eight

Lark and John Morales worked in tandem to transfer jurisdiction to the family courts of Richmond County, allowing us to finalize PJ's adoption—a blessing as I stared squarely at my first final exams in seventeen years.

A new ad litem attorney introduced himself at our house, a former litigation expert and seasoned grandfather named Jim Archer. Jim reviewed the process with me—one I knew well from our previous legal transactions.

"I'm here to represent PJ's interests, but more important, I'm here to lay eyes and ears on his life with you, to confirm you can provide a healthy home for him," he told me. "From what I have read and from what I see today, I have no doubt you will care for his every need."

Before he left the house, he and PJ had become fast friends. Seeing them together made me long for my father. PJ would've enjoyed the man I'd known before the stroke.

A week later, we assembled at the courthouse and finalized the adoption. We celebrated afterward with my new BFF Adam and our children at Chuck E. Cheese's and wrapped up before naptime.

A FEW DAYS LATER, ADAM and Alice came over for a playdate. "Your house looks great. Your schoolwork's nearly done for the year. Think it's about time to blow off some steam?" Adam asked.

"As cold as it's been, I can stand the steam just fine." I laughed.

"We know a guy. Handsome, divorced, and no kids." Adam bent to inspect what his daughter had picked up, and shaking his head, peeled a piece of lint out of her mouth. "We don't put that in our mouths."

"My carpet's clean. Besides, whatever happened to 'God makes dirt, and dirt doesn't hurt,' hmm?"

"That only works for a kid who doesn't put every speck she finds into her mouth. Should've named her Hoover, the way she sweeps up."

"A little fiber is healthy, right?"

"Eh." He returned to the chair beside me. "Back to you." His eyes locked on my face like high beams. "We're having a pre-Hanukkah dinner, and . . ." His voice pitched into song. "Kyle's inviting Will Rothman so he can meet you."

"Tell you what, find me a guy as nice as you and I'll consider."

"They broke the mold." He raised his hands in surrender.

"Where were you when I was sixteen, getting knocked up?"

"Summoning the courage to come out to my parents? So much for all my anxiety. They had already figured it out." He laughed. "They were unbelievably kind—even my dad. Kyle's dad, not so much."

"Ouch."

"Haven't given up on the old guy. Gotta believe he loves Kyle, so he'll find the grace to get over his insecurities and accept him . . . and our family."

"We'll pray for him."

"Is that a Texas thing? Praying for lost causes?"

"How'd you guess?" I said, feeling understood.

He checked on Alice and turned back to me. "You don't want to meet our handsome friend . . ." Adam blinked like an owl. "So, who's got your heart?"

I hesitated to explain my relationship with Harlan. "There's this guy. He's . . . traveling right now."

"Traveling? What is he, a carnie?"

"Forest ranger . . . or, he was. Now he's finding himself."

"That might take some time. What's the commitment potential with . . . what's his name?"

"Harlan."

"Pardon me for offering advice, but if I were Harlan, I'd—"

"Be living a lie?"

He snickered. "I wouldn't let you out of my sight. If a guy wants you, he'll move heaven and hell to be front and center. As long as I've known you, which, admittedly isn't all that long, you haven't mentioned Mr. Wonderful."

"He wanted me, but I needed to find myself, so I set him free to wander the universe."

"Where is he, on the International Space Station?"

"Florida."

"Is he good to you?"

"Oh, yeah." I turned to PJ, standing in front of me. "Awesome with my kids, too." I bit my lip. "It happened at a bad time—right after Meg's dad died. We were becoming friends, before. Can't lie—we had chemistry. It was like we were singing the same song even though neither of us had read the words before."

"I get it. When do you expect him to wrap up the world tour?"

I shrugged.

"If you change your mind, send up a flare before the dinner party and we'll modify our seating arrangements."

Short of flagging down help on the side of the road, no such flares are in my future.

THE SATURDAY BEFORE FINALS WRAPPED up, Meg stayed the night with us. We parked our studies until PJ went to bed. For a few hours, I had my babies within arm's reach. Pizza was delivered, blankets were tented, and *Moana* was on the TV. Life was grand.

At some point after PJ went to bed, Meg was particularly glued to her phone. Finally, she pried herself from it. "Mom? Can I make dinner here Thursday night?"

"Don't you have a test on Friday?"

"I told you—no test in philosophy."

"Cut me a break. I can barely remember my own test schedule."
I laughed. "Of course you can. Put whatever you need on the list
on the fridge, and I'll buy the groceries."

"I'm taking care of it, Mom."

"What are you making?"

"Diego's hooking me up with a recipe."

"I'm sure it'll be delicious."

"Oh, and okay if I invite somebody?"

"Somebody? Like the somebody you've been texting?"

"Snoop much?"

"Not snooping. You're pretty obvious when you're tapping
away at that phone. Is he cute?"

"Eh." She lifted a shoulder.

Clear as mud.

⚘

MEG ARRIVED ON THURSDAY WITH three grocery bags and excitement all over her glorious face.

Diego, now a chef-in-training, had sent detailed instructions for
a pork dish requiring twine and spices I'd never seen.

Meg whirled around the kitchen, chopping and boiling vegetables, baking breadcrumbs, and tying a stuffed pork tenderloin with
twine, pausing only to exchange a plethora of messages with her
unnamed dinner guest. This was going to be an important dinner.

*Better prepare for the next phase of your baby girl's life, Mom.
Won't be long before you two are choosing flowers and wedding cake.*

⚘

WITH MEG'S KITCHEN TAKEOVER IN full effect and PJ down for a
nap, I plopped on the couch, inhaling the delectable scents floating
through the house. The dormant fireplace stared back at me. I
thought it would be nice to start a fire, but short of my class notes,
I had nothing to burn.

It'd been a few days since I'd heard from Harlan—not surprising, as he had been on a deep-sea fishing trip in the Gulf with an old business associate. That didn't stop me from ringing him.

"So good to hear your voice." Harlan's voice sent warm fuzzies through my chest. "Ace all those tests?"

"Hmm. I think I passed, if that counts?"

"Bet you did well."

"Hope my professor is as optimistic about my performance. Where are you?"

"Let's see, where am I?" he teased, not offering an explanation.

A bit put-off by his non-answer, I didn't press for details. Jealousy stirred, and I regretted making the call.

"Still there?" he asked.

"Uh-huh. Meg needs me in the kitchen, so I'll let you figure out where you're going."

"Okay. Miss you."

"You too. Bye."

I stared at the phone, willing it to burst into flames so I could toss it into the fireplace.

"Mom," Meg hollered.

I found her digging in the freezer.

"I forgot those frozen cocktail onions for the sauce."

"Substitute minced onions. They're in the spice cabinet."

"Diego says minced onions are the antichrist's making. I need the real ones." Meg threw up her hands. "It's fine. I need more experience driving in the snow."

Not tonight, you don't. "I'll go. PJ will wake from his nap soon, so keep an ear out for him."

"Got it. Thanks, Mom. Promise they'll be worth it."

I bundled up and crossed the driveway to reach the unattached, uninsulated garage. *What was I thinking when I agreed to leave the ever-warm Hill Country?*

THE CAR HAD NEARLY REACHED the grocery store by the time the heat kicked in. When I climbed out, my feet crunched over the snow and the fog of my breath filled the air like smoke.

"Hey, Mrs. Dietrich," a cashier greeted me inside. Perhaps I hadn't completely acclimated to the weather, but I had become acquainted with a few of the folks at our neighborhood Kroger.

Experience had taught me that a quick stop at the grocery store usually becomes more, so I pulled a cart from the storage lane and darted toward the houseware aisle.

Ahh. Two lonely Firestarter logs left on the shelf. Come home with me, gentlemen.

Next move was a walk to the back to restock our milk. Seemed we couldn't ever keep up with PJ's milk habit.

The snowy weather enticed me to toss in a package of refrigerated chocolate-chip cookie dough for good measure. An aisle away, I bought the makings for hot cocoa, including mini marshmallows for a post-dinner treat.

Meg's friend will be so impressed. God, I hope he's not a jerk. In that case . . .

I considered returning those items to their shelves, then shook my head.

Meg wouldn't date a jerk.

My phone rang as I crossed to the frozen food cases.

"Where are you?" Meg asked.

"The store."

"Did you find the frozen onions?"

"Haven't gotten that far."

"Which store are you at?"

"The Kroger around the corner. What is this? The grocery store police? I'll hurry."

"Don't hurry so much you speed. It's icy out there."

"Okay, Mom," I deadpanned.

"Ha-ha. Just come home."

"Be right there. Love you."

"Love you, Mom."

I was filled with a surge of pride as I dropped the phone into my bag. *Who needs a man when you have everything I do?*

As I pushed the cart down the frozen veggie aisle, the annoying, wordless holiday music that had been playing overhead ended abruptly, right in the middle of "We Three Kings."

But then Dan Fogelberg's "Same Old Lang Syne" began to play overhead—words and all—and I took it as a good omen. Harlan and I had come full circle. It was time to acknowledge the truth. Some relationships are meant to end.

Searching the cold cases, I mumbled along with the song. *There!* Below a pile of pre-cut bell peppers and mushrooms were fist-sized bags of frozen cocktail onions. I tossed two into the cart and released the glass door.

"Hey." A man's voice sounded over my shoulder, and a hand touched the back of my right sleeve.

That one small word—spoken by a big voice—poured over me like warm caramel. My body resisted turning toward it.

"Sissie?"

I caved and turned around.

Harlan's crow's feet bent as his mouth angled into a sexy grin. A few more grays had made themselves at home on his head, but those eyes were as spellbinding as ever.

"Wh—wh—what . . ." Unable to form words, I sighed. "How are you here?"

"Planes, trains, and automobiles." He laughed, but I couldn't share in the joke. He straightened his shoulders and pulled in a full breath. "Hope I'm not too late."

"Too late for—"

He cocked his head to the side. "Has the snow turned into rain?"

"Has what?"

"You know? From the song? Has the snow turned into rain?"

Is Harlan really standing here asking me about a Dan Fogelberg song in the middle of a grocery store in Virginia?

"Remember? About the grocery store?" He pointed to the ceiling as Kenny G played out the end of the song. "Thought it was an old favorite of yours?"

"Uh-huh." I looked at my hands and turned up to him. "Did you do this?"

"No." He took a closer look at my face. "You're frowning. Did I do a bad thing, surprising you?" His brows pitched up in a hopeful way.

"How did you—"

"Questions are complicated, answers are—"

"Simple." *Meghann Elisabeth, your fingerprints are all over this.* My eyes rose to take in his face.

He drifted closer, an arm reaching around me like the leading edge of a storm. His hand coasted to my chin and a finger teased my jawline. My skin grew hot. *Frozen food department, be damned. I'm not moving an inch.* "How'd you find me here?" I asked.

"Little bird told me. Actually, that little bird's been working pretty damn hard getting me here."

"Meg?"

"We made a deal. I helped her with calculus, she helped me with . . ." He raised his hands.

"How long are you here?"

"How long do you want me?"

If he's the one, tell him. A kick of courage hit my gut. I swallowed, searching for the right words. Finally, I looked him dead in the eyes. "I needed to get away."

"Okay," he said, looking defeated.

"I've never allowed the dust to settle long enough to look in the mirror, at what I need, who I'm supposed to be."

"Alrighty, then." He rocked on his heels.

"I know now."

He leaned in and his eyes roved over my face, like he was scouring my expression for meaning.

I shook my head, untwisting my panties. "Harlan, I'm glad you're here."

His pursed lips softened, and he bent toward me. His thumb brushed my bottom lip. "Kiss you?"

"Uh-huh."

That kiss, strange and startling, threatened to thaw every carrot, pea, and potato along the aisle. But Meg was at home waiting on me.

"Do you have plans for dinner, because we're having—"

"Actually . . ." He pointed a finger at me.

"Right." I smacked my forehead, finally getting it. "Little bird." I made a clicking sound with my mouth. "Can't believe she did this."

"Wasn't my idea, I swear. Your girl's got a way about her—a little stubborn, a little insistent? Smart as a whip. Might take after her mom."

"You think?" I scrunched my eyebrows, pausing for effect. "Be straight with me—is this another one of your stopovers like last time?"

"Told you. I'm here as long as you'll have me. Meg said you have a comfortable couch I can sleep on."

"Did she, now? Well, I should warn you. I'm in college, and I have these kids." I wiped my brow theatrically. "They keep me plenty busy."

"Put me to work. Boss me around. Send me after groceries. Tell me what to cook for dinner. I can mow the lawn, wash the laundry. Sissie, I got an A in home ec. Learned how to sew on buttons, and cook a mean omelet, too."

"You do make a mean omelet." I nodded appraisingly. "As I recall, you're fairly skillful at a few other things, too." I felt a blush rise up my neck and took a step backward. "Need a ride?"

"What with the snow, I brought my truck. Just in case you turned me down. You know how the song goes."

"I wouldn't make you walk. We're not *that* couple. We're the relationship that came next for those people." The words slid out of my mouth faster than I could contain them.

"So we could be looking at the one that works out?" he asked.

I was about to answer when he dropped his gaze to his jacket pocket and pulled out a buzzing phone. He resumed eye contact with me while he spoke into the receiver.

"I found your mom, but I can't get her out of here. You're right. She can be stubborn. Okay. See you in a few." He slid the phone back into his pocket with a sly grin. "Shall we?" he asked—his question telling me all I needed to know.

Right there, in the frozen food aisle, the answer was simple. I chose him.

Harlan loaded the two grocery sacks into my car and got into his truck, not without kissing me one more time. We climbed into our respective cars, and he followed me back to the house. In the snow and ice, the route lasted longer than usual, giving me plenty of time to think about the road that led me here.

I'd come a long way since that guidance counselor urged me to determine my life's purpose. I didn't find my purpose in a college brochure or by following someone else's example. I found it in hundreds of small moments and a handful of big ones—some tragic, others exhilarating.

Della was right. I had bloomed where I was planted.

Nearing my house, I slowed in the driveway, pausing to soak it all in—wisdom earned from the distinguished university of hard knocks, the opportunity to earn a real degree, my perfectly unplanned family, my inconveniently timed love affair with Harlan, and my little home—alight with love that evening as Meg and PJ waved into the darkness. Through a series of bewildering events, I had received everything I never knew I wanted, and for the moment, we were (mostly) the Dietrichs, alive and well on Seminary Avenue.

Acknowledgments

It has been an honor to work with Brooke Warner's team at SparkPress and She Writes Press. Shannon Green's exhaustive coordination and Krissa Lagos's expert editing made those final versions shine. Through Women on Writing, Margo Dill's early editing helped me create a richer story.

Thanks to Ann-Marie Nieves at Get Red PR for sharing your expertise and putting me at ease about this wild ride. You are an author's best pal.

Since moving to Kansas, my local indie bookstore has supported my path to publishing. Sincere thanks to Sarah, Rebecca, Kris, and the rest of the Watermark Books team. My optimal writing day would find me in one of Watermark's leather chairs with one of Jeff's lattes by my side.

To my Summit Sisters, especially to SS#1 (Jules) for reading through my manuscripts and introducing me to Colleen McCullough's *The Thorn Birds* when I was barely a teen, showing me what grown-up books could offer.

I would be amiss if I didn't express my gratitude to my WTAMU family, especially the professors who gave me opportunities and learning experiences that inform my writing today. Dr. Trudy Hanson, a Renaissance woman, taught me about feminism and the many forms it can take. Dr. Russell Lowery-Hart continually demonstrates the importance of showing up for one's community through his work to breach gaps in educational opportunities. Dr. James Hallmark encouraged me not to give up on graduate school after MS took my confidence, and his better half, Becky, counseled me on the hazards of cat ownership and the importance of coffee. I treasure you both.

Kristan Higgins, I owe you big time. You're right—babies declare their futures.

The writing community makes the roughest days not so bad and makes the best ones even better. You're some of my favorite people: Camille Pagan, Barbara Claypole White, Molly Harper, Kelly Farmer, Leah DeCesare, Amy E. Reichert, Lainey Cameron, Trish Doller, Alison Hammer, and Phoebe Fox, the lovely WFWA patio writers, Every Damn Day Writers, and the Tall Poppies.

Erin Spencer and the One Night Stand Productions team took their time to create a lovely audiobook. Xe Sands—thank you for lending your voice to make Sissie's story better than I'd ever imagined.

Sadly, I had hoped to include my mother-in-law in these acknowledgments, but Vonnie Wilkerson passed away in May 2021. Instead, I hope to honor her with this message: Love your friends and family while you're able; always keep a jar of red nail polish on hand; and when creating something, don't be afraid to put a bow on it.

Hugs to my Kansas pickleball pals for making room on the courts and in your hearts for a Texan and her books. Love you all!

Marissa—you've known me longer than almost anyone else, and no one will ever beat us at Taboo. Sharla—through all those committees and raffles, you were the big prize.

Linds, Jamie, Brad, and Kenz—each of you shares a uniquely special spirit with the world and I'm so proud of you. Mike—you are my true north.

To each of the bookstagrammers, bloggers, and book club members who build buzz and host discussions around novels, you are our unsung heroes.

A very special thank you to the people who bring our books to life—the readers and audiobook listeners. You make our work matter. Thank you for sharing your most precious asset: your time.

About the Author

Kris Clink called Texas home for most of her life but now lives in Kansas, where she and her husband have filled their empty nest with two spoiled-rotten pups. Kris's debut, *Goodbye, Lark Lovejoy*, is the first in The Enchanted Rock Series. When not writing, she hosts the *Kris Clink's Writing Table* podcast.

You can visit Kris online at www.krisclink.com or on Facebook at @krisclinkbooks.

Author photo © Kacy Meineke

About SparkPress

SparkPress is an independent, hybrid imprint focused on merging the best of the traditional publishing model with new and innovative strategies. We deliver high-quality, entertaining, and engaging content that enhances readers' lives. We are proud to bring to market a list of *New York Times* best-selling, award-winning, and debut authors who represent a wide array of genres, as well as our established, industry-wide reputation for creative, results-driven success in working with authors. SparkPress, a BookSparks imprint, is a division of SparkPoint Studio LLC.

Learn more at GoSparkPress.com

Selected Titles From SparkPress

SparkPress is an independent boutique publisher delivering high-quality, entertaining, and engaging content that enhances readers' lives, with a special focus on female-driven work. www.gosparkpress.com

Goodbye, Lark Lovejoy: A Novel, Kris Clink, $16.95, 9781684630738. A spontaneous offer on her house prompts grief-stricken Lark to retreat to her hometown, smack in the middle of the Texas Hill Country Wine Trail—but it will take more than a change of address to heal her broken family.

Charming Falls Apart: A Novel, Angela Terry, $16.95, 978-1-68463-049-3. After losing her job and fiancé the day before her thirty-fifth birthday, people-pleaser and rule-follower Allison James decides she needs someone to give her some new life rules—and fast. But when she embarks on a self-help mission, she realizes that her old life wasn't as perfect as she thought—and that she needs to start writing her own rules.

That's Not a Thing: A Novel, Jacqueline Friedland. $16.95, 978-1-68463-030-1. When a recently engaged Manhattanite learns that her first great love has been diagnosed with ALS, she is faced with the impossible decision of whether a few final months with her ex might be worth risking her entire future. A fast-paced emotional journey that explores whether it's possible to be equally in love with two men at once.

And Now There's You: A Novel, Susan S. Etkin. $16.95, 978-1-68463-000-4. Though five years have passed since beautiful design consultant Leila Brandt's husband passed away, she's still grieving his loss. When she meets a terribly sexy and talented—if arrogant—architect, however, sparks fly, and neither of them can deny the chemistry between them.

The Sea of Japan: A Novel, Keita Nagano. $16.95, 978-1-684630-12-7. When thirty-year-old Lindsey, an English teacher from Boston who's been assigned to a tiny Japanese fishing town, is saved from drowning by a local young fisherman, she's drawn into a battle with a neighboring town that has high stakes for everyone—especially her.